the wrong man

A NOVEL OF SUSPENSE

KATE WHITE

HARPER

NEW YORK • LONDON • TORONTO • SYDNEY

HARPER

THE WRONG MAN. Copyright © 2015 by Kate White. All rights reserved. Printed in the United States of America. No part of this book may be used or reproduced in any manner whatsoever without written permission except in the case of brief quotations embodied in critical articles and reviews. For information address HarperCollins Publishers, 195 Broadway, New York, NY 10007.

HarperCollins books may be purchased for educational, business, or sales promotional use. For information please e-mail the Special Markets Department at SPsales@harpercollins.com.

FIRST EDITION

Library of Congress Cataloging-in-Publication Data has been applied for.

ISBN 978-0-06-235065-7

15 16 17 18 19   OV/RRD   10 9 8 7 6 5 4 3 2 1

To Yvon Le Fichant and David Minka,
fabulous friends on three continents

the wrong man

chapter 1

For some reason she couldn't understand, Kit woke on the last morning in Islamorada with the urge to do something a little dangerous in her life. Not like shark-cage diving or parasailing over the turquoise blue Florida Bay. She hadn't lost her *mind*. She just longed for something that would make her heart pump harder and her breath catch in her throat.

Maybe it was because her vacation, a combination getaway and business-scouting trip, had been nice enough but had offered up no surprises, none of those unexpected discoveries you secretly yearned for on a trip. Oh, she'd done a kayak tour of the mangroves and she'd treated herself to a hot stone massage. But those were hardly the kind of activities that left you breathless, even though the massage therapist had stressed that the stones were actually "certified lava shells," as if having them kneaded into your back was comparable to hiking along the rim of a volcanic crater.

Or, maybe the urge was tied to her birthday. She'd turned thirty-five the week before, had broken up five months before with a sweet, nice guy who'd been all wrong for her, and during the days leading up to the occasion, she'd goaded herself to use her birthday as an impetus to go bolder, to be more of a badass at times. As she'd left the office for the airport eight days ago, Baby

Meadow, her seventy-one-year-old interior decorating partner, had quoted a line of Mae West's that kept echoing in Kit's head: "Good girls go to heaven but bad girls go everywhere."

But even as she toyed with the idea, she heard an internal warning. Wasn't the problem with a little danger that you had no guarantee it could be contained? It was like a match tossed on dry brush. Maybe things only smoldered for a while, the embers glowing softly through the night until a light rain doused them at dawn. But with the right wind conditions, those embers could begin to flare, creating flames that would thrash higher and higher in the darkness. Until they torched everything you owned.

She stepped out onto the small, stone patio of her hotel room and discovered that the early April sky was cloudless, and the jungle-like grounds of the hotel—dense with palm trees and sawgrass—looked lush and seductive, in shades of deep green that she rarely liked to use in her work but always felt spellbound by in nature. A gecko darted up the trunk of a tree. Time to get moving, she told herself. It would be crazy not to make the most of her last day.

She dressed quickly—a bikini covered with a sarong and T-shirt—and headed for breakfast, her iPad tucked under her arm. The hotel was a small boutique one, almost motel-like in style but charming and Caribbean in feel. Her room was in one of a half-dozen white clapboard buildings separated from the main building by winding sand pathways. As she came around a bend in the path, she overheard snippets of conversation. It was a man talking, probably another guest up early, too, and after a moment she realized he was on a cell phone. There was a hint of consternation in his tone.

"I don't want to wait much longer," Kit thought she heard him say. And then, as she rounded the bend, his words were more distinct: "I'd rather have a few regrets than none at all."

He was late thirties, she guessed, about six foot two with dark red hair cut short in a kind of Navy Seal style and a closely cropped beard and mustache. Dressed in a pale, long-sleeved shirt and cream-colored pants. He caught her eye and then looked away, lowering his voice at the same time.

As she passed him, she reflected on the last comment he'd made. Perhaps that should be her motto in life, she thought. But how did you guarantee a few regrets didn't balloon into too many?

Breakfast was included in the price of her room, and she went a little nuts—glistening red papaya, half a muffin, a cheese and mushroom omelet, and a foamy cappuccino—telling herself to get her money's worth. While eating she knocked off replies to a few emails and checked the news online.

She lingered longer than she'd planned. With half an eye directed toward a headline on her iPad, she grabbed her tote bag and left the restaurant, eager to reach the beach.

And then *bam*, she collided hard with someone. Her fault for trying to still read the darn iPad. She looked up to see that her victim was the red-haired man she'd passed on the path.

"So sorry," Kit said. She felt like an idiot.

"It's my fault, too," he said politely. "My mind was elsewhere."

She wondered if it had been on the conversation he'd had earlier. Well, whatever, decent of him to let her off the hook. He held her gaze tightly for a couple of beats, with eyes that were a light but piercing blue.

"Have a nice day," she said. He nodded and they both went on their way.

She walked the beach and started shooting photos with her Samsung, mostly of the luscious white sand. She loved to catalogue shots of things whose names were the same as colors—like sand, olive, lavender, ash, or bone. It was fascinating to see how many variations there were, and to liberate them all from the confinement of their names. Later, she read and ate lunch under a palm tree by the small, turquoise-bottomed pool. Then she changed into street clothes and took a taxi to a shop in town.

It was on the main road that ran through the island, a kind of honky-tonk strip, but there were a decent few stores, some of which she'd already perused, scouting for her client. The woman had vacationed as a girl in the Florida Keys and wanted the same vibe for a Jersey Shore cottage she'd recently purchased. That was actually part of the reason Kit had picked Islamorada to begin with—killing two birds with one stone. But now she was shopping just for herself. One of the stores specialized in fanciful exotic stuff, including a mounted sawfish bill that she'd practically drooled over.

The place was nearly empty but she liked that. She started down an aisle, relaxed in the moment. And then there he was again, Mr. X, the red-haired guy from the morning, wearing a tight, heather blue T now instead of the long-sleeved shirt. It was as if she'd conjured him up, the way a magician pulls a dove from his sleeve.

"Hello again," he said, suddenly seeing her. His eyes held hers the way they had earlier.

"Oh, hi. Sorry again about this morning. No injuries, right?"

"No, none at all. Though I should warn you. I hear they're going to make that illegal in some states—walking while reading a tablet."

"Good to know," she said, smiling. "I'll leave my iPad at home—or use a designated reader."

He didn't say anything for a moment, just looked at her, as if weighing a decision.

"Are you hunting for souvenirs?" he asked finally.

"Sort of. What about you? You don't seem like the type who goes for mirrors with seashells hot-glued to the frame."

She wasn't sure why she'd teased him that way. It was a tactic she sometimes relied on with awkward male clients, to entice them to open up.

"I'm going to take that as a compliment," he said. "I was actually trying to find a gift for my big sister's birthday. Any ideas? She'll be forty-one. Nice taste but on the casual side."

She wondered suddenly if he might be trying to pick her up. But she'd never been drawn to red-haired men. Weren't they supposed to be brooding or even wildly mercurial, the type who'd think nothing of bashing another man over the back of the head with a bar stool?

"Will you need to pack it in your luggage?" she asked. "If that's the case, you might want to think small."

"She's got a place in Miami. I'm headed there by car tomorow so I can take it with me."

"So size isn't an issue?" she said.

"Not really. But don't women hate gifts in large packages? They assume you've brought them a juicer or an emergency kit for their car."

"You're so right," Kit said. He looked, she thought, like the kind of guy who'd never given anyone a juicer in his life, and if he needed juice himself, he'd just crush a half-dozen oranges in one fist. Maybe he *was* a Navy Seal, decompressing after a raid on a terrorist cell or Somali pirates. "Okay, let's see, then . . ."

She turned to scan the store and then headed down an aisle, with him trailing just behind her. After a minute or so, she spotted a hammered metal frame tucked behind a group of decorative boxes.

"What about this?" she said, easing it out. "A woman can never own enough frames. And this one would work with any style."

"Even causal? Though maybe a better way to describe my sister is a touch Bohemian."

"Yes, this would mix with that." Kit smiled. "I'm actually a decorator."

"Ahh. Well then, *sold.*" He accepted the frame from her. "I'm Matt Healy, by the way," he added like an afterthought.

She was standing so close to him that she could see the light freckles on his face. There was something about him that was both rugged and refined—the cropped beard and mustache contrasting with the sophisticated air. And then there were those freaking blue eyes. When she'd handed him the frame, she'd noticed there was no wedding ring on his hand. Though, of course, that didn't mean a thing.

"Kit Finn," she said.

"Here on vacation?" he asked.

"Partly. I'm also checking things out for a client. How about you?"

"Uh, business and pleasure, too, I guess you could say. I sold my company recently and I'm trying to figure out what my next move should be. . . . I actually drove down here from New York this time."

"And how was *that*?" she said, raising an eyebrow. "I'm from the city myself but I don't think I could handle a drive that long."

"Well, let's just say it was an experience." She sensed him deliberating again, caught between two thoughts, and then he glanced at his watch.

"I'd love to buy you a cup of coffee as thanks for helping me," he said, looking back at her, "but I have a business call in a few minutes, and then another at four. Maybe later?"

"Sure," she said. Though later seemed right up there with, "Why don't we grab a bite together the next time we're both in Bogotá."

"Do you have a card at least?" he asked.

She pulled one from her wallet, handed it to him, and, as he slid the card into his pants pocket, she said goodbye. Who knew? Maybe he'd at least need an interior designer at some point.

As he paid for the frame, she inquired of someone else behind the counter about the price of the sawfish bill—outrageous, unfortunately—and left the store. Heading up the street in the steamy air, she felt herself longing for a dip in the pool.

And then as she strolled, lost in thought, Matt Healy was suddenly hurrying up to her from behind.

"Hello, again," he said. "This may be presumptuous on my part, but would you like to join me for dinner tonight? I was planning on eating at the hotel."

"Yes, I'd like that." Why not? she thought. To her surprise, she realized she found him attractive. And maybe having dinner with a total stranger would satisfy that yearning she'd had earlier for a little bit of danger.

"Great. Then why don't we meet on the restaurant patio? Say, eight-thirty?"

After parting from him, she walked to one more shop, and then arranged for a cab back to the hotel.

Matt was already seated on the patio when she arrived for dinner. His back was to the bay, and though it was too dark to see the water now, there were scattered points of light farther out— boats, she assumed. Ones that seemed to be on secret missions.

As she wound her way to the table, she noticed he was reading on his phone, holding it close to the hurricane lamp on the table. For a moment a frown flickered across his face. As if sensing her presence, he suddenly glanced up and took her in. She'd worn her blond hair in a messy bun, with a few loose pieces hanging around her face. And she'd picked an outfit that she thought was sexy enough but didn't look like she was trying too hard: white jeans, silver sandals, and a lavender-colored halter, which she knew worked well with her light green eyes. Baby liked to call it "the wisteria effect."

Matt rose to greet her, setting his phone facedown on the table.

"It's nice to see you again," he said.

He was wearing a navy blazer over a collarless off-white shirt. He pulled out the chair across from him and gently cupped her elbow, guiding her as she sat down. His touch was like an electric spark and she felt it shoot all the way through her.

"Did your phone calls go okay?" she asked.

"Yes. Yes, they did, thanks."

He asked if she wanted to share a bottle of red wine, and she told him, "perfect." Good girls go to heaven, she thought, but bad girls drink Bordeaux.

"So how did you end up becoming a decorator?" he said after the waiter moved off.

"I got a job as an assistant with the mother of a friend of a friend, and it was love at first sight." She laughed. "With decorating, I mean, not the mother."

"You'd never had an inkling before that?"

"I guess I did without putting my finger on it. I was the prop person for all the plays in high school, which I adored. And I have this funny memory of when I was around ten. My mother took me with her to visit her sister one afternoon, and after the two of them went out to the backyard, I felt compelled to rearrange the entire living room. When they came back inside later, they got these utterly terrified looks on their faces, like that scene in *The Sixth Sense* when the mother turns around and every one of the kitchen drawers and cabinets have been yanked open."

"That's very funny," he said, chuckling. "That scene nearly made me jump out of my seat when I saw it. Is interior design something you study in school?"

"Uh, that's one route," she said quickly. "But you also can

work at a firm and more or less apprentice with people far more experienced. That's the way I did it."

"I imagine your clients can be difficult at times. People with money are often pretty demanding."

"My business is just a tiny one, and the clients aren't what you'd really call wealthy. They have good jobs and nice apartments, and they're at a point where they can finally hire an interior designer to pull things together better. I guess you could say I'm kind of a starter decorator for most of them.

"But that's enough about decorating," she added. Her partner Baby always said that if you wanted to make a straight man impotent, just start gushing about floor plans, poufs, and color palettes. "I don't want to bore you to tears."

"I honestly enjoy hearing about stuff like that," he said. "I studied sculpture in college."

"Really?" she said, surprised. There was that contrast thing at work again. Rugged and yet also refined. "What kind of medium?"

"Metal mostly. A lot of copper. Not huge pieces, just table size.

"Do you still do it?"

"I've just started again. Part of why I got rid of my business was to have time for it. Just for my own pleasure."

"What kind of business were you in?"

He paused in the way he seemed to have of waiting a beat before speaking. "A tech business. Trust me, if I elaborated, we'd *both* be bored to tears. It was a way to make money . . . and guarantee some freedom for later."

They ordered, and over dinner they fell into an easy conversation, talking about art they both enjoyed looking at, and places they'd traveled and loved. He was funny at moments, and a good listener, listening and questioning, in fact, more than he spoke. Was it a seduction ploy? she wondered.

There was, she also decided, an intriguing contradiction to

him: self-possessed without being braggy, engaged but at the same time slightly mysterious. He made her a little nervous, yet in a way she liked. It felt good to be on her toes a bit with a man.

She was attracted to him, she realized. Even the damn red hair.

"No, no, dinner's my treat," he insisted when the check arrived and she attempted to contribute. He scribbled the tip amount and signed his name. She took a final sip of coffee, and when she looked up, she caught him scanning the patio, his eyes narrowed, as if searching for someone. The waiter to hand back the check to? she wondered. Was he eager for the night to end?

"I'd love to continue the conversation," he said. "How about a walk along the beach."

"Sure," she replied, trying not to sound as ridiculously eager as she felt.

But no sooner had they stepped onto the sand and she'd kicked off her sandals, than it began to drizzle.

"The gods aren't being very accommodating," he said, glancing upward. He took her elbow, guiding her back onto the patio. That spark once again. It was lust, she realized, and it was making her pulse race. "How about plan B? We could grab a drink at the bar. Or—there's bottle of white wine in my room. I have a suite so we could sit in the living room."

She didn't want the evening to end. But did she want to *sleep* with him? Because by going back to his hotel room, she was saying that sex was a possibility. She'd play it by ear, she decided. See where the chemistry led.

"I'm up for a glass of wine," she told him. "But just one. I'm leaving at seven a.m., and I still have to pack"

Once they were in the living room of his suite, he slipped out of his blazer and reached for the bottle of white wine on top of the mini bar. Without the jacket, she could see how fit he was, and imagine how muscular he must be under his shirt. She felt a fresh rush of desire flood through her.

"Let me get some ice to keep the wine chilled," he said, grabbing the bucket that had been provided.

As soon as the door closed behind him, she let her gaze run over the room. Nice to have a suite, she thought. The bedroom door was closed and he hadn't left much in the living area, just a few items on the desk. She stepped closer. An iPad in a leather case. A slightly rumpled *New York Times* perched on the edge. A Moleskine notebook, closed. And a Mont Blanc pen.

She plucked up the pen and with the other hand fished around in her purse for her own Mont Blanc. It had been a gift from her father, a way, he'd told her, to say he was sorry for everything, though no apology had ever been necessary.

The pens were identical, she saw. Black and gold fountain pens. Maybe that was a sign of something, she told herself.

And then, she heard footsteps outside the door. Startled, she dropped her purse and one of the pens on the floor. She quickly scooped up both items, and as she did, her elbow knocked the newspaper off the desk as well. She went into scramble mode, and she'd just managed to put everything back in place when she heard the key turn in the lock. That would have been nice, she thought—*caught snooping.*

Back in the room, Matt opened the wine, poured them each a glass, and crossed to her. After handing her the wine, he didn't step back. He was standing so near, she could feel the heat from his body.

He took her free hand and pulled her to him. Then, he leaned down, his gorgeous mouth nearly touching hers. She closed the gap and kissed him.

His lips were both soft and firm and when he pulled away a moment later, she already felt hungry for more.

"I've wanted to do that since I first set eyes on you," he said.

"In that shop in town?"

"No, when you accosted me on my way out of breakfast. Maybe even when you came around the corner earlier, while I was on the phone."

"You're not thinking I'm a stalker, are you?" she teased.

"If you are, I don't care."

He set his wineglass down and kissed her again, more urgently this time, cupping her face with one hand. She accepted his tongue as he slid it into her mouth, savoring the taste of it. Suddenly, he was pressing his body deeply into hers and running a hand along the outside of her halter, just grazing her breast. After a few moments, he pulled back and ran his eyes over her face.

"I'd love to go to bed with you, Kit," he said.

Ah, they'd arrived at that point much faster than she'd predicted. And yet, she found herself definitely entertaining the idea. Not her usual M.O., for sure, but her body seemed to have its own agenda tonight.

"That's a very interesting proposition," she said, still deliberating.

"But I also need to be perfectly honest with you," he said, before she could answer. "If we go to bed, there's no way—at least right now—that I could take things beyond tonight, even with us both living in New York."

"Are you saying there's someone serious in your life?" That would be a deal-breaker for sure. She would even regret the dinner.

"No, no," he said, shaking his head. "There's no one. I haven't had a girlfriend since I broke up with a woman nine months ago. We were pretty serious but she ended up too homesick for Melbourne to stay in the States."

"I take it then that you're up for only casual dalliances these days," she said, looking him in the eye. "No strings attached."

"Yes." His expression turned serious, almost grave. "But it's a little more complicated than that, than me not feeling ready. I'm very attracted to you, Kit. But there's a problem I need to turn all my attention to in the next weeks—even months. It's going to consume most of my time and my energy."

So there'd be no chance of ever seeing him again. But would it be so wrong to go for it, she wondered. This morning, she'd challenged herself to be a badass, to try something a little dangerous, and couldn't this be it? The proverbial night to remember.

She looked off, considering. Yes, she told herself. Take a chance.

"All right," she said. "But you'll just have to promise not to mind when my cell phone alarm goes off at five-thirty."

"Not a problem. I plan to still be having sex with you then anyway."

She flushed at the thought.

"You don't happen to have any condoms, do you?"

"I've got some in my dopp kit." He laughed. "Old but not past the expiration date."

He led her into the spare white bedroom and began to peel off her clothes, then his own. He was in fabulous condition, taut and lightly tanned. He laid her on the bed and moved along her body slowly with both hands and mouth, exploring, teasing, making her writhe in pleasure.

She'd never gone to bed with anyone for the first time without experiencing a twinge of self-consciousness, from being naked and exposed. But she felt none of that now. It was like dropping from a trapeze into a circus net, and relishing the pure, glorious thrill of the fall.

His prediction had been right. They'd barely finished making love for a third time when the alarm went off. She forced herself out of bed, gathered up her clothes, and slipped into the bathroom. When she emerged a few minutes later, Matt was out of bed, too, pants on, waiting to walk her to the door.

"That was a fantastic night, Kit," he said, a hand against the doorframe.

"Yes," she said. "It was."

He kissed her softly goodbye.

She had too much last-minute packing to reflect on any of it. She took a six-minute shower, tossed items into her suitcase in a crazy rush, and grabbed a coffee to-go in the lobby.

The car service was right on time, and as the driver headed toward the highway, she finally leaned back and replayed the night. It had been exquisite, it made her blush even to think about it. She had no regrets about her decision to spend the night with a stranger. Just regret over the fact that she'd never set eyes on him again.

Halfway to Miami, as endless palm trees whipped by outside the car, her cell phone rang.

The screen flashed the name of the hotel, and she wondered if there'd been confusion over her bill.

"Good morning," a man said when she answered. For a moment she couldn't place the deep voice.

"Did you get off on time?" he asked. And then she realized: it was Matt Healy.

"Yes, thanks," she said, taken aback. "I'm in the car now."

"Look, Kit, I know I pleaded no entanglements last night. But I have to see you again, in New York."

She took a breath.

"I'd like that, too," she said.

"I'll be there on Thursday. Why don't I cook you dinner? I'm not exactly Bobby Flay, but you won't leave starving."

She didn't care if he fixed her a fried eel sandwich.

"Perfect."

"See you Thursday then," he said after giving her his address. "seven-thirty."

Once they'd signed off, she realized she was smiling stupidly to no one in particular.

It was nearly 4:30 by the time she reached home. She had a one-bedroom apartment in a five-story building on Elizabeth Street in Nolita, named because it was just north of Little Italy. She was crazy about the area, a hip but friendly neighborhood of narrow streets, low-rise buildings, and old churches, as well as trendy boutiques and cafés. Last year, when the studio apartment next door became available, she and Baby had decided to rent it as office space.

She dropped her suitcase in the apartment and entered the office through the adjoining doorway that the super had given them permission to create. Baby was at her desk, staring quizzically at a pile of fabric swatches.

"*There* you are," Baby exclaimed, touching one of her lovely hands to her chest. "Dara saw that your flight was late."

"Just by an hour," Kit said. She'd been in too good a mood to let the delay bug her. "It's great to see you, Baby."

"Same here. I take it you had nice weather. You've got some gorgeous highlights."

Baby was a blond fanatic. She dyed her gray hair a gorgeous champagne color and wore it like a prized crown.

"I'll tell you all about it, but first fill me in. Everything okay?"

"Well, I'm up to my ass in ikat," Baby said, nodding toward the fabric pile. "After this particular job I refuse to do another throw pillow in it for as long as I live."

Kit laughed. "What about West 87th Street? You said in your email there were some problems."

"Oh, the husband's suddenly bullied his way into everything. He thinks blue is for sissies and that the slipper chairs in the bedroom look like they were made for Tinkerbell. Says he's a 'Mission furniture kind of guy' and thinks the place should have a *huskier* feel. The man actually said that. I once had a woman say she wanted a bedroom like a harlot's, but in forty plus years I never heard anyone ask for *husky*."

"I thought the wife said she had free rein."

"Apparently she did until the bills started to roll in."

"You'll work it out," Kit said, smiling. "You always do."

Baby was brilliant at many things but one of her specialties was negotiating what she called ICDC: Intense Couple Decorating Conflict.

"Where's Dara?" Kit asked, referring to their assistant.

"I had her run to the D&D building, and she's going home from there."

"Don't stay late on my account, Baby. We can do a real catch-up tomorrow, and I'll go through paperwork tonight."

The next few days rushed by. Kit spent a good chunk of her time on site at a Greenwich Village apartment she was decorating, checking on the paint job the contractors were doing in the study. It ended up perfect, a gorgeous, gleaming shade of aubergine. When the clients, the Griggses, saw the final results on Thursday they were agog. Kit felt both thrilled and relieved. The wife, Layla, had turned out to be a fussbudget, and Kit had been micromanaging the project even more intensely than normal.

But she knew there was another reason for her good mood. Her dinner with Matt Healy was just hours away. She felt herself craving both his company and his touch.

She chose a pale gray jersey dress for the night, one that was loose fitting, but clung in the right places. And she picked the sexiest bra and panties she owned.

She treated herself to a cab uptown so she wouldn't feel frazzled. The building turned out to be a high-rise luxury, not far from Lincoln Center. She gave Matt's name to the concierge and he nodded, lifting the intercom phone out of its cradle.

"Is he expecting you?" he asked.

"Yes," she said. She felt a rush of nervous excitement.

Before the concierge could buzz the apartment, a woman interrupted, asking about a package delivery.

"18C," the concierge told Kit, confirming what she already knew. "I'll tell him you're on the way up." Then he redirected his attention back to the other woman.

Kit rode the elevator to eighteen, feeling her pulse rate accelerate. "*Easy*, girl," she told herself. "You don't want to be foaming at the mouth when you arrive." After finding the right apartment, she pressed the buzzer. The door began to swing open and she smiled expectantly.

But the man standing on the other side of the threshold wasn't Matt. Kit's eyes darted toward the number on the door. Yes, this was C. Had she heard the letter incorrectly?

"I'm sorry," she said. "I'm looking for Matt Healy. I must have the wrong apartment."

"Well, I'm Matt Healy," the man said. "Who are you?"

chapter 2

For a moment she couldn't process what he'd just said. Instead, as she stared at the man's unfamiliar features, other phrases kept tumbling through her brain: wrong apartment, wrong building, wrong street, wrong day, wrong *something*.

But then, finally, his words computed: *"I'm Matt Healy."*

So where was the other Matt Healy? The one who was supposed to be serving her chili or stir-fry or whatever guys whipped up when they invited you for dinner? It felt as if she'd accidentally exited a building from a different door than the one she'd entered and was on the wrong street now, momentarily discombobulated.

"I—I don't understand," Kit stammered. "Is this some kind of joke?"

He smiled. Pleasant seeming, not acting at all cagey. For the first time, she really took in his appearance. Nice enough looking. Strawberry-blond hair. Blue eyes. He was dressed casually, in an untucked, long-sleeved dress shirt and a pair of brown cords, but he exuded a buttoned-up vibe. Lawyer/banker type.

"Well, not a joke *I'm* playing," he said. "Why exactly are you here?"

"To see a man I know named Matt Healy. We had plans."

He shrugged. "Like I said, I'm Healy and I don't believe we've ever met."

"But the doorman," she said, really flummoxed now. "He—he told me to go right up."

"Yeah, I know. He rang to say someone named Kit was on the way up. I said I wasn't expecting anyone but by that time you'd hopped on the elevator. I figured he got the name wrong, and it was probably a friend of mine dropping by to say hi."

Instinctively, she bit her lip, trying to think, trying to make sense of the rabbit hole she seemed to have fallen down. Maybe, by a freakish chance, there were two guys named Matt Healy in the building. But this was the apartment number Matt had given her. A revelation fought its way across a threshold in her mind. Had she been *played*? Tricked for some reason she didn't understand?

"Look," the guy said, "maybe there's an explanation. Do you want to come in for a minute and we'll try to sort it out?"

Down the long hall, the drone of a TV leaked beneath the door of another apartment but that was the only sound. No, she certainly didn't want to come in.

Shaking her head, she wondered what to do next. Her confusion began to morph into anger. If the man she'd had dinner with hadn't wanted to see her again, why set up this whole charade tonight?

The guy flipped over a hand in a kind of "I'm-as-stumped-as-you-are" gesture.

"I'm sure this isn't any fun for you," he said, "but let me at least help. I bet there's more than one Matt Healy in New York. How did you get the address?"

"From him. We met in Florida a few days ago and he invited me for dinner."

He took a slow breath and brought his hands to his mouth steeple style, holding them there. She wondered if he might be amused by her predicament, but his expression was intense and a couple of seconds later he raised an eyebrow in alarm.

"Oh God, I think I know what's going on," he said. "A week or so ago, someone robbed me. I mean, they stole my wallet. I cancelled my credit cards but the thief would still have my license, which of course has my address on it."

It felt as if someone had kicked her legs out from under her. Did this mean that the man she'd slept with was a thief? She could see him clearly in her mind's eye. Confident, self-possessed, a bit mysterious. But no way had there been a hint of anything *criminal*.

"I really should go," she said. She wanted to get as far away as possible from apartment 18C.

"No, wait." The guy's voice was almost pleading. "I can understand why you don't want to come in. For all you know I've got the real Matt Healy hogtied in here. But I don't and I really need to hear more details from you. This guy may have stolen my identity. Would you be willing to go someplace public with me? There's a little bar a few doors down from the building."

"Okay," she said finally. Though the idea had nada appeal for her, it seemed unfair not to help him.

"Let me just grab my jacket," he said.

"I'll meet you in the lobby," she told him. She needed a minute alone and a chance to think.

In the elevator, she flopped back against the wall and groaned. Maybe there *was* an explanation. Somewhere the real Matt Healy had to be waiting for her, maybe right this minute popping a cork from a bottle of wine or stirring a stew pot in anticipation of her arrival.

She checked her phone, where she'd programmed Matt's info when he'd called on her way to the airport. She groaned again as she saw that she was definitely at that address. There was a chance, of course, that she'd taken down the details incorrectly. But it was too huge a coincidence that a building she ended up in erroneously would have an occupant with the same name in the very same apartment.

What if the guy in the apartment really wasn't who he claimed to be? An imposter. But about a minute later, when he hurried around the corner from the elevator bank into the lobby, the concierge nodded at him and called out, "Evening, Mr. Healy."

There seemed little room for doubt now. She'd been hood-winked.

They stepped outside and Healy—yeah, she had to start thinking of him that way now—gestured toward a building a couple of doors down. As they reached the entrance she saw that it was an Italian restaurant, one of those faux rustic ones with yellow and white checked tablecloths and chairs with woven twine backs. The kind of spot you'd pick for a second date, not where you'd debrief a person about a con artist. There was a small bar, though, and Healy suggested they grab stools there rather than a table.

The bartender greeted him by name, just as the concierge had. Kit realized glumly that unless she was part of some mas-sive Bourne movie kind of conspiracy, the guy sitting next to her *was* who he claimed to be. And the man she'd met five days ago wasn't. When she'd first encountered him shopping in Is-lamorada, she'd thought of him as Mr. X, and now he was no more than X again.

Healy asked what she wanted to drink and she told him a cappuccino. She'd briefly considered a glass of wine, just to take the edge off, but she needed a clear head to come to grips with what had happened. He ordered a scotch and water himself and took a quick swig as soon as it arrived.

Healy had seemed unruffled when she'd first shown up on his doorstep, but she could sense his tension now—in the stiffness of his body, the way he jiggled the plastic straw that had been in his drink.

"I appreciate this," Healy said. "When I lost my wallet I thought cancelling six credit cards and ordering a new license was the worst of it, but the situation is clearly more complicated. What did this guy tell you he did for a living?"

"That he'd run a tech business but had recently sold it. Is that what you do?"

"No, I'm a portfolio manager at a hedge fund. You said you were in Florida when you met this guy. Where exactly?"

"Islamorada. He was staying at the same hotel I was."

"And he told you he was headed back here? Did he say when?"

"Today—and he promised to make me dinner." Of course, the missing meal was hardly the issue. She'd slept with a man, formed a connection with him, and had been hoping for more. And it had all been a sham.

Healy's body seemed to tense even more.

"Sounds like he might actually still be there, in Islamorada."

"He said he was going to Miami," Kit said. "But I guess that might have been a lie, too."

Yes, maybe it *all* had been a lie. Certainly if he was busy pickpocketing people, he hadn't recently cashed in on a tech company. But what about the drive south, being a sculptor, the Boho sister in Miami, the girlfriend who'd moved back to Melbourne? It stood to reason that every detail had been make-believe, part of a devious scheme to sound enchanting and lure her into bed.

Healy ran his finger around the rim of the glass, saying nothing for a moment. She was sure he was wondering if she had slept with the guy in Florida and was smarting now from being stood up and made a fool of. Well, she *was* smarting. She felt humiliated.

"When was your wallet stolen?" she asked.

"Uh, about ten days ago, at a party in Dumbo. I had it in the pocket of my sports jacket and I made the mistake of laying the jacket over a chair when the place got hot. An hour later when I went to pay for my cab home, I realized the wallet was missing. The hosts checked around but couldn't find it. I figured that some unsavory guest had seen me shed the jacket and gone through the pockets."

"And you cancelled the cards right away?" she asked.

"That night."

In her mind Kit conjured up the image of X summoning the bill at the hotel restaurant. She was pretty sure he had simply signed so that the dinner was charged to his room. But, of course, he would have needed a card to check into the hotel.

"So, if your cards were cancelled right way, he couldn't have used one of them to check in," she said. She wasn't sure why she was bothering to play Veronica Mars with Healy because all she wanted was to give him the info he needed and beat it out of there.

"Right, but if it's the same guy and he's using my name, he's got some game going on," Healy said. "Tell me exactly what this dude looked like. There were a lot people I didn't know that night, but maybe I can place him."

"Dark reddish hair with a close-cropped beard. Blue eyes. About six one or two." Describing him only heightened her annoyance. How stupid she'd been.

Healy took another drink. There was a privileged, preppy aura about him, though she couldn't tell if he came by it naturally or had cultivated it over time. In her work, particularly during the years she'd done stints at two big interior design firms prior to starting her own company, she'd met more than a few people who, after hitting it rich, acquired the trappings of old wealth—not just clothes and Bottega Veneta handbags but signet rings and clipped, patrician accents—that allowed observers to make grand assumptions about their background.

"I've got a favor to ask you," Healy said suddenly. "Would you be willing to drop by my office tomorrow and talk to our head of security?"

The last thing Kit wanted to do at this point was become part of some manhunt. She didn't respond immediately and she could tell Healy sensed her reluctance.

"Look, I hate having to involve you in this whole thing," he added, "but if this guy is posing as me, it could turn into a huge nightmare, and not just for me personally. It could ripple over to my business. I want the firm to be in the loop."

"I've got a pretty full work day," Kit said truthfully.

"Is there *any* time you could squeeze it in? It's really important."

"Well, I guess I could stop by at noon," she said, realizing she'd feel guilty if she declined. "But let me confirm the time with you."

"Great, I really appreciate this," he said.

"What about the police? Don't they have to be informed about this latest development?"

"Yes, I'll take care of that and they'll probably be in touch with you. But let's talk to my security guy first. Do you have a card?"

Healy seemed credible enough, but still, the whole situation was weird.

"Why don't you give me *your* card," she said. "And I'll call you early tomorrow."

His expression read worried, worried that she wouldn't follow through.

"All right," he said. "I don't have cards with me but I'll write down the details." He asked the bartender for a pen, scribbled his contact info on a cocktail napkin and turned it over to her.

"I know it's a pain, but I really need your help. This could screw up my life if I don't deal with it."

She nodded. She felt sorry for him, though not as sorry as she felt for herself at the moment.

A few minutes later she parted company with Healy on the street. It was drizzling lightly, and she considered taking a cab or Uber home, but she hated blowing another thirty bucks on the night. So she rushed to the subway stop and hopped onto a downtown train, at least securing a seat.

As the train hurtled through the tunnel, she stared down at her lap. Inside she was churning, her feelings all in a big, messy tangle. Anger dominated, running roughshod over everything else. She'd been duped, and the mean, nasty way X had done it infuriated her.

She was furious at herself, too. Not for sleeping with a stranger. She was hardly going to slut shame herself now that it hadn't worked out in her favor. What she hated was that she'd been such a freaking dummy. After years of dealing with the public, she considered herself to be clever at reading people, at assessing right from the start if a potential client would prove to be high maintenance or need to be massaged a certain way—or even try to stiff her when it came to the final bills.

It was a skill she had actually cultivated, reading books on body language and interpersonal relationships. Her father had been taken advantage of in business when she was seventeen, forcing him to declare bankruptcy and throwing their whole life as a family into a tailspin, and she'd sworn to herself that she'd never be deceived that way. *Ever.*

She thought suddenly of the comment X had made after he'd asked her to bed. He said that in the next weeks he'd need to focus all his attention on a critical matter, and he'd looked troubled by the thought. Was that because he was on the run? Nothing, however, about his comment or his manner then, had set off alarm bells for her. She'd simply assumed he was dealing with a personal, private challenge.

There was something else churning inside her, something she hated to acknowledge. *Disappointment.* Not only had the sex with X made her body feel as if it was on fire, but she had *liked* him, had found him more interesting than any man she'd met in ages, and had loved the effortlessness of being in his company. There'd be no repeat.

It was still drizzling out when she ascended the steps of the Spring Street station, and the air felt raw. She had a four-block walk ahead. Tightening the belt of her trench coat, she quickened her pace. All she wanted was to be home, curled up in bed with something warm to drink.

She turned onto her street and saw that it was almost empty, except for two people climbing into a van halfway up the block. A question suddenly recurred, one she had asked herself in Healy's corridor.

Why had X *punked* her that way? Con artist or not, he'd seemed so thoughtful toward her. Though he'd been open about wanting sex, there'd been no pressure on his part, and he'd offered her a reason to pass. Besides, once he'd conveyed on Sunday night that he wasn't interested in any entanglements and she'd accepted the fact, why not just leave it at that?

Had he derived some sadistic *pleasure* from doing it, chuckling malevolently as he imagined her arriving at Matt Healy's building all lit up and then leaving with her tail between her legs. The thought chilled her.

He had her business card, she realized, a breath catching in her chest. It listed only her work address, but that, of course, was also where she lived.

She tried to tamp down her fear. She'd been tricked but there didn't seem to be any real reason to be alarmed. X was probably still in Florida, onto another play by now. She pitied the next girl in line.

Her building was just a few yards away now, and she made a dash toward it. The lobby was empty, forlorn almost, and she jangled her keys nervously as she waited for the elevator. When she was finally inside her apartment, she shut the door closed with such force that a framed print nearby bounced against the wall.

chapter 3

She threw the bolt on the door and set the chain.

After kicking off her boots, she grabbed her laptop and searched online for Ithaka, the hedge fund Healy had jotted down on the napkin. She quickly found the firm's official website, tapped on it, and seconds later was staring at a bio of Matt Healy, complete with photo. It was the same guy she'd just met. There was no doubt now that he'd been telling the truth and that X had tricked her.

She thought of one more step she could take, mainly to satisfy morbid curiosity. X had introduced himself as Matt Healy and she wanted to know if he'd presented himself to the hotel that way or just to her. She called the hotel and asked for Matt Healy's room.

"I'm sorry," the operator said after a pause. "Mr. Healy has already checked out."

So he'd definitely posed as Healy. But how had he paid the hotel bill? The real Matt had said that he'd cancelled his cards. Wouldn't X have needed a credit card to check in? Had he somehow managed to get a new card under Matt Healy's name, using the identity he'd stolen?

Even if she had the answers, none of them would shed any light on why he had duped her into going to apartment 18C.

She told herself to feel lucky that she'd escaped Islamorada with only her ego bruised.

She tugged off her gray jersey dress and hung it back in the closet. It looked mopey and morose on the hanger, as if its feelings had been hurt, too. She couldn't help but picture herself three hours ago, shimmying into the dress and pairing it with a long silver pendent. How pointless all her efforts had been.

She forced herself to the fridge and rooted around for food. There was half a chicken breast, left over from a rotisserie bird she'd bought the day before, a bag of mesclun greens, and a chunk of blue cheese, not quite ripe enough to kill an STD but almost. As she stood at the kitchen counter, fashioning a salad from what she'd found, she thought of the meal she'd eaten that night with X—conch chowder, blackened red snapper, a slice of key lime pie, all so different from her usual fare.

There was something else that was troubling her, she realized, something that the memory of those dishes forced her to recognize. Her Florida trip was supposed to have been a turning point, the beginning of a more daring, more adventurous chapter in her life. Not so much a *new* Kit really, but the Kit she'd once been as a girl, before everything had unraveled in her family's life. Well, so much for being a bit of a badass. Maybe she should take the whole episode as a warning.

The irony was that in her work she rarely held back. She'd started her own business, and when it came to the actual design work, she liked to turn things on their ear, like painting a wall to resemble awning stripes or upholstering a couch with the fabric inside out.

That was one of the reasons she'd been so excited about teaming with Baby, a bold decorator who advocated that every room have at least "a dash of clash." She always pushed the envelope, like choosing Fanta orange for the accent color in a posh Upper East Side apartment. The two of them loved tossing wild-card ideas back and forth.

"Oh, you naughty girl," Baby would say to her.

But in other aspects of life, including love, Kit had always played it ridiculously safe. Risks scared her pants off, or rather, for the most part kept them on. She thought of herself as the total opposite of a woman who was buttoned-up all day at the office but after sundown turned into a whip-wielding domina-trix, with a name like "Madame Darke" or "Nurse Payne." After a gutsy day at work, *she* turned into "Miss Goody Two Shoes."

Of course her friends would probably have been surprised to discover she thought of herself that way. They referred to her as *spunky*—or at least most of them did. Kit suspected that after her bland, lame relationship with Jeremy, a few might have begun to revise their sense of her.

She crashed at eleven that night. The sound of a couple ar-guing on the street below woke her just after one, and it took her over an hour to fall back to sleep. She kept thinking of X, wondering how she could have done such a bad job of reading him. A few memories surfaced: X on the phone on the walk-way, sounding slightly aggravated. Maybe he'd been talking to a cohort. X casting his gaze around the restaurant right after they'd finished eating. At the moment she'd supposed that he was searching for the waiter. But it could have been the instinct of a criminal who was always on the watch.

First thing the next morning, she emailed Matt Healy and told him that she'd drop by his office at noon. The sooner she got it over with, the better. She dressed casually—she planned to shop a good part of the day—grabbed a yogurt, and unlocked the door that led to her office from the apartment. The point of the door wasn't simply for her convenience. Both she and Baby occasionally used the living space for client meetings—it was a great way to show off the kind of nontraditional aesthetic they subscribed to—and the inner door gave them easy access back and forth.

Baby had beaten her into the office that morning. She'd laid trace paper over an apartment floor plan and was plotting out where the furniture ought to be positioned.

Baby had spent nearly four decades as one of Manhattan's top decorators—not quite in the same league as Bunny Williams or Mario Buatta, but in demand by tons of well-heeled clients. She'd retired at sixty-four, planning to travel, entertain, and relish life, but when her adored husband Dan had died five years later, she'd decided that the best way to tackle grief was to jump feet first back into work. After meeting Kit at an event and getting to know her, she'd suggested partnering with her—and investing a small amount of money in the business. Kit had been ecstatic. This time, though, Baby had no interest in her projects being splashed in the pages of *Elle Decor* or *Architectural Digest*. She wanted out of the limelight and that's why a small boutique business had appealed to her.

In the two years they'd worked together, she and Baby had become not only colleagues but also friends, often reaching out to each other for personal guidance. The day after her return from Florida, Kit had reported on her dinner under the stars with the man calling himself Matt Healy—and had admitted to spending the night with him. As soon as Baby set eyes on Kit this morning, she arched a brow mischievously, eager for a full report about the date.

After dropping into her chair, Kit blurted out what happened.

"That's perfectly dreadful," Baby declared. "The man should be shot."

"Yes, but so should *I*. It was just so stupid of me to believe he was the real deal."

"It's not like you let someone convince you the moon landing was faked. Thinking an attractive, educated-seeming man is who he claims to be isn't stupid. It's a mistake any woman could make."

"I appreciate your saying that, Baby. But it was a lapse, a big one. The guy was a freaking con artist. I hate the thought of making a bad call like that."

Baby tapped her hands together softly, her red nails gleaming.

"I don't know if I ever mentioned this to you, but I was married briefly in my twenties before I met Dan. These days they call that a starter marriage, though back then the euphemism was 'too young to know better.' The man was a real cad and he cheated on me within months. For years, even after I married Dan, I beat myself up about it, really doubted my judgment. What helped me was to finally step back and ask myself what the warning signs might have been and why I missed them."

"*Had* there been warning signs?" Kit asked.

Baby scoffed. "Does French kissing the maid of honor at the rehearsal dinner count? Unfortunately I didn't learn that until much later. But there had been subtle signs from the very start, ones I'd chosen to ignore. Put this behind you, Kit. But there may be something to learn from it."

Kit nodded glumly. The only lesson she'd gleaned so far was that taking a risk had blown up in her face.

"That said," Baby added, "it's time for you to meet someone new and wonderful. Why don't you finally give Match a chance?"

"But I thought you said it was full of losers and lunatics."

"Oh, in my age category—also known as the court of last resort—it's positively swimming with them. I had a date two weeks ago with a man who told me he would never travel to Italy because the Italians inject sleeping potions into their train compartments so they can rob you while you are unconscious. But you're in an age category with far more options. Plus, it's a numbers game. You have to cycle through a certain number of bad ones for something good."

"Maybe I'll give it a try," she said half heartedly. She *did* want to meet someone. It had been five months since her split with Jeremy, a mutually agreed upon one, and she felt hungry for a real connection with a man, hungry, she had to admit, for love. But getting there seemed like such an awful lot of effort, something you needed to work at like a second job. That was part of the reason the night with X had been so gratifying. Instant attraction. No game playing. Or at least that's how it had presented itself *then*.

"Just a word of caution," Baby advised. "Don't believe anyone who announces in the first email that his baggage is small enough to fit in the overhead compartment."

"Ha," Kit said, smiling. "I'll watch for that."

Baby's face clouded.

"You don't have any concerns that this man will try to track you down, do you?"

Kit sighed. "I have to admit, I've felt anxious since last night. But I'm banking on the fact that he's one thousand miles away. And at noon, I'm going in to meet with the security chief at Healy's firm. Who knows? Maybe there's something they can do."

"I'll be eager to know how it goes."

Kit turned her attention to work. Beyond the Griggses' Greenwich Village apartment, she was juggling five or six other projects, including a one-bedroom Murray Hill condo for a recently divorced, fifty-something tax attorney named Barry Kaplan with the simplest of demands ("I just want a place women will dig and doesn't have any of those little towels and soaps in the bathroom you're never supposed to actually use"); a two-bedroom rental in Chelsea that a picky couple insisted be spectacular on next to nothing; and, of course, the Jersey Shore cottage that was supposed to have a Florida Keys vibe.

She knew the last project would make it difficult to put X out of her mind, but at the moment it had to be her priority. Following her return last Monday, she'd forwarded the owner, Avery Howe, some of the photos she'd snapped in Florida and explained that she'd soon be following up with a plan.

But something about the whole project had her stymied. Avery, the thirty-nine-year-old head of a hip, boutique PR firm, insisted she wanted a beachy Key West vibe in the cottage. That would be easy enough to pull off, but everything Kit knew about Avery seemed to contradict what she claimed to long for. Could anyone who wore earrings with two huge Chanel C's on them and carried designer handbags too large to fit under the airline seat in front of her be happy in rooms decorated with bamboo shades and bleached coral?

Kit grabbed a sheet of paper and made a Venn diagram. In one bubble she scribbled down words Avery had tossed out during one of their exploratory meetings, words that also fit with the clippings Avery had pulled for her: spare, serene, creamy, bleached wood. In the other bubble she listed words she associated with Avery's personal style: chic, sophisticated, glittery, over the top at times. Then she stared at the empty intersecting section and wondered what could fit there.

Nothing came immediately to mind. She made herself a cappuccino in the office kitchenette and as she stared at a small milk mug, one she'd brought back as a souvenir from a trip to Sweden, she suddenly had a crazy brainstorm. What if she went for beachy but mixed in touches of Gustavian design? It was a Swedish style from the 1800's that called for cream colors, as well as splashes of pale gray, blue, or yellow. But it also featured crystal chandeliers and gilded mirrors. Done right, Gustavian could be both spare and glittery. It could give Avery what she *swore* she wanted as well as what she probably yearned for without knowing it.

Perfect, Kit thought. She sent Avery a long email describing the concept.

Dara, Kit and Baby's assistant, arrived promptly at nine. She was wearing a fuchsia-colored turtleneck sweater that worked fabulously with her dark brown skin and hair. After they exchanged hellos, Kit asked Dara to start putting together Pinterest pins on Gustavian design for her to share with Avery.

"Oh, that era rocks," Dara said. "And I'd love to know more about it."

"You never cease to amaze me, Dara," Kit said. And it was true. Dara was not only mature for twenty-four, but she also had far more understanding of decorating history than Kit ever possessed at her age.

"Well, it's all that Swedish blood of mine," Dara said kiddingly.

At 11:15, Kit slipped on her coat, said goodbye to her office mates—letting Dara assume she was off on an errand—and headed toward the subway. She still felt unsettled about her experience in Islamorada and wasn't looking forward to revisiting it.

Ithaka was located on West 43rd, in a nondescript high-rise, but when Kit stepped off the elevator onto the twenty-ninth floor, she discovered that the reception area was sleek and modern; one entire wall was covered in glowing white Plexiglas with the word Ithaka in gray. She gave her name to the receptionist and a minute later Matt Healy appeared. He looked spiffier today, dressed in business casual—black slacks and a crisp button down shirt—but she could sense the edge still. Maybe the identity theft was weighing heavily on him.

"Thanks so much for coming," he said. "Let me take you to Steve Ungaro's office. He's our security chief and he very much wants to speak to you."

"You'll be in the meeting, too, won't you?" Kit asked.

"Unfortunately, I won't be able to stay. I'm leaving momentarily on a business trip. But I'll make the introduction and you can fill Steve in."

Okay, that was a curveball, but there seemed to be no point in protesting. She followed him into a large open area. Along the outside were glass-walled offices, which she assumed were for higher-level players; the middle space was clearly the trading area—six or seven rows of desks, back-to-back with the ones in the next row. Each desk had four to six computer screens mounted above it, bright with multicolored charts and graphs and long streams of numbers, none of it easily discernable from a distance. Most of the desks were occupied by men, some dressed like Healy in business casual, others in jeans and hooded sweatshirts, and most wearing headsets. What surprised her was how hushed the atmosphere was. No ringing phones. Barely any conversation.

Kit wasn't very familiar with hedge funds or how they operated. But she'd read enough to know that they were part of a high-stakes world where someone could make millions in a day, and also lose that much, all with a single trade.

As she walked along the outside passageway, most people kept their eyes glued to their computer screens, though one woman, talking on the phone in one of the glass offices, took her in from top to bottom. Maybe, Kit thought, I don't look hedge-fund-y enough in my jeans, turtleneck, and black riding boots.

Ungaro's office was at the far end, and as she entered the room with Healy, the security chief rose in greeting. She'd imagined that he'd be beefy and bodyguard-like, but in his business casual pants and dress shirt, the slim, fit-looking Ungaro could have exchanged places with any of the other staff she'd spotted. Except for his age. He was about fifty, older than most of the other people she'd spotted, and with a rogue tuft of gray in his thick, dark hair.

Healy made the introduction, said goodbye, and then exited, closing the door behind him.

"Thank you for coming in, Ms. Finn," Ungaro said. "We're most appreciative. Our executives are privy to highly sensitive information, and we certainly don't like the idea of one being impersonated."

"I can understand," she said.

"Please, have a seat. Matt shared some of the details but if you can walk me through them, I'd appreciate it."

His tone was all friendly, but she knew it was probably purely for the benefit of his mission. He wanted the facts and he knew it wouldn't do any good to put her on the defensive. She suspected that beneath that easygoing manner was a guy who got the job done at all costs.

After settling into the chair across from Ungaro, she explained how she'd first seen X at the hotel, then encountered him at the shop, and later had dinner with him, skipping the part about accompanying him to his room. That was nobody's business but hers. She also provided a description of X.

Ungaro took notes while she spoke, but he glanced up from time to time, obviously trying to read her. Despite what Healy might have shared with him, it was clear he was reserving all judgment until he'd evaluated the situation himself.

"Did this man talk about his work at all?" Ungaro asked.

"Not really. As I told Mr. Healy, he mentioned he'd recently sold a tech business, but he didn't say much about it."

"By any chance do you have a photograph of him?"

"No, sorry, I don't," she said. The last thing she would have done is ask X if she could grab a selfie with him as a souvenir of their one-night stand.

Ungaro let his writing hand fall limp and leaned in toward the desk. His expression morphed from purely neutral to sympathetic.

"This is a tough question," he said, "but I need to ask it. Do you think there's any chance this man who called himself Healy could have targeted you?"

"*Targeted?*" she said. "I'm not sure what you mean." But the very word had made her stomach knot.

"You see him in the hotel and then he just happens to pop into a small shop at the same time you're there. Perhaps that wasn't as random as it looked."

"Well, it seemed perfectly random at the time," she said, still trying to figure out what he was getting at. "It's a small town and there are only so many shops there."

"I'm just wondering if he felt there was something to gain from talking to you. . . . Information, for instance."

"What information could he possibly want to extract from me?" Kit exclaimed. "I'm a *decorator.*"

She opened her purse, located a business card and handed it to Ungaro. "There, you can see for yourself. Even if he tied me up and put a gun to my head, all I'd be able to tell him was how to make his ceilings look higher—or what to do if he ended up with two shades of red that didn't match."

"I didn't mean to concern you," Ungaro said, sensing her agitation. "You've been quite helpful, and I should let you go."

"Thank you."

"By the way, what *do* you do with two shades of red that don't match?"

Oh, that was funny, she thought. Was he really hoping for a decorating tip? Maybe he was just trying to gauge if she knew her stuff.

"You add a third shade of red. And then the eye isn't bothered by the discrepancy anymore." She rose from the chair, eager to split. "Am I supposed to talk to Mr. Healy again?"

"He has a trip scheduled so I offered to walk you out," Ungaro said, rising himself.

"All right. Please tell him I said good luck sorting this out."

"I will. Just one final question, something that puzzles me." He was watching her intently now. "Why do you think the man you met created this whole ruse of inviting you to dinner at Mr. Healy's apartment? If he'd sensed eagerness on your part to meet again and he felt he had to placate you, why not just stand you up at a restaurant?"

"I've wondered the same thing," Kit said somberly. "But I have no clue. Inviting me to his apartment actually exposed the lie."

He cocked his head. "I'm afraid I'm not following."

"If he hadn't done that, I would have never discovered that he was an imposter."

Out of the corner of her eye, she saw the office door swing open and to her surprise, another man entered the room. He was slightly older than Ungaro, late fifties and handsome, with hooded eyes and thick silver hair. *Now* what? Kit thought.

"Ms. Finn, I'd like to introduce you to our CEO, Mitchell Wainwright," Ungaro said. He didn't seem surprised by Wainwright's appearance and Kit suspected it had all been orchestrated in advance.

Wainwright reached out to shake her hand. His grip was powerful, as if he could crush her fingers in the time it took her to plead for mercy.

"Matt Healy explained the situation to me. We're grateful for your cooperation."

"Thank you," she said, edging toward the door.

"I was just seeing Ms. Finn out," Ungaro said. "She's been very helpful."

"I'm headed to the front," Wainwright said, "so why don't I accompany her." A statement more than a question.

She didn't care who showed her out as long as they got it over with. After nodding goodbye to Ungaro, she strode with

Wainwright along the outside of the bullpen. His barrel-chested body seemed to give off power, the way a stove gave off heat, and she saw at least a half-dozen people discreetly lift their eyes from their computer screens. They were keeping tabs on the silver fox who ruled the empire.

Wainwright didn't say a word, just walked along in tandem, practically hugging her side with the force of a magnet. But in the reception area, he finally opened his mouth to speak.

"So how was the weather when you were in Florida?" he asked.

"The weather?" she said. Why would he care? she wondered. "Sunny. Nice."

His eyes were coppery brown–colored and small, like two pennies, but he used them to hold her gaze, and his stare was as fierce as his handshake had been.

"I like to get down there to play golf a couple of times a season," he said. "But unfortunately this year, I haven't had much chance."

"Well, maybe next year," she said, realizing as the words spilled from her mouth how lame they sounded. But she didn't care. "If you don't mind, I'd like to use the ladies' room before I leave."

"Of course," he said, and pointed to a door just down the corridor. "Good day and thank you again."

In the bathroom, she ran a paper towel under cold water and dabbed her cheeks, which were warm to the touch. She felt troubled still by the comment Ungaro had made, about X potentially targeting her. Could X really have followed her that day? But if he had some motive in mind—to go to bed with her or even to steal *her* wallet—then why not immediately ask her to dinner at the hotel? His invitation had seemed like an afterthought.

The door to the ladies' room opened quietly and a woman

stepped inside. It was the same one who had eyed her earlier. The woman approached the mirror and began to reapply her lipstick, a shade that might have been called black cherry. She was tall, with slightly wavy, raven-colored hair that grazed her shoulders, and gray eyes that were set far apart. Her slim pants and cobalt blue silk blouse might look low-key, but Kit could tell at a glance that they were pricey, designer-made. And then there were the diamond studs in her earlobes, bright enough to burn someone's corneas. The fact that she had an office clearly indicated that she had plenty of clout at the firm.

"I'm Sasha Glen, by the way," the woman said, turning to her abruptly. "Have you just started here?"

"I'm only visiting," Kit said, amused by the comment. The chance of her working at a hedge fund was about as likely as Baby decorating a Park Avenue living room with a pair of La-Z-Boy recliners.

The woman turned back to the mirror and stroked the lipstick deliberately once more across her mouth. She continued to gaze at Kit, via the mirror this time. "Oh, yes, I think we met at the holiday party," she said after a moment. "You're dating Matt, right?"

That seemed like a presumptuous remark to make to a stranger.

"You must have me mixed up with someone else," Kit said. "I had an appointment with Mr. Healy today, but I barely know him."

"My mistake," the woman said. She dropped the lipstick back in her purse. "Have a nice day."

I will, Kit thought, as soon as I've escaped from here.

She tossed the paper towel in the trash and hurried to the elevator bank. She felt relieved to finally be descending toward the lobby. The rest of the afternoon was spent roaming the D&D building as well as two stores that carried pieces inspired by the

Gustavian period. She was still waiting to hear if Avery Howe liked the concept for her cottage, but she wanted to be prepared to kick into gear once she received the okay.

By the time she reached the office, it was after seven and both Dara and Baby were long gone. She let herself into the apartment, feeling the same rush of comfort and pleasure she always experienced when she walked through the door. Though the open living space wasn't huge, she'd worked hard to make it dazzling.

She started to turn toward the island in front of the kitchen area when she suddenly froze, staring at her midnight-blue velvet sofa. Something wasn't right.

The seven accent pillows were in a neat row, just as she liked them. But they were in a different order than she'd left them in that morning.

Someone had been in her apartment.

chapter 4

She crossed the room to the sofa and stared at the pillows. She was sure her imagination wasn't going cuckoo on her. When she'd left the apartment that morning, the pillow with the Union Jack—a whimsical touch she'd added—was in the middle of the arrangement and flanked on each side, from outside in, by a pillow in fake zebra, one covered with kilim fabric, and another in solid red. She was ridiculously particular about the order and always kept it that way. But now the Union Jack pillow was one spot over from where it should be.

Stepping back, she anxiously examined the room, searching for anything else that seemed weirdly *off*. But nothing else was out of place.

Maybe, she reassured herself, Baby had used the apartment for a meeting with a potential client or a new one, and the pillows had gotten shuffled around. Clients were often curious to see a designer's home, dropping broad hints like, "So what's *your* place like?" But Baby always let Kit know in advance if she'd be taking advantage of the space. She'd said nothing about a Friday meeting.

Kit tried Baby's cell, but it went to voicemail and she left a message asking her to get in touch. She tried Dara next. But as the phone rang, she realized that of course Baby must have used the apartment and she was totally overreacting. What other explanation could there be? That some psycho with an uncontrollable urge to *fluff* had snuck in and rearranged the pillows? Clearly, she'd been so unsettled about the Florida experience that she was now practically jumping at the sight of her own shadow. She was about to break off the call when Dara answered.

"Since I missed you this afternoon, I just thought I'd make sure nothing came up," Kit said, fudging.

"It was actually fairly quiet," Dara told her. "Though Corey stopped by and left off the latest drawings for you." Corey was one of the freelance draftsmen she and Baby assigned work to.

"Good. I actually haven't popped into the office yet, so I didn't see them. Why don't I let you get back to your Friday night? You and Scott doing something fun?"

"We're going out later to hear a friend's band play."

"Enjoy—oh just one more question." As long as she had Dara on the line, Kit couldn't resist asking.

"Did Baby meet with a new client today? It looks like she might have been in my apartment with someone."

"She didn't mention anything, but a prospect may have dropped in while I was out. I went tile shopping for Baby at three and headed home from there."

"Oh, right. Okay, I'll catch up with Baby later."

"Is anything the matter?"

"No, no. It just looked like someone had been on the couch." Dara laughed. "Maybe Baby snuck in a power nap when we were both gone."

"Well, let's not bust her if that's the case," Kit said, laughing, too.

She'd no sooner signed off than Baby phoned.

"I'd been planning to call *you* tonight," Baby said. "How was the meeting?"

"What? Oh, at Ithaka you mean. Thanks for asking. I've had bikini waxes that were more pleasant, but it's behind me now. I'm going to banish the Florida mystery man from my brain, once and for all."

"Good for you. By the way, I don't know if you've seen it yet, but I left a message on your desk from a potential client. A doctor. He said he'd also email you, but I took down his info."

Kit had her hands full but she never turned down business. If necessary, she could hire a freelancer to help her shop any new projects that materialized.

"That's great. Have you got a new prospect yourself?" Kit said.

"No, I'm up to my ears at the moment. Why do you ask?"

"Oh, just me being anal. The pillows on my couch look re-arranged and I thought you might have taken a meeting in the apartment."

"Oh I *did* use your place," Baby said. "But it was with Miss Fancy Pants, my Sutton Place client. I left you a note about that, too. She swung by at 3:30, desperate to see swatches. We mainly used the dining table to spread out the fabrics, though she sat on the couch once while I was getting organized. She must have scooted the pillows around."

"Not a problem," Kit said, feeling her body sag with relief.

"Wait, were you worried someone else had been there?"

"No, no," Kit lied. She didn't want Baby to see how on edge she was still feeling. "Have a great weekend."

Before fixing dinner, she slipped into her office. She found the drawings Dara had mentioned and the messages from Baby. Checking her email, she discovered that the doctor, Keith Holt, had indeed sent her a message. He wrote that over the course of a week, he'd heard people talking about her at two different dinner parties and that he'd been impressed by her website. He asked if she could come by his place next week to discuss the possibility of working on his apartment.

Nice, she thought. She offered him a few slots on the calendar, but suggested they speak on the phone first. She'd learned over time that making a connection with a potential client by telephone in advance reduced the chance of the client cancelling the appointment and postponing it indefinitely.

There was also an email from Avery, who had written to say she was "over the moon" about the concept for the cottage that Kit had sent her earlier. Kit grinned as she read it.

But at the end of the email she discovered a hitch. Avery mentioned that her aunt with the house in Key West had a selection of antiques she wanted to pass on to her and Avery needed to know which pieces, if any, would work in the cottage. She hoped Kit could make a quick trip to Key West and tag what she thought should be shipped north. Avery would foot the bill, though Kit knew she'd expect her to travel as inexpensively as possible.

The last thing Kit wanted was to be in Florida again any time soon, but Avery's project was a substantial piece of business and she couldn't refuse. For a moment she considered finding someone in Key West to photograph the pieces and email them to her. But that wasn't the best way to evaluate furniture and she didn't want Avery to incur the cost of shipping items that in the end might not work.

She wrote Avery back, saying that she would be happy to make the trip and would head down there next week. With that out of the way, they could begin serious shopping immediately afterward, which would help guarantee that the cottage would be ready by the start of summer.

Leaning back in her desk chair, Kit realized how much the

thought of returning to the Keys unsettled her. Not that she worried about running into X. Even if Miami hadn't really been his next destination, he'd probably hightailed it out of the Keys. But deep down, her emotions about Islamorada were still in a tangle, and too many questions continued to gnaw at her. Who *was* X? Why had he made love to her, asked to see her again, and then hoodwinked her? And how had she been so easily deceived? Being in the hot Florida sun would force it all to the surface again.

By the end of the weekend she had relaxed a little about the trip. She decided to fly south Thursday or Friday afternoon and return the next day, which would amount to just less than twenty-four hours away. And she'd do her best to keep her focus on the project.

Monday was bleak and rainy, a typical early April day, and she, Baby, and Dara hunkered down for the morning. At about eleven, as Kit was reviewing the contractor's punch list for the Greenwich Village apartment, the phone rang. Dara answered and Kit heard her ask who was calling. Instinctively, she glanced up and caught a frown forming on her assistant's face. Dara scribbled a few words on a piece of paper, told the caller, "Let me see if she's here," and then pressed the hold button.

"Kit," she said, worriedly. "It's the police. From Miami. A detective named Linda Molinari wants to talk to you."

It felt to Kit as if someone had locked an arm around her from behind and was pressing hard against her chest.

"A *detective*?" she said. "Did she say what she wanted?"

"No. Do you want me to ask her?"

Kit shook her head. "I'll take it," she said. She picked up the phone on her desk and identified herself.

"Ms. Finn, this is Detective Molinari from the Miami-Dade Police Department," a woman said crisply.

"Hello," Kit replied, at a loss for more than that. What were you supposed to say when a detective rang you up out of nowhere?

"You're an interior designer in New York City?"

"Yes, I am."

"I'd like to ask you a few questions if you have a minute."

"Okay," she said. What was going on, she wondered, anxiously. Nothing about the detective's tone suggested she was calling to investigate changing the color palette at the police precinct. "Can I ask what this is about?"

"I'll fill you in momentarily. Have you been in the Miami area recently?"

"Uh, not Miami," she said. "I was in Islamorada about a week ago on vacation, but I flew in and out of the Miami airport."

"What day did you return to New York City from your trip?"

Kit could feel her nervousness intensifying. Didn't cops ask those kinds of questions when they were investigating you in relation to criminal activity?

"On Monday. A week ago today."

"Do you come to this area frequently?"

"No, not generally. I mean, I'm actually going to have to fly through Miami this week, but just for business purposes."

"While you were on your recent trip, did you give a business card to anyone?"

"Yes, yes I did," she said, fumbling through her memory. While scouting, she'd handed out cards to a couple of shop managers in Islamorada, and she related that to the detective.

"Were any of them male?"

"One of them was." And then, with a jolt, Kit remembered. She'd also given a card to X that day at the store. Had he dragged her into his troubled life somehow?

"And there was one other person," she added, trying to keep her voice calm. "A man at my hotel who I had dinner with. Why?"

She was aware of Baby watching her, signaling with her expression that she was there to help if needed. Dara had gone back to bill paying, attempting to appear nonchalant, but Kit could detect how on alert her body was.

"Can you describe him, please?" Molinari asked.

"Um, late thirties. About six one or two. Blue eyes and reddish hair. Please tell me what's going on."

"Ms. Finn, we're investigating a hit and run involving a man who fits that description. He had no identification on him—no wallet, nothing—but he was carrying your business card in his pocket."

Kit gasped and grabbed the side of the desk with her free hand. "The man I had dinner with put my card in his pants pocket," she said. "Is—is he okay?"

X must have been seriously injured, in a coma, perhaps, and not able to talk. She realized that she would have to fill the detective in on what she knew about him from Healy, and that it might very well lead to his arrest.

"What was this man's name?" Molinari asked.

"I—I have no idea," Kit said. "I mean, he told me his name was Matt Healy, but since then I discovered that it wasn't true. He may have stolen someone's wallet. It's very complicated."

She overheard Baby whisper something to Dara, and the two of them whisked themselves out of the office and into the small kitchenette.

"I've got all the time you need," Molinari said.

Kit ran through the story quickly, leaving out any mention of going to bed with X, and feeling a twinge of shame as she described how she'd been tricked.

"Can you just tell me," Kit said at the end. "Was he badly hurt?" She couldn't help it. She felt the urge to know.

A pause.

"The hit and run was a fatality," Molinari said finally. "And it may have been premeditated."

Kit tried to respond but no words came out. X was dead. She

could still see his face in her mind, feel his naked body next to hers, feel him *inside* her.

Maybe he'd been entangled in something bigger than pickpocketing and it had led to his death. The detective was talking, but Kit could barely hear the words.

"Ms. Finn?"

"Yes, I'm sorry. It's just a shock. Can you repeat what you said?"

"You mentioned that you were going to be in the area this week. I'd appreciate it if you could meet with my partner and me while you're here."

"But I'm only flying *through* Miami," she protested. "I'll be connecting there for a flight to Key West."

"Could you allow a few hours between flights so we could meet at the medical examiner's office?"

"You want me to look at the *body*?" Kit said, stunned. That would be horrible. X had duped her, but that didn't mean she wanted to see him lying lifeless on a slab in the morgue.

"You wouldn't be looking at the actual body. Only a photograph."

"Is it possible to just email the photo?"

"No, that's not allowed unfortunately."

"But I wouldn't be able to identify him regardless," Kit said. "I have no idea who he is."

"You'd be able to confirm whether or not it's the man who misled you. We have to solve this case, and you're one of the few leads we have. The ME's office is just fifteen minutes from the airport."

She scrambled for a response. The way the detective had phrased the request made it sound as if there was no actual requirement for Kit to acquiesce. But something told her it would be smart to be helpful, to appear willing to cooperate.

"I was thinking of flying down Thursday or Friday," she said after a moment. "Would that work for you?"

"Could you make it tomorrow instead?"

"*Tomorrow?*"

"We need to move quickly."

"Uh, okay," she stammered. "Let me see about flights and get back to you shortly."

Before signing off, Molinari provided her contact info.

The call over, Kit just sat there, too stunned to move. X was dead, possibly murdered. And the whole ugly mess seemed to be blowing back on her.

After a minute, she forced herself out of her chair and into the galley kitchen, where Baby and Dara were leaning against the counter, silently sipping their cappuccinos.

"Dara, could you give Baby and me a minute," she said.

"Sure," Dara replied, agreeably, but Kit could tell she was wigged out about what was happening. As soon as Dara had closed the kitchen door behind her, Baby grasped one of Kit's hands.

"What's going on?" she asked. Her pale blue eyes had darkened in worry.

Kit spilled out the story, her voice catching at moments.

"Do you think the body they found is definitely the man you met in Florida?" Baby asked.

"The description fits and the only other man I gave a card to was a sixty-something shop owner who wasn't an inch over five foot four. And my infamous one-night stand said he was headed toward Miami. Of course, now I have no reason to believe that detail, but I suppose even liars tell the truth sometimes." She covered her face with her hands. "I can't believe what I've gotten myself into."

"They can't *force* you to identify the body, can they? It's not like you're a relative of the man's."

Kit sighed.

"I just don't want the cops mistakenly thinking that I played a role in anything he was up to, especially if he was killed on purpose. Talking to them in person should help them see me for who I am."

"You may be right," Baby said. She tapped her nails on the countertop a few times. "And once you've met with them, you can put this crazy thing behind you."

"Yes, hopefully."

"I know this is going to sound awful—and as my mother always advised, one should never speak ill of the dead—but I'll say it anyway." That was another thing Kit loved about Baby, even though it occasionally caught her off guard, Baby told it like it was. "At least now you won't have to worry anymore that this man could turn up again. I know that concerned you."

Baby was right. If X had been killed, there'd be no worry that he would surface once more in her life. And yet the thought of him dead rattled her.

After they both returned to the main room, Kit phoned Avery and asked if she could arrange for her to survey the aunt's home as early as Wednesday. No problem, she was told. The aunt was now in an assisted living facility but a neighbor would be able to show her the house. After checking flights, Kit called Detective Molinari back and made arrangements to meet her at the Dade County Medical Examiner's at one o'clock the next day. She could hardly believe it. She *would* have a chance to set eyes again on X, but she'd be staring at a photo of his corpse.

By nine the next morning she was air bound. Being on the plane felt totally surreal. She thought suddenly of the Magritte painting of a pipe with the words "*Ceci n'est pas une pipe*"—this is not a pipe—written below the image. This was Tuesday but nothing about it *seemed* like Tuesday. Underneath her anxiety and dread, she felt a dull, aching sadness.

As promised, the Medical Examiner's Building turned out to be only a short drive from the airport. The cabbie pulled into the driveway and dropped her in front of the large brick building. As he hoisted her roller bag out of the trunk, he eyed the structure with a slight grimace, as if fearful of being exposed to something contagious. She thanked him, shrugged off her trench coat, and draped it over one arm. She'd worn leggings, thinking they'd be a good transition outfit from New York to Florida, but the temperature was in the mid-eighties and the leggings had begun to stick obnoxiously to her thighs. Dragging her roller bag, she ascended a long ramp and spoke her name into an intercom. She was buzzed into the lobby by a woman sitting at a desk behind a glass barricade.

The reception area caught her by surprise. She'd expected something grim with a ghastly smell seeping through the walls or ducts. But there was deep blue carpeting and upholstered furniture in a cheery yellow fabric, the kind of look you'd expect at a dental center. No bad smell either, just icy cold air from the AC. Who were they trying to kid? Somewhere, probably in the bowels of the building, were rows of steels drawers with dead bodies lying inside.

There was no sign of Molinari at first, but then suddenly a woman came along beside her, wearing a buff-colored pantsuit and matching the description the detective had provided—fortyish, short, dark haired with streaks of gray. A badge, secured to her waistband, peeked out from just past the opening of the blazer. And there was a bulge further along the waist, where Kit realized her gun must be.

"Ms. Finn?"

Kit nodded.

"Thank you for coming all this way," Molinari said, putting her hand out. Friendly enough but clearly, Kit saw, the no-nonsense type.

Kit shifted her coat from her right arm to her left, and shook the detective's hand. She wondered if Molinari noticed how sweaty her palm was.

"We can speak afterward," the detective said, "but I wanted you to view the photos first. That way we'll know if we're on the same page."

In a moment they were joined by an African American woman who identified herself as an investigator with the ME's office and led them to a "family viewing" room just off the lobby. The lights were low and there were just a few pieces of furniture—a small couch, a coffee table, and a couple of pleather-covered chairs. Baby, Kit thought ruefully, would have flinched at the sight of them. She claimed that she was allergic to pleather and her tongue swelled if she found herself within twenty feet of it.

"Why don't you have a seat?" the investigator said, directing her to the sofa. Kit did as asked, lowering herself onto the hard surface. She wondered how many millions of tears had been shed in the room.

While Molinari stood just to the right, the investigator joined Kit on the couch. For the first time Kit noticed that the woman carried a manila-colored envelope. She laid the envelope on the table and slid the flap open with her thumb.

"There are two photos," the investigator said. "One face forward and the other a profile."

Please, no, Kit thought, I don't want to see this. Her whole body felt limp, as if her bones had begun to melt. Out of the corner of her eye, she saw the investigator slide two photos from the envelope and lay them on the table.

"Ms. Finn?" Molinari said. "Why don't you take a look now."

She grabbed a breath and directed her full attention to the first photo. Only the head was visible, surrounded tightly with blue draping paper, so that it looked like a stage performer popping his head out between the curtains for a pre-show peek at the audience. Her hand flew to her mouth in shock.

"Omigod," she exclaimed.

"It's him?" Molinari asked.

"No," Kit said, her voice sounding nearly strangled. "It—it's Matt Healy. The *real* Matt Healy. The one I met in New York."

chapter 5

Molinari stared at Kit, her lips parted in confusion.

"Wait," she said. "Are you saying this is the man whose wallet was stolen, the one working at the hedge fund?"

Kit glanced briefly at Molinari and then wrenched her attention back to the photo, still struggling to grasp the truth. There was no mistake. Though Healy's eyes were closed and his skin almost clay-like in color, she was certain it was him. But it made no sense. What had he been doing in Miami—with her business card in his pocket?

"Yes," she said, bewildered.

"You're certain it's not the other man?"

"The other man had red hair but a brownish red, not strawberry blond. And some facial scruff. It never occurred to me when you described the victim that it might be Mr. Healy."

"And you gave him a card, too?" Molinari asked.

She shook her head. "Uh, no. I gave a card to the man in Florida but not to Matt Healy."

Molinari studied her for a moment, questioningly. An alarm buzzed in Kit's brain. Did the detective think she was lying?

"Why don't we stop by my office so we can sit down and talk, okay?" the detective said.

"My flight—it's at four."

"I'll be sure you make it. This is important."

Kit nodded in consent. Better to cooperate, she realized. She'd somehow stumbled into a horror show and she needed to be careful, make Molinari grasp that she was an unwitting bystander who knew absolutely nothing and had played no role.

They returned to the lobby. Molinari suggested Kit wait there, where it would be cooler, while she retrieved the car. Kit stood by the window, watching the detective put her phone to her ear as she hurried across the parking lot, probably filling a colleague in on the body I.D. Someone would surely be designated to get in touch with Matt Healy's family and the higher-ups at Ithaka while Molinari was busy questioning her.

The lobby was empty and utterly silent now, but Kit could hear her heart thumping in her chest. She was still struggling to come to terms with what had just happened in that sad little room. She'd stood there dreading the sight of X's body, and then suddenly she was staring at a photo of Healy's face, his mouth parted in a terrible grimace. It was like plunging your hand into what you think is ice-cold water, knowing it's going to sting, and then finally realizing it's scalding hot instead. She barely knew Healy but she felt shaken by his death.

What exactly had he revealed to her about the trip he was taking? Just that he was headed out of town on business but he'd never said where. She wracked her brain for more. Suddenly she recalled that at the bar in the Italian restaurant she'd told Healy about X's plans to visit Miami.

And then another memory: she'd handed her business card to Ungaro at one point. Based on what Healy had said about not being able to join the meeting, she'd assumed he was going right away, but he might not have taken off until later, and Ungaro could have turned the card over to him.

What if instead of leaving town on business, Healy had actually hightailed it to Miami in search of X, and managed to find

him? Could X have murdered Healy? If that was the case, Kit
had unwittingly set off a grisly chain reaction.

Kit felt fear snake its away around her ankles. If X had killed
Healy, that shifted everything about the past days. It meant that
the man she'd been to bed with—and been so charmed by—
wasn't just a thief, he was a killer. In the Ithaka meeting, Ungaro had suggested X could have purposely targeted her, and Kit
had wondered if he might have been after her wallet, too. But
maybe he'd been after something more, something she wasn't
even aware of.

I have nothing for you, she wanted to scream.

She laid her coat on her roller bag and walked the length of
the window, trying to quell her thoughts. She was leaping way
too ahead of things. There was no proof yet that Healy had even
been murdered. His business trip could have very well been to
Miami and this was all a bizarre coincidence. But these assur-
ances did nothing to ease her distress.

It took Molinari a few minutes to pull up the car, a dark Ford
Taurus. She leaned across the seat and eased the passenger door
open for Kit.

"You doing okay?" Molinari asked as she maneuvered out of
the parking lot. Though the AC was now blasting, the car was
hot as hell inside from sitting in the sun and Kit wished she could
rip off her sweaty leggings and heave them out the window.

"It's just hard to make sense of it," she said. "But I remembered a couple of things you need to be aware of."

She related Healy's mention of a business trip, and her memory of handing over her business card that day at Ithaka.

"I thought you said you hadn't given him a card," Molinari
declared.

"Well, I hadn't given *Healy* a card," Kit said, wishing it
hadn't come out so defensively. She didn't want to seem in any
way suspicious. "But I gave one to that Mr. Ungaro, the security

chief I mentioned to you on the phone. And maybe he passed it on to Matt Healy."

"We'll need contact information for him and Healy's boss."

"I just have their names and the main number for Ithaka, but I'll give you that."

"It could be that Healy's business dealings were in Miami and his death is a standard hit and run," Molinari said, reiterating Kit's own thought. "But it's the kind of coincidence I don't like. When you spoke to Healy, did he ever indicate he might try to track down the person who'd stolen his wallet?"

"No, not at all. Needless to say, he was upset about the possibility of his identity being stolen, but he made a big point of wanting me to talk to Ungaro, like it would be the security chief's responsibility to look into it—not his."

"And this meeting was Friday, you said?"

"Uh huh. At noon."

"Let's finish discussing this at the office," she said. "I'd like my partner to join us for the interview, and it's important for me to get some notes down."

That would make the experience so *official*, Kit thought anxiously. She told herself that she would have to summon a way to chill. If she acted flustered, the cops might suspect that her nerves were due to the fact that she was concealing the truth.

The drive to the station took about ten minutes. They rode in silence, past endless white buildings that seemed to pulse in the bright sunlight. Minutes later, as they stepped off the elevator onto Molinari's floor, Kit couldn't shake the false sense that she *was* guilty of something.

Molinari offered her a chair in a bullpen area of desks, all belonging, Kit assumed, to detectives—several talking on their phones, others typing or confabbing with colleagues. The mix was about thirty percent female. Kit was introduced to Molinari's partner, Detective Todd, who had just ended a call. He was nice looking, maybe late thirties, wearing a short-sleeved white linen shirt. He seemed like the kind of guy who coached kids' soccer on the weekends.

"What can I get you to drink?" Todd asked. "Coffee?"

"Just water, thanks," she said. As he rose to fetch it, she suddenly felt overwhelmed with fatigue.

"Give me a sec, too, will you?" Molinari asked. She crossed the room and spoke quietly to an older man at the far end. Probably, Kit figured, a boss who was eager for an update. She glanced worriedly at her watch. If she wasn't out of there in thirty minutes, she would surely miss her flight.

The two detectives returned almost simultaneously. After handing Kit a plastic glass of water, Todd perched on the edge of his own desk and Molinari sat at hers, typing notes on the computer. She asked Kit to start from the very beginning and describe X as best as she could and anything that he said or did that might be pertinent.

She shared everything she recalled about X personally, including his supposed plan to head to Miami. She mentioned the dinner, just as she had with Ungaro, but nothing about visiting his room. As far as she was concerned, it was totally irrelevant. Matt Healy's death had zero to do with her getting butt naked with X.

"Did you see what kind of car he was driving?" Todd asked.

"No, and I'm not sure if it was his own or a rental."

"Any other details about his background that might be pertinent?"

"What difference would it make?" Kit asked. "It would probably all be a lie."

"You'd be surprised," Molinari said. "Humans have a crazy need to reveal themselves, and sometimes even con artists slip in facts that are real."

Kit shook her head. "There's nothing more than I've told

you. Except that he said he had a sister who lived in Miami. But he never said where."

Molinari then mentioned that the New York City police would most likely be in touch with her in the near future.

Great, she thought. It just goes on and on.

Surreptitiously Kit checked her watch again, and saw that she was out of time. When she glanced back toward the two detectives, she caught them exchanging a look and wondered what it could mean. Molinari leaned forward.

"You've been very helpful," Molinari said. "But we need a bit more of your time."

Oh God, Kit thought. Was this going to explode somehow? She stared at Molinari, waiting in dread.

"We'd like you to work with a sketch artist for us."

"But I'll miss the flight," Kit exclaimed.

"Why don't you give us your info and we can see if there's another option available tonight. And Detective Todd will drive you to the airport."

Kit nodded wearily in consent.

"Are you thinking that the man I met could have actually killed Matt Healy?" she asked. By chance, the buzz in the room had quieted almost instantly and her words carried across the bullpen.

"We don't know," Molinari said. "At this point we're still determining if the hit and run was premeditated. But as I told you earlier, I don't like coincidences."

"Do you think *I* have anything to worry about?" Kit asked.

Molinari toggled her head back and forth, as if she were weighing the question.

"Right now there's no indication this man is after you," she said, "but it wouldn't do any harm to be cautious."

And what did cautious mean? Kit thought glumly. Was she supposed to look over her shoulder every place she went?

They managed to find another flight for her, an hour and a half later, and so she sat down with the sketch artist, describing X. It wasn't hard. He was still strangely vivid in her mind, as if she'd stood looking into his eyes just moments ago.

When the artist finally showed her the results, she caught her breath in surprise. It was *him*, staring straight at her. This time, though, there was no charm to his eyes, only a hint of malevolence. Had the artist interpreted that from something she'd said? She nodded and slowly let out a ragged breath.

Even with the ride from Detective Todd, she was running about ten minutes late when she reached the airport, and the security line seemed to snake forever. She desperately wanted to call Baby and fill her in, but she had to put all her energy and attention into reaching the gate in time.

It wasn't until the plane was in the air that she finally sank farther back into her seat and allowed a little of the tension to seep from her body. But she knew she couldn't fully let go. There were still so many unknowns, an ugly nest of them, and her emotions seemed all bunched up, too. If it turned out X had indeed killed Healy, his dark shadow would loom even larger in her life.

How stupid she'd been to say yes to that dinner, to say yes to the crazy lust that had left her weak in the knees. She grimaced at the memory of her foolishness. And how ironic in the end, she thought. X had suggested that the night would have to be one with no strings attached, but since then there'd been nothing *but* strings. No matter what she did, she couldn't untangle herself from them.

Once Kit was finally in Key West and ensconced in her hotel room, she called Baby, who'd already left two worried messages.

"This is perfectly mind-boggling," Baby said after Kit poured out the story. "Why would this fellow Matt Healy take the risk of trailing a criminal, especially when he had a security person at his disposal?"

"There's still a chance he was in Miami purely on business. And his death was just a horrible accident."

"Can't you ask that security chief you spoke to whether Healy was supposed to be in Florida?"

"The police will get in touch with Ithaka, and it wouldn't be smart for me to interfere. Besides, I want to distance myself from this whole nightmare as much as possible."

"Good point."

"Baby, one thing I can't ignore. This story is bound to end up in the New York papers, at least in the tabloids. There's a chance it might even mention me and the firm. I'm really sorry."

"Oh don't worry about that, dear. As my mother used to say, 'Bad breath is better than no breath at all.'"

Kit managed to laugh, despite how agitated she still felt.

"You're back tomorrow, right?" Baby asked.

"Yes. I'm going to check out Avery's aunt's house first thing in the morning and then be on a plane early. The sooner I launch my butt out of this state, the better. Plus, I'm meeting that doctor at seven tomorrow night."

"I'll probably still be here when you arrive, so I'll see you then. But call if you need to vent beforehand."

"Will do," Kit said, more than grateful for having Baby in her corner.

Good restaurants supposedly were everywhere in Key West, but she had no interest in venturing beyond the hotel dining room. She knew there was little chance X could have discovered her whereabouts, but in her mind he seemed ready to emerge from behind every corner, just as he had in the shop in Islamorada. For a moment she flashed back on what Baby had suggested the other day, that she step back, determine the warning signs she might have missed, and then freaking *learn* from them. But though she'd pressed herself, she'd had no luck summoning any warning signs about X. Yes, he'd been a little mysterious at moments, but that had hardly hinted at a sinister side. In so many ways he had seemed the kind of man she'd been searching for.

She took a book with her to dinner and ordered a glass of white wine along with a small pot of moules marinière.

She'd done what she had to do to put this all behind her. Relax, she told herself. But the mussels tasted as if they'd been barnacled to the hull of a freighter for the past year and she couldn't enjoy them. She returned to her room still hungry and fretful, and woke the next morning in the same state.

The taxi ride to the aunt's home took only a few minutes. The house was enchanting from the outside: sea blue with yellow shutters and a deep wraparound porch. Though much of the furniture was dark and imposing, at odds with the Key West vibe Avery wanted to incorporate, Kit spotted a few framed prints and small accessories that could work.

At noon she was buckling her seat belt on the puddle jumper to Miami. She had a short layover at the airport there and spent the entire time at the gate with her nose in her iPad. She let out an audible sigh when the wheels of her plane finally touched down on the LaGuardia Airport runway.

She stopped by her apartment first, dropping off her roller bag, and then let herself into the office. Dara and Baby were both still there, glancing through a catalog together. She felt joyful at the sheer sight of them.

"Welcome back," Dara said. She flashed a smile, but there was an undercurrent of concern in her tone. Kit knew she must still be wondering about the call from the cops and the earlier-than-planned trip to Florida.

"Good to be here," she said, and nodded to Baby in a way that divulged she was doing okay.

"So did you run into Bogie and Bacall down there?" Dara asked. Unlike many girls of her generation, Dara knew plenty about popular culture from the decades before she was born.

"No sightings, unfortunately. Anything going on since we last texted?"

"No, just that the doctor confirmed his seven o'clock. You've got his address, right? East 84th Street."

"Yes, I'm going to head up there before long," she said.

"I could take the meeting if you want," Baby said as Dara stepped into the bathroom. "You must feel spent."

"Thanks, but I'm eager to do it. I want to dive back into work and just feel normal again."

And she did feel almost normal the minute she stepped into Keith Holt's foyer. She always loved the rush that came from meeting potential clients and contemplating the chance to transform their homes. From checking the forty-three-year-old out online, she'd learned that he was a respected orthopedic surgeon, affiliated with one of New York's top hospitals.

He looked younger in person than he did in photos, with deep brown eyes and brown hair graying a little along the sides. He greeted her warmly, though she suspected that based on his demanding profession, he didn't suffer fools gladly.

"Can I offer you a glass of wine?" he asked as he led her into the living room.

"Are you going to have one, Dr. Holt?"

"Please, it's Keith," he corrected her with a smile. "And yes, absolutely. It's been a nutty day."

He was still in a suit, a nice-fitting navy one, so she assumed he'd only just walked in from work.

"Then I will, too," she said. "It's been a nutty day or two for me, too." She wondered what he'd think if he knew she'd been busy corpse-viewing at the Miami morgue rather than scooting around town with fabric swatches and floor plans.

While he stepped into the kitchen to fetch the wine, she quickly studied his place, a classic prewar apartment in a building with good bones. The design had clearly been orchestrated by a professional decorator or someone fancying themselves as one: deep red sofa, armchairs in a red and gold print, and a quality Turkish rug, in coordinating colors. More than a few nicelooking pieces of art on the wall. Holt had said on the phone that he was divorced so this might be the place he'd shared with his wife, and he was ready to expunge any traces of his former life. She'd had more than a few clients who were eager to purge the past.

"Thank you," Kit said, accepting the wine. "You told me a little about your situation on the phone, but I'm anxious to hear more."

"I'm just itching for a change," he said. He'd sat down opposite from her and crossed one leg over the other. "As you can see there's nothing wrong with my apartment—in fact, people often comment on how nice it looks—but I had it done when I divorced six years ago and I just went along with everything the decorator suggested. I've come to realize that it doesn't feel like me in the least."

There was something else that might be bothering him, she realized, without his even being aware of it. The place felt *busy*. She subscribed to the ideas that every room should have at least three colors but none in equal proportion. In this place the red was in constant battle with the gold, so much so that it could make your head throb.

But she'd never knock another decorator's work to a potential client.

"What *would* feel like you, do you think?"

"Something far less traditional and *nice*. A place where the art I'm collecting could stand out. Something really gutsy."

The word gutsy always made her heart leap. And done the right way, it wouldn't have to induce a migraine.

For the next half hour she encouraged Holt to tell her more

about himself and what he enjoyed most: He reeled off a list of his hobbies—tennis, running, eco-traveling—as if he had little patience for talking purely about himself. He was far more effusive when he discussed modern art and the type of visuals he was drawn to. When they were done talking, Kit was given a tour of the apartment.

Holt clearly didn't have kids, she realized. The guest bedroom looked as if it hadn't been slept in in ages, and the only photographs in the apartment showed the doctor standing with groups of fellow hikers in front of places like Machu Picchu and Kilimanjaro. A risk taker for sure.

Back in the living room, Kit explained her billing process. She also fished her iPad out of her tote bag and showed Holt several apartments she'd decorated that most aligned with what he seemed to be yearning for.

"These are awesome," he said. "I'd love something bold like this."

She smiled, trying not to appear overly eager. As Baby always advised, "Never seem hot to trot. Cast the client as the pursuer and yourself as the agent provocateur." But there was no denying it would be a terrific project to snag, not only for the challenge but also for the billable hours it would entail.

"Question," he said, suddenly looking pensive. "Is there a way to do this without getting rid of everything I have? I'm the kind of guy who preaches sustainability and now here I am talking about tossing out all this good stuff, like some petulant trophy wife."

"You don't actually have to get rid of everything," Kit said, appreciating his concerns. "Some upholstered pieces can be recovered and you have wood furniture that could be painted and lacquered to look ultramodern. Besides, you may want to keep a few antique pieces in the mix, just as they are. A great room always has both yin and yang."

"I like that—yin and yang." Holt looked off briefly, as if studying something on the inside of his brain, and then returned his gaze to her, tapping his knees with his hands. "Well, this has been quite inspiring," he said, rising. "Why don't I think it over and get back to you."

No surprise there. That was what most people said at the first meeting. They wanted time to mull over their decision, even meet with other decorators first. But she'd really sensed that Holt was going to go to yes right then and there. The fact that he hadn't left her oddly deflated as she rode the elevator to the ground floor.

Her mood didn't improve when she emerged later from the subway station and checked her phone. Ungaro, the Ithaka security chief, had left a message asking her to give him a call, saying it was urgent. By now, of course, he'd been informed about Healy's death, and she was sure he wanted to hear her version of events.

She wasn't going to call him, she decided, hurrying up the block. This was a matter for the police now and it was time for her to completely back off.

The corridor outside her apartment seemed totally forlorn that night. Often she could hear jazz coming softly from the large apartment just to the right side of hers or the yummy smell of an exotic dish. But the tenants, a couple in their forties, had said they'd be on vacation for ten days.

After dinner she tried to distract herself by leafing through some of her art books. In high school, she'd planned to study art in college; at least she had before everything went to hell. As she paged through a section on German post-impressionism, she spotted a painting she hadn't thought of in ages but one that had had an impact on her years before: Kandinsky's *Murnau: Street with Horse-Drawn Carriage*. It had been painted when the artist first began to break free of traditional constraints, and he'd let the bold, fanciful colors of the horses bleed through the lines.

Despite her best efforts, her thoughts were torn back once again to where she least wanted them to be. A man may have died because of her. Not directly, but still, if she hadn't showed up at Matt Healy's door, he might never have flown to Miami.

And the same awful questions began nagging her again: Was X really a murderer? Why had he sent her to Matt Healy's apartment? And the most paralyzing question of all: Was there something more he wanted from her?

chapter 6

She woke the next morning from an anxious dream, though all she could remember was wading desperately through water, unable to move more than an inch at a time. And that the water had been turquoise blue, like the water in the Keys.

Still in her pajamas, she checked online for any news of Healy's death. So far there was just a small item on the *Daily News* website, stating simply that he was a New Yorker and had been struck by a car while visiting Miami. It made it sound as if he were a snowbird or tourist who fate had conspired against.

She wondered when she'd hear from the New York City police. Though she hardly welcomed the call, she prayed it would be today. Then that would be behind her, too.

After breakfast, and before either Dara or Baby had even arrived at the office, she grabbed her coat and headed for Greenwich Village, to check once more on the project there. Yesterday the bedroom floor had been sanded and stained, and when she arrived she was grateful to see that none of the polyurethane had splashed onto the floorboards or at least if it had, the contractor had done a good job of touching up the paint. The female client, Layla Griggs, had turned out to be someone with little patience for even the slightest blunder.

Afterward, she caught a subway uptown and met Avery at the

D&D building for the first round of furniture shopping. Avery looked dazzling, dressed in a flared spring coat that was nipped in at the waist and lined in a leopard print, which revealed itself along the collar. At their first meeting Kit had been struck by the resemblance between herself and her client, though with Avery everything just seemed more, well, *dramatic*. Her hair was generally blown out so that it was super smooth and shiny with the ends flipped up. She never seemed to leave the house without a spray tan, and she wore so much gloss over her nude lip color, you could practically see your reflection in it. While Kit never imagined herself playing things up that way, she admired Avery's go-big-or-go-home approach to life.

"I've just got an hour," Avery reminded her.

"No problem," Kit said, though Avery had promised two on the phone. "The main goal today is for me to show you pieces I think could work. If you like the general direction, I can shop on my own going forward and just show you photos."

They made a decent amount of progress, despite the time constraints and the fact that Avery stopped frequently to check messages or send a text, and once to take a phone call from an associate at her PR firm.

"I couldn't represent someone who looked like that," she told the person. "It's not about the sound bite anymore. It's about the image."

Overhearing the call, Kit remembered that before she left on vacation, she'd toyed with the idea of hiring someone right out of college to help her for a few hours each week with the social media efforts for her business, but she'd been so preoccupied with the X situation, the idea had flown from her head. She had to get back on track.

A few minutes later, as they surveyed dining tables, Avery paused and looked at Kit.

"I know my aunt's dining table is too big for my house,"

she said, "but did you see the sideboard in the same room? I always loved that piece. She used to let me set the table, and that's where all the silver was kept."

Kit had seen the sideboard. It was dark and huge and hulking. If it were placed in the cottage, it would look like a water buffalo grazing against the wall. But she knew she had to pay heed to what Avery was saying. If you tried to ride over a client's wishes, you might get your way, but there was a chance your client would never truly be happy with the end results.

"I *did* see it," Kit said. "And it's lovely. But beyond the expense of shipping such a big piece up here, I worry that it will eat up too much space in the cottage and work against the open feeling you're trying to achieve."

Avery sighed.

"I hear you," she said. "It *would* be too big, I guess."

"You mentioned once that your aunt had given you her silverware when she moved out of her house."

"Yes, and I was thinking of keeping it at the cottage. I plan to entertain a lot there."

"What if we try to find another sideboard for the dining area? Something more minimal but still with drawers. It won't take up as much space but it will add a bit of elegance. You can keep the silver there and think of her when you use it."

"That's a possibility," Avery said. "That could be nice, in fact." Kit could sense her warming to the idea even as they spoke.

After Avery departed in a mad dash to the office, Kit stopped at several more of her favorite design houses and then headed to the small restaurant on the top floor of the building to grab lunch and review her notes. Between what she'd seen with Avery and the items she'd found on her own, she had most of the basics figured out: sofa, armchairs, an ottoman, dining table and chairs, and the guest bedroom furniture. The next step would be picking out fabrics for the upholstered furniture and the curtains.

Her phone rang just as her lunch arrived, and she saw with annoyance that it was Ungaro again. She pressed decline. There was nothing she could tell him that he couldn't learn from the police. Of course, if she *did* speak to him, she might be able to glean if Healy had gone to Miami on business, but that information would come at a price. She'd be further ensnared with Ithaka. And she couldn't let that happen.

When she returned to the office later in the day, she raced through emails. With a twinge of disappointment, she noted that there was no message from Dr. Holt.

Her phone rang and she checked the screen before answering, making sure it wasn't the security chief again. No. But the second she said her name into the phone, her brain spit out a piece of information. The prefix was the same as Ungaro's.

"This is Mitch Wainwright," the caller said, his voice deep and imposing. "Have you got a few minutes?"

It was a question that came out more like a command and Kit's body tensed in frustration. Ungaro had sicced the big boss on her, and she'd stupidly picked up the phone.

"Yes, but literally just a few minutes. I'm very sorry about Mr. Healy, by the way."

"It's a tragic loss for the firm, and for his family, of course. Are you aware that Mr. Ungaro has made several attempts to reach you? We'd like you to come in again for another conversation."

He had to be kidding. Don't let him bully you, she warned herself.

"I can't imagine how I can be of assistance," Kit said. "The police are the best people for you to communicate with at this point."

"We've been in touch with them, needless to say. But we'd like to talk to you, too. There are details that only you can provide."

It felt as if he was standing in the room with her, backing her into the corner with the sheer force of his presence.

"I don't really know what you're referring to. All I did was identify the body."

"It's interesting that you happened to be in the area again."

"*Interesting?*" she said. That was the last word she would have used to describe her trip to the morgue. "I had business in Florida and I simply agreed to help the detective in charge while I was there."

"How were you aware they needed your help?"

She hated how he was pressing her.

"Mr. Wainwright, this is a police matter now, and they're the ones you should be discussing this with. It's not appropriate for me to be in the mix of things anymore."

"But you *are* in the mix. You seem to be smack in the middle for some reason."

She was speechless. What was this guy implying? That she might be connected to Healy's death?

"Look, Ms. Finn," Wainwright interjected into the silence. "We got off on the wrong foot with this call. The firm simply wants as many answers as possible. We're at a disadvantage being a thousand miles away from where one of our people was killed. But we need to be certain this case ends up solved."

There was no legal reason she had to fill in the blanks for him. But maybe, she decided, it would be better to cooperate. She could relay to him and Ungaro the bare basics about her trip to the medical examiner's office and then she wouldn't have to talk to them again. Besides, it might assuage some of her guilt. She was still plagued by the worry that her appearance at Healy's apartment might have set in motion the events that led to his death.

"All right," she said. "I could come by later today, at about five. But from that point on you'll need to speak to the police about this matter."

"Five works for me," he said. "And, by the way, please come to the thirtieth floor instead of the twenty-ninth this time. We'll have a bit more privacy there."

Did he have a private office up there, she wondered, away from the high-stakes hurly-burly? Whatever, she'd just have to get in and out. And assisting Ithaka might prove to be a benefit to her in the long run. The firm would surely put pressure on the authorities to move quickly. If X were arrested, she wouldn't have to fret about him any longer.

A few minutes later, Baby returned from a job site.

"Something's up," she said as she sat down at her desk. "I see a worry dent in your forehead."

"It's thanks to my endless date from hell," Kit said. "Every day there's a crazy new development." She shared the details of the recent phone call from Wainwright.

"Well, *that's* nervy," Baby said.

"I can't totally blame them for wanting information, but after this afternoon, I'm done."

Baby pursed her lips, a thought clearly brewing.

"What?" Kit asked.

"Dan used to say that when you're facing a battle, you don't go in with a wooden stick. You go in with a gun."

Kit snorted. "Wait, you're not suggesting I pack a firearm for the meeting, are you?"

"No, but I'm wondering if you should consult with a lawyer. I doubt you could end up in any legal difficulty, but it might be smart to have a pro helping you navigate things with both Ithaka and the police. It's getting very complicated."

This time Kit groaned. "I'll be honest, the thought crossed my mind in Miami. There's nothing like sitting in a police precinct to summon the "L" word to your mind. But there was no hint from the police that they suspected me of being in cahoots with the fake Matt Healy. And I just don't want to throw the money away. Even a few hours of consultation would be a huge chunk of change."

"Well you wouldn't be throwing it away if it worked in your favor."

She nodded, weighing Baby's words.

"Let me mull it over. I certainly don't think I need one for the meeting at Ithaka. But if things get ratcheted up, I'll definitely consider it."

"Wear your black suit today," Baby suggested. "There's something about it that just says, 'I refuse to be intimidated.'"

Smiling, she promised she would. Though she couldn't imagine Wainwright being the least bit cowed by a cropped gabardine blazer and pencil skirt.

An hour and a half later, as the elevator whisked her to the thirtieth floor of the midtown building, she could feel her dread ballooning. It'll be over soon, she reassured herself.

The receptionist tapped Kit's name into an iPad, nodded, and then led her down a long, hushed hallway. From what Kit could see, there were no glass offices up here, no trading floor either. It all seemed very corporate.

Finally the receptionist came to a stop and swung open a mahogany door on the right. Inside was an empty executive conference room. One wall was lined with floor-to-ceiling windows that faced a stunning canyon of midtown Manhattan office buildings. Kit wondered about all the deals that had been cut in the room, as well as the scheming and conniving that had transpired there. Her father had been undone in business and she couldn't look at a room like this without being reminded of that.

"Please have a seat," the receptionist said, gesturing toward a rectangular table big enough to accommodate ten. "Mr. Wainwright will be with you shortly."

The woman started toward the door and then looked back.

"Would you like something to drink?" she asked.

Kit politely declined. A glass of water would be nice but she refused to be beholden to Ithaka for even that.

A minute later, Wainwright entered with Ungaro in tow. Ungaro was dressed in business casual again, but the silver fox was in an expensive suit, as if the day entailed important meetings out of the office. He took a seat directly across from her, and Ungaro settled into one to his right. There was no mistaking the message. Wainwright would be in charge of the questioning today and Ungaro would be playing sidekick.

"We don't want to take up much of your time, Ms. Finn," Wainwright said, holding onto her gaze with his penny-shaped eyes. "We'd simply like to hear about your trip to Florida."

Kit took a breath.

"There's really not much to tell," she said. "The Miami-Dade police called me to say they were holding the body of a hit-and-run victim who had no ID on him but was carrying my business card in his pocket. I told them I thought it might be the man I'd met in Islamorada. When I explained he'd had red hair and blue eyes, they said that matched the victim. I mean, Matt Healy's hair was really strawberry blond but someone could consider it red. It never crossed my mind that Healy was the actual victim."

"And you offered to fly down and identify the body?" Wainwright said. "That was very generous of you."

There was an edge to his tone, challenging.

"No, that's not how it happened. As I mentioned to you on the phone, I had business back in Florida, and when I told the main detective that, she asked if I would come to the morgue and confirm that the victim was this—this stranger I'd met. It seemed like the right thing to do so I agreed."

"Can you tell us anything more about mystery man?"

"I'm sorry, but I can't think of anything that I haven't shared with you already."

"This is a delicate question but we have to ask," Ungaro interjected. He'd been taking notes since she started speaking but stopped at this point, his pen poised. "Was this man ever in your hotel room?"

She couldn't believe they were going there. "No, he wasn't," she said. "But I can't imagine why it would matter if he had been."

"We were just curious if he might have had access to your belongings and stolen something," Ungaro said.

She shook her head. "Nothing was missing."

"Was he already at the hotel when you arrived?" Wainwright asked.

"You mean at the hotel restaurant—the night we had dinner?" she said, wondering what difference that made either.

"No. We're curious if he was staying at the hotel when you first checked in or did he arrive afterward."

Her stomach tightened. His question harkened back to what Ungaro had suggested in the previous conversation: that X might have tailed her to the shop in town, his sights set on her. Were they wondering if he'd even followed her to the hotel?

"I don't have a clue," she said. "I spoke to him for the first time on the last day I stayed there, as I was leaving breakfast. And then we had dinner that night. I'm sure the hotel could tell you exactly when he checked in and out."

A loaded few moments of silence followed, as both men studied her.

"But you told us previously that you had only *seen* him at the hotel and that you spoke to him for the first time at the store in town," Wainwright said.

There it was again, that challenging tone of his, as if she was a witness for the other side. And they seemed obsessed with minutiae.

"The store was the first place we had an actual conversation,"

she said. "We only exchanged a few words when
into each other after breakfast. It—it just seemed to
cant to mention before."

She sounded slightly flustered, she realized, defensive. But
they were making her nervous, the way they were eyeing her
like two hyenas preparing to circle.

"When you say bumped into each other," Ungaro said, "are
you using the phrase as a manner of speaking? Or are you saying
this man *physically* bumped into you?"

"Yes, we bumped into each other physically, but how is that
relevant?" Why were they so fascinated by it? she wondered. "I
was reading my iPad and wasn't paying attention."

"All right, thank you, Ms. Finn," Wainwright said abruptly.
"We're grateful for your cooperation, and we shouldn't take up
any more of your time. I'm sure you're busy."

"I'd appreciate one piece of information from you in return,"
Kit said, rising. "Can you tell me if Mr. Healy had business in
Florida?"

Neither man looked at the other, but she sensed a message
being telegraphed from one to the other.

"Yes, he did," said Wainwright after a moment. "We have a
client in Miami and he was planning to see him."

"Then maybe this was all a terrible coincidence," Kit blurted
out, feeling a rush of relief.

"Perhaps," Wainwright said. "But we want to cover all our
bases. We need to be sure Mr. Healy's killer is brought to justice."

Minutes later, as the elevator whisked her solo to the ground
floor, she couldn't help but feel discombobulated. If Matt Healy
had a legitimate reason to be in Miami, then his death might
have no connection to X, and she could relax. But Wainwright
had paused before answering and his reply might have been a
lie, a cover-up. And then there were those questions suggesting

that she may have been targeted. Was it actually X who had bumped into *her*, trying to force an exchange? Perhaps he *had* followed her to the shop. But what could he have wanted from her beyond sex?

It was still light out when she emerged from the building and she took a west side subway downtown and then walked the rest of the way home. The day had been lovely, truly spring-like, but she'd barely noticed it. Moments from her apartment, her phone rang. The number was blocked.

"Hello," she answered, not willing to identify herself.

"Is this Kit Finn?"

"Yes," she said, stepping into a building doorway so she could hear better. Maybe it was a potential client with a private number.

"This is Detective Steve Patchel from the 84th precinct in Brooklyn. I'm following up on information you provided the Miami police."

Okay, she could at least get this out of the way on the same day.

"I've been expecting your call."

"Miami–Dade will be investigating the fatality, but we're trying to offer whatever background we can," Patchel said. "According to Detective Molinari, Mr. Healy told you that his wallet had been stolen at an apartment in Dumbo. Did he say when exactly?"

"I spoke to him last Friday and he said it had happened ten days before. He'd been at a party there, and he assumed another guest had taken it."

Patchel was momentarily silent. Kit wondered if he was going to insist she come to Brooklyn and talk to him in person.

"Here's the problem," he said finally. "I've checked the files. There's no record of Matt Healy ever reporting a stolen wallet."

chapter 7

Kit froze in place, trying to process what the cop had told her.

"Maybe he reported it in Manhattan," she said. "That's where he lives—I mean lived."

"But that would have turned up in our system, too. There's nothing on file in the entire city."

Her heart skipped. Was Healy a liar, too?

"Are you saying that he made it up?" she asked. "That he was never pickpocketed?"

"No, it's possible that his wallet was stolen, but people don't always take the time to file reports on crimes like that because, frankly, it's too much of a hassle, or they don't see how it's going to help. They won't get their cash back and they can just cancel their credit cards and order new ones. You said he thought it was stolen at a private party?"

"Right. Apparently there were a lot of people there that he didn't know."

"Maybe he didn't report it because he was afraid it might blow back on the hosts. You know, embarrass them."

"Okay, I see what you're saying." But still, it seemed weird.

"Regardless, there's not anything I can do from my end without a report. Thanks for your cooperation, though."

After he signed off, she lingered for a moment in the doorway. The revelation from Patchel gnawed at her. There was something about the situation she wasn't seeing.

She thought back to her first conversation with Healy, at the bar of the Italian restaurant. She'd stressed that he needed to call the police in regard to what she'd shared, assuming he'd already informed them about the stolen wallet. She distinctly remembered that Healy said he was planning to contact the police with her news but wanted to check with security first. So maybe he hadn't called them about the wallet initially. Why not get in touch, though, after she'd dropped the bombshell? Even if Healy hadn't had the time before heading to Miami, Ungaro could have done it. Maybe the security chief had advised against reporting the incident to the cops. But for what reason?

Whatever the backstory, she'd told Wainwright and Ungaro everything they wanted to know. The New York police had just made clear they required nothing from her. It was *over*, hopefully. And except for a few bad memories, she could move on.

As soon as she reached home, she plugged her iPhone into the speakers and played music, hoping to slip into a better mood. It didn't help that the weekend was looming and she had almost nothing planned, other than a rendezvous with the treadmill at the gym and her weekly phone call to her parents. She realized that in the months since her break-up with Jeremy, she'd allowed her personal life to become as exciting as a soft-boiled egg.

In the first weeks after the split, there'd been a flurry of activity. She'd signed up for an iPhone photography course and downloaded advanced Spanish lessons from Pimsleur. Her friends knew that the break-up had been mutual, knew she'd sensed for ages that Jeremy was a nice, safe harbor rather than someone she truly loved and longed for a life with, but they'd still been generous with invites for everything from pub crawls to concerts. They'd arranged blind dates, too. Most had been attractive, decent guys, the type who never left you flabbergasted because they failed to call when they promised they would or made goo-goo eyes at the waitress's boobs with you sitting right next to them. And yet she hadn't felt a magic connection with any of them.

Within two months she could see herself beginning to pull back, declining invitations. Plus, her business was at full throttle and it was easy to convince herself that she needed to be working weeknights and weekends, too.

Of course the trip to Islamorada was supposed to be a kick in the butt, the launch of a feistier, more adventurous girl. Or rather relaunch. Up until she was seventeen, she *had* been that girl—whether it was traipsing around Manhattan on her own to museums and galleries or traveling during summers in special volunteer programs to South America.

In the end, Islamorada seemed like a warning that she was better off playing it safe. And yet she couldn't let her life become an intolerable bore. She picked up the phone and called her friend Chuck, an associate at the last big interior design firm she'd worked at. She not only adored Chuck, but he was also always game for last-minute invites.

"Well, hello Miss Kit Kat," he said. "I've been meaning to call you, but it's just been insane around here this month."

"Any chance you could cut out from work early tomorrow? I was hoping I could interest you in a little gallery hopping in Chelsea, if you don't already have plans that is. We could have dinner afterwards."

"Oh, I'd adore that. I was supposed to have a date with a new guy I've been seeing, but he just called to say he needs to review his tax forms before he submits them this month. Who does *that* on a Friday night? You can ease the sting of rejection."

"My pleasure."

"Oh, and both partners are away this week, so I could start as early as four."

"Perfect," Kit said. They agreed to meet at the Gagosian Gallery on West 24th Street and grab a bite afterwards in the area.

So she'd pulled the weekend out of the fire, at least. As for her romantic situation, that was a far tougher challenge. She'd never actually been what you'd called lucky in love. Before Jeremy there'd been a fairly long drought, preceded by two and a half years of living with a man who was smart and decent and attentive, but had never roused any real passion in her. Like Jeremy, he'd been a safe bet, a situation that at first had seemed alluring, but had come, over time to feel nearly suffocating. When he eventually told her about a job offer in Silicon Valley and his desire to take it, she'd felt mostly relief.

Baby worked from home most Fridays, and it was just Dara and Kit in the office the next day. As Kit opened her email, she discovered, to her delight, a message from Keith Holt saying that he'd like to sit down for a second discussion.

"Are you ever available weekends?" he'd written.

"Definitely," she replied. "I could even meet you tomorrow afternoon if that's good for you."

He responded a few minutes later, saying that he had to be downtown in the afternoon and wondered if that area would be convenient for her.

She suggested that he stop by her office. That way she could show him more of her work if necessary, and even offer him a glimpse of her apartment. They agreed on two o'clock.

Midafternoon, she looked up from her work and caught her assistant's eye.

"Why don't you split now, Dara?" she said. "Get a head start on the weekend."

"Thanks, but I'm still doing research for the Avery Howe job."

"That can wait until Monday. Besides, I'm leaving early today myself."

Dara's expression clouded.

"Is there anything I can do—I mean, do you need me to help with anything?"

Kit sensed that Dara was distressed about all the undercurrents in the office this past week.

"Oh, no, I'm just headed to a few galleries."

The last thing she wanted to do was drag Dara into the mess, but she also didn't want her fretting over the weekend.

"Look, Dara," she added. "I know I've been a bit mysterious at moments this week, but you shouldn't be concerned. It was simply a little personal drama I stupidly stepped into. Fortunately it's behind me now."

"Thanks, Kit. I was just worried for you. I didn't know if a client had done something crummy or tried to screw you over."

"No, nothing like that," Kit reassured her. She smiled. "Besides, if a client ever tried to screw with us, we could just put Baby on the case. The person wouldn't stand a chance."

"Ha! Okay, so I'll take you up on your offer about splitting early. I'm just going to finish up a couple of emails."

Dara departed a few minutes later and Kit was out the door shortly afterward. It was another gorgeous spring day, and this time she let herself relish it. She took a subway to the east twenties and then walked west to Chelsea, past endless bodegas, delis, restaurants, and flower shops. People were dashing rather than walking, charging toward their weekends. And so was she. For the first time in days she didn't feel as if she existed in an alternate universe.

Chuck arrived at the gallery just a minute after her, dressed in the outfit that had become more or less his uniform: a crop-jacketed suit, polka dot tie, and brogue shoes worn without socks. His prematurely gray hair was spiked up in front, also a signature for him. They hugged warmly.

"Don't you wonder?" he asked, after they'd entered Gagosian, "why the people at the front desk in galleries *always* act as if you're tearing them away from their jobs when you ask a question. It's like you've interrupted them as they're about to negotiate the sale of a de Kooning or a Rothko. I thought it was their freaking job to be there for the people walking in the door."

Kit laughed. "Oh, good, I thought it was just me that generated that kind of please-don't-annoy-me response from them."

"Shall we just browse now and catch up over dinner?"

"That sounds like a plan," Kit said. They'd been friends for six years and though Chuck had told her he could simultaneously gab and engage in almost any other function at the same time, even a tooth extraction, he knew Kit preferred quiet when she looked at art. She liked to fully absorb what she was seeing.

They spent a half hour at Gagosian and then decided to head to two more galleries before dinner. At the third they separated for a bit so Chuck could check out woodprints she had little interest in.

She positioned herself in one of the rooms, where each wall was dominated by a huge canvas by the same artist. She tried to do what an artist friend had once suggested: examine each corner and let it tell you something about the middle.

As she studied the most dramatic piece, she sensed someone come up alongside of her, just a few feet away. For a moment she thought it was Chuck, back from the woodprints and eager for food and booze, but out of the corner of her eye, she could tell that the person's hair was long and black. She glanced over.

It was someone she knew, she realized, though for a moment she struggled to place her out of context. And then, with a start, her mind caught up.

She was staring at the woman from the hedge fund, the one

who'd come into the ladies' room. She couldn't escape from those people, Kit thought in frustration, no matter how hard she tried.

The woman turned, too. Kit noticed her gray eyes flicker with recognition.

"Hello," the woman said, slowly drawing out the last syllable, as if deliberating the reason for Kit's presence. She was wearing a perforated black suede anorak over another pair of sleek black pants. An expensive fragrance wafted off her, a floral scent with a hint of something resinous, like amber.

"Sasha Glen, from Ithaka," the woman added. Kit realized she'd been staring blankly at her, and the woman had assumed she hadn't placed her yet.

"Right. Hello."

"By the way, I'm sorry about the other day," Sasha said. "I had you totally confused with someone else."

"Not a problem." She wanted to move away, to not be talking to this woman anymore, but there was no point in being rude. She glanced toward the door to the rear gallery space, wondering where Chuck was.

"Mitch told me you're a decorator."

"*Mitch?*" Who was that and why was he telling this woman anything about her?

"Mitch Wainwright. The man who runs Ithaka. I saw you talking to him last week and he said you might be redecorating some of the space."

Kit tried to keep her face neutral as her mind raced. Wainwright had obviously lied to Sasha Glen about why she'd been in the building. But it made sense that he'd want to be discreet about the real reason for her appointment.

"That's kind of up in the air," Kit said, covering for him.

"It'd be a plum assignment," Sasha said, kind of girlfriend-to-girlfriend–like now. "Do you do residential jobs as well as commercial ones?"

"Mostly just residential." She glanced over the woman's shoulder, wishing that Chuck would materialize.

"You must have heard the terrible news, of course. About Matt Healy's death."

"Um, yes," Kit said, trying not to sound flustered. "I saw it in the newspaper. How tragic."

"We were in separate areas, but it's still a shock. How well did you know him?"

She'd already told Sasha in the ladies' room that she barely knew him. Was this some kind of test?

"Not very well at all." She needed to extricate herself from the conversation as quickly as possible.

"But he was the one who introduced you to Mitch, right?"

"Yes—sort of. If you'll excuse me now, I need to catch up with a friend. We're supposed to be somewhere for dinner."

"Of course. By the way, I've just bought a new place and I'm in dire need of a decorator myself. Are you taking on new clients these days?"

Of course she was taking on new clients, but the last thing in the world she wanted was further involvement with this woman or anyone else at Ithaka, even if it would help pay the bills.

"I'm sorry, I'm not," Kit said. "I've got a few big projects that are eating up most of my time."

"That's a shame," Sasha said. Reaching into her woven black leather handbag without even looking down, she pulled out a silver business card case. "Why don't you at least take my card? If your schedule opens up, give me a call."

Again not wanting to be rude, Kit accepted the card.

"Of course. Have a nice evening."

Kit headed toward the rear exhibition room, eager to find Chuck. The encounter had creeped her out. It was clear that the woman must have tried to ferret out information from Wainwright about why Kit had gone in to speak to him that Friday. And tonight she'd been trolling for even more info.

Two rooms later, there was still no sign of Chuck. Kit texted him: "Where r u?"

"Sry, mens rm," came the reply. "C u up front."

She weaved through the crowd back to the front of the gallery and Chuck was already standing there. Sasha was nowhere in sight.

"Want to try to grab a seat at the bar at Cookshop?" he said. "I've got a ferocious craving for that fried kale they serve as a snack."

"That works for me."

They double-checked for the cross street of the restaurant on her iPhone and set off by foot in that direction.

"Was that a client I saw you talking to at the gallery?" Chuck asked after they'd reached the restaurant and seated themselves at the bar.

"No, just some woman I met briefly the other day." For a split second she thought of coming clean about what had happened to her recently. She'd trusted Chuck with more than a few secrets over the years, including her growing qualms about her relationship with Jeremy, and his advice was always wise. But she sensed that sharing the story would cast a pall over the evening. Besides, discussing the drama was not going to help put it behind her.

"And not someone I'd ever want as a client," she added.

"I wouldn't want to have a nonfat *latte* with that chick, let alone decorate her apartment. She looks way too high maintenance. But speaking of work, how's it going?"

Kit tapped the bar a couple of times with her knuckles.

"Knock on wood, business has been strong. I've begun to get some nice word-of-mouth referrals—there was one just this week. By the way, I brought my iPad to show you that one project you'd asked me about."

"Great. I'm so freaking envious of you."

Chuck, four years younger than Kit, had just begun plotting how to go out on his own one day.

"Are you doing plenty of networking? You want to use this time to develop as many leads as possible so they'll be there when you start your own firm."

"I'm trying, but you know how it is at McCaverty-Swain. I'm working twenty-four–seven. They think nothing of calling you at eleven o'clock at night and asking, "What do you think of a pop of canary yellow in the kitchen?"

"How's Mavis, by the way?" she asked. Mavis Swain was one of the firm's senior partners, a grande dame in the old-school style. "Is she under control these days?"

"Absolutely *not*. You should have heard her last week. We've signed these new clients, a fiftyish couple wanting to upgrade the look of their apartment. They've got dough, needless to say, but they're hardly major league. Mavis is having me shop the project so I've been in tow at the sessions so far. Last Thursday we met the husband for the first time. When he heard that the window treatments were going to cost thirty grand, he got all red in the face and started blustering about how outrageous that sounded. Mavis leaned back in her chair, said nothing for a second, and then finally asked him, 'Mr. Hartley, do you remember what you paid for your current window treatments?' He shrugged and said he couldn't recall the exact amount but he was sure it wasn't more than five grand. You know what Mavis said in response? 'It *shows*.'"

"Omigod," Kit exclaimed, laughing. "I've seen Baby come close to biting a contractor's head off on a few occasions, but she'd never treat a client disrespectfully. How did the guy respond?"

"Let's just say he didn't look pleased and they took off a few minutes later. I had to fight the urge to grab the woman by the ankles and restrain her from leaving. I need projects so I don't end up downsized out of there. But two hours later, the wife called and announced that Mavis could spend what she wanted on the drapes."

That was the thing with Mavis, Kit thought. She had this way of reading clients and knowing just how far she could take it with her behavior. But she also had family money and could afford to let a client go. For a moment, Kit reflected on her own parents, now living in their tiny condo in Oxford, Maryland.

"But enough about Mavis the Maleficent," Chuck announced. "Tell me about Florida. How did the trip work out?"

It felt as if she'd been poked in the chest. No matter how hard she tried to avoid it, everything seemed to circle back to Islamorada and to X.

"Lovely," she said. Again, she felt tempted to spill but caught herself. "A great little hotel. Gorgeous scenery."

"Did you ever wish Jeremy was there with you?"

Kit sighed.

"No, and I feel guilty admitting that. The poor guy. I kind of wasted a couple of years of his life."

"Don't be ridiculous, Kit. First of all his apartment looked a billion times better after you helped him with it. I mean, his toilet seat had its own *hoodie* when you first started dating him."

"Don't blame him for that. His mother stuck it on there, and he didn't want to hurt her feelings by taking it off."

"He should have incinerated that thing. Beyond that, he just wasn't right for you."

"I tell myself I want some totally gutsy guy but isn't that asking for trouble in the long run?" Kit smiled ruefully, thinking of X. "I mean, can you ever really trust that kind of man? Maybe I should call up the Poppin' Fresh Doughboy and see if he's available."

"Trust me, Kit Kat, I'm no man genius but I know there's a guy out there who's perfect for you, who's in between Poppin' Fresh and a real bad boy, someone who's thrilling to be around but isn't going to knock up the housekeeper or end up with a ton of D.W.I.'s."

The kind of man she'd thought X might be. But so much for that.

"I intend to hold you to that prediction," she told Chuck. "What about your new honey? Is he a keeper?"

"Not really. He's like twenty-six and fun to hang with, but he seems kind of clueless. He actually told me that the way to get frozen French fries extra crispy is to set the oven to 'clean.' That's why I'm skeptical he's home doing his taxes tonight!"

They ordered dinner and chatted for the next two hours about clients, show houses they'd seen recently, and what former colleagues were up to. Kit also gave him a look at the project he'd asked to see.

It was after nine by the time they left. A brisk wind had come up and they both buttoned their coats against it before hugging goodbye. Chuck, who lived in the Village, headed off on foot and Kit grabbed a cab going east. As Manhattan rushed by in a blur, she found her thoughts dragged back to Sasha Glen and the way they'd bumped into each other, seemingly out of the blue. She thought, too, of a comment Detective Molinari had made about coincidences, that there were some she just didn't like. Had running into Sasha been simply a coincidence? Or could Wainwright and Ungaro have arranged for their employee to keep tabs on her?

The idea pissed her off. She'd told them everything she knew so what would be gained by spying on her? Did they think she knew more than she'd let on?

It *had* to be coincidental, she reassured herself. Occurrences like that happened, even in a city as big as New York. And if they were going to tail her, they'd hardly put a woman in Louboutins on the case.

Moments later, Kit let herself into her building and rode the elevator to the fifth floor. Talked out from her night with Chuck, she looked forward to crawling into bed with a book and just drifting off to sleep mid-page.

But as she stepped closer to her apartment, she jerked to a halt. There was something pinkish brown poking out on the right side of the doorframe. Cautiously she forced herself a step closer. She saw then that the pinkish color was shards of raw wood and that the frame was gouged and splintered, as if someone had wacked at it with a sharp object. Then she saw the door. It was ajar, by a couple of inches, and there was a huge, ugly dent where the lock was.

Her skin pricked with fear. Someone had broken into her apartment. And she realized that they might still be inside.

chapter 8

Run, she commanded her legs. She spun around and nearly hurled herself down the hall toward the elevator. No, there wasn't time, she realized as she started to jab the call button. She kept going, to the stairwell entrance. After yanking open the door, she jerked quickly to a stop and listened, wondering if the intruder could be lurking below. It was silent. She flew down the stairs, her feet barely touching the steps and her palm skimming over the handrail at light speed.

By the time she reached the lobby, her heart was beating so hard that the sound filled her head, like a piston churning. She pushed open the main door and frantically glanced up and down the street. There were a half-dozen people at various points along the block, but they seemed *ordinary*, people just going about their business.

She dashed ten yards up the street and ducked into the entranceway of another building. Her hands had begun to shake and for a few seconds she fumbled uselessly in her purse until she finally found her phone. She called 911.

"What is your emergency?" the operator asked.

"Someone's broken into my apartment," Kit blurted out. "They—they might still be inside."

The operator asked for the address and apartment number. She also wanted to know where Kit was at that moment.

"Outside. Um, on the street."

"Do not attempt to reenter the residence. Wait outside. The police will be there shortly."

As soon as the call ended, Kit could feel a sob catch in her throat. Her *home*, all her lovely things. She couldn't stand the idea of a stranger in there, pawing over her possessions, stealing what she'd worked so hard for. Instinctively, she let her hand brush the outside of her tote bag, remembering gratefully that she'd lugged her iPad with her tonight. And her Samsung camera was tucked in her purse. Thank God for small favors, she thought grimly.

Burglary, she knew, was always a possibility in New York, particularly in a non-doorman building. But she'd taken pre-cautions: the best locks she could afford for both her apartment and the office. The *office*. In dismay she remembered that she'd left the inner door—the one from her apartment—ajar, so that meant the burglar would have had easy access to her workplace. Fists clenched, she kept her eyes riveted to the front of her build-ing, waiting to see if anyone suspicious looking emerged.

And then a thought poked through her brain, sharp as a stick. What if it wasn't just a regular burglary? From the moment Matt Healy had opened his door and explained to her about the theft of his wallet, she'd worried that X might have another card to play with her. And he knew where she lived.

But what could he possibly want from her apartment? He'd stolen Healy's identity so maybe he'd hatched a plan to steal hers, too, and market it to someone else. She pressed her hands to her cheeks in alarm, realizing that if she'd shown up earlier, she might have come face to face with him.

The local precinct was super close to her, and it took under ten minutes for the squad car to arrive. Two uniformed cops emerged, one a male Hispanic, and the other a thirtyish white woman, with a brown ponytail sticking out from the back of her cap. Kit hurried from the doorway to greet them and then explained what had happened, words tumbling out of her mouth.

"And you think someone might still be in there?" the male cop asked her. His badge read Tirado.

"I couldn't tell," Kit said. "The door was open a couple of inches, but I didn't hear any noise. And no one's come out of the building."

"What's the apartment floor plan like?"

"It's just a one bedroom with an open kitchen. But I rent the studio next door—to the left—as an office. There's an inner door to it from my living room."

"How long had you been out tonight?"

"Um, about six hours."

"All right," the female cop told her. "We need you to stay down here for a few more minutes. Once we clear the apartment, we'll have you come back up to the floor."

Kit nodded, and watched the cops stride purposely into the building. Part of her wished she could accompany them. As much as she dreaded confronting whatever havoc awaited her inside, not knowing what had happened was even worse.

She retreated once more to the doorway of the nearby building. The temperature had dropped, and the wind was even choppier now, but inside her coat, her top was damp with sweat.

With the cops gone, she felt vulnerable again. She kept her eyes on the street, on anyone passing by. A small crowd began to mill around the squad car, curious, even as jaded New Yorkers, to discover what was brewing inside the building. If it *was* X who had broken into her apartment, she wondered anxiously if he might be still hovering nearby. Again, questions ping-ponged back and forth in her brain: What would he have been looking for? Was he some kind of sociopath? She was just lucky she hadn't been home.

It was about ten minutes before the female cop emerged from the building. Kit hurried from the doorway to meet her halfway, her pulse racing in anticipation of news.

"Whoever was in your apartment is gone now, so you can reenter the building," the cop told her. "But you'll have to wait in the hall. CSU needs to go through your place first and dust for prints."

"Was it a burglary?" Kit asked anxiously.

"It appears that way. I should warn you, though, it's a mess in there."

Kit's heart sank. She dreaded the thought of seeing her home violated that way. But a crazy part of her felt relieved by the fact that it might be a standard-issue break-in after all.

"What about my office?" she asked. "Were they in there, too?"

The cop nodded solemnly.

"But it doesn't look like they bothered with much in that room. You'll know better when you take a look."

Her *laptop*, she thought suddenly, fighting the urge to wail. She'd left it on her desk. Everything of importance was stored on Dropbox—but that offered only minor consolation. As for her co-workers' laptops, she was pretty sure Baby had taken hers home on Thursday, and she just prayed Dara had done the same with her own today.

"I—I should call my super," Kit said, as she accompanied the cop into the building. "The door will have to be replaced."

"He has a set of keys I assume?"

"Yes, but he lives in a different building, not far from here."

"Who else is a lawful key holder?"

Kit explained that two people worked with her, and as they

rode the elevator to five, she provided Baby and Dara's contact info.

Stepping from the elevator into the corridor, Kit saw Officer Tirado standing just outside the apartment. She forced herself to take in the splintered doorframe again. She had a sudden, horrible image of an intruder bashing away at it.

She took a few steps closer to her apartment.

"Ms. Finn, please," the female officer said, lightly raising a hand, "we need you to remain out here for a while."

But the door was fully open now and Kit was close enough to glimpse the inside of her apartment, at least the first ten feet or so. Her heart sank. The drawer from the small table in the entranceway had been yanked out and lay upside down on the area rug, the contents scattered. A floor lamp, which had been next to the table, was now on its side, the lampshade askew. It looked as if there'd been a minor explosion, spewing objects pell-mell around the room.

"Understood," Kit said, beginning to retreat. "But—can you just tell me how they got in?"

"Most likely with a crowbar," Tirado said. "It's a typical approach. Burglars just wedge it in there a few times and pull. If the door is kind of flimsy, like this one, it only takes a couple of minutes."

She'd paid all that money for a good lock, never realizing the door was lame. Reluctantly, Kit retreated farther down the hall near the door to her office, which was still closed.

While the two cops murmured to each other, occasionally pausing to speak into their walkie-talkies, Kit called the super and told him the news. Clearly upset, he promised to show within the hour. Next she phoned Baby. Though she'd kept her cool while talking with the super, Kit's voice trembled as she broke the news to her partner.

"Dear lord," Baby said. "But you're okay?"

"Yes, though I'm afraid once I get in there, I might burst into tears. I hope you and Dara took your laptops home with you."

"I did, and I assume Dara must have because she can't live without hers. Kit, do you want me to come down? I could probably be there in twenty minutes or so."

"Thanks, but there's really nothing you can do. I don't even know what I'm dealing with yet, and I won't until they let me inside."

There was a long pause, and Kit glanced quickly at the screen, wondering if the call might have been dropped.

"I've got to ask this question," Baby said finally. "Do you think this could be related to what else has been going on, with that nasty man from Florida?"

"They're saying right now it looks like a run-of-the-mill burglary and I'm just hoping that's the case. Look, I'd better go. I need to contact one of my girlfriends and see if I can crash on her couch tonight. But I'll call you after I've been in the office and assessed the damage."

"Don't be ridiculous," Baby said. "You're staying with me. I have a perfectly lovely guest room, and the sheets in there probably make anyone else's feel like horsehair."

"Baby, I couldn't impose." Yet even as she said the words she knew that's where she wanted to be. Baby's Park Avenue apartment building was like a fortress and she'd feel totally safe there tonight, to say nothing of it being far more comfortable than bunking down on someone's pullout sofa with a mattress as thin as a cheese singlet.

"I won't discuss it another moment. Just give me a heads-up when you're due to arrive."

"Thank you, Baby."

About ten minutes later, she heard the elevator begin to groan and two men in lightweight overcoats spilled out along with a man and woman in CSU jackets. One of the overcoated guys introduced himself as Detective O'Callaghan while the other three people disappeared into the apartment. He was about fifty and from his weary, lined face, it looked like he'd probably witnessed the aftermath of a million bust-ins, but he at least seemed sympathetic as Kit described her discovery.

"I see you've got four apartments on the floor," O'Callaghan said. "Do you know if your neighbors are around?"

"The first door here is actually to an adjoining office of mine. The neighbors in apartment A go away every weekend and the ones in B are on vacation."

O'Callaghan shook his head, frustated on her behalf.

"The intruder either got lucky or he'd done his homework. You see anyone suspicious in the building lately or notice any unusual occurrences?"

"Occurrences?" Kit asked, not sure what he meant.

"Burglars often case a building before they attempt to break in," he said. "They might leave a pizza flyer tucked into your door and then wait to see how long it's there for. That gives them a hint to your schedule."

"Nothing like that," Kit said. "But there's something I need to tell you."

O'Callaghan's ears practically pricked up as she spoke. Kit shared what had happened to her over the past week, including Healy's death. Though she'd told the story several times already, she still cringed as she described how X had tricked her.

"Wait, you kind of lost me in Miami," the detective said. "You're saying you think the break-in might have something to do with this guy down there?"

"I have no way of knowing. It just seems like such a freaky coincidence."

"Okay, why don't I get all this down a little later," he said. "Right now I want to take a look inside with my partner, and then we'll have you make an inventory of what's missing."

He plucked a pair of latex gloves from his coat pocket, snapped them on, and entered the apartment. It was another fifteen minutes before he reemerged, with the CSU pair trooping out behind him. Before the team departed, O'Callaghan had one of them take a set of her fingerprints for comparison.

"You ready to go inside now?" O'Callaghan asked.

"Yup," Kit said. By this point she felt totally drained, but she was also desperate to learn what was missing. Taking a breath, she followed O'Callaghan down the hall and into the apartment. The other detective met them at the entrance and conveyed that he was headed to the other floors to canvass the building while at least some people were still awake.

It was a total shambles inside: cabinet doors flung open, cushions from the sofa and armchairs upended, contents from drawers flung every which way. And there was an eerie black coating of fingerprint dust over many areas.

In an instant, Kit felt her despondency morph into outrage. *Damn* them, she thought.

"I know it's tough, but try to take a close look," O'Callaghan said. "You'll need to make an inventory of what's gone."

Nodding, she grabbed a pad and pen from her purse and began taking stock.

She started with the kitchen area. Her iPhone speakers were gone, she realized. And so was the jar she kept spare change in. It *did* look like a burglary, she thought. Maybe a junkie desperate for drug money.

She turned and surveyed the living/dining area.

"It's so hard to tell in all this disarray," she told O'Callaghan, "but it looks like they stole a set of silver picture frames." They'd been a gift from a client, the kind of splurge she wouldn't have indulged in for herself.

To her surprise, her small flat-screen TV was still in position.

"Why wouldn't they have taken that?" she asked, pointing.

"Best guess? We're probably talking one guy here, and besides the fact that he'd want to enter and exit in in a hurry, there was only so much he could carry. What about jewelry?"

Kit nodded gloomily toward the bedroom. Steeling herself, she led the way, with O'Callaghan behind her.

The chaos was even worse in there. Clothes and bedding were strewn on the floor and the drawers of her dresser were hanging down like slack tongues. She could see that the tray she kept costume jewelry on had been overturned, and though a few odd earrings were scattered on the floor, it appeared that most of the pieces had been taken.

She strode over to her bookcase. She had only a few pieces of really nice jewelry, including a bracelet and earrings from Jeremy, and they were stored in a hollowed-out book on her shelf, a trick she'd learned from Baby. To her relief, she saw that the book was still there. She tugged it from the shelf, flipped open the top, and found the pieces safely tucked inside, along with her passport.

She sighed gratefully. "Everything's here."

"Fortunately most of the guys who pull this crap aren't book readers," O'Callaghan commented.

"Can I check my office now?" Kit asked, her dread building again. She was sure her laptop would be gone.

And it was. After threading her way back through the mess with O'Callaghan, she saw that it was missing from the top of her desk. That's a thousand bucks, she thought woefully. At least she'd shut it down before leaving, requiring a password to reopen it.

She glanced around the room. Just as the patrol cop had said, the thief, or thieves, hadn't really bothered much with the office. The desktop computer on Dara's desk was still in place, and the printer remained on a side table. File drawers, locked by Dara for the weekend, were closed and all the piles of fabric samples and drawings looked untouched. Besides her laptop, nothing appeared to be missing.

She knew she should consider herself fortunate. It had scared her to think of her workspace disrupted. What she could afford even less than the loss of her belongings was any downtime in her business.

"Anything other than the laptop?" O'Callaghan asked.

"Not that I can tell."

She returned to her apartment with O'Callaghan, just as the second detective, a Lieutenant Lopez, walked through the main doorway. He reported that he'd managed to speak to a half-dozen residents, rousing some of them from bed, and unfortunately no one had seen or heard anything suspicious. And no one else had been burglarized.

Why target *me*? Kit thought despondently. She was starting to feel the full impact of the evening. Her limbs ached and her head was throbbing.

"Now that Detective Lopez is back," said O'Callaghan, sliding onto a stool at the kitchen island, "take us through this Miami situation." He withdrew a pad from his suit jacket pocket. "This way he's in the loop, too, and I can get it all down."

Kit ran through everything again. O'Callaghan pursed his lips, clearly trying to digest it all. What could she expect? The story sounded crazy even to her as she recounted the details.

"We'll certainly take all that into consideration," said O'Callaghan. "But to be honest, this looks like a straightforward burglary to me."

He slid a card from his wallet and handed it to her, saying he would be in touch if there was anything to report and she should do the same. Kit told herself to accept his version of events and to thank her lucky stars.

As O'Callaghan rose, ready to leave, her super, Andre, poked his head through the doorway of the apartment. Kit motioned for him to enter. His mouth dropped open in shock as he absorbed the scene in front of him.

The detectives introduced themselves to him and explained how the door had been jimmied. Then they indicated they needed to move on, reminding Kit that they would require fingerprints from her two co-workers. She thanked them profusely for their help.

"My son is on his way, and we will take care of this," Andre said as soon as the police departed. "But do you have any other place to stay tonight?"

"Yes, with a friend," she said. "But Andre, I need a better door this time or I'll never feel safe here."

"Yes, I promise," he said. "I will order a customized door, with a steel plate so it can't be jimmied."

"How long will it take?"

He pressed his chubby lips together momentarily, as if afraid to say.

"About a week."

"A *week*? What do I do until then?"

He said that he and his son would barricade the apartment with wood tonight and first thing tomorrow morning they would install a temporary door with metal pins that would insert into the floor at the bottom and into the doorframe at the top. It would be up by noon and she could return at that point.

"All right," Kit said, knowing a better door would soothe her nerves only so much. She was sure an alarm system was probably out of her price range—she'd investigated one when she first moved in—but she was determined to make calls tomorrow and at least find out. "I'm going to leave as soon as I pack a few things."

As Andre waded around the apartment, scooping up a few objects here and there in an attempt to at least rescue them from the floor, Kit tossed a change of clothes into a duffle bag, along with a handful of toiletries. Then she returned to her office. As much as she wanted to just flee the scene, she needed to grab her insurance file. There were calls that would have to be made first thing tomorrow.

It was hauntingly quiet in there. Quieter it seemed, than on so many other nights when she'd snuck into her office after dinner to take care of business. Staring at the three empty desks and the small pine worktable topped with a lovely bowl of dried pomegranates, she found it hard to believe that so much mayhem lay just a few feet behind her in the apartment.

She collected the necessary documents from the filing cabinet, grateful to have been so persnickety over the years about keeping hard copies. Then she pulled out the top drawer of her desk, searching for a binder clip in order to secure all the papers together. As her hand hovered above the open drawer, she caught herself.

Something was off. The contents in the organizing tray—paperclips, pushpins, stamps, Post-its, etc.—were neatly organized, just as they always were, but they looked different somehow. Different from how they'd been arranged when she'd last opened the drawer that afternoon. The staple remover was now on the left side rather than the right. The pad of neon pink Post-its was turned lengthwise rather than vertically.

The thief had been in the drawer, she realized. The thought of his hands in there, pawing through her things repulsed her. She wondered what he'd been hoping to find tucked inside. Perhaps an envelope of petty cash. Or an iPod?

And yet something confused her. Why would the burglar be such a neatnik all of a sudden? Back in her apartment, the table and dresser drawers were hanging by a thread or yanked out entirely, with their contents cast about, but in the office it appeared as if nothing had been touched, save a laptop whisked from a desk. The drawer had clearly been searched but then carefully reorganized.

Maybe, she thought, there'd been two burglars tonight with two different M.O.s—one who got his kicks out of trashing places and another who didn't.

Or, there was a whole other explanation. She straightened her body and held it still, as if listening for a sound from afar. In her living space, where the thief had absconded with most of the items of value, he'd announced his presence brashly, as if to say, "See what I'm doing, bitch." But in her office he'd barely left a footprint. As if he was trying to convey, "This room doesn't matter to me." When it really did.

With a jolt, she thought suddenly of the rearranged pillows earlier in the week. What if that hadn't been done by Baby's client but rather by an intruder, who'd cased her apartment, hoping to leave no footprints? And then returned another night.

She lifted her gaze and stared at her desktop. There was a small stack of opened letters, all addressed to her, and also a Post-it with a message from Dara that said, "Kit, we're out of milk but I'll pick up a quart on Monday morning." Anyone looking would know at a glance that this desk was hers.

Eyes back to the drawer. Something, she realized, was missing from one of the little black compartments. A flash drive she'd dropped in there the day before, one she'd been planning to send to a client so he'd have extra photos of his newly renovated one-bedroom apartment. She couldn't imagine what value that would hold for anyone other than the client.

A thought began to form in her mind and lodged there, chilling her. What if the person had broken in not to steal but to *search*?

For what, though? Financial data? About her—*and* her clients? With a shudder she realized, she didn't have a single clue. But X's face formed clearly in her mind again.

chapter 9

It was close to 11:30 by the time Kit left for Baby's, with Andre still working wearily on the door. She made sure that he planned to leave notes for her neighbors on the floor so they'd be aware of what happened and could take whatever precautions they wanted to. By the time she was in a cab, her nerves felt as if someone had taken a grater to them.

Baby opened the door fully dressed in a cream-colored blouse, navy pants, and a thick red leather belt, as if she was coming from a brunch at the Colony Club. She held a half-filled cocktail glass.

"You poor thing," Baby said, welcoming Kit into the apartment. She nodded toward the glass. "I was fretting so much, I resorted to a second vodka. What can I get you? You must need a stiff drink at this point."

"Actually, I'd kill for a cup of caffeine-free tea if you have it," Kit said. "I hate to sound like a wuss, but I feel too wired for anything else."

"Okay, just give me a minute."

"But first can I borrow your laptop? I need to get on Dropbox and erase information in some of our files. Whoever stole my laptop may know how to hack in."

While Baby busied herself in the kitchen, Kit took a seat in the study, logged onto Dropbox and quickly forwarded Baby her current client files, each of which contained credit card info used for purchases. Then she deleted those files on her own laptop. She also sent Baby her most important personal files and trashed those on her computer as well.

Finished, she wandered back to the living room and collapsed onto one of the pair of brown leather sofas. She glanced distractedly around the dazzling space: walls painted a turquoise blue, known officially as Benjamin Moore's California Breeze; curtains made of Indian bedspreads; huge, ravishing botanical prints on the wall; and in one corner an Egg chair in shocking red, because, well, just because Baby could. What always amazed Kit about the apartment was that it managed to be not only jaw-droppingly gorgeous, but also totally inviting. Tonight, however, she was so churned up inside that she could hardly relish its charms.

She leaned her head back wearily against the sofa and stared at the ceiling. Two hours ago she'd been eager to accept O'Callaghan's assurance that the break-in had probably been a run-of-the-mill burglary, but based on the missing flash drive and the discreet search through her desk drawer, her gut now told her that she'd be a fool to believe that. Something else was going on.

And X had to be the one behind it. He was an identity thief, after all, and only days after meeting him, her home had been searched for possible data. A coincidence too big to ignore. From the moment she'd been tricked by him, she'd felt his dark presence looming in her life. It was like being hunted by a predator who'd tried to hide behind a floor-length curtain, and yet despite his efforts, you couldn't miss the terrifying outline of his body on the fabric and the tips of his shoes protruding on the floor.

The image of Healy's corpse suddenly flashed in her mind. What if her own life was now in danger?

"Here we go," Baby said, returning to the living room carrying a tray laden with a small teapot, a cup and saucer, and a plate of butter cookies. Baby always set a mean tray. "According to the box, the tea is 'Cozy Chamomile,'" she said, "so maybe it will help a little."

"Thanks, Baby. Just *being* here is helping me. Though it's going to be a while before I feel anything close to cozy again."

"Tell me what they stole," Baby said. While she settled into an armchair close by, Kit took a long sip of tea and then returned the gold-rimmed porcelain cup to the saucer.

"They made off with my speakers, most of my costume jewelry, some silver stuff, and, of course, my laptop. It doesn't appear, at least, that they took anything of yours, but you'll have to check when you get there."

"I spoke with Dara already and, like me, she didn't have anything of real value lying around. I just feel so bad for *you*. You're insured, right?"

"Yes, with an annoyingly high deductible." Kit blew out a long breath. "But to be honest, the stolen stuff isn't at the top of my worry list right now."

"What do you mean?" Baby asked. She'd had her cocktail glass halfway to her mouth as she'd posed the question and now it was paused in midair, like a freeze-framed image from a video.

"I don't believe it was really a routine burglary tonight."

"But the cops—you said they thought it *was*."

Kit explained about the searched drawer and missing flash drive, as well as her theory that the ransacked living room might be a ruse to distract her and the police from the real intent behind the break-in. Just talking about it all made her anxiety level spike.

Baby frowned, her expression a mix of worry and confusion. "I remember you asking Dara to put those pictures on a flash drive so you could send them to that client of yours, Stan what's-his-next-name, the one with the bad hair plugs. But why would anyone else want photos of his apartment?"

"They don't," Kit said, shaking her head. "I think the person may have been searching for confidential information about me, and probably our clients as well. If he'd done his homework, he would know interior designers keep client credit card numbers on file, and he probably wanted access to those. By making the burglary seem like it was the work of a druggie looking for stuff to pawn, he buys time to hack into my computer, extract the info, and use it."

"Dear God. Do we need to alert our clients?"

"I've deleted their files from my Dropbox account, so no one would be able to access them from my laptop now, but it may be too late. I think we should let clients know what happened and tell them to keep an eye out."

"Let me do that tomorrow. You've got enough on your plate at the moment. And I can smooth any ruffled feathers."

"Thanks so much." Kit looked off, thinking, gnawing on the tip of her finger.

"What?"

"I just hope this doesn't cast too much of a pall over the business."

"These things happen. It's New York City after all."

Kit nodded tentatively.

"There's something you're not saying, Kit. What is it?"

"I'm not so sure this is just about living in New York City. Remember what you asked earlier? About the man from Florida? I'm worried this actually *does* have something to do with him."

Baby pulled her arms across her chest. She was doing her best not to seem rattled, but Kit knew that this update had to be disturbing.

"Did you find anything specific pointing to him?" she asked.

"No, but the one thing I know for sure about him is that he's been using someone else's identity, so identity theft could easily be his main line of work. And then, of course, there's the timing. This guy sends me to Healy's apartment. A few days later Healy turns up dead. And then a few days after that my apartment is ransacked. It just screams that there's a connection. I'm even wondering if he was in my apartment once before, the day I noticed that my pillows had been moved. He might have been casing the place."

"You're going to talk to the police about this, right?"

"Yes, for sure. I've already told them what happened in Florida. But even with this new little theory of mine, it's hard to believe the cops can do much. No one has any idea who this guy I call X really is or how to find him. And there isn't a shred of proof he's behind this."

"So what recourse do you have? What if this Mr. X decides to—I don't know, come back and look for more?"

Kit pushed herself off the sofa and began to pace back and forth in front of it. Something had begun to stir in her, but she couldn't yet define it.

"I—I'm going to have to find out what I can myself," she said finally.

Her words came only a beat or two after the thought had crystalized, catching her by surprise. Did she really mean what she was saying? *Yes.* She couldn't sit around any longer, waiting for one devastating event after another to domino through her life.

"Am I hearing you right?" Baby asked. "You can't get involved in this, Kit."

"But I already *am* involved. From the moment I left the Ithaka offices that first time, I've told myself again and again, 'It's behind me now.' And then there's always been one more aspect I've had to contend with. This isn't going to stop. For some reason I don't understand, I'm smack in the middle of an ugly mess and it's up to me to extricate myself."

"Whoa, wait a minute. I hate to go all Judge Judy and get

really tough, but you just can't do that. Taking action could be terribly dangerous."

Kit smiled wanly. "I know. And I'm scaring myself a little. But I feel even more frightened about the alternative: doing nothing and waiting for fate to play its hand. I have to look out for myself—and our business."

"But *how*? You mean more security for the office and your apartment?"

Kit shrugged helplessly, still not certain herself. "What I think I need as much as security is information. I can't begin to get out of the mess until I know what I'm actually up against."

"I understand how you feel, but I don't like the idea of you hunting down information," Baby said, looking dismayed. "What exactly would that entail?"

"I'm not really sure." Kit reached down for her cup and took a last swig of tea. "We're both bushed. Why don't we head to bed, and then tomorrow I'll consider everything when my mind is fresh."

"Well, I'm counting on the fact that at the first light of dawn, you'll come fully to your senses."

Baby led Kit to the guest room and they hugged good night.

After washing her face and changing into a nightshirt, Kit slid between the bed's luscious percale sheets, hand stitched with custom embroidery. Her body ached with fatigue and she yearned for the release sleep would bring, but within seconds she could tell that her brain wasn't going to cooperate. There were too many anxious thoughts—and unanswered questions—bouncing around in there for her to let go.

Despite Baby's pleas, Kit was determined to secure information that could help reveal X's agenda, and she knew that the first light of dawn wasn't going to revise her thinking. The very first step, of course, would be following up with the New York detectives. But then what? A call to Molinari for starters, she decided. And this time she'd be less passive. She'd ask for more details about Healy's death and an update on the investigation.

Healy. For the past few hours, all of her attention had been focused on X, but for the first time she realized that if she wanted to learn the truth, she needed to consider Healy, too. He'd been a victim of X's as well, maybe in the most horrific way possible. According to Wainwright and Ungaro, Healy had headed to Miami on business. But Healy might have lied to them about the actual purpose of the trip.

And yet if Healy had gone in pursuit of X, the trip could hardly have amounted to more than a wild-goose chase. All Healy would have known was that X *might* be in Miami. Unless, of course, he'd somehow dug up additional info.

She thought back to their conversation at the restaurant bar. She'd given Healy a decent description of X. Perhaps based on that, he'd talked to the hosts of the party in Brooklyn and figured out who the pickpocket was, and from there, determined where X might be staying.

For the first time she realized how stupid it was of X to send her to the apartment that night. Surely he would have known that she'd describe him to Healy. But, of course, X wasn't stupid. He hadn't seemed that way for a second. There had to be something else at play, something she just couldn't see.

What if X's main motive had never been to punk her? Perhaps she'd been sent to Healy's for another reason. To deliver a message, or even a *warning*, that she didn't know she was giving.

She thought back again to her initial meeting with Healy. When she'd first arrived at his place, he'd seemed mildly amused by her plight, but his expression had clouded the moment she'd mentioned her encounter in Florida, and by the time they were in the bar, he'd been visibly agitated. She'd assumed it was because he'd begun to conclude his identity had been compromised, but alarm bells clearly had gone off for him just from hearing about the mystery man in Islamorada.

It dawned on her then that Healy might have known X. She remembered what the cop had said: that Healy had never reported his wallet stolen. Maybe the missing wallet story had all been a lie, too. Healy and X might have been in league together and later fallen out, which had resulted in Healy's murder. The thought chilled her.

Finally, too disturbed to focus on it any longer, she chased the thoughts away and finally drifted off into an anxious sleep.

By 10:30 the next morning, Kit was in a cab headed downtown with Baby in tow. Baby had insisted on joining the cleanup effort, and though Kit hated ruining her partner's Saturday, she was both grateful for the help and eager to have Baby inspect her desk for any kind of disturbance. They'd called Dara earlier from the apartment and she promised she would meet them after a doctor's appointment and before a wedding she was due to attend late in the afternoon. Kit had also used the early morning to alert the insurance company and leave voicemail messages for both O'Callaghan and Molinari.

When they were halfway to Kit's apartment, Molinari returned the call.

"I was just hoping for an update," Kit told her.

"An update?"

"Yes, about the case. Did you find out any more about how Matt Healy died?"

"There's no reason not to tell you because we've just released a statement. Mr. Healy's death was a homicide."

Her heart nearly stopped

"How—how could you tell?" Next to her she felt Baby's body stiffen, as she sensed something was up.

"Primarily from the tire tread marks. Mr. Healy was crossing the road and the driver clearly accelerated in order to strike him."

Kit tried to fight off the image but it bullied its way into view regardless: Healy crossing an intersection, turning his head at the sudden sound of an engine being gunned, the look of terror on his face as the front hood razored into him, hurtling his body into midair. She could almost hear the awful thud.

"Do you have a suspect yet?"

"We don't at this time, unfortunately. The person you met in the Keys is still a person of interest, but we haven't had any luck locating him. Based on your sketch, the hotel staff confirmed he was staying there under the name Matt Healy, but he's vanished without a trace."

"There's something you should be aware of from my end," Kit said. "My apartment was broken into last night. The police have categorized it as a routine burglary, but in light of the timing, I'm worried it could be more than that."

"I'm in the middle of something right now, but why don't you give me the name of the detective in charge and I'll reach out."

Kit tapped onto O'Callaghan's contact info and read off the phone number. Molinari said a quick goodbye, promising to follow up.

"Not good," Kit whispered and turned to Baby. "Healy was definitely murdered."

Baby said nothing, just grasped Kit's hand and held it tightly. Kit appreciated the gesture. With each day she seemed to find herself ever deeper into the plot of a film noir. It was like a dream she'd had once in which a piece of paper, something she wasn't meant to lose, had blown out of her hand and as she tried to rescue it, the wind kept snatching it farther and farther away, first through a field and then, to her alarm, into the woods, which grew darker and more sinister with each step she took, until finally she was horribly lost, stumbling over tree roots and rocks with the paper no longer anywhere in sight.

It's like that now, Kit thought. She was looking for a piece of paper with all the answers and she couldn't save herself until she found it.

As soon as the taxi pulled onto her street, Kit was flooded with fresh dread. She hated the idea of seeing the chaos again, but postponing the moment wouldn't do any good at all.

Stepping off the elevator, they found an exhausted-looking Andre in the hallway, dressed in the same clothes he'd been in the night before and limply dabbing a paint brush at the now patched-up doorframe. The temporary door was fully installed, with the promised pins into the floor and upper doorframe. Andre turned over the key and Kit made sure that there was no difficulty opening the door with it. Then she and Baby entered the apartment.

Baby threw her hands up in disgust as she surveyed the scene.

"Let's go check your desk," Kit said quickly.

They stepped over and around the items still on the floor and Kit unlocked the door to the office. Her breath caught in her chest as she fumbled on the wall for the overhead light switch. She wondered if she'd ever again walk into her darkened apartment or office without a rush of fear.

Baby went straight to her desk, glanced over the top and then opened the drawers one by one.

She shook her head slowly back and forth. "I don't have your gift for neatness, but nothing appears to be missing."

"Flash drives?"

"I didn't have any in here."

They returned to Kit's apartment and began to tackle the upheaval, Baby focusing on the living room while Kit restored the bedroom and bathroom to order. As she worked, she realized that an older camera of hers was also missing. But that didn't change her mind about the motive of the intruder.

By the time Dara arrived at noon, dressed in jeans and carrying a pizza, Baby and Kit had the apartment back to normal.

"I'm so sorry I couldn't be here earlier," Dara said, dropping the box on the kitchen island. "I thought I'd at least pick up food."

"Thanks, I'm famished," Kit said. "But why don't you take a look at your desk before we eat?"

Dara checked her top drawer first. She had the impression, she said, that someone had rustled through there, but nothing was missing. She took a set of keys from her purse, and opened the bottom drawer, where she kept petty cash and anything valuable. She had locked it, per usual, at the end of the workday. She glanced through and announced that everything appeared just as she left it.

"I thought New York was supposed to be so much safer these days," Dara said worriedly as the three returned to Kit's apartment.

"Yes, but stuff still happens," Kit said. Baby shot her a questioning look, obviously wondering how much should be revealed to Dara. But Kit didn't want to alarm her assistant any more than necessary. "Are you nervous about working in the office, Dara?"

"No," she said, though not convincingly. "But I'm freaked about you being here at night."

"The super told me on the phone this morning that he's ordering a security camera downstairs above the entrance, and he's going to have his son come by periodically during the day just to keep an eye on the building. That should help. And as a precaution, let's agree that for the time being, no one will stay alone in the office. We'll arrange our schedules so that two people are always here together."

Both Dara and Baby nodded, looking relieved at the suggestion.

Dara departed just a few minutes later, saying that she would swing by the police precinct to be fingerprinted before returning home to change for the wedding. As the door clicked shut behind her, Baby turned to Kit.

"Why don't you grab some extra clothes and come back uptown with me now," Baby said, her face etched with worry. "Despite the super's precautions, I think you should bunk down with me for a while."

"Thanks so much, Baby, but I'm going to bite the bullet and stay here. Every day I delay sleeping in my apartment will make it tougher to finally do it."

Besides, Kit despised the idea of being uprooted from her home.

"But what if this man isn't done searching?"

"That's why I need to get some answers. If I can figure out what's going on, maybe I can better protect myself."

"Kit, please," Baby said. "I was hoping you'd woken up this morning and scared yourself silly with that idea of snooping around."

"I just want to see what I can dig up about Matt Healy. I've started to wonder if he and X were connected, maybe working together. The more I learn, the better."

"Where do you start? The Miami police are hardly going to let you in on their investigation. You had to call them just to find out his death was ruled a homicide."

"I know. And those guys at Ithaka aren't going to blab either. That place looks like an impenetrable fortress. I—"

She paused and lifted her eyes.

As she'd uttered the words, she sensed an idea beginning to push toward the surface of her mind, as if it had been slowly gnawing its way through the tangle of thoughts. She suddenly realized who might spill at least a little of what she needed to know.

chapter 10

"Wait, what are you thinking?" Baby asked.

"Umm, nothing, just letting my mind wander," Kit decided not to spill, knowing she'd only make Baby fret more. She took a last bite from her pizza slice, which she barely tasted.

"Just be careful, Kit. I don't want to think of you running around playing private detective."

Kit smiled. "Well that would be tough for me to do considering the only rod I generally pack is one you hang drapes from. But look, I've already taken up enough of your Saturday, Baby. Why—"

A buzzer sounded suddenly, making them both jerk. It had come from the office. Someone was ringing up from the lobby.

"Are you expecting anyone?" Baby asked warily.

"No," Kit said. She wondered if the cops were back, following up from last night. She hurried into the office, with Baby behind her, and answered the intercom.

"Hi, it's Keith Holt," a male voice said. "I'm here for our appointment."

"Oh, right," Kit stammered. She had completely and utterly forgotten. She buzzed him in, spun around, and blurted out the situation to Baby.

"My brain's so fried from this whole experience that I forgot that he was coming by today," Kit added. "I can't believe I've been so stupid about a client."

She also felt like a grungy mess from the cleanup.

"You'll pull it together," Baby reassured her.

"Would you mind staying one more minute? Meeting you could help seal the deal."

"Of course. But if I don't get the chance to tell you while he's here, promise me you'll consider coming back to my place later."

In the time it took the elevator to transport the doctor to the fifth floor, Kit threw on a new top, doused herself with fragrance, and undid her hair from the braid she'd fastened earlier. She also lit two fig-scented candles in her living room. None of it did anything for her state of mind, however, and as the doorbell to the office rang, she told herself she was going to have to suck it up and manage to be mentally present.

Holt was dressed down today compared to their first appointment, wearing dark brown pants and a hip-length navy jacket, and yet he still managed to exude that almost palpable aura of self-assurance she'd beheld at their first meeting.

Baby gave him a taste of her charms and then, after a few minutes, announced that she needed to head back uptown.

"Why don't we go over to my apartment," Kit said after Baby had left. "It'll be more comfortable there." Besides, she knew it could be a bonus for him to see it.

After they entered her living space, Kit gestured toward the dining table.

"Please have a seat," she said. "And, uh, let me take your jacket."

She realized she felt oddly disoriented, like an actor who'd just dropped a line in a play and was scrambling for what to say next. The break-in was still clearly weighing on her.

"Your place is terrific," Holt said as he slipped out of his jacket. "I really like what you've done with it."

"Thank you. It's not a huge space, but that made the challenge even more fun. Can I get you something? An espresso? Or cappuccino. I have sparkling water, too, if you'd like."

"An espresso would be terrific."

"Um, sure, just give me a minute to get the machine going." Kit detected a flicker of puzzlement in Holt's eyes.

"Is this still a good time?" he asked.

"I'm sorry if I seem a bit flustered," Kit said, realizing she was doing a lousy job of disguising her lingering distress. "I was robbed last night and I still feel slightly rattled from the experience."

"That's terrible," Holt said. "Were you injured?"

"No, no. I guess I should have said burglarized, not robbed. It happened when I was out for the evening."

"Did they get much?"

"A fair amount. And yet, maybe not what they were really looking for."

He cocked his head, his expression quizzical.

"It's weirdly complicated," she told him. "But to answer your other question, this *is* a good time for me to meet with you. I'd so much rather be talking to you than focusing on what happened."

"Great," he said. "But I tell you what. You sit and I'll make the espressos."

Kit laughed. "No, please."

"I insist." He nodded toward the counter. "I own the same kind of machine."

She settled into one of the dining chairs as Holt took over. It wasn't until she'd spread out her legs beneath the table that she realized how much her whole body ached, partly from all the picking up she'd done earlier.

"Cups are to the left," she called out.

"Yes, I see," he said. From the distance of the table, she

watched him work, his hands moving with utter confidence and control. Surgeon hands, she thought. There was something comforting in that.

A minute later he approached the table, carrying two bright white espresso cups in their saucers. As odd as it was to have a near stranger waiting on her in her apartment, Kit couldn't deny how satisfying it was. She was in dire need of a little tlc at the moment.

"Now that I've made you wait on me hand and foot, tell me what you wanted to discuss," Kit said, smiling. "I take it you had additional questions."

"I did actually. As I mentioned, I really like your portfolio. But I'm curious about how you work with clients. During my last experience with a decorator, I felt so shut out."

He's definitely open to hiring me, she realized. Whatever mental fatigue she'd succumbed to, she knew she had to get the better of it pronto.

"If you hired me, the first thing I'd do is have you collect tear sheets from shelter magazines," she said, leaning forward. "Pictures of rooms that appeal to you. I'd also want you to print out images from online. Famous paintings you love, favorite travel photos, anything that grabs you. Next I'd analyze them to get a sense of what you're drawn to on a visceral level. And then I'd present you with possible design ideas and listen to your feedback."

She was a hundred and ten percent sure the guy didn't have a Pinterest account, so she hadn't suggest using *that* as a tool.

Holt nodded, absorbing her words. "I like the sound of that. Why don't we go ahead then?"

Well, well, she thought. That's literally just what the doctor ordered.

She smiled once again. "I'm delighted. I'll put a letter of agreement together and send it to you Monday."

"Excellent." He took another sip of his espresso, cupping the bowl with his long, strong fingers rather than primly holding onto the handle.

"Weekends must be nice for you," Kit said. "Considering how intense your job is."

"I do value my weekends, and it's good to have the break. But I also love performing surgery. They'll have to drag me out of the operating room one day."

There was a fierceness to his tone that reinforced the passion he obviously felt.

"What area of the body do you focus on?"

"Knees primarily. My specialty is in skeletal issues impacted by rheumatoid arthritis." He smiled. "Not very sexy sounding, I know, but it's a major issue with an aging population."

"As a surgeon, you must handle stress awfully well. Is that hardwired or something that you've worked at over time?"

As he considered the question, he stroked the side of his jaw slowly back and forth with his thumb. "Probably both. I was always fearless as a kid. But you need to learn ways to shut out the world when you're operating. I use my time at the scrub sink to prepare mentally. Scrubbing is such a rote activity—the way you use the brush methodically over each plane of your hands— and it helps me visualize what's ahead and begin blocking out distractions."

Intriguing, she thought. The fearlessness. But also the discipline, and the ability to compartmentalize. They were qualities that could draw you to a man initially, but she wondered whether they might frustrate the hell out of you over time, when you suddenly saw that you were being denied access to what you yearned to know the most. Had that played a role, she wondered, in the demise of his marriage?

"I'm going to scrub my dishes with a whole new attitude," Kit said.

Holt's espresso cup clicked against the saucer as he set it back in place. "I should let you return to your Saturday."

"Trust me, this has been a wonderful diversion," she said, rising from the table with him. "And thank you for the opportunity."

"One last question before I go." He stared off for a moment, thinking. "Would it make any sense at all for me to start from scratch?"

"From scratch?"

"Buy a new apartment in a totally modern building and go from there."

"That's one possibility, of course," she said. If he went that route, it would be an even bigger—and more lucrative—project for her in the long run, and yet it would entail a lot of upheaval for him, which he might not appreciate once he found himself in the thick of it. "Why don't you start pulling those clips I mentioned? Once I have a sense from those, we can discuss all the options."

After closing the door behind him, she listened to his footfalls recede. Stepping back, she studied the temporary door. It looked sturdier than the old one and yet hardly crowbar resistant. A wave of panic plowed into her from behind. She would be all alone tonight in the apartment. And every night going forward. She knew she had no choice but to suck it up and take the necessary precautions.

She checked her watch. It was time to trudge to the Apple store in order to purchase another MacBook Air. But there was a matter she had to deal with first—the idea that had wiggled into her brain while she was talking to Baby.

She dug in her purse and pulled out the card Sasha Glen had given her last night. After mentally rehearsing what to say, she made the call.

Sasha picked up on the second ring. There were bustling

background noises, as if she might be in the midst of a shopping spree.

"Hello, this is Kit Finn. We spoke at the gallery in Chelsea."

"What can I do for you?" Sasha asked. Pleasant, but not nearly as eager to chat as she'd been last night.

"I wanted to follow up on our conversation. A client I was about to take on just called to say he was being transferred to California and won't need my services after all. You had said you were looking for a decorator and I'm open to talking if you're still interested."

"Hmm," Sasha said, as if the idea had lost its luster overnight. "You've caught me at an awkward time."

Damn, Kit thought. She'd convinced herself the woman was nosy enough that she would jump at the opportunity.

"I'm sorry to call out of the blue this way. I have your card so why don't I send you an email with my info. If you want to chat at a later point, feel free to follow up."

An excruciating pause followed.

"It's not that I'm uninterested," Sasha said. "I'm just in the middle of something. Can I have you come by my place and take a look?"

"Of course," Kit said, surprised by the turnaround. "When would work for you?"

"Unfortunately weeknights are bad because I'm usually dining with clients."

"Well, weekends are fine for me. Would . . . tomorrow work?"

"Not now," she said, and it took Kit a moment to realize the woman was addressing another person. "Uh, yes, tomorrow's good. Let's say two." She rattled off her address and then announced she had to go.

When the call was over, Kit stood for a few moment in the middle of her living room, grasping the phone in her hand. She wasn't sure how much information she would glean from the meeting, but it was a start at least. She was *doing* something.

The rest of the day was a crazy rush, and her body practically vibrated with anxiety. Where are you *now*? she wondered, thinking of X. If it was indeed him who had broken in, she prayed that he'd moved on, having realized she'd deleted any client information of value to him. But she kept *sensing* him, the man hiding behind the curtain.

After a trip to the mobbed Apple store on Prince Street, where she purchased a new laptop, she took the subway to a store that sold security supplies, which she'd researched online before leaving her apartment. A home security system remained out of her price range, but she needed *something* to make her feel safer. The store claimed to sell affordable devices that could provide a small amount of comfort. She ended up buying three hanging door-handle alarms. They supposedly emitted an eardrum-splitting sound if someone so much as jiggled the handle on the other side.

"Trust me," the salesperson told her. "When this thing starts to shriek, no one is going to stick around."

While racing around downtown, she'd called her friend Amy, explained about the burglary, and asked if she could glom onto Amy and her boyfriend's plans for the night. The answer was yes, of course. She tagged along on their dinner to a Thai restaurant. Kit had hoped the evening would be a distraction, but Amy was intent on warning her how burglars often targeted the same place twice, and trying to convince her to stay with them. By the time the couple dropped her off after dinner, she felt even more on edge.

No sooner had Amy and her boyfriend departed than Kit hung and set the alarms—on both the outer and inner doors to the office and on the main door to her apartment. Going through the process seemed to escalate rather than diminish her fear. What if it really *was* X who had broken in and what if he planned to return? Part of her regretted not taking either Baby or Amy up on their offers. But even if she stayed with one of them for the rest of the weekend, she'd have to return home at *some* point.

For the next hour or so she alternated between trying to watch TV and leafing aimlessly through decorating magazines. Baby called at 10:30 just to check in.

"I'm okay," Kit lied and informed her about her purchase of the door alarms. "I just have to remember to turn them off before you and Dara get here. Otherwise we'll all have heart attacks."

"I've got a better idea for the future," Baby said. "Fall madly in love with Dr. Holt and move in with him."

Kit snorted. "You think he's a catch?" she asked. "I guess I've been so preoccupied with everything, I was evaluating him only as a potential client."

"Yes, I think he's a catch. Handsome and successful. And he couldn't take his eyes off you."

Kit laughed and said goodnight. Afterward, she considered Baby's comment. Holt *was* attractive, and probably brilliant, but in light of where her most recent infatuation had landed her, she was hardly in the mood for another.

At midnight she crawled into bed, but it was after two before sleep finally overtook her. She slept fitfully and when she awoke, her heart was beating hard, as if her subconscious had spent the night in a state of watchfulness and agitation.

After making a cappuccino, she took it with her to the couch, where she sat with her legs tucked under her, forlornly watching through the window as the early morning light began to seep above the downtown rooftops and wooden water towers. She wondered if she would ever feel at ease in her home again.

For the first time she realized it wasn't simply the break-in that had knocked her off her heels. The experience had tapped into memories from the year she was seventeen, when she'd felt unsafe in the world for the first time. It had begun one weekday afternoon, when she'd returned from school to find her father unexpectedly at home and visibly shaken. He'd seemed preoccupied through much of the winter, but she'd assumed it was related to normal work issues. The business he owned, a highly successful plumbing-fixture company, placed plenty of demands on him.

That day, however, her father explained haltingly that there were far more than normal business headaches causing his distress. A man her father had brought in as a new partner two years before had embezzled hundreds of thousands of dollars from the company and fled the state. Not only was the business in ruins, but her parents' personal assets, long intermingled with the business, were gone as well.

She'd nearly ceased breathing as she digested the news And though she knew she should be concerned about her parents, the first question she blurted out, one she couldn't contain inside her, was, "What about *college?*" She'd been accepted early decision to Penn, where she'd planned to study art history. Because her parents were—or *had been*—fairly affluent, they were going to be paying full fare.

"We've already called the college," her mother said. "They might be able to pull together a small financial-aid package for you, but there's no way they can contribute everything. Honey, we're sick about this, but we just don't have the money."

It felt as if she'd been standing on the deck of a boat with everyone else below ship, and a huge wave had sent her hurling into the water where she was now fruitlessly screaming for help and straining desperately to stay afloat.

Her parents quickly sold their house, as well as most of their lovely possessions. Their next home was a tiny one-bedroom apartment, with Kit in the bedroom for the time being and her parents sleeping on the pullout sofa.

Kit spent the spring trying to convince a few state colleges to give her a financial package, a mix of aid and loans, but it was too late in the game to pull it off for fall. It would have to happen in the next calendar year. Following graduation, she'd found an assistant job at an interior design firm in New York. After throwing herself a pity party that stretched for at least three months, she realized that she loved the work, and from that point on there was no looking back. She took courses in design at night but, as her career took off, it seemed unnecessary to go back for a full-time degree. Besides, in light of what she'd lived through with her parents, she didn't have the stomach for taking on huge college loans. And yet even now, she still flinched when someone asked about her college background.

There were two things she had taken away from that awful year her father went bankrupt. Nothing was ever going to hold her back from creating the life she wanted. And she would never let anyone outsmart her and ruin what she'd built. If X was after her or her business, she had to shut him down.

She forced herself off the couch and began to plot how to handle the meeting with Sasha. She needed to find out what she could about Healy, particularly what he was doing in Florida. But she couldn't make it seem obvious or Sasha would smell a rat.

Early that afternoon, she took the subway uptown and walked several blocks east. Sasha lived in one of the many white brick high-rises that dotted the Upper East Side, though this one looked newly renovated and tres chic. After being cleared by the concierge, she took the elevator to the fourteenth floor.

She was glad she'd bothered with her outfit because Sasha looked impeccable. She was wearing slim black pants, a tight-fitting, black V-neck sweater, and large gold earrings shaped like bamboo. It wasn't until Kit had stepped fully into the apartment that she saw that the woman had a phone to her ear. After closing the door, Sasha motioned with a free finger that she would need a minute.

Discreetly Kit eyed her surroundings. She was standing in a large foyer that featured not a lick of furniture or a single piece of art. The walls had been painted a pale gray, maybe Benjamin Moore's Balboa Mist or Dove Wing, suggesting that the apartment might have once been a model that was shown to prospective buyers. Over Sasha's shoulder, Kit caught a glimpse of the living room. It was two spaces really, with a double-sided fireplace partially dividing them. Shockingly, there was hardly any furniture there either, just a white leather couch, a glass coffee table, and a few framed black-and-white photos leaning against the walls.

"It's going to have to be handled," Sasha said into the phone, her voice authoritative and yet slightly strident. "But I need at least twenty minutes to get there."

"This is extremely rude on my part," she said to Kit after disconnecting. "But something's come up and I need to reschedule with you."

Kit fought to keep her frustration at bay. All this way for nothing. But she couldn't settle for nothing. She had to leave with *something*.

"Don't worry about it," she said easily. "I know things can come up. . . . Does it have to do with Matt Healy's death?"

"What makes you ask that?" Sasha said.

"I—I just figured that the company must still be reeling from what happened. I'm sure plans have to be made."

"Actually, I'm dealing with a client matter today. But you're right—people *are* reeling." Sasha stared at Kit intently. "How about you? Has his death affected you?"

"Uh, yes, of course," Kit said, momentarily flummoxed. Sasha seemed to have no filter. If she wanted to know something, she just asked it. "As I told you, I didn't really know him, but it's always unsettling when someone you're acquainted with dies."

"Apparently it was a homicide. We just heard this weekend."

"How dreadful," Kit said, faking surprise at the news.

Sasha reached for the door handle. Kit knew she had only seconds left to extract the detail she needed.

"Was he in Miami for business—or just pleasure?" Kit asked.

"Actually, no one seems to know why he went there. We don't do any business in that area."

Kit's breath quickened at the comment. So Ungaro and Wainwright had lied. She wondered if they had simply been covering for Healy because they thought the truth was none of her business.

"Sounds like a personal trip then."

"He didn't say anything to you?" Sasha said, narrowing her eyes. "You talked to him that day. According to his assistant, he'd originally been booked on a flight to Ann Arbor and then changed his plans at the last minute."

"No, he just said he was going out of town."

Sasha swung open the door. "I'm sorry but I really *do* have to scoot. I'll call you when my schedule opens up again."

"Of course," Kit said and quickly left.

Out on the street she started walking fast, with no destination in mind, just fueled by her agitation. The fact that Healy had altered his original plans and headed to Miami added credence to the idea of him on a hunt for X, as well as the possibility of X getting wind of it and gunning him down with his car.

She replayed the brief encounter with Sasha. Abruptly cancelling the meeting seemed odd, but Kit sensed it had been legitimate. Just as she had an agenda for being with Sasha, she suspected that Sasha had an agenda for her as well, and the woman wouldn't have bailed unless she had to.

She stopped finally and looked up at the street sign. She'd reached the corner of 59th Street and Third Avenue. It would be good to find a café where she could order a cup of tea and try to subdue her free-floating dread, but the places around her were packed with people lingering over a late brunch. It wasn't far, she realized, to the old Antiques Center, which was open on Sunday afternoons. She decided to head in that direction. For the past week she'd had her eye out for a crystal chandelier for the dining area in Avery Howe's cottage, and Baby had mentioned seeing a couple of good ones at a booth in the mall.

The Antiques Center wasn't a place she shopped often. The three-level space of endless glass-walled stalls felt frozen in the 1970's, and many of the vendors were pushy, refusing to let you browse in peace. Baby complained that there was so much dust she needed Benadryl just to step inside. But Kit sometimes popped in when she was at the end of a project and in search of a few finishing touches—like the odd Asian stool for a seating area or a ginger jar to add a little history to an entranceway.

She walked the last few blocks and entered the mall. Inside, in the windowless interior, it could have easily been six in the morning. Not only were there few customers wandering along the dim, narrow corridors, but also many of the stalls were closed, probably, she realized, a common occurrence for Sundays. She glanced distractedly at some of the ground floor stalls, stacked to the ceiling with dishes, glasses, paintings, busts, and endless knickknacks. She descended two flights to the lowest level where the shop Baby had mentioned was located.

It was even more deserted down there. Only two stalls in the main corridor were open, both run by old Chinese men who she knew from experience liked to squabble over customers. The chandeliers, Baby had said, were at Hanson's, which was down the corridor to the right and around the corner. Just bag it, Kit thought. The place was creepy today. But it seemed crazy not to check out the chandeliers as long as she was within yards of them. Even if the booth turned out not to be open, the chandeliers might be visible from the front window.

After nodding at one of the Chinese vendors, who was sitting quietly outside his shop, threading something in his hands, she wandered in the opposite direction, past a small pool with a fountain in the middle of the hall. The repetitive splash of water was the only sound.

She reached the end of the corridor, swung left, and saw that Hanson's was indeed closed. But even from this end of the hall she could spot two chandeliers hanging just on the other side of the glass window. She hurried to the end of the corridor and peered inside the stall. One of the chandeliers was clearly too big for the cottage, but the other would work nicely. After digging out her phone, she snapped a photo through the glass. She'd call Monday, ask for the price, then haggle to lower it.

She dropped her phone back into her purse and as she started to turn, she caught a flash of movement in the glass, the reflection of something moving behind her in the corridor. She spun around, her heart knocking hard. There was a man at the intersection of the two corridors, dressed in black, with a baseball cap on his head and a scarf obscuring the lower part of his face. By the time she was fully around, he'd darted away.

But she'd caught enough of a glimpse to see the hair on the sides of his head. It was dark red and closely cropped. Just like X's.

chapter 11

Panic surged through her. Was it *X*?

Instinctively she turned back toward the shop, looking for a place to flee. But she was cornered. The only way out was down the corridor. And he might be right around the corner, poised to ambush her.

She grabbed a breath and yelled, "Help." She knew there was little chance of anyone hearing her besides the old Chinese vendor, but it might be enough to jar the man in black into taking off. She called out again and then froze, listening. She thought she heard footsteps receding, muted by the carpeting.

After a minute she edged up the corridor. She froze just before the corner, straining to hear. The only sound was the splash of the fountain, and the frantic thumping of her heart.

Finally, she took one more step ahead, twisting her head to the right. The man she'd glimpsed was now nowhere in sight. There was just the Chinese man farther down the corridor, standing now and staring in her direction. She hurried toward him.

"Did you see a man?" she blurted out. "In a baseball cap?"

"I didn't see anyone. Just heard you yell out."

"But—were you outside here?"

"No, inside. I was inside."

She bolted up the two flights of stairs to the ground level, her head swiveling back and forth as she moved. She needed to know for sure if the man was X or not, but there was no sign of him anywhere. Outside, she halted in front of the building and frantically searched the street with her eyes, checking doorways, the bus shelter, the clusters of people at the corner buying Snapple and roasted nuts from a food stand. It was New York City, so *everyone* was in black. But she saw no one dressed like the stranger in the corridor.

She took a moment to catch her breath and headed west, choosing 59th Street because it was crowded. She kept turning and looking back, making sure she wasn't being followed. She checked on the subway platform, too, and in the car she boarded four minutes later. There was no one suspicious looking, just people winding down their Sunday afternoons, some with strollers, one with a fold-up bike. In relief, she let her body sag into the seat.

She knew she wasn't imagining the flash of dark red hair, but she hadn't glimpsed enough of the man's face to know for certain if it was X. Could it simply have been another shopper? Her nerves were so frayed, her mind might be playing tricks on her. And yet if it were another shopper, why would he run when she spotted him?

Back at her apartment building, she glanced behind her before unlocking the door to the lobby and then made sure that the lock engaged after she entered. Her heartbeat had finally slowed on the subway ride, but now, in anticipation of reaching her apartment, it began to rear up again, like a startled horse.

She took the elevator to five. Her dread felt thick and heavy, and the low, mournful groan of the elevator did nothing to help. Before stepping off onto her floor, she blocked the closing door with her hand, making it buck, and stared down the hall. The new door to her apartment was still intact. *I'm okay*, she told herself. *I'm okay.*

New key in hand, she dashed toward her apartment. Thankfully the tenants in A, who fled Manhattan each weekend, would be back tonight. That would at least provide a measure of comfort.

She jabbed the key quickly into the lock.

And then, behind her, she heard the sound of the stairwell door being sucked closed, followed by a whoosh, someone moving quickly. She jerked to the right.

It was X, standing two feet away, dressed all in black, his head uncovered. Her knees started to buckle from fear.

"Hello, Kit," he said quietly, but he made the *t* sound at the end of her name so hard there was no way to hear it other than as a threat.

"Please don't hurt me," she said.

"I won't—as long as you cooperate."

"Yes. Yes, of course."

"Why don't we go inside," he said, shoving the door fully open with one hand. She thought of screaming as she'd done earlier, but there was no one to hear this time. Just do as he says, she told herself desperately. X grasped her arm so hard it pinched and prodded her inside. Then he shoved the door closed behind them.

She knew for sure now that it had been him earlier. He'd probably been trailing her all day, and after she spotted him, he must have taken a cab downtown, followed someone into her building, and waited in the stairwell for her return.

"Just—just tell me what you want," she said. Was it her personal info to steal? Or her clients'? He'd surely been the one who'd broken into her apartment, and had probably targeted her from the beginning, just like Ungaro had guessed.

He stared hard at her. Those blue eyes, the ones she'd been so beguiled by, were menacing now, measuring her with cold calculation, as if she were a foe who needed to be brought to her knees. He looked away finally, taking in the apartment. She tried to gauge if it was possible to reach into her purse without him noticing and tap 911 on her phone.

But then his eyes lasered back to her.

"Over there," he said, cocking his head toward the island that separated the kitchen from the rest of the living space. "Let's sit down." He'd dropped her arm but he was right behind her, his body giving off an energy that urged her on. She made her way to the island and perched on the edge of a stool, just trying to anchor herself in some way. As her feet touched the cross-bar on the lower part, she realized her legs were trembling. Get control, she told herself. She had to figure out what he wanted and tell him enough to make him leave.

"Now, give me your phone," X said, as if he'd read her mind seconds ago. She fumbled in her purse for it and handed it over to him. As he thrust the phone in his jacket pocket, she saw that his scruff was fuller. And he looked weary. He was probably on the run, frenzied. The trick would be for her to play this as shrewdly as possible, to do nothing to add to his feeling of desperation.

"Is it information you want?" she asked. "Is that it? Please, just tell me."

His eyes narrowed again, this time quizzically.

"No, I don't want information," he said. "What I want is my pen."

"Your *pen*?" His request seemed utterly ludicrous, as if he'd forced his way into her apartment and demanded her recipe for spinach frittata. And then, she could sense a memory beginning to surface, like something coming loose from a tangle of weeds at the bottom of a pond. His room at the hotel. While he was hunting down ice, she'd checked out his pen, held it next to the one her father had given her.

"You mean the Mont Blanc pen? On the desk in your hotel room?"

"Yes, exactly," he snapped angrily. "And I want to know why you took it."

"I admit—I saw it there. But I didn't take it."

He took a half step closer to her, making her breath quicken.

"Don't lie to me. You took it and left another one in its place."

She looked off, desperately thinking. Had she accidentally switched her pen with his when she'd dropped things to the floor? But the pens had been near identical. How would he have even known? And why in the world would he care?

"Uh, I picked up your pen when you left the room. I have one, too, just like it, and I had mine in my hand. Maybe—maybe I mixed them up by mistake."

He scoffed. "You just happened to be carrying a Mont Blanc fountain pen around?"

"Yes, I swear."

Quickly, she reached into her purse. She had the pen in there, nestled somewhere at the bottom. If she turned it over to him, maybe he would leave and never come back.

"What are you doing?" he demanded.

"Showing you." She fished through her purse until her fingers lighted on the pen. Why, she wondered again, was it so freaking important to him?

"Here," she said, thrusting it toward him.

He took the pen, his fingers grazing hers. It was hard to believe that the same hand touched her days ago, making her ache with longing. How could she have been so wrong about him?

For a moment X just stared at the pen. Then, grasping both ends, he tugged until it came apart in two.

Shocked, Kit saw that it wasn't a pen at all—or at least on the inside it wasn't. There was a flash drive where the cartridge should have been. So he *had* broken into her apartment—and snatched the flash drive in her drawer. He'd been looking for the one she'd mistakenly switched with hers. Maybe he used it to keep track of identity data he stole from people.

"So that's what I'm supposed to buy?" X said, as he thrust the pen back together. "That you picked up my pen out of pure curiosity and accidentally switched it with yours?"

The truth finally hit her. He thought she had targeted *him*, that she was some kind of con artist herself, and had been after his stash of information. Oh, that was rich, she thought, anger suddenly overriding her fear. The grifter who'd put her through hell over the past few weeks was accusing her of being no better than him.

"You can't honestly believe that I accepted your dinner invitation so you'd ask me back to your room and I could steal your secret pen? And if I *had* stolen it, why would I show up for a second date with you?"

"Then what you're saying is that you're just a run-of-the-mill busybody?" he said, practically sneering.

"Call it whatever you want. But if you *must* know, I—I was just struck by the fact that I had the same pen as yours and I took mine out to compare it. Stupidly, I . . ." She let the words trail off.

"What?"

"Stupidly I thought it meant that there was some kind of—I don't know—connection between the two of us."

He raised his chin, studying her, weighing her words.

"You don't look like the type of girl who would bother with a fancy fountain pen," he said coolly.

She hated the thought of sharing anything personal with him, but she needed him to believe her. That might be the only way to get him to go. "It was a present from my father, years ago. I almost never use it, but I always keep it with me."

She saw his shoulders release, as if he'd lowered his guard a hair.

"And what about *my* pen?" she asked. Maybe she was crazy to ask, to rock the boat in any way, but she wanted it back.

"We'll have to see about that." He glanced toward the kitchen area behind him. "What have you got to drink around here, in the way of booze?"

Oh no, she thought. This wasn't over. He had the flash drive, but he wasn't budging.

"Nothing really."

"*Nothing?*"

"Just some white wine—in the fridge. But, please, you have what you want. Can't you just leave now?"

"In a minute."

Did he mean it? And would he go without hurting her? She knew more about him now, knew that he was in New York, knew where he stored his information. Surely he would realize she'd share all of it with the cops the moment he departed.

He stepped toward the refrigerator, yanked open the door, and scanned the inside. Then he tugged the bottle of Pinot Grigio from a pocket on the door.

"Corkscrew?" he asked.

"In that drawer," she said, nodding toward it.

He popped out the cork, drew two glasses from the cabinet, and splashed wine into each. Her anger surged back.

"I don't want any wine," she said.

"Well, I hope you don't mind if I do. It's been a tough couple of weeks."

"Would it matter if I minded?" she asked, her voice tinged with resentment. "You thought nothing of taking all my other stuff."

His expression darkened.

"What do you mean?" he demanded.

"What do you *think* I mean? Friday night. When you broke in here."

"Are you saying you were burglarized?"

"I'm not a fool. I know it was you. And it wasn't the first time. You snuck around in here a week ago as well, didn't you?"

"It wasn't me. I've never been inside this place before now." He swung his gaze around the room, as if the walls could tell him something. "What did they take? I need to know."

"Jewelry, some frames. My laptop. And a flash drive."

"Shit," he said. He fisted one hand and tapped it into his other palm a few times. "They were after *this* flash drive."

Did he have competitors or enemies? she wondered. How would they know she had the pen?

"Are you suggesting that the person who broke in thinks I'm in cahoots with you?" she asked.

He took a long drink of wine, and she could sense his mind racing.

"I'm not sure what's going on," he said eventually. "Someone may have seen us together in Islamorada and thought you knew something. Or—the night you went to Matt Healy's apartment, is there a chance you were being followed?"

Her stomach clutched at the mere mention of Healy's name. X might be back in New York now, but as far as she knew, he could have been in Florida last weekend and run Healy down with his car.

"*Followed?* I have no idea." She added sarcastically, "I guess I was too busy thinking about the night ahead to wonder if I was being tailed."

"It was never my intention to dupe you, Kit. I just wanted to see you again."

His expression had softened and his eyes lingered on her face. Careful, she warned herself.

"So you could get your *pen* back?"

"When I called you that Monday morning, I hadn't realized yet that there'd been a switch. My only intention was to have dinner with you."

Despite the weariness etched on his face, he was as attractive as she'd remembered. Don't be stupid, she told herself. She couldn't let him try to charm her—or con her a second time.

"Why send me to Healy's? Why play that whole game?"

"It wasn't a game. I'd been staying with him and I was supposed to be back there by Thursday night."

She was the one scoffing now. "Oh, please. How gullible do you think I am?"

"Okay, I'll admit I lied to you about my name and about my background. I never owned a tech business. Until a month ago, I was a portfolio manager at the same firm as Matt. It's called Ithaka. He and I were friends."

The words were so improbable it took her a moment to process them.

"So why pretend to be him?" she asked.

"There was a reason for that. Matt knew I was using his name."

She shook her head in disbelief. If Matt had been X's friend, why had he claimed his wallet had been stolen? X was surely trying to dupe her all over again, probably so she wouldn't run to the cops. But maybe, she realized, she should go along, let him think she'd fallen for it. That way he'd feel less threatened by her, by what she knew.

Before she could respond, he clasped her forearm. She flinched at the tightness of his fingers.

"Kit, I need you to believe me," he said, relaxing his grip.

Crazily enough, she saw a flash of concern in his eyes. Though she knew he might be an even better actor than she'd given him credit for.

"Why?"

He took another slug of wine and set the glass down on the

small island. "Because the stakes are high. Matt Healy is dead. Someone is after me and they may have been after Matt, too. And those same people probably showed up here, looking for the flash drive."

Could at least part of what he was saying be true? That he *hadn't* broken into her apartment?

"Who are *they*?" she asked.

He met her eyes again and then he pressed his lips together, momentarily hesitant. She sensed a turn in the action, that something was about to shift.

"I'm in a precarious situation, and it seems I've dragged you into it without meaning to," he said. "I could share more information with you, but you clearly don't trust me. And I'm still trying to decide if I believe *you*. So the best thing for me to do right now is to split and leave you alone."

He still seemed to think that she knew more than she did. But at least he was *going*. And from what she could guess, he wasn't going to harm her.

Turning around, he scrutinized the kitchen countertop and then grabbed a small notepad and a ballpoint pen. He tore off a piece of paper and scribbled down a phone number.

"Here," he said. "I'm going to do what I can to let it be known that I've got the flash drive and you don't. But if you find yourself in any danger and you want me to help, call me."

As she accepted the slip of paper, his fingers brushed against her again.

"And just for your information," he said. "It's a burn phone, which means it can't be traced."

He tugged a black baseball cap from his jacket pocket and secured it on his head. After a final swig of the wine, he took a deep breath and pushed off from the counter, ready to make his way toward the door. He still had her phone, she realized. Was he going to keep it?

Again, he seemed to read her mind.

He wrestled the phone from his pocket and passed it to her.

"Are—are you going to be in New York for a while?" she asked. She wasn't sure why she needed to know. And she doubted he'd tell her the truth anyway.

"Like I said, Kit, we've got trust issues. So why don't I just keep that to myself. If you decide you're willing to trust me, you know how to reach me. But I'll know from your voice if you've got the cops waiting."

She stared at him, at a loss for words.

He turned and strode toward the front door, leaving her standing by the island. Reaching for the handle, he glanced back at her. Even with the brim of the hat pulled low, his eyes found hers and held them.

"By the way," he said. "My name is Garrett Kelman. And just for the record, I felt it, too."

And then he was gone. She rushed toward the door and pressed her ear against it, listening. Footsteps moving away. Then nothing. Kit quickly positioned the door bolts into the floor and ceiling, and hung the alarm on the handle.

Her legs had stopped their awful trembling, and yet she could still feel a faint reverberation in them, like a guitar string plucked moments before. She moved back to the island and took two quick gulps from the glass of wine that X had poured for her. Her thoughts and feelings—fear, anger, relief, confusion— seemed flung about in a crazy mess. She wanted to accept what he'd told her, wanted to believe that he hadn't killed Healy. But as far as she knew, he'd simply spun her a whole new set of lies because the moment had called for them.

She grabbed her phone. She needed to call O'Callaghan. But even as part of her brain was commanding her to do that, another part resisted with an almost magnetic force. What would she say to him exactly? "You know that man I told you I had dinner with in Florida? The man with the phony name who I said might have burglarized my apartment? Well, he came to see me. To get his *pen*. Which I took from his hotel room. Oh, and he says he didn't break into my place."

She'd sound like a total nut job. The Miami police would think so, too. They might even be suspicious of her, wondering what she was up to, weaving all these cloak and dagger tales together.

And what if, just *what if*, X had been telling the truth.

She grabbed her new laptop from the bedroom and carried it to the island. With her fingers racing, she typed Garrett Kelman, Ithaka, into the search bar. A handful of links popped up, most from within the past two years. But just because the name existed, it didn't mean it belonged to X.

The first couple of links were to databases of business people, what a prospective client or employer might use to verify contact info. One listed a Garrett Kelman as an employee of Ithaka, though it appeared to be a dated entry. No photo. The third link was to an article in *Institutional Investor*. A Garrett Kelman was quoted in it. But no photo there either.

The last link was to a society website, one she'd actually checked out a few times when tracking down info on potential clients. It was always loaded with party pictures. She held her breath and clicked.

And then there he was. X. Standing with four or five other people on a wraparound terrace. Dressed in a navy blazer and gray pants. Looking relaxed and smiling broadly. So different than how he'd been today. But it was definitely him.

According to the caption, the event was a fund-raiser for a charity, with Ithaka as one of the sponsors. And then there was his name: Garrett Kelman.

Okay, he wasn't lying this time, at least about his name and where he'd worked. But what about all the rest? If he'd been using Healy's name for some crazy reason that the two men had agreed on, it made no sense that Healy would insist that he was being impersonated by a thief and then have her spill the whole story to Ungaro. And surely based on her description of the Florida mystery man, Ungaro might have guessed she was describing a former employee. Or Healy may have even told him.

Other questions followed. What was on the flash drive masquerading as a pen? What kind of "precarious situation" was X involved in? And most important, who were *they*? Even if X left her alone from now on or she turned him in to the police, *they* would still pose a danger.

She wondered briefly if Sasha might shed any light on things. She could call and try to nudge her into rescheduling their appointment. But Sasha had her antenna up big time, and would have her suspicions aroused if Kit suddenly tossed out the name of a former colleague, particularly one who might have left under suspicious circumstances.

Kit glanced at her watch. On Sundays she often made pasta for herself, but she had little appetite tonight. Besides, cooking would entail running out for groceries and she'd worry that *they* were out there, the people X had alluded to. They might be watching her the way X had clearly been, and even worse, planning to hack their way back into her apartment now that they'd discovered that the stolen flash drive wasn't the one they'd been searching for. And there might be no appeasing *them* with a glass of Pinot Grigio.

Damn, she thought, clenching her fists. She had to figure out who they were and what was really going on. Only once she'd done so could she go to the police with real information and not just vague references to a mystery man.

She splashed more wine into her glass and took another sip. As she set the glass down, her fingers grazed the edge of the glass X had used. Next to it lay the slip of paper on which he'd scribbled the number for his burn phone.

Which version of him was she supposed to buy? Garrett Kelman, a con artist who'd tricked her in Florida, forced his way into her home to obtain what he wanted, possibly murdered a man, and was now trying to trick her with a new, improved version of himself?

Or Garrett Kelman, not a criminal mastermind at all, just a man who had unintentionally drawn her into harm's way and was now offering information of value if she'd only "trust" him? She hadn't a clue.

She thought of the words he'd said as he'd departed: "And just for the record, I felt it, too." There was no denying that she'd experienced an electric jolt at that moment, and some part of her wanted the Florida fantasy back, might always yearn for it, but as far as she knew, the man she'd been attracted to two weeks ago was nothing more than a phantom.

She covered her mouth and breathed into her hand. Inside she was churning.

I have to call that number, she thought. I have to talk to him again. The idea of another encounter with X frightened her—he hadn't hurt her this time, but there was no guarantee that he wouldn't in the future.

And yet she knew it was the only way to lay her hands on the information she needed. It was the only way to ultimately escape the danger she was in.

So much, she thought again, for no strings attached.

chapter 12

That night she hardly slept. She jerked awake every hour or so, startled, as if roused by a sound that was out of place. Each time she lay in the twisted sheets straining to hear, wondering if X had returned and was creeping around her apartment. She told herself that he couldn't be, that the door alarm would have begun to shriek.

After waking again just before six, it was clear to her there was no chance of falling back to sleep. She made coffee and sat at the island, replaying her encounter with X. She still didn't know what version of the man she was supposed to believe.

What she *did* know was that over the past few days she'd fallen behind in her work and she needed to snap into gear. Of course, this would require faking it around clients, pretending that life was perfectly peachy when the world really seemed to be spinning off its axis.

She showered, dressed, and, yogurt in hand, let herself into the office. Outside on Elizabeth Street, a vehicle rumbled along the pavement, probably a van making an early morning delivery to a local shop, but that, and the hum of the refrigerator in the galley kitchen, were the only sounds. Everything seemed normal. Except it wasn't, of course.

She texted the contractor at the Greenwich Village apartment and told him she would be stopping by late that afternoon to do a check on the work. Originally she had planned to pop in there on Saturday or Sunday, but that was before people had wreaked havoc in her life.

Next she emailed her client Barry Kaplan, the fifty-something bachelor who she'd mostly ignored for the past couple of weeks. She wanted to do good by him. His wife had filed for divorce the moment the last kid was out of college, and he still seemed shell-shocked from the break-up. But Kit's mind had been in such a muddle lately, she hadn't been able to come up with a concept for his apartment. She informed him that she was still pulling thoughts together but hoped to have a proposal for him shortly.

Then there was Keith Holt. That would be a rewarding job, both creatively and financially. She emailed him a letter of agreement and reminded him to begin collecting tear sheets and pictures. "Don't overthink it," she told him. "Just pick images that grab you instantly."

Finally, at around eight, she turned her attention to the Avery Howe project. She'd already managed to pull together ideas for furniture, but she had yet to make a dent in fabric selection. She started searching fabric houses online, hunting for material in bleached blues and yellows, as well as subtle prints. As soon as Baby and Dara arrived, she would head uptown to pull swatches.

Though a dread of slipping behind had managed to keep her focused on her work for an hour or so, Kit's thoughts eventually found their way back to Kelman. The choice was obvious. She *had* to meet with him, and she needed to make the call today. Right now he seemed willing to communicate with her but that could change, particularly with him on the run, and she couldn't allow the opportunity to escape.

If only she could validate more of what he had told her

yesterday. Yes, he was Garrett Kelman, but had he really been Healy's friend? She wondered if there was any way of proving that. Knowing he'd told the truth about his relationship with Healy would ease her fears a little. It would reduce the likelihood in her mind that Kelman had mowed Healy down with his car.

An idea started to take shape. Healy's building had a concierge, and if she handled it shrewdly, she might be able to extract from him whether X had stayed at the apartment. She didn't even have to double-check the address. It was still etched in her brain. She decided that as soon as she collected fabric samples, she would swing by the building and try to elicit the information from the concierge.

At just after nine, a key twisted in the lock to the office door. Even though she knew it was either Baby or Dara, Kit still jumped at the sound. A moment later, Baby stepped into the office. Her expression, until she spotted Kit at her desk, was hesitant, wary, as if she was on guard for the worst.

"Morning," Kit said, smiling. She didn't think she'd ever been happier to set eyes on Baby.

"You okay?" Baby asked, dropping her spring coat onto one of the wrought iron pegs in the entranceway. "I was barely able to sleep thinking about you all alone here."

"I'm hanging in there."

As Baby entered the main part of the office, she caught sight of the door alarm, which Kit had removed earlier and set on a small table.

"Oh goodness, so this is your fancy new alarm system?"

"Yup, pretty impressive, right? Maybe they should try using these at the White House."

"Are you sure you don't want to come back to my place?"

"I appreciate the offer, Baby, but I think I'm okay for now. But there *is* a new development I want to share with you." Kit had decided last night that as much as she hated burdening Baby, she needed to loop her in about Garrett Kelman's visit. "Why don't you make your cappuccino, get settled, and then I'll fill you in."

Baby raised one of her perfectly arched blond eyebrows, both curious and concerned. "I'll make my cappuccino," she said. "But I'll be damned if I'm settling in before I hear what's going on."

She returned from the kitchenette two minutes later and plopped into the chair by Kit's desk.

"Don't tell me you've been playing Nancy Drew after you promised me you wouldn't."

"A little bit, but that's not the big news."

Haltingly, she described her encounter with X. Baby listened, stunned, one hand on her chest.

"Dear God," Baby said when Kit finished. "You've called the police, of course."

Kit bit her lip.

"No, I haven't," she said. She raised a hand. "But before you're tempted to beat me with a rubber hose, hear me out. If I talk to the cops again, there's nothing concrete I can really report. So they could end up deciding I'm a bit of a nut job, the way I keep blabbering about this mythical man that only I get to see—like Big Foot or something. Plus, I'd have to admit that I took his pen. It was an innocent mistake, but it could sound suspicious and make the cops wonder what I'm really up to, if I'm trying to throw Kelman under the bus to protect myself. And if they start looking into me, it could impact our business."

"Then what *do* you do?"

"I'm thinking that the best strategy is for me to learn more about what's really going on so I have credible information to share with the cops. And the way to do that is to convince this Garrett Kelman that I trust him."

"But that sounds so dangerous, Kit. The man forced his way into your home last night."

"But in the end he didn't hurt me—or even threaten me.

And I need to get ahead of this. I'm worried that if I don't, the people who broke in will come back for the flash drive. They've surely discovered by now that the one they took has nothing but photos of leather club chairs and a bed with a nail-headed upholstered headboard."

"Wait, I thought you assumed Kelman had broken in."

"I'm not so sure now. When he stepped through the door, he seemed to be taking it all in, like it was his first time there, and when I told him about the burglary, he looked alarmed. Besides, he knew that flash drive was in the pen, so why steal the random one in my drawer?"

"Kit, you know I think you have good instincts, but I don't like this. The man could be lying all over again."

"I know. But like I told you, some of what he shared last night turned out to be true. And I'm not going to reach out to Kelman until I've investigated him further. There's more research I plan to do this afternoon."

For a moment Baby said nothing, just tapped her gleaming pink nails in a nervous dance on the desktop.

"I had a colleague named Garrett once," she said finally, arching a brow again. "British. He claimed the name meant 'he who rules with a big spear.' That's not what this is about, is it?"

Kit snorted, and then broke into a smile.

"He didn't seem to have a weapon on him last night, and in regard to that other spear you may or may not be referring to, my lips are sealed."

Baby offered a grim smile back.

"Just promise me that if you sense any danger whatsoever, you'll call the police. And if you don't, I will."

"Got it. You'd mentioned yesterday that you were going to be here most of the day. Is that still your plan? Because I need to go out for a while, and I don't want to leave Dara alone."

"Yes, that works for me. Plus, I have a potential client stopping by this morning, someone renovating a boutique hotel here in New York. Could be a nice piece of business that we'd work on together. I also want to field any calls that might come in today from clients concerned about their credit card information."

"Any fallout from that?" Kit asked, sensing now that there had been.

"A bit, but I didn't want to tell you last night before you went to bed. I emailed all the active clients, the ones who we've kept the card numbers for, and I told them to contact me with any questions. Several people called back, two in a tizzy, and one of those was your Greenwich Village client, Layla Griggs. She wasn't pleased about the idea of having to apply for a new card."

Kit felt fear tug at her, like an undertow. This whole crazy mess wasn't going to stay contained to her personal life. It was engulfing her work, too, sabotaging her relationship with clients. She had to *fix* it.

"From the little I learned last night, the person or people who broke in weren't looking for client info after all," she told Baby. "Can you convey that to clients even if they've already cancelled their cards?"

"Don't worry, I'll put out any fires. And what do these people expect anyway? If everybody from the NSA to Sony Pictures can get hacked, we're hardly immune."

Dara arrived a few minutes later, dressed for spring in a lemon-yellow top, but beneath the warm hello she offered, her mood seemed subdued. She's scared, Kit thought. And not only because the office had been broken into. Dara clearly knew there was more to the story than she was being told.

Midmorning Kit grabbed her trench coat, bid her colleagues goodbye, and headed out. She took the subway uptown and for several hours prowled the D&D building, searching for fabrics with the most intense focus she could summon. She pulled about thirty samples and planned to whittle the selection down even more once she returned to the office.

With the swatches stuffed in her tote bag, she emerged from the building just before two. She scanned the surrounding area, searching for anyone not in motion, who might be standing there appearing aimless but with a secret agenda. She couldn't ignore the comment X had made, that someone might have followed her to Healy's, and she couldn't take any chances now. She darted across Third Avenue and, making sure no one seemed to be watching, flagged down a taxi. As the car headed west, eventually crossing Central Park, she glanced behind her several times, making sure the same car wasn't always on their tail.

After alighting in front of Healy's building, she drew a compact from her purse, along with a lipstick. She touched up her makeup and smoothed her hair into place. She also mentally reviewed what she planned to say to the concierge.

As she dropped the makeup back into her purse, her phone sounded. Glancing at the screen, she saw that the call was from Detective O'Callaghan—she'd programmed his number into her phone on Friday night. Though he was most likely returning her call, the sight of his name flustered her.

"Sorry not to be back to you sooner," he said once she'd answered. "I was off this weekend. What can I do for you?"

"I was just checking in," she said, trying to buy a sliver of time to think. As she'd told Baby, she wasn't going to reveal X's visit, but she wondered if she should at least tell O'Callaghan what she'd originally planned to, that a flash drive was missing from her desk drawer. No, she decided. It would be better to wait until she had more facts. "I wondered if you had any leads yet."

"Unfortunately I don't. Your two colleagues came by the precinct to be fingerprinted, and we were able to eliminate theirs as well as your own from the apartment and office. Unfortunately, it appears that the perpetrator wore gloves."

"Well, you'll let me know, though? I mean, if you do hear anything?"

"Of course. There is one interesting detail I wanted to discuss with you."

Her heart skipped. Could the man possibly intuit over the phone that she was holding out on him?

"Okay."

"Since the perp wore gloves, we found smear marks in certain areas of your apartment. But there were also a fair amount of them in your office. It seems like he spent more time in there than met the eye."

"Oh," she said, holding her breath. "That's interesting."

"Any idea what he might have been looking for?"

"Uh, petty cash maybe. I didn't look super closely in there because, other than my laptop, very little seemed disturbed. But I'll check again."

"Please do. If you notice anything else is missing, it's important to let us know," he said.

"Oh, I will for sure," she said, sounding too rushed, she realized. "Thanks again for calling."

After O'Callaghan had disconnected, Kit stood on the sidewalk in a patch of muted April sunlight, wondering just how stupid it had been to withhold information from a detective. At least she'd given herself an out. Depending on what happened, she could always pretend she'd done a second search later and had made a discovery then about the flash drive.

After mentally readying herself, she entered Healy's building and strolled decisively toward the concierge desk. There was a chance that the same guy she'd seen before would be on duty again, but she was hoping he wasn't. If he recognized her it wouldn't necessarily be a problem, but he might also remember her name—these guys were good at such stuff—and that would spoil her plan.

She was in luck, however. It was another man, this one short and stocky with a gleaming bald head. The lobby was empty, except for a porter polishing the brass fixtures, and the concierge smiled at her receptively. The name on his badge said Bob Dolan.

"Hello, I'm Sasha Glen," Kit said, assuming the most knowing air she could muster. "I'm with Ithaka, the firm Matt Healy worked for before his death."

Dolan grimaced.

"Terrible thing," he said. "Out of the blue like that. And what was he—thirty-eight, thirty-nine?"

"I know. We're all very distraught at Ithaka. I was hoping you could help us. We're planning a memorial service for him and we want to make sure we invite everyone that was close to him."

"Gosh, I'm afraid I wouldn't be any help there. We don't keep tabs on people's personal lives. The only thing I've been told is that his mother and stepfather went to Florida to collect the body, and at some point they're coming here to deal with his belongings."

"They'll be invited to the service, of course, and we have their contact information. But there's a friend of his we're trying to reach, a former colleague from Ithaka who stayed with him here."

Dolan wrinkled his brow. He'd been eager to engage when she'd first approached him, but she could sense his antennae shooting up now.

"Would you happen to have some identification?" he asked.

"Of course," Kit said and drew Sasha's business card out of her purse. She handed it to Dolan, who gave a quick nod as he read what was written on it.

"I think you may have been misinformed," he said. "Mr. Healy didn't have any roommates."

"But this person—his name's Garrett Kelman—he would

have stayed with Mr. Healy for just a short time. We're desperate to reach him because he may not be aware yet that Mr. Healy is dead."

He flicked his head to the left, as if he was about to shake it in a "no," and then caught himself.

"Actually, he did have a buddy with him for a few days a while back." She saw him reach behind the reception counter for something and next she heard the sound of pages being flipped. Some kind of log, she guessed.

"Okay, I see it here," he said. "A Mr. Kelman was given access to the apartment for several days about three weeks ago. But that's all the info I have. You don't have a cell phone number for a former employee?"

So one part of Kelman's story held up. It also meant that Healy had deceived her.

"Um, unfortunately the number we have isn't in service anymore," she said. "But thank you for your help. Do you mind if I take the card back? It's the only one I have on me today."

As she left, she sensed him watching her, wondering too late if she was a reporter or someone nosing around for all the wrong reasons. But she'd snagged what she'd come for and that was all that mattered.

Out on the sidewalk she exhaled and desperately tried to corral the thoughts ricocheting in her brain and then make sense of them.

Last night she'd confirmed that Garrett Kelman had worked at Ithaka, and now she'd learned that, yes, he'd also been a friend of Matt Healy's. That added credence to his claim that he hadn't broken into her apartment.

But though Kelman had been honest with her in certain regards, she still had no reason to completely trust him. The man might not be the mastermind of an identity-stealing ring as she'd once suspected, but he was clearly in trouble and on the run. And he could very well be Healy's killer. Maybe they'd even been involved in illegal stuff together and had argued, fallen out with each other, which could explain Healy's strange claims about Kelman being a pickpocket.

Most disturbing of all: if Kelman *hadn't* broken into her apartment, someone else definitely had. She was back to the idea of *them* again, unknown persons who'd come looking for the flash drive, trashed her apartment, and might very well return. How in the world would she ever stop them?

It was time to call Kelman. She couldn't put it off any longer.

She cast her eyes up and down the street. A man with a bull-dog approached on the sidewalk, practically dragging the dog behind him. "Max, for the love of God, come on," he implored. "You're going to tear all the skin from your paws."

Behind him a row of taxis idled in the street, waiting for the traffic light to change. From the third taxi in line, a man probably in his fifties let his eyes linger on her. Then he quickly glanced away. Was that just a New York moment? she wondered. Or something to be freaked about? She wouldn't be able to stop questioning everything around her until she figured out the truth.

She moved a few yards up the block to the corner and stepped out of the sun, under the awning of the same Italian restaurant that she had gone to with Healy. Because of the fairly mild weather, the front door had been left ajar, and a sweet gar-licky scent wafted outside. Kit dug into her purse for her phone and called up the number she had programed in for X. Her heart raced in anticipation.

He answered on the third ring. Just "Yes?" in that deep, sure voice. She had a memory suddenly of hearing it during her car ride to the Miami airport, and the erotic rush she'd experi-enced from knowing she'd be granted another chance to taste his mouth again and feel his body press against her. But what difference did any of that make? He'd never been the man she thought she'd made love to that night.

"It's Kit Finn," she said. "You said you'd be willing to talk again. I want to do that."

A pause.

"Why the change of heart?" he said finally. "You seemed awfully eager to get me out of your apartment and be done with me."

"I know now that you were telling the truth yesterday, about who you are. I checked it out."

"Okay. But why am I suddenly supposed to trust *you*?"

"You just are," she said, anger swelling. "I didn't take your pen on purpose. There'd be no reason in the world for me to do so, and I think you know it now."

"Is that right?"

How nervy, she thought, as she heard the tinge of sarcasm in his voice. It was Kelman who'd upended *her* life, not the other way around.

"What are you getting at?" she demanded. "Are you still trying to suggest that I'm some kind of Bond girl, someone who set out to double-cross you in a tropical resort?"

She heard him chuckle lightly, which only riled her more.

"The bottom line is that you've endangered me," she said. "By sending me to Matt Healy's apartment for what I *thought* was a date, you've made me an accomplice and it's put me at risk, and my business, too. I wish I could just tell the police about you and walk away, but if what you said about these other people is true, that's not going to help me. I can't extricate myself without you. Besides, I have information that could be of value to you as well."

He said nothing for a moment and she wondered if, miffed by her tone and her comments, he'd disconnected the call. She briefly pulled the phone from her ear and saw there was still a connection.

"I want the truth," she said. "You owe me that."

"All right," he said finally. "But I can't meet you until to-morrow night. Pick a bar or a restaurant near you, where we can sit in the back and not be seen."

"There's a place called Jacques on Prince Street, and it's fairly dark inside."

"Seven o'clock."

"All right."

And then the call disconnected.

So it had worked. She had challenged him and he'd bitten, and she finally had a shot at learning what she was really en-snared in. Their meeting, however, was over twenty-four hours away, and until then she would have to find a way to make her heart stop hurling itself against her chest—but without ever let-ting down her guard.

It was nearly four by the time she climbed the steps from the Spring Street subway station and began the short walk to her building. To her relief she heard music when she reached her floor, coming from apartment A. One of her neighbors must be working from home.

She reached the entrance to the office, turned her key in the lock, and pushed open the door.

And then she saw the man. He was standing just beyond the entranceway, where it opened onto the main room. A total stranger. He turned and looked at her, his dark eyes hard. Her hand was still on the doorknob and she gripped it tight. Adren-aline coursed through her body, urging her to fight or flee.

chapter 13

"Who are you?" she demanded.

He didn't answer, just stared at her, his pupils weirdly dilated. She caught a movement out of the corner of her eye and turned to see Baby standing to her left. Her partner appeared startled, but not alarmed.

"What's going *on*?" Kit asked.

Before anyone could answer, Dara emerged from Kit's apartment, improbably carrying a glass of orange juice. She hurried toward the man and handed him the juice, which he downed in two quick gulps. It was like a scene out of *Alice in Wonderland*, Kit thought, people in the wrong places doing things that made no sense.

"Much better," he said, handing the glass back to Dara.

"That's a relief," Baby said. "Kit, let me introduce you to Steven Harper. He's the hotel developer I mentioned earlier. He was worried he might be having a hypoglycemic attack and needed juice"

"Oh, I'm terribly sorry," Kit said. Though her brain was playing catch-up, her heart hadn't stopped pounding from the shock of finding a strange man in the office. "I just wasn't expecting anyone to be here besides you and Dara."

"Not a problem," Harper responded, reaching to shake her

hand. He was tall, at least six foot three, dressed in gray slacks and a sports jacket. His deep tan had an orangey undertone that made it look fake, as if he'd had it airbrushed on earlier that day at a tanning salon.

"Here's a card with our website address on it," Baby said, handing it to Harper.

He turned to Kit. "I'll admit, I'm impressed with the work you and your partner do. Are you game for a project where every square inch of the property has to be astonishing?"

"Of course," Kit said, forcing a smile. "We don't like projects unless that's one of the requirements."

"I'll be in touch," he said to Baby, "and then you can make a formal presentation."

"My suggestion?" Baby said as she swung open the door for him. "You should meet with a number of designers at this time." She was following her never-seem-like-the-pursuer strategy. "It always helps to see what else is out there."

As soon as Harper departed, Dara grabbed Kit's attention to review a few matters and then packed up to leave, looking almost relieved to be taking off. Baby hung back, clearly eager to talk.

"I'm so sorry I sounded rude when I first walked in," Kit said. "It just caught me off guard to find a stranger here. I thought you were meeting with the hotel guy this morning."

"That was the plan but he had to postpone it because of a business issue, and then he obviously got caught in a rust storm on his way here. Have you ever seen a tan quite that shade?"

Kit smiled. "I hope I didn't jinx things with him."

"I'm sure you didn't. The bottom line is that he seemed impressed with our work and my instinct tells me we're definitely a contender."

It was typical Baby to take things in stride. And yet Kit

worried that underneath that unflappable demeanor Baby might be starting to lose patience with the predicament she'd suddenly found herself in. She'd been forced to double up in the office as a safety precaution, warn clients that their credit card accounts might be endangered, and coexist with a partner who looked wigged out most of the time. That was hardly what Baby had in mind when she'd decided to plunge back into the field.

"How nice *that* would be. And I promise, Baby, I'm going to extricate myself from this situation so it doesn't wash over on the business anymore."

"Any news?"

Kit told her about confirming one more aspect of X's story and her plan to meet with him the next night.

"I'm still not happy with that idea," Baby said, shaking her head.

"He's got information of value," Kit told her.

"So does Vladimir Putin, but that doesn't mean I want you cozying up to him."

Kit swore she'd be extremely careful.

Later, she ordered Chinese food for dinner but only picked at it. Her thoughts were consumed with the upcoming rendez-vous with Kelman. She worried she was banking on it more than she should be. What if, when push came to shove, Kelman refused to pony up all the info she needed to know? And then there'd be the added challenge of determining how much to actually believe.

And yet right now, the meeting was all she had.

As planned, Baby used the next morning for shopping and Kit and Dara worked out of the office. With input from Dara, Kit narrowed down the fabric choices for Avery's cottage: white with blue piping for the living room sofa; a pale blue and white stripe for the bleached, rounded-back dining chairs; a subtle lavender floral print for the guest room duvet; various shades of white and cream for the master bedroom. Next Dara mounted swatches onto boards along with photos of the suggested furniture. The fabrics were subtle, almost muted-looking on the boards, but Kit knew that once they were mixed with teardrop chandeliers, gilt-framed mirrors, and billowing, sheer white curtains, the end result would be enchanting.

"Oh, I forgot to tack on a sample for the living room rug. Hand me that piece of sisal, will you?"

"Tell me why you chose that."

"With so much white and cream in the room, it needs to be grounded."

"Ah, got it. Do you think Avery can concentrate long enough to recognize how exquisite this is going to be?" Dara asked.

"She seems to trust me and she's got nice taste, so I suspect she'll say she loves it," Kit said. "Ideally you want people to be fully engaged, to visit the showrooms with you and sit in the chairs so they know exactly what they're getting. The big problem with clients like Avery, the ones who don't have the time or patience to do that as you go along, comes when you reach the very end. They finally focus and make statements like, "Wait, when did we decide to use so much *white*?"

"And what do you do then? Besides want to bitch slap them?"

Kit smiled. "Tap dance a bit. At least I do, and Baby does, too. Some designers will just announce, 'It is what it is,' but I try to fix what I can. For instance, if they think there's not enough color, I'll add a bit more with accessories. Speaking of clients, what did you think of Steven Harper, the hotel developer?"

"Mr. Man Tan, you mean? Baby had me research him but I couldn't find much. Just that he's an investor who's gotten into hotels only recently. But it could be a sweet piece of business, that's for sure."

"How about personally? You spent more time with him than I did."

"That's the catch. He seems awfully high maintenance. When he said he needed O.J., he expected me to jump."

Kit had picked up the same vibe as Dara, even in her brief encounter. But Baby was an expert at dealing with the blustery and demanding clients and she'd be the one handling Harper for the most part.

She emailed Avery next, informing her that she had completed the boards and was eager for her reaction so she could start ordering furniture and fabric. Avery wrote back minutes later saying she was "crazy busy," but could send a messenger for the boards tomorrow.

Once Baby returned, Kit grabbed her coat and flew out of there. She made an inspection of the most recent work at the Griggs' Greenwich Village apartment and then headed farther uptown to shop for a Gustavian floor clock for Avery's cottage. Each time she emerged from a different place, she found herself checking the street, watching to make sure no one was watching her. All she wanted was for her life to be normal again, the fear to be gone. She checked the time. Four hours until her rendezvous at Jacques.

As she exited the last store on her list, feeling the now familiar wave of discomfort that happened each time she stepped onto the street, Keith Holt called her.

"Have you got a minute?" he asked. In the background she could hear echoing footsteps and snatches of conversation, as if he might be standing in the middle of a hospital corridor.

"Of course. What's up?"

"I was actually hoping we could meet today, perhaps for an espresso. I've put together the clippings and I'd love to deliver them to you."

Yikes, she thought. She'd counted on the fact that with the

demands of Holt's job, the clipping task would keep him busy for at least a week or two, buying her time to catch up with her other projects.

"I'm actually just finishing a shopping expedition for another client."

"Where are you at the moment?"

The bluntness of the question caught her off guard.

"Uh, the Upper East Side."

"I bet you're not far from the hospital. I could meet you in a half an hour or so."

She hardly had time for that, but Holt was now officially a client and clients didn't appreciate the words, "I'm sorry I can't."

"Sure," she said. "That works for me. Just tell me where."

They met at a small café around the corner from the hospital, nearly empty now, though the air still seemed to pulse from a lunch crowd that had dispersed just a short time before. Holt was already seated and as Kit approached, she spotted the folder on the wooden table. He was in a sport jacket today, wheat colored with threads of blue woven through, and a crisp blue shirt. Handsome, just as Baby had pointed out.

After rising to greet her, Holt flagged the waitress with just a tilt of his chin. Once the espressos were ordered, he turned his attention back to Kit.

"I hope I didn't browbeat you into coming. I'm just anxious to know what you think."

He lifted the folder off the table and offered it to her.

"It seems like you had fun with the project," Kit said. "I'll want to spend time going through these, but can I take a peek now?"

"Please, be my guest."

She opened the folder and began to sift through the clippings. The mix, she saw, included not just pages from shelter magazines, but also two magazine travel stories and photocopies of about ten pieces of art. Kit thumbed through them, struck immediately by the contrast between what she was viewing and a comment Holt had made at their first encounter.

"Why are you smiling?" he asked.

"You have two Agnes Martin paintings in here."

"I told you I loved modern art."

"I know, and I like Martin, too. But it's not quite what I was expecting from you. You said you wanted your apartment to be gutsy, but at a glance I can see that a lot of what you chose is wonderfully pared down and subtle. Perhaps you really crave something with a calming effect. Which would make sense considering how demanding your work is."

He reached to take the folder back and thumbed quickly through it.

"I see what you're saying," he said, nodding softly. "And this may be the *real* reason my current apartment irks me. Not because it's so nice but because it's just too busy with all that red and gold."

"That's a great point." This was what gave her the biggest rush of all in her work, even more than the kick that came from deciding to pair a bunch of wildly different prints or painting a tiny room chocolate brown in order to draw attention to its size rather than distract from it. She loved helping people recognize that what they'd convinced themselves they wanted wasn't necessarily so, and that there was something else entirely that would capture their fancy.

Holt leaned back in his chair, his brown eyes pensive. "How are you doing, by the way? I felt so bad for you on Saturday."

"It's just like you always hear about these situations. You feel so *violated* when someone breaks into your home."

"I have a colleague whose apartment was burglarized and the police actually recovered some of her jewelry at a pawn shop. Maybe that will happen in your case, too."

"Fortunately they didn't find my nice jewelry. All in all, whoever broke in was probably disappointed with their take."

"Bad for them but good for you."

They spoke a few more minutes, with Kit urging him tele-pathically to drink faster. The meeting with X was only hours away and it weighed on her nerves. Finally, with another nod, Holt signaled for the check.

"I'll be anxious to hear your final verdict on the clippings," he said as they rose simultaneously from the table. "In fact, here's an idea. Would you be free to meet for dinner later? We could discuss them further."

Was he asking her for a date? she wondered. Maybe he *was* the kind of guy she should consider seeing, just like Baby had suggested, but now was certainly not the time. Plus, he was a client, and that could make it thorny.

"I'd love to," she said, "but I need to get back to the office and then I have to run out at seven for a meeting. But let's plan to review everything soon."

"Of course," he said, looking mollified. "I look forward to it."

As they stepped outside, she saw that the sky was smudged with gray but the forecasted rain had yet to break through. She bid goodbye to Holt and started for the subway.

"New development," Dara announced when Kit finally ar-rived at the office. "I packed up the boards for Avery but she never sent a messenger. Turns out she's at the Crosby Street Hotel this afternoon for an off-site brainstorm meeting with her team, and since she's so close, she says she wants to pop by and pick them up herself at 6:30. Want me to hang around?"

"Thanks, Dara, but I don't mind handling it. I'll be here until just before seven." However, even as she said the words, a ping sounded on her phone, indicating a text. With a start she saw it was from X.

"Need to meet at nine instead. Same place."

That didn't sit well with her. It meant waiting even longer, but at least she'd have more time if Avery ran late. She texted back "okay."

After Dara and Baby took off, with Baby whispering for Kit to call her after the meeting, she paced the office, waiting for Avery. It wasn't until a quarter to seven that the buzzer rang.

"*Sorry*," Avery blurted into the intercom, sounding more irritated than apologetic. "Traffic's a bitch."

A few minutes later she swept into the office in a cloud of fragrance that hinted at rose petals and bitter orange. Her look was more subdued than usual: the humidity had knocked some of the volume out of her hair, and, probably because of the off-site meeting with her staff, she was dressed simply in black leggings, black booties with heels, and a long, taupe-colored sweater.

Kit turned over the three boards to her, which had been carefully wrapped by Dara, and though she knew Avery was probably in a hurry, she updated her briefly on the progress she'd made scouting for not only major pieces but also lamps and accessories.

"Will it all be ready by the beginning of summer?" Avery asked.

"Yes, most of it, as long as I can order the fabric right away. I've lined up a painter for you, and he's going to start next week, so I'll work with your assistant about securing access. I'll be driving down there every week to supervise."

Avery smiled. "Fabulous. Now I just have to meet a new man to invite for the weekends."

"Just give a few parties this summer and ask people to bring along some men you haven't met. Those billowing curtains I promised you are going to be pretty seductive."

Avery smiled. "I'm counting on it. But look, I'd better dash." No sooner were the words out of her mouth than the rain finally arrived, and Kit and Avery turned in unison to the sound of it pelting against the window glass.

"You'll never find a cab now," Kit said. "Let me order you an Uber."

"I've got a car," Avery said, as if it would be ludicrous to think otherwise. "But what I desperately could use is an umbrella. I've got to run in and out of a few places."

"Let me grab you one."

Kit reached into a basket in the entranceway, found a small fold-up umbrella and handed it over. Avery looked at it glumly.

"Maybe I should bag the stops," she said. "It's so damn windy out, I'm going to get drenched even with an umbrella."

"Do you want my trench coat?" Kit asked, making sure the reluctance didn't show in her voice. She hated to part with the coat, but she also didn't want to leave a client in a jam.

"You sure? I could send it over by messenger tomorrow."

"Of course." Kit tugged her tan trench coat off the peg and passed it to Avery, who momentarily set the boards down before slipping into the coat and tightening the belt around her. "I'm dying to hear what you think about the boards."

"Well, I'm dying to see them. I'll be in touch."

Kit opened the door for her and Avery hurried out.

For the next two hours Kit tried to busy herself with work. Thirty minutes before she was due to leave, she changed into jeans, boots, and a khaki green jersey top. She stared at her reflection in the mirror. The color of the top played off her eyes in a way someone couldn't help but notice.

Oh, that's hilarious, she thought. She was going to meet a man who had imperiled her life and she was subconsciously trying to dazzle him. She nearly tore off the top and wiggled into a black knit turtleneck instead. Just before it was time to go, she threw on an old rain slicker. With her trench on loan, that was the best she could do at the moment.

Outside her building she paused in the doorway for a minute, more fraught with nerves than she'd even anticipated. The heavy rain had stopped but there was a light drizzle now, and the air was misty. She glanced up and down the wet streets, making certain no one suspicious was lingering nearby. And then she took off, checking several times over her shoulder on the short walk to Jacques.

The restaurant was a French bistro with cracked plaster walls, a tiled linoleum floor, and faded red toile curtains. It was half empty tonight and Kit immediately spotted Kelman, sitting alone against the back wall. She drew a breath at the sight of him. As if sensing her presence, he looked up, met her eyes, and rose. Just as he had when she'd crossed the restaurant in Islamorada.

Reaching the old wooden table, she slid into a chair across from him. He was dressed in black jeans, a stone-colored T-shirt, and his black leather jacket.

"What would you like to drink?" he asked, sitting back down again. He had a mug of beer in front of him, the outside of the glass wet with condensation.

"A white wine," she said.

It was hard to believe that two weeks ago she had sat with him on that lovely candlelit terrace with the dark bay as a backdrop. And that she'd toyed in her mind with all sorts of possibilities: that he might kiss her later, that she would see him back in New York, that something would develop between them. But nothing, nothing like this.

A waitress took the order and Kelman didn't speak again until she returned with the wine.

"I'm glad you reached out, Kit," he said finally.

His tone had shifted since Sunday; gone was the hostile edge. Clearly he'd given up on the notion that she had a devious agenda. Still, she would need to be careful.

"You said that you had information that could benefit me," she said. "I'm ready to hear it."

"Frankly, I'm still surprised you decided to meet. On Sunday, the only thing you seemed interested in was getting me out of both your apartment and your life."

"What choice do I have?" she said, feeling a swell of indignation. "I'm scared and I need your help."

"I *want* to help. I realize you're in this mess because of me."

"And what *is* the mess exactly? I deserve to know."

"Okay. But I need you to realize that I'm in a highly volatile situation and there's a chance you'll be in even more danger because of what I have to tell you."

Her body tensed from dread. *Was* he involved in something highly illegal? She had to know, one way or the other.

"Consider me warned," she said.

"Like I told you Sunday, I worked at Ithaka as a portfolio manager. After about four years, I decided to leave—the place was no longer a good fit for me for a variety of reasons. So that I wouldn't lose my bonus that year, I decided to hand in my resignation after the first of the year, though just knowing I'd be resigning was a relief. And then, right before I left, something happened."

He took a swig of beer and when he pulled the mug away, she saw that his expression was grim.

"One day, purely by accident, I stumbled on the fact that some serious illegal trading had gone on in the firm about six months previously. It involved our holdings in a pharmaceutical company that was testing an experimental drug for leukemia."

He was speaking in a hushed voice, and Kit leaned in closer to hear, to try to fully fathom what he was telling her. She'd assumed for days that X was an identity thief and a con artist, and now the truth, if it *was* the truth, was totally different. It felt like being a passenger in a car that had flipped over on its hood, and trying desperately to figure a way out when everything was upside down.

"These illegal trades—they hadn't aroused any suspicions up until then?" Kit asked.

"Apparently not, and I knew I had to report what I'd discovered to the SEC. I'm not trying to paint myself as some hero, but the whole thing disgusted me. I had my suspicions that even the head of the company might be involved."

Wainwright. She thought of the power that emanated from his pores, the way he'd pressured her into coming to the office.

"Wait," Kit said. "Was Matt the one doing the illegal deals?"

Kelman shook his head adamantly.

"No, no. It was two other portfolio managers—Gavin Kennelly and Tom Lister. At some point Kennelly and Lister apparently approached a doctor who was on the board monitoring trials for this leukemia drug. It's okay for portfolio managers to use doctors as consultants, but it's not legal for a doctor to share confidential information or for anyone at a firm to accept it. But over time they corrupted the guy, paid him to tip them off about the findings."

"And you learned all this how?"

"The doctor's in his eighties and he's losing it a little. One day in January he called the office and mistakenly ended up with me instead of Gavin Kennelly. Maybe the receptionist just heard him say the name wrong. But as soon as he started talking to me, it was clear that he was waiting for a final payment that was due him. He never realized he was talking to the wrong guy. I just played along."

"How did you figure what the payment was for?"

"First I researched the doctor's background and saw his connection to the drug. Then I started digging. I have a pretty strong tech background, and before I got promoted to portfolio manager I helped design the database and the user interface. I got into the system and saw that we'd dumped all the stock we had in the pharmaceutical company about a week before it was announced that the drug wasn't going to pan out, which prevented about 150 million dollars in losses. I put what I found on the flash drive."

It sounded credible on the surface but she'd believed Kelman in the past, and look where that had landed her.

"Kit, I deceived you in Florida, but this is the truth," he added, knowing exactly what was in her mind.

"So where does Healy fit into this?"

"After I saw what had happened, I asked Matt about it. He's a buddy of mine, and I thought he might have had his own suspicions since he was friendlier with Kennelly than I was. All he knew was that Kennelly had seemed preoccupied lately. The main thing we wondered was whether the CEO was involved because the numbers seemed too big for him and the compliance officer not to have noticed. I was on my way out the door at that point, so Matt said he'd do some of his own probing. Once we knew more, we could go to the authorities."

"Funny you found time to slip off and get a tan in the middle of all of this."

"My trip wasn't about that. Right after I left Ithaka, my doorman tipped me off that for a couple of days he'd seen the same guy take off from across the street the minute I left the building. I figured that the firm might have gotten wind of my snooping and had hired a private detective to see what I was up to. Insider trading convictions mean big fines and long prison terms and the last thing they would have wanted is me blowing the whistle. Matt suggested I lay low and crash at his pad, which I did for a few days, but in the end I decided it would be smarter to leave town until we were ready to pull the trigger. I drove down south, paid cash for everything, and checked into the hotel with a credit card Matt loaned me for that purpose.

When I met you, I gave you Matt's name because that's what I was going by at the hotel. After I called you, I figured I could explain the situation back in New York."

"And you were really coming back the week we met?"

"Yup. I was going to ditch the rental car and fly this time— Thursday morning. Matt hadn't had any luck, and I thought it was stupid to wait any longer. It was probably crazy to call you that day, but I wanted to see you again. At the time there didn't seem to be any harm in having you come to his apartment."

She stared at the table, not wanting to meet his eyes. If the comment about wanting to see her again was a tactic to make her lower her guard, she refused to bite.

"But when your plans changed, why not call me?" she demanded. "Why let me bungle my way through that encounter with Healy?"

"After I left the Keys, I rented an apartment for a couple of nights in Miami, an Airbnb thing. On the night before I was headed back, I woke to the sound of a prowler in the living room. I tried to fight him off, but he clocked me and managed to take my laptop, phone, iPad, anything that might hold data. I'm pretty sure the guy must have been hired by Ithaka. Up until that point, I didn't know how far they would go to protect themselves."

"And the magic pen?"

"They didn't get it. It was on my bedside table, and as far as I knew at the time, it was still the right one. After that night I was scrambling. It didn't seem smart to go back to New York then. I'd tossed your card and programmed your info into my cell so I didn't have it anymore. I had the same problem with Matt's cell number. I finally reached him Friday morning and explained what had happened.

He looked pained as he uttered Matt's name, as if the death was still weighing on him. But she wondered if it could all be an act in order to keep her quiet. Matt had been up to something and he'd tried to throw Garrett under the bus. What if he and Garrett had been partners on the insider trades and had decided to quit the firm while they were ahead. They might have eventually ended up at cross-purposes, one threatening to betray the other. There was still a chance that it had been Garrett who had killed Matt.

"Did you know Matt was coming to Miami?" she asked.

"Yes. I switched to a cheap hotel after the break-in and when we spoke on Friday, he volunteered to fly down and meet me so we could strategize. He said he'd be staying at a friend's— someone who was out of town—so he'd be under the radar as well. By then I'd checked the pen and realized you'd taken mine. I felt like a fool telling Matt you'd absconded with the flash drive. But at least he had access to the system at the firm, and I could help him duplicate my efforts."

"What could you possibly think I wanted with the flash drive?"

"I figured the break-in had been round two of Ithaka trying to get their hands on any evidence I had in my possession, and that you had been round one. Though what I couldn't understand was how you knew the flash drive was hidden in the pen because I'd kept that detail to myself. Needless to say, I was flabbergasted when I heard you'd shown up for the dinner. Neither Matt nor I could guess what your game was."

"Did you ever see Healy in Miami?"

"No. He was supposed to come by my place. When he never showed, I was in a panic wondering what had happened. He didn't answer his phone. The next day I heard that a man fitting his description had been killed. I was almost positive it had to be him."

If he was telling the truth, he had no idea that Matt Healy might have betrayed him.

"And you think his death could be related to all this?"

"Yes," he said solemnly. "Yes I do. And now I've shared plenty. You said you had stuff to tell *me*."

"Just one more question. When you finally talked to Healy, what did he reveal about the encounter with me?"

"Since he hadn't heard from me in a few days, he was worried something had happened. Said he realized the person you'd met must have been me and that there might be a message he was supposed to interpret from your visit, but couldn't decipher what it was. And that he'd tried to make it all seem like a bad misunderstanding."

She shook her head.

"That's not what happened. Healy told me his wallet had been stolen and the person I'd met in the Keys was probably the pickpocket."

Kelman frowned. "Maybe that was the first story he could think of. Don't forget, he had no idea why you'd shown up."

"But then explain *this* to me. Healy had me go in to Ithaka and tell both Mitch Wainwright and the head of security the whole story."

"That doesn't make any freaking sense," he said, taken aback. "Why would he open a huge can of worms that way? That was practically confirming to Wainwright that I was up to something."

"I have to ask you, Garrett." It was the first time, she realized, that she'd said his real name. "Are you sure Matt Healy didn't turn on you?"

He brought his fist up and held it to his mouth. Either truly perturbed by the revelation—or just brilliantly pretending to be.

"It's hard to imagine," he said. "But what you just told me— it's disturbing," he said.

"The SEC will have to know about this, too. I take it you've talked to them now that you have the flash drive again."

He took the last swig of his beer and set the mug down.

"No, not yet."

Kit looked at him, stunned.

"But what are you waiting for?" she demanded. "They need to be informed, and so do the cops. Both the ones here and in Miami."

"In light of how complicated the situation's become—especially with Matt's death—I'm working out a slightly different strategy with my attorney."

And what could *that* mean? she wondered. Delaying seemed utterly crazy to her. It would only increase her vulnerability and his as well. She needed time to think, to determine if what he was telling her was true—and how to convince him to drag his butt to the authorities *now*.

"I'll be right back," she said. "I'm just going to use the restroom."

The only bathroom was in the back of the restaurant, down a short, dark corridor. After peeing she washed her hands and then let the cold tap run, while she played back what Kelman had told her. His story, though overly complicated, might be true. From the little she'd read about insider trading cases, she'd learned that they *were* complex, and the stakes were very, very high. And yet Kelman might be spinning yet another tale for her. In the past few weeks she'd been fed bullshit stories about former tech businesses, stolen wallets, and business trips to Palm Beach, and she knew now that the words counted for next to nothing.

She looked in the mirror and saw that her face was flushed, in large part because of how agitated she felt. If Kelman's story was true, and Ithaka had broken into his Miami rental, it meant they'd probably broken into her place as well. And they may have killed Matt Healy. She was now in more danger than she'd ever imagined. She had to convince Kelman to move faster. It was time to tell him about her trip to the Miami police because learning that he was a person of interest in a homicide might light a fire under him.

She ran a paper towel under the stream of cold water and dabbed at her face.

A woman was waiting for the bathroom when Kit emerged into the narrow corridor. She eased by the stranger and turned the corner into the main part of the restaurant. And then she halted, perplexed. Garrett Kelman wasn't at the table. She spun outward, scanning the room. There was no sign of him anywhere. The men's room? she wondered. But there was just the one bathroom.

She hurried to the table. Her wineglass was still at her place, and Garrett's empty beer mug was just across from it. And in the middle of the table, tossed down as if in a rush, were three ten-dollar bills.

He was gone.

chapter 14

He's played me again, she thought furiously. How could she have been so incredibly stupid to fall for it again?

Staring at the tabletop, she tried to process what had just happened. Clearly Kelman's only motive for meeting her had been to tap into whatever details she was privy to. He'd offered up the story about illegal trading as a warm-up, to entice her into talking, and then once he learned what Healy had done, he bolted.

For a moment her gaze lingered on the clump of ten-dollar bills. Thank God for small favors, she thought mockingly. At least he hadn't stiffed her with the check.

"Will there be anything else?" a voice from behind her inquired. She turned to see the waitress eyeing the scene quizzically. Kit realized that the woman probably assumed there'd been a lovers' spat and Kelman had stormed off.

"No, nothing else. But—can you tell me? Did the man I was with say anything before he left?"

"He didn't even ask for the check. I just saw him toss the money onto the table and then he took off in a rush."

Kit muttered thank you and wiggled back into her slicker. Out on the street she punched her hands into her pockets and looked over the street, over the faces of passersby and into the dark slivers between buildings. What was she supposed to do *now*? she wondered. Call the police? The update she could offer O'Callaghan would sound even more absurd than the one she could have presented Sunday. "You know that mystery man, the one who I thought broke into my apartment? I decided to have a drink with him and he kind of stood me up again. I'm now two for two."

She started off for home, walking at a clip, checking behind her every few moments. It had stopped drizzling, but the air was still misty, almost cottony.

And then, as she passed in front of a row of shops closed for the night, a hand grabbed her arm, like an attack dog rocketing from the darkness, and yanked her into a doorway. She started to scream but the other hand clamped down on her mouth. She struggled, thrusting an elbow toward her assailant and trying desperately to free herself.

"Kit, shhh, it's me," a male voice whispered hoarsely. She twisted her head around. It was Kelman. He lowered his hand from her mouth and brought a finger to his lips, urging her to be quiet.

"What are you *doing*?" she demanded, her voice low.

"While you were in the restroom, I noticed someone suspicious come into the restaurant. I didn't want him to see me with you."

"Someone from Ithaka?"

"No. It was a guy I could have sworn I'd seen on the subway when I came down earlier from the Upper West Side. I slipped into a doorway and watched, and he ended up leaving the restaurant right after me."

Was it the truth? she wondered. That was the question she had to ask herself constantly when she spoke to Kelman.

He slumped his shoulders wearily. "I don't know, maybe I'm just so edgy from this whole thing, I overreacted. Why don't we head someplace else? We need to talk more."

"Where?" She hoped he wasn't going to say back to her apartment because that was the last place she would ever go with him.

"Let's find another bar."

For a moment she hesitated, wondering if it was a trap. But the street was still busy with people and as long as she stayed in public with him, she wouldn't feel vulnerable. Besides, there were more answers she needed. And most of all, she had to convince him to go to the authorities without further delay.

After shooting glances up and down the street, he took her arm, stepped from the doorway, and began to lead her west, in the opposite direction from both Jacques and her apartment. At Mott they turned left. She didn't like the way he still had his hand on her arm, as if he'd taken temporary ownership, and she was about to tug it away. But as if sensing her thoughts, he dropped it.

They headed south in silence, the only sound their footfalls on the slick, glistening pavement. Two or three times Kelman checked behind them. Once, she looked back, too. No furtive strangers. Just neighborhood types and a few obvious tourists.

"Why don't we duck in here?" he said when a small dive bar appeared on the right. She nodded, seeing that there were at least a dozen people inside. He swung open the door for her and took one last look down the street as they entered. After sliding into a booth, he flagged down a waiter. Kelman ordered another beer, and this time she asked for a club soda.

"Kit, I have to know more about that night you met Healy," Kelman said after the waiter moved away. "The things he told you. Clearly something isn't right."

She looked off, thinking. What if, as she'd surmised earlier, he wanted to know about Healy because they'd been involved in a crime together and he was now facing the ugly truth that Healy had betrayed him? And even if Kelman was being honest about everything, where was all this talk really getting her?

"What is it?" he asked.

"When you were at my apartment, you said you had information that could *help* me. But so far all I've learned is that you've dragged me into even more trouble than I imagined. And you don't even have plans to go to the authorities yet."

"I didn't say that. I said I was working out a strategy. In fact, that's the reason I was late tonight. I met with a lawyer, and the plan is for me to come forward by the end of the week."

She stayed silent, still deciding. Her tidbits of information were bargaining chips, and it seemed stupid to cash them all in now.

Kelman leaned toward her across the table. "Please, Kit. I need your help. If Matt was on the wrong side, I have to share that with the authorities. And in the end that *will* help you."

She didn't trust him. But at that moment, the advantages of telling him seemed to outweigh those of withholding what she knew.

"Okay," she said finally.

She saw his body relax, some of the tension drain from his face.

"When I first showed up at Healy's, he seemed almost amused," she said, "as if I was just some damsel in dating distress. But as soon as I told him I'd met this other Matt Healy in Florida, he became alarmed, and that's when he offered up the wallet story. I suppose there's a chance it was the first thing he could think of. After all, he hadn't heard from you, didn't know why I'd suddenly popped up on his doorstep. But then he went into elaborate detail about being pickpocketed. And he said it was essential that I share my experience with his security chief at work."

Kelman raked a hand through his cropped red hair, clearly shaken. "He never said a word to me about fabricating that kind of story. He told me he just sent you away, telling you he knew nothing about why there'd been a mix-up."

"How did you finally get hold of him?" she asked. There were parts of the story that still weren't making sense to her. "You said you didn't have his cell number."

"I managed to make contact through the Ithaka office. I didn't want to phone Matt myself because I knew his assistant would recognize my voice and might tip off someone on the staff about it. So I convinced this woman on the beach to do it with my disposable phone. She left a message for Healy to call back on that number. I had her use a phrase he would recognize, and he phoned about thirty minutes later."

"When you spoke to him, why not ask for my contact info."

"I did. He said you refused to even give him your name. . . . Tell me about the meeting at Ithaka."

"I met with Ungaro first. He wanted to know all about the Florida mystery man I'd been with. In hindsight it seems he must have surmised, from the description I gave, that it could be you I was talking about. Or Healy told him."

"And Healy was in the meeting, too?"

"No. I'd assumed he would be, but when I arrived at the office he explained that he was headed out of town—to see you as it turns out. I met with Ungaro alone, and Wainwright stopped by just as we were finishing. And then they pressured me into coming in a second time, after Healy was killed."

"Why?"

"Wainwright presented it as if they wanted to make sure that justice was done, that they needed to be totally in the loop about Healy's death."

Kelman's shoulders sagged. If he was lying to her tonight, he was doing a pretty good job disguising it.

"It does sound like Healy turned on me," he said. "Whether he was in on the illegal trades himself or just trying to prove to Wainwright that he was fully on his team, he clearly wanted to expose me, otherwise why have you go in there? Christ, he probably even tipped them off to where I was staying in Miami. And that would also explain why *your* place was broken into. Matt must have told them I thought you'd taken the flash drive."

"And that explains why Wainwright wanted to see me another time. He was probably hoping to get a better read on me."

"Exactly."

"If Healy was betraying you, why would he go through the ruse of flying to Miami to discuss a game plan?"

"Maybe to learn more about what I thought your game was. Or to convince me to delay a meeting with the SEC, which would buy more time for Ithaka."

"Does Ithaka have clients in the Miami or Palm Beach area?"

He narrowed his eyes. "No. Why do you ask?"

He didn't need to know her reason. But his answer revealed that Wainwright had definitely lied to her and that the revelation from Sasha Glen was probably accurate.

"Just curious. Since Healy had to cancel his plans and head to Florida, I wondered if he'd tried to kill two birds with one stone."

"What do you mean, change his plans?"

"He apparently had intended to fly to Ann Arbor on business Friday. But he aborted that trip after hearing from you."

Kelman's mouth parted in surprise and he reached out across the table, laying his hand on Kit's arm. She felt her body tense in response.

"*What* did you say?"

"That he changed his itinerary after talking to you."

"No, about Ann Arbor."

"That's where I heard he was originally headed."

Kelman clenched a fist and tapped it against his mouth. His mind seemed to be racing, trying to make pieces fit.

"What?" she asked.

"You know who's in Ann Arbor?" he said.

"No."

"The member of the advisory board who Kennelly corrupted. He's a professor emeritus with the university. So I bet Matt *was* part of the illegal trading scheme."

He looked stricken by the revelation. Betrayed by someone he trusted and also played for a fool. But had it been one thief against another? She still didn't know.

"So who ran over Healy?" she asked. "His death has been ruled a homicide."

"It has to be someone from Ithaka—or hired by them."

"But why? Whether he was in on the illegal trades or he just wanted to cover his ass by letting Wainwright know you were blowing the whistle, there'd be no reason to murder him."

Kelman ran a thumb over the lip of his beer bottle, thinking.

"I don't know," he said after a moment. "They may have wanted one less player in the mix. Or maybe I was the one who was supposed to die. Healy and I had vaguely similar coloring, and if someone was hired to take him out using a photo, he might have been mistaken for me."

Yes, she knew all about that kind of confusion.

"Frankly, I'm mystified they'd go this far," he added, flipping his palms over. "Trying to steal the flash drive is one thing, but murder is a whole other ballgame. There've been a lot of these insider trading cases and as far as I know, they don't come to violence. The bad guys are so cocksure of themselves, they assume that even if someone blows the whistle, they'll manage to weasel out of trouble."

"Of course," she said quietly, her heart starting to pound, "there's someone *else* with a motive for killing Healy. Someone besides the people at Ithaka."

She had to get it on the table, see how he'd react.

"Who?" he asked.

"You." Her voice was just a whisper now. "Maybe you discovered Healy had betrayed you. You could have told him to meet you on the street in Miami and waited in your car, ready to mow him down."

His body went totally still and all the expression drained from his face. He stared at her, pinning her eyes so tightly with his that it almost hurt. She would have liked to tear her gaze away but she didn't. She needed to read him, find a tell of his that would help reveal where truth ended and lies began.

"Is that what you believe, Kit?" he asked, his voice disarmingly soft. "That I'm a cold-blooded killer? That you went to bed with someone who murdered a friend a few days later?"

His eyes never left hers as he spoke. But she knew that didn't mean anything, not with Kelman. He was the master of looking at you and not letting go, and she assumed he could do that whether he was being honest or lying through his teeth.

"I didn't say I believe it. I said it was a possibility. . . . *Did* you kill him?"

He stared for a few moments more. In the dim light, his blue eyes were now the color of slate.

"No," he said. "No, I didn't."

"You should know that the Miami police consider you a person of interest in Healy's homicide," she said. She was tipping him off, but if his story was legitimate, it seemed wrong not to.

"How do you know that?" he asked. "I mean, it makes sense. I even wondered if Ithaka would try to implicate me. But what makes you so sure?"

"The police found my business card in one of Healy's pockets and called me about it. At first I thought you were the victim—the description seemed to fit, and I'd given you my card after all. I told them about my encounter with you. Later, after they had me I.D. the body and I saw that it was actually Healy, I helped them do a sketch of you."

"Oh great," he said. "That's just the extra nightmare I need."

"You can hardly blame me. The only thing I knew about you at that point is that you'd totally deceived me."

"You're right," he said, letting the sarcasm fall away. "And I *can't* blame you. But this complicates everything."

"Then all the more reason to go to the police. To clear your name so it doesn't interfere with what you're trying to do about Ithaka."

Kelman checked his watch rather than answer.

"It's late," he said. "We should split."

He paid the bill and they stepped outside. It had begun to drizzle again, and the street was quiet now, except for a few stray people rushing through the dark, as if hoping to beat a potential downpour.

Kelman turned left, in the direction they'd come, and she sensed by the way his body led that he had every intention of accompanying her. Not so fast, she thought.

"I'll take it from here," she said.

"I can't let you go alone. I'll walk you most of the way and then watch to make sure you get in okay. So if someone's lurking around your building, they won't see me with you."

That was funny, she thought as they started to walk. She was being escorted home by someone she'd just considered might be a cold-hearted killer. But at least for now he scared her less than the unknown, the person or persons who had broken into her apartment, who might be the real ones behind Healy's death. Besides, she still had a question, and she could ask him it as they walked.

"Did you follow me that day in Islamorada?" she asked, after they'd gone half a block. "Into the shop where we talked?"

"Why do you ask that?" Even in the dark street, she could see his expression grow perplexed.

"Ungaro wanted to know. It's clear he thought you might have."

"Really? You mean to force an encounter with you for some reason?"

"Yes."

"Oh, I get it. Healy told them that I was claiming you'd stolen the flash drive, but they might have entertained other explanations—that I could have marked you and used you as some kind of unsuspecting mule to sneak the flash drive out of the area."

That, she realized, could explain their interest in the fact that she and Kelman had literally run into each other early in the day.

"So you didn't follow me that day?"

A pause. The only sound was from her boot heels scuffing the pavement.

"I didn't say that. The truth is I *did* follow you. But not for the reason Ungaro suggested. I saw you go into the store, and that's why I went there, too. You'd intrigued me from the moment I saw you that morning. I should have left you alone, Kit, but I didn't. I wanted you."

His voice was seductive. It was a kind of quicksand, she told herself, and she needed to be careful. She ignored the comment and picked up her pace, anxious to be home.

A half block from her apartment building, Kelman touched her arm, signaling for her to stop. "I'll watch from here," he said.

She nodded and started to turn.

"Wait," he said, suddenly. "This is yours."

She turned back. In his hand was the pen, the one her father had given her. As she accepted it, his fingers brushed against her own. She met his gaze. Under the street lamp, his eyes were back to being that piercing blue. It was utterly crazy, she thought. After everything, there was still something about Kelman that made her want him, too.

"Text me when you're in your apartment," he said as she started to turn again. "I want to know you're safe."

"You know when I'll feel safe?" she said. "When you call to tell me you've been to the SEC and the police. And not a second before then."

"Point taken. I know it's hard for you to trust me, but I'm going to make good on what I've said. All I'm asking is that you give me a few more days."

She nodded tentatively and then darted across the street. As she covered the last yards to her building, she could almost feel his eyes on her back, like a magnetic force.

As soon as she'd slammed the apartment door behind her, she flipped on the lights, checked around the space, and then set the alarm on the door. Only then did she text Kelman.

Her brain felt ready to explode from all the information she'd heard tonight, and from the constant weighing she'd done of Kelman's words, trying to assess the veracity of everything he said. She was also frustrated. She'd gone out hoping that it would be a turning point for her, that she'd somehow be able to dig out from under, but as she'd told Kelman, little he'd said was truly of help to her.

And she felt scared, too—more than earlier. If Kelman's story was legit, they were both up against a powerful entity, one with the money and resources to truly hurt them.

Even though it was after eleven and she'd risk a headache from drinking wine this late, she pulled a bottle of Pinot Grigio out of the fridge, a fresh one she'd added the day before. She poured a glass and took it with her into the bedroom. On the way she grabbed her laptop from the coffee table.

First she emailed Baby to say she was safe. It was too late to call but she wanted Baby to see the message first thing in the morning. For the next half hour, she Googled insider trading cases. There had been a number of high profile ones in the past few years, mostly involving male defendants, and the vast majority had ended in conviction. And Kelman was right. The penalties in every case were huge fines and daunting prison terms, the kind that took forty- and fifty-something men away from their growing families for years. It wasn't hard to imagine someone doing their utmost to guarantee that didn't happen to him.

The cases were complicated, too, often involving weeks of testimony. That seemed to back up Kelman's claim that he had to be shrewd about what he came forward with and when.

Also of interest: Whistleblowers could receive a financial award from the SEC, and it could amount to millions of dollars. She realized that was a possible motive for X to kill Healy—so he'd be able to keep all the money for himself.

Kit took a sip of wine without tasting it and leaned back against the headboard of her bed. She still didn't know whether to believe Kelman's story—maybe parts of it were true and others not—but there was one thing she knew for sure. Kelman might have his game plan but she wasn't going to be held hostage to it. If she felt in any danger, she would act. For the first time she realized that something in her had changed over the past few weeks. She'd become determined not to spend her life waiting in the wings.

The next morning she was at her desk early again, trying to focus on work and catch up. Most of her attention was devoted to the Barry Kaplan concept. Doodling with a pencil, she suddenly had a vision of a purple velvet sofa off-set by earthy Irish matting on the floor. It would look stunning, but Barry would probably find it too designer-y, not masculine enough. Perhaps, she thought ruefully, she should suggest a tiki bar in the middle of his living room.

Frustrated, she stuffed his folder back in a drawer. Maybe her head would be clearer in the afternoon.

Dara arrived at nine, looking more laid back than she had earlier in the week, though, as Kit knew, nothing had changed for the better. She wondered if the right thing would be to insist that Baby and Dara work from home for the foreseeable future.

"I see Avery picked up the boards," Dara said, glancing toward the spot on the wooden table where they'd been stacked.

"Yes, she blew in here just as the rain started."

"When's she planning to get back to you about them? We have to start placing orders if things are going to be ready by summer."

"Hopefully today, though with Avery you can never be sure."

The office phone rang and Dara glanced at her screen. "Speak of the devil, that's her calling. Want me to get it?"

"No, I will. Let's hope it's a good sign that she's responding so quickly." She grabbed the receiver and answered.

"This is Chloe Marzilli, Avery Howe's assistant," a voice said after Kit answered. Avery liked to have her assistant place her calls, Hollywood-mogul style, but it suddenly dawned on Kit that the assistant wasn't about to put Avery on. She was pretty sure she knew the real reason for the call.

"Good morning," she replied. "Are you calling about my coat?"

"Excuse me?"

"The coat I loaned Avery."

"No, not a coat," the girl said breathlessly.

"Oh, sorry. Does she want to speak to me?"

"She's not here—that's why I'm calling. We don't know where she is and I was praying you might have a clue."

Kit's body tensed, as if she'd heard the sound of a window splintering during the dead of night.

"What do you mean?" she asked.

"She's totally missing. I can't reach her on her phone. The driver from last night said he dropped her off at your place just before seven and never saw her again."

chapter 15

Kit's mind scrambled, trying to dislodge what Avery had conveyed last night about her plans. She'd mentioned that she needed to pop in a few other places—that's why she'd borrowed the coat.

"Yes, Avery was here, but just for a short while," Kit said. "From what she told me, she had additional stops to make but she didn't say where."

Dara had halted what she was doing by this point and was watching Kit, her expression concerned, as if she knew just from the snatches of conversation that something was brewing, and it wasn't good.

"But why not get in the car—or at least tell the driver?" the assistant asked, her voice almost in a wail. "The guy waited like two hours and the dispatcher said they tried her cell a zillion times. She never answered."

"Maybe the stops were close by and she decided to walk and never went back to the car."

But even as she uttered the words, Kit realized how stupid they were. It had been practically raining sideways at the time, and even if Avery *had* decided to travel to the next location on foot, she would have dropped the fabric boards in the car instead of lugging them around with her.

"The driver says he was reading the paper so if she walked past him he might not have seen her, but it isn't like her to just ditch the car," the girl added. "No one's heard from her, she hasn't been tweeting, and she never showed for her eight a.m. meeting."

A voice began to whisper hoarsely in the back of Kit's mind: This has to do with me somehow. This has to do with everything bad that's been happening.

"Have you been to her apartment?" Kit asked. But of course they would have checked there.

"Yes, someone from the office went up there after she missed the meeting and we couldn't reach her on her cell. The night doorman doesn't recall ever seeing her come in. Plus, the clothes she was wearing yesterday aren't in her apartment."

"You need to call the police," Kit said. "And—I'll go outside and ask around. At shops along the street. Maybe someone saw her."

"Okay," the girl said, her voice trembling now.

"Keep trying her cell, too," Kit said. "Maybe she had an accident or medical emergency."

"Yeah, okay."

Kit signed off, promising to be back in touch soon. She quickly related the news to Dara.

"Did she look okay when she was here?" Dara asked anxiously. "I mean, you hear of people suddenly going into these crazy fugue states. Wasn't there an NYU student that happened to?"

"She seemed okay to me, just busy. From what I've heard it takes the cops a while to act on a missing persons report, so what we need to do is hit the street and ask if anyone at a store or restaurant saw her after seven o'clock. We'll split up to make it faster. Can you print out a couple of photos of Avery from the Internet to take with us?"

Kit could feel her dread blooming, but she commanded herself to chill, to think this through. Sure, Avery was a control freak, someone who ran her business fastidiously, but there was an impromptu side to her that surfaced now and then. Kit remembered that when the two of them had gone on their first idea-gathering mission together, Avery had suddenly ducked into a bakery and bought a box of macaroons for them to nibble on. Maybe last night her head had been turned unexpectedly and she'd given in to a spontaneous urge.

Across the room the printer began to whir and Dara snatched the pages, turning one over to Kit. Dara grabbed her coat and Kit a sweater and the two of them stepped out into the corridor. As Kit locked the door, she caught Dara looking at her almost pleadingly, desperate to know what was really going on. Kit didn't want to share the fear that seemed intent on sucking her breath away.

"Why don't you head south," Kit said. "And if you recognize people from the neighborhood, ask them, too. I'll go in the opposite direction."

"Right."

And then, a sound reached her ears, like the pinging of one of those gradual alarm clocks that slowly permeates the outside edges of your sleep. She froze. From Dara's expression, Kit could tell that she'd heard it, too. It was the ringtone for a phone. *Bamboo.* She used that one herself, and she'd heard it on Avery's phone, too.

"Where's that coming from?" Dara said.

Kit turned her head slowly to the right.

"The stairwell," she said. "Dara, you stay here. I'll check."

"No, I'm coming with you."

"Only if you stay far behind me, okay?"

Kit forced herself toward the stairwell door. Slowly she pushed it open. There was no one in sight, either on the steps to the roof or those leading down to the landing. But she could hear the ringtone clearly now. It was coming from below, probably just outside the door to the fourth floor.

Suddenly the sound ended, mid-riff, as if someone had just answered the phone.

"Avery?" Kit called out feebly.

Silence. Something bad was waiting down below. Kit braced herself and made a move for the stairs.

"Stay right here," she urged Dara without turning around.

She took the stairs haltingly, grasping the handrail for support. As she reached the landing, she held her breath and slowly pivoted, letting her gaze fall to the stairs beyond.

She spotted Avery's legs first. They were splayed upward from the ground onto the first few steps, with both knees bent. She was facedown, her face mashed into the pale concrete floor and her wheat-colored hair fanned out on each side. The trench coat— the one Avery had borrowed—was bunched up around her torso. For a split second, it seemed to Kit as if she was staring at herself. She moaned in despair. Please, she begged, let her be alive.

She descended a few steps and called out Avery's name again. No response. No movement. Behind her she could hear Dara scurrying down the stairs.

"Omigod," Dara yelled as she reached the landing and caught a glimpse of Avery's body. "Is she dead?"

"I'm not sure," Kit said, but by now she'd honed in on the blood. Dark as chocolate, it had formed a pool to the left side of Avery's head. There were smears of it, too, on the package of fabric boards, which lay just above her, the wrapping paper partially torn.

Kit fished her keys from her purse and tossed them to Dara. "Go back and call 911, okay? I'm going to go down there to check."

"I don't want to leave you alone."

"I'm all right, just hurry."

Kit knew you weren't supposed to touch anything in a situation like this, but if Avery was still alive, she had to take action. She eased down the steps. At the same time she heard Dara scramble up the stairs and tug open the door.

Kit reached the fourth floor and crouched next to Avery, her heart thumping hard. Now that she was so close, she could see that Avery's hands were purplish red, and small pools of blood had formed beneath the skin. Not good, she thought, anguished. Holding her breath, she reached out and gently touched the center of Avery's left hand, the fingers of which were still slightly tangled in the strap of her handbag. It was cool, almost cold, like a shell dug from wet sand at the shoreline.

A sob caught in Kit's throat. She turned and tore back up the steps. In the corridor she almost collided with Dara, who was just pulling a phone from her ear.

"Help is coming," she said. "I told them we didn't know if she was alive or not."

"She isn't. It looks like she hit her head pretty badly. We better get back to the office and wait there."

How had this happened? she wondered, fighting to stay calm. Had Avery slipped, the consequence of trying to juggle the fabric boards as she navigated concrete steps in her high-heeled boots? But why in the world would she have taken the stairs?

Once back inside, Kit urged Dara to sit at the wooden table.

"Should we call Avery's assistant and let her know?" Dara asked quietly. She seemed eerily subdued to Kit, overwhelmed by what had happened.

"That was my first instinct, but I don't think we should do anything until we clear it with the police."

"Okay," Dara said. She reached up and pressed both hands to her temples.

"Dara, listen to me." Kit said, "As soon as you're done talking to the police, I want you to go home and work from there until this is resolved, okay? While we're waiting for the cops, think about what supplies you might need to take with you."

"Uh huh. But what about *you*? I can't just leave you here."

"Don't worry, I'm thinking I can work out of Baby's place," she said. "I'm going to run over to my apartment for a minute or so. I'll call Baby and make sure she doesn't head down here."

It was essential for her to talk to Baby in private, but after entering her apartment and placing the call, Kit reached only voicemail. She left an urgent message.

Disconnecting the phone, she sank onto one of the stools by the kitchen island. She couldn't stop picturing Avery splayed out at the base of the stairs, all that vibrant energy of hers gone without a trace.

Why, Kit asked herself again, had Avery taken the stairs, especially when she had so much to carry? The building elevator could be wonky at times, and that might have forced Avery to the stairwell, but it had been working when Kit went out later. And how had Avery's fall turned so deadly?

A thought that had been gnawing at her subconscious finally chewed through: What if it wasn't an accident? What if Avery had been pushed down the steps? Had an intruder done it? A mugger? But the motive couldn't have been robbery—her purse was still with her. Unless the assailant had panicked once Avery fell and didn't dare waste time untangling the strap of the purse from her fingers.

Kit pictured the body again: There was the wheat-colored hair, the same color as her own and styled more simply last night, closer to the way she wore hers. And then the borrowed trench coat.

Her stomach twisted. What if someone had meant to hurt *her*, and in a case of mistaken identity, had killed Avery instead?

Don't go there yet, she told herself. There was still a chance it was all a horrific accident. She had to stay calm, wait for the facts. But she also knew she had to reach Kelman, fill him in. She tried his burn phone but he didn't answer. She left a message telling him that there was an emergency and she needed to talk to him immediately.

As she tucked the phone into her skirt pocket, another thought broke through, this one with the force of wood splintering. Could Kelman be the killer?

But no, it wasn't possible. He'd been waiting at the restaurant for her, eager for information. He would have hardly tried to kill her before hearing what she had to say. But Avery's death was going to shift everything. Kelman would have to change course and go to the police *now*. This would be a test of how much she could really trust him.

She forced herself to the sink, turned on the tap, and splashed water toward her face, just to wet her mouth. She needed to get back to Dara. She also had to figure out how to handle the police. They would have to be told about the break-in and they'd, of course, wonder if the two situations were linked. But there was no way she could come clean about her encounters with Kelman, not yet anyway. She had no proof of anything to offer them, just a story about her meeting more than once with a murder suspect. She might very well implicate herself.

The safest strategy, she decided, would be to volunteer the bare minimum and answer their questions carefully, keeping certain details under wraps for now.

Dara was still at the table when Kit returned, staring listlessly across the room, a pad and pen lying in front of her. Kit walked over and set a hand on Dara's shoulder to comfort her.

"How are you doing?"

"It's just so awful. She's probably been lying there since last night, right?"

"I assume so. People on the top two floors never use the stairs unless the elevator's out, so clearly no one came across the body."

"What *happened*, Kit? Did she trip, do you think?" From Dara's anguished tone Kit knew she was really asking what Kit had wondered, too: Could she have been pushed?

"I just don't know. Maybe we'll have a better sense after the police come."

Dara reached up with her hand and rubbed a tear away. "Even though you were standing right next to me, for a split second I felt like I was looking at *you* at the bottom of the stairs. It was horrible."

So she had been struck by it as well. The resemblance.

"I know. She——"

Kit's words were cut off by the scream of a siren, and then the sound of a car lurching to a stop in front of the building. Kim looked down from the window and saw a patrol car below.

"It's the police," Kit said. "I'm sure they'll want to talk to you at some point, but why don't you just sit here for now and I'll meet them."

Her buzzer rang and she told the police to come up. Steeling herself, she opened the office door and waited. A short time later, two female patrol cops stepped off the elevator.

"Someone's injured?" one of them said.

"We—we thought she might still be alive, but she isn't," Kit said, her voice catching. She pointed to the door down the hall. "She's in the stairwell. Her name's Avery. Avery Howe."

"And you are?" one of the cops asked.

"Kit Finn. I have an interior design firm here. She came for an appointment last night and never made it home."

"Okay, we're going to send for detectives," she replied. "Someone will be with you shortly."

Kit backed over the threshold into the entranceway but kept the door ajar. She watched the two cops slip into the stairwell.

What seemed like only moments later, an EMS crew arrived, and disappeared into the stairwell, too. There's no one for them to save, Kit thought bleakly. About fifteen minutes afterward, the buzzer rang again and this time it was detectives. By now her stomach was in knots.

"I'm Detective Burke," one of the two suited men said, when she greeted them at the door. He was white, mid-forties, with a slim, chiseled face and shaved head. He gestured toward a younger-looking black man whose thin mustache seemed almost fake, like something you'd glue on for a play. "This is my partner, Detective Wingate."

Kit nodded and quickly explained what had happened. Burke's gaze lingered on her face, unsettling her.

"Why don't you step back inside," he said finally. "We'll have questions for you in a few minutes."

Kit retreated back into the office, where she filled Dara in. She made them each a cup of tea and then joined her assistant at the table. Dara hadn't made much progress on the list of what to transport from the office, so Kit scribbled items down, forcing herself to concentrate. She had her phone next to her and she kept checking the screen, willing it to ring. She needed to talk to Baby, and to Kelman. Oddly, even the office phones were silent.

Twenty minutes later, she heard a rap at the door. Kit jumped up and swung it open. Detective Burke stood there, alone this time. The stairwell door had been propped open and she could hear the sound of commotion coming from the floor below, a blend of voices and shoes scraping on cement.

"You said this is your office?" Burke asked, glancing over Kit's shoulder at the setup.

"Yes, though my apartment's next door."

She stepped out of the way so he could enter and then introduced Dara, who had risen from the table.

"So which of you found the body?" Burke asked. His voice was totally flat, emotionless. Kit warned herself to be on guard.

"We found her together," Kit said. "Avery's assistant had called to say she was missing, that no one had heard from her since she was dropped off here last night. We were going out to make inquiries in the neighborhood, but before we got on the elevator, we heard a phone ringing from the stairwell. And that's how we found her. I should tell you that I touched her hand. Her, um, left hand. I was trying to see if she was still alive."

Burke glanced over at Dara.

"What's your role here, Ms. Taylor?"

"I'm Kit's assistant."

"And were you both here last night when the victim left?" he asked.

Kit saw Dara swallow hard before answering, and it wasn't hard to grasp why. Burke was the kind of cop, Kit thought, who could make you feel like you'd robbed an armored truck an hour earlier and had just been stopped for questioning at a roadblock.

"No," Dara told him. "I'd left a few minutes before."

"It was just me here at the time," Kit said, and Burke returned his gaze to her. One of his eyes was slightly drooped and hooded more than the other, making it seem as if he was squinting from a waft of smoke, or maybe suspicion.

"My partner and I need to interview you each separately," he announced. "So Ms. Taylor, why don't you sit tight for a few minutes? Is there another room where I could speak to you privately, Ms. Finn?"

"Yes, we can talk in my apartment."

He accompanied her through the doorway, directing her without saying a word toward the couch in her living area. There was an energy around him that was almost palpable, like something muscling her. Be careful, she warned herself again. She couldn't let him drive the conversation anywhere near Miami or Garrett Kelman.

They were barely seated when his partner, Wingate, entered the room and took the other armchair across from the couch. He seemed warmer, friendlier, but she was aware it could be that good cop/bad cop routine she saw at play in TV crime shows.

"Let's start from the beginning," Burke said, fishing a notebook from his suit jacket pocket. "What time did Ms. Howe show and what was the purpose of her visit?"

"She arrived around 6:45," Kit said. "I was aware of the time because she was supposed to show up at 6:30, and I was watching the clock. As I mentioned earlier, she's—she was a client, and she stopped by to pick up several fabric boards. They're in the package lying near her body."

"Does it surprise you that no one saw the body until this morning? Don't tenants here take the stairs?"

"Well, people on two and three sometimes do. But generally not the ones on four or five."

"Why do you think Ms. Howe took them, considering all she was carrying?"

Kit shook her head. "I don't know. There's a chance the elevator was temporarily out of order. That happens sometimes." She was about to add that it was working later that night, but that would necessitate mentioning she'd gone out just before nine. And she didn't want to raise that fact if she didn't have to.

"Did she seem okay to you? Not wobbly or anything?"

"Wobbly?"

"Could she have been drinking before she got here?"

"I doubt it. She'd come from an off-site brainstorming meeting for her company." But as soon as Kit spoke the words, she forced herself to think back, replay the encounter. It would be just like Avery to celebrate the end of a daylong event with wine or champagne, even a tray of margaritas. But from what she recalled, Avery had presented as a hundred percent sober.

"She was a little rushed, but otherwise fine," Kit added. "She said she had a few other stops to make."

"Was she alone?" It was Wingate, speaking for the first time.

"Yes—though she had a car waiting for her," Kit explained. "That's how her assistant knew to call here. The driver reported that she never went back to the car."

"When she left, did you see anyone in the hall?" It was Burke again. "Or hear any noises afterward?"

So was he thinking foul play? she wondered.

"No, nothing like that."

"Does she have a boyfriend, do you know?"

"From what she said, she wasn't seeing anyone."

Burke didn't speak for a few moments, just glanced down at the notes he'd been taking and then back at her, leveling his squinty gaze and holding it there. It made her think of a cat hunched in the grass, watching a little bird bobbing along and calculating when to pounce. She had to fight the urge not to touch her hair or her face or to twitch in her seat.

"How about the two of you?" he said finally.

"Excuse me?" she asked. What was *that* supposed to mean?

"You and Ms. Howe. Everything good with the two of you?"

She almost gasped in surprise. Was he toying with the idea that *she'd* pushed Avery down the stairs? That they'd had a tiff over a fabric choice Kit had made or a charge on the bill, and it had turned physical?

"Yes," she said, trying to keep her voice calm, not defensive. "I was decorating a cottage of hers on the Jersey Shore, and she was a very nice client to work with."

Had it sounded forced? She couldn't tell. Burke just kept staring.

"There's something you should know," Kit added in a rush she regretted. "My apartment was broken into last Friday night. Burglarized. The detective I dealt with is named O'Callaghan—from this precinct."

When they touched base with O'Callaghan—and surely they would—he'd of course raise the Miami incident, but she wasn't going to be the one to bring it up.

Wingate shifted his position ever so slightly. "So are you thinking the guy came back?" he asked. "That he was planning to hit another apartment in the building and then saw a different kind of opportunity when Ms. Howe came out of your apartment?"

"I wasn't thinking anything specific—I just thought you should know, that you might even hear it from Detective O'Callaghan. And there's something else. Avery was wearing my trench coat. She'd borrowed it because it was starting to rain."

They both studied her, and she could sense them summoning a picture of Avery in their minds—her body type, her hair color—and comparing the image to her.

"You thinking someone assumed it was you?" Wingate asked finally.

"I don't know. I just thought I should tell you."

"You got a boyfriend yourself?" Burke said.

"No. No I don't."

"How about a disgruntled ex? Or even a disgruntled client? Anything like that?"

"Nothing like that, no."

It felt as if they were moving around her in smaller and smaller concentric circles, inching closer and closer to the spot she didn't want them to reach. She saw the next question coming before Burke had even opened his mouth.

"And you were here last night? At home?"

"I ran out—at around nine," she said, her breathing growing shallow. "To take a walk. Just for an hour or so. And—and the elevator was definitely working then, by the way."

She'd nearly tripped over her words. Could they sense she was concealing something? She wondered if they'd press her for more details, force her to out-and-out lie.

But the next question was for her phone numbers, and then Burke snapped his notebook shut, done at least for now. The two men rose in unison. She sensed that a message, indecipherable to her, had been telegraphed between the two of them.

"We're going to talk to your assistant now," Burke said. "Why don't you wait in here and we'll be back to you in a bit."

"Okay, but what about Ms. Howe's assistant? Is it okay for me to call her now and tell her the news?"

"Just give me the contact information," Burke said bluntly. "We're the ones who take care of that."

As soon as they'd gone, Kit checked her phone. If it had rung from the kitchen island she would have certainly heard it, but she wanted to be sure. Nothing from Baby or from Kelman. Frustrated, she ran a hand through her hair. She left a second message for Kelman.

She glanced around her apartment. She'd toughed it out here since the burglary, but there was no way she could stay after today. It would be back to Baby's, she decided, grateful that the offer still stood. After grabbing a duffel bag from the closet, she began to toss in clothes and items to cover her for the next few days. Nearly finished, she glanced at her watch. Fifteen minutes had passed. What was taking the cops so freaking long? She wondered how poor Dara was faring.

As she was stuffing a bottle of shampoo into her toiletry bag, she heard a knock on the doorframe. Returning to the living area, she found Burke emerging through the door from the office.

"When you found the body, you just touched the hand?" he asked.

"Yes." Why was he asking that?

"So you never saw the face?"

"No, but I—I'm sure it's her."

"The investigator from the ME's office is going to need you to come back in the stairwell and make an official I.D."

Inside she groaned in protest. This was crazy. At the rate things were going, identifying corpses was going to become a full-fledged hobby of hers.

She nodded solemnly and followed Burke, this time leaving through her own apartment door. There was now a strip of bright yellow caution tape strung across the stairwell doorway and Burke lifted a section with his jacketed forearm so she could duck underneath. On the landing below was a man, dressed from head to toe in white, examining the wall.

As she took her first step on the stairs, a burst of light startled her. Another followed two seconds later. She realized that someone must be photographing the scene. From farther down, on the fourth floor, she could hear people talking in low tones, their words indistinguishable. And then, as if a switch had been flipped, there was silence. She sensed people waiting, expectant. Instinctively she froze in place, one foot hovering above a step. An unseen woman began to speak.

"I'm sure you noted that she fell head first," she said, her voice echoing a little against the stairwell walls. "And it's *very hard* to do that without somebody's help."

So that was it then, Kit thought, fear gushing through her. Avery had been shoved down the stairs.

ered and congealed around the edges. Her eyes were closed. Kit felt a crushing wave of grief.

"Yes, that's Avery Howe," Kit said.

"Thank you," the investigator replied. "I'm sorry for your loss."

As Kit nodded in reply, the door from the corridor pushed open and two people in navy blue coveralls came into sight, holding a stretcher trolley. Behind them was one of the female patrol cops and Kit could hear her talking to someone who was obviously a tenant.

"You need to stay in your apartment for now, ma'am," the cop said. "We'll be coming by door to door to make inquiries."

It was going to turn into a total zoo, Kit realized, and there would surely be press, too.

"You ready for us?" the guy with the stretcher asked the investigator.

"Give me a couple more minutes."

Burke grasped Kit's elbow again and piloted her back up the steps. She felt a sudden wave of nausea—from the smell of sweat in the stairwell, from the thought of Avery's mottled, lifeless face.

"Are Dara and I free to go now?" she asked when she and Burke reentered the corridor on the fifth floor. "I'd prefer not to stay here right now."

"Yes," he said, studying her again, making a silent evaluation. "But we may need to speak to you again as the investigation unfolds."

She nodded and gratefully watched as he retreated once more into the stairwell. Back in the office, Kit found Dara standing with a phone pressed to her ear and three big shopping bags at her feet, two of them already brimming with files.

"Baby," Dara mouthed. Kit motioned for the phone.

"Dear God," Baby said. "Do you think she tripped? That's what Dara said might have happened."

"The cops aren't divulging anything," Kit said grimly. "Let

Kit didn't budge, just stayed there with her foot raised, straining to hear what came next, but the speaker's words were quickly engulfed by the murmuring of other people's voices, everybody talking at once again.

"Here we go," Burke said, his grip on her elbow urging her down the steps. She let him guide her, because all she could concentrate on was what she'd just overheard. Avery hadn't tripped. She'd been pushed. One of the investigators had practically said so. But *why*? Or had the person really meant to hurl *her* down the stairs?

She and Burke reached the fourth floor. Detective Wingate was there, as well as a man taking pictures. Crouched next to Avery's body was a woman, also dressed in one of those white crime scene suits. Kit guessed she was the investigator from the ME's office and clearly the person she'd overheard.

"I'll only need you for a second," the woman said to Kit. "Just to make an official I.D. for me, okay?"

As the woman stepped to the side, Kit saw that Avery's body had been turned over and her face was now in view. The skin was mottled with reds and purples, just like her hands were, and on the left temple was an ugly gash, with dark red blood puck-

me wait and take you through everything in person." She wanted to share the troubling comment she'd overheard in the stairwell but not in front of Dara, not yet anyway. "Are you still okay with me crashing at your place—and can we run the business from there for a bit?"

"Of course. Come as soon as you're able."

"I'll head up there shortly then. I want to be long gone from here before any reporters descend."

"Speaking of press," Dara said after Kit disconnected, "we've already gotten one call. From Channel 7. They seemed to know that Avery was here last night—maybe they heard it from her assistant. I told the woman I wasn't familiar with any details. I figured that was better than, 'No comment,' which sounds like you know stuff but have been told to keep your mouth shut."

"Good girl," Kit said. She paused, thinking. She wanted to know what Burke had asked Dara but a little voice in her head warned her to not come across as overly eager, that it might make Dara uncomfortable. "Did everything go okay with the detectives?"

"Yeah, I guess. I mean there wasn't much I could tell them. They wanted to know what time Avery was expected, what time I split—and whether the elevator was working when I left. I said it was."

"I'm sure she came up in the elevator—she would have mentioned it to me if she'd had to trudge up the stairs. And it was working when I went out two hours later."

Dara grimaced. "There's some other stuff they were asking about—they wanted to know if I talked to you last night after I left here and whether you said anything about your meeting with Avery when I showed up this morning. It was creepy, Kit. They can't possibly think you had anything to do with Avery falling, can they?"

"No, no," Kit said. "They're just being cops, covering all their bases." But she harkened back to Burke's question—"You and Ms. Howe. Everything good with the two of you?" Had they sensed she'd been withholding information and thus become suspicious?

"Oh, I told them about the burglary, too," Dara said. "That was the only other thing we really discussed."

"Yes, I included that, too." She thought suddenly of the call last week from Detective Molinari and wondered if Dara had mentioned that to Burke. Kit guessed that for now at least she hadn't. Dara would err on the side of discretion.

"It seems you're all packed up," Kit added. "Just give me a few minutes to grab my stuff and then we'll split."

As Kit threw the last items into her duffel bag, she tried to piece together what little info she had. For some reason Avery had taken the stairs and then, from the sound of it, been attacked there.

A name came to her with sickening clarity: *Ithaka*. She recalled the two men whom Kelman had mentioned, the ones behind the illegal trade. If they were behind the break-in, they—or whoever they'd hired—might have returned, intent on silencing her this time. And then killed Avery by mistake.

She thought of the error she'd made over the phone with Molinari, hearing words like red hair and blue eyes and just surmising it had to have been X lying in the morgue. It would have been easy for someone in the dim light of her stairwell to see Avery from behind and assume, because of the hair, and the body shape, and the trench coat, that it was her instead.

Avery's killer had probably been hiding on the steps up to the roof and descended as soon as he saw her emerge. It would have taken a few seconds to reach her and that would explain why she was pushed from the landing between the fifth and fourth floors.

But that didn't make sense, she suddenly realized. How would someone know Avery would take the stairs? So maybe the person had actually accosted Avery by the elevator and forced her into the stairwell. Kit tried to summon the moments just after Avery had swept out of her office. She'd been preoccupied then, her attention immediately turned to the meeting ahead with Kelman. And yet if there'd been any kind of altercation in the hallway, she certainly would have heard it. Maybe the assailant had used a gun. A paid killer would have been armed, which would also explain why the wrong person had been targeted—he'd have been working with a photograph or a description. But then why throw his victim down the stairs rather than fire a bullet into her head.

She shuddered, overwhelmed by both remorse and dread. She'd spent the past few days determined to obtain answers, confident she could dig herself out of the hole, but the old questions had been replaced by even scarier ones. Would the killer return once he realized his mistake? Was there any way at all to save herself? It felt as if she'd been sucked into quicksand and was struggling futilely to heave herself above the muck.

She wondered why the hell Kelman hadn't called her back. Though it seemed unlikely that he was the killer—she could still picture the expectant look on his face when she'd arrived at Jacques—there might be other wrongs on his conscience causing him to retreat back into the shadows now. She felt a wave of fury toward him. He'd set it all in motion two weeks ago and now Avery was dead.

But that wasn't the full picture, was it? She'd set it in motion, too, by saying yes to his invitation, by going to bed with him, by picking up a pen that didn't belong to her.

Finally she tugged the zipper on her duffel bag closed and stuffed her new laptop into its carrying case. She threw the bolt on the main door to the apartment and then checked the living space. This was her sanctuary, she thought mournfully, and she was being expelled from it.

When she and Dara emerged from the building, they found that a small crowd of people had already congregated outside, drawn out of morbid curiosity to the official vehicles lined up along the curb and the two patrol cops guarding the front. Miraculously, a free cab sailed by the moment they stepped on the sidewalk and Kit shot her hand up for it. At the other end of the crowd, a guy with a lanyard and name badge around his neck—probably a reporter—spotted them and darted in their direction, running along the perimeter of rubberneckers. But they were in the cab and moving before he could reach them.

They barely spoke on the ride. Dara had withdrawn again, silenced by her bewilderment. The most telling indication of her distress was that she hadn't protested when Kit had volunteered to drop her first and then head to Baby's apartment on her own. Under any other circumstances, Dara would be insisting on helping Kit lug the bags up to Baby's.

"I'll call you in a little while, okay?" Kit said when they pulled up in front of Dara's building. She was trying to sound reassuring but she knew her voice was strained.

"Thanks, Kit," she said, reaching for the door handle. "Oh, by the way, one client called when you were packing, someone I guess you're in the process of signing. Sasha Glen."

That was a surprise. After the abruptness of their meeting last week, she'd suspected she might never hear from Sasha again.

"Did she say why she was calling?"

"Just that she wanted to set up another meeting. I told her you'd be in touch."

"Thanks for letting me know.

But better to leave that one alone. She needed to keep her distance from anything to do with Ithaka.

It took another fifteen minutes to reach Park and 89th Street and by then Kit was ready to jump out of her skin.

Baby hugged her as soon as she'd set all the bags down in

the foyer. It felt good to be comforted and yet at the same time Kit couldn't help but detect a stiffness in Baby's arms. Maybe, she thought, it was simply Baby's nerves betraying themselves, but Kit was still worried that it could actually signal the first inkling of impatience with the nightmare she'd been dragged into. Baby had a brilliant reputation, one she'd burnished over decades, and, despite her imperturbability—her ability to remain unbothered by lying vendors or lard-ass contractors or even a client in the throes of a massive hissy fit—she'd never allow that reputation to be besmirched. A break-in was one thing; a client dying violently at the office was in a category all to itself. There was a good chance this new development would bite them both in the ass, and Baby might not be up for that amount of trouble.

"I sensed you didn't want to say much in front of Dara so tell me everything now," Baby said. She led Kit into the living room, where they both collapsed onto the sofa.

Kit spilled out the story, including the remark she'd overheard from the medical investigator and the fact that Avery had been wearing her trench coat.

"I could have been looking at myself lying there," Kit said, still so distraught at the memory. "And Dara noticed it, too."

"Dear God. So you think someone actually meant to attack *you*?"

"Yes, maybe, and poor Avery ended up dead instead. I mean, it makes no sense that someone would come to the building intent to kill *her*."

Baby's face tightened even more in concern and she tapped her fingers a few times, as if she were urging her thoughts to form.

"Did you end up meeting with that man last night—Garrett Kelman?" she asked after a pause.

"Yes, at around nine, and what he told me plays into Avery's death somehow, I'm sure." She briefly described her conversation with Kelman—the claims he'd made about insider trading at his company and his supposed intention of going to the authorities later in the week.

"I just don't know whether I can believe him," Kit added. "At certain times he seems credible, and yet he's given me no proof that anything he's said about Ithaka or his role in the situation is true. But if he *is* being honest, it means that an Ithaka employee could have killed Avery or sent someone to do it."

"How did he seem to you last night?"

"Weary. Shaken by the news that his pal Healy might have been on the wrong side. I just can't evaluate whether it's the real him or he's putting on an Oscar-winning performance because he needs access to what I know."

"But was he—rattled at all? Frantic?"

"Frantic?" Kit said, at first not understanding, and then she got it. Baby was wondering if Kelman was Avery's killer.

"I know what you're suggesting," she added, "and I've considered it, too. But if he believed he'd just shoved me down a flight of stairs, why hang around in the restaurant for me?"

"To give himself an alibi? He might have assumed you'd told someone you were meeting with him. If the cops tracked him down, he'd be able to say he was waiting for you but you never showed."

"Okay, that's valid," Kit said. "But the whole point of meeting me there was to obtain information he seemed eager for. It doesn't make sense that he'd kill me before getting his hands on it."

Baby looked at her almost imploringly. "What if he actually thinks you know too much at this point? That could make you a liability as far as he's concerned."

Kit rubbed her forehead, thinking. "There are other reasons he's not a good suspect," she said finally. "I was meeting him at nine so why would he start hiding in the stairwell before seven o'clock? And most of all, he knows what I look like. Though Avery bore a resemblance to me last night, I don't think Kelman would have mistaken us."

The last point seemed the best proof of all. She'd been to bed with him, he knew what every inch of her looked like.

"I just hope you're finished having any contact with him," Baby said.

Kit tossed her hands up. "I can't be done just yet. I need to give him an ultimatum, make him go to the police *now*, not later. I don't trust him, but I also don't think he would hurt me. He's had his chances and hasn't taken them."

Baby inhaled deeply, her breasts swelling insider her crisp white blouse, and let out a long sigh.

"What?" Kit asked.

"I worry that this man's got a bit of a hold on you—like the Death Star. You can't help but be drawn in his direction."

For the first time all day, Kit found herself smiling.

"Wait, don't tell me you're a *Star Wars* fan, Baby," she exclaimed.

"Well, in the 80's I certainly was. Though after marrying a scoundrel the first time, I decided to go for men who were more Yoda than Han Solo. But you get my point, Kit. I'm worried this Garrett Kelman fellow has some sway over you. Because of your previous—well, *encounter* with him."

Kit smiled again, wryly. "You mean lust has blinded me?"

"Exactly."

"I swear the only thing I'm interested in right now is rescuing myself from this nightmare. But I don't want to tell the police what I know without any evidence or corroboration from Kelman. Burke already seemed slightly suspicious of me and talking about a mystery man that only I get to see could make it worse."

But she wondered if there could be any truth to what Baby had said. Did she feel some kind of pull from Kelman that she couldn't resist?

"I promise, I'll be extremely careful," Kit added. "For now, why don't we discuss business, before the shit hits the fan on that front. Avery's death is going to be in the news, and it's going to emerge that she'd been at our office."

Baby suggested they strategize over lunch. Kit grabbed a pad and followed Baby to the kitchen, where she took a seat at the hammered metal table by the window. She had little appetite, but she gratefully accepted an iced tea.

"The first thing we need to do is figure out how to handle the press inquiries," Baby said. "I know I said that bad breath is better than no breath at all, but this is the kind of breath that could fell an elephant. We need to enlist a pro to help."

"I agree we have to be smart about this, but a PR person—especially one who does crisis management—isn't going to be cheap. How can we possibly swing that?"

"I have a friend who I think will give us some advice for free. She'll need a room done at some point and I'll make it a barter deal."

Baby also recommended that for the next few weeks they focus on only existing clients or those hovering on the horizon, and not accept any brand-new business. Keeping a low profile, she said, meant less exposure, fewer questions asked.

Kit understood her reasoning, but the strategy troubled her. The firm would be fine for the short-term, but it would mean a dip, perhaps a substantial one, in future revenue. And they'd be dinged by Avery's death. Kit had already invested many hours working on the project and there was no way, in good conscience, for her to collect on that.

"What about the hotel job?" Kit asked. "You wouldn't want

to turn that down, would you? And how do we pay Dara if we don't take new business?"

"The door's already open on the hotel project so if it *does* materialize, we should definitely go for that one. It will pay extremely well, and we'll both have to be involved. As for Dara, we'll just have to watch the budget. There might be a point where we'll need to ask her to go part-time for a while."

Kit groaned. She hated the idea of throwing Dara such a curveball.

"This will blow over eventually," Baby said. "We may just have to lay low for a few weeks."

"Right—as long as nothing else happens." But even as she said the words, she knew she couldn't bank on them. Whoever was wrecking havoc in her life wasn't *done*. "Baby, you don't deserve any of this. If you want out, just say the word, and I'd totally understand."

She meant it, but the idea made her reel. She couldn't help but be reminded of her father, his business unraveling, their life going inexorably to hell with the speed of a bullet train.

"Don't worry, I'm not going to be cowed by any of this," Baby assured her. "But there's one more strategy I'd suggest immediately. We should call all our existing clients."

"And inform them of what's going on?" Kit said, taken aback. That didn't seem shrewd at all.

"No, no, just find an excuse to touch base, demonstrate to them that life is normal. Then when they do learn of this, they'll know we're still business as usual. And some of them may never get wind of it. Not everyone reads the tabloids."

Kit nodded in agreement. While Baby settled in her study, Kit set up her phone and laptop at the mahogany table in the dining room. Before starting to reach out to clients, she checked the office voicemail. She and Dara had decided earlier that rather than have calls to the office forwarded to either of their cell phones—and risk being caught off guard—they would simply check for voicemail messages throughout the day. To her dismay there were half a dozen calls from media outlets about Avery Howe's death. She jotted down the info to pass along to Baby's friend if she came on board.

Next she jumped online. There were already a couple of posted items about the death, one stating that "PR Maven Avery Howe" had died in a mysterious fall and that police were investigating. To her dismay, a *Daily News* post was even more specific. Avery Howe had died "while at the Elizabeth Street offices of Finn-Meadow, an interior design firm she was working with."

She hurried into Baby's study and broke the news.

"I've already spoken to my friend, and she's volunteered to return media calls," Baby said. "She says the best strategy is to appear cooperative, but direct attention away from the firm as much as possible."

"How do we do *that*?"

"She says by giving them a name of someone else to talk to. Like that detective you like so much."

"Perfect," Kit said, pleased at the idea of sending them all Burke's way.

Back in the dining room, Kit took a deep breath and started on client calls, the first to Layla Griggs. The Greenwich Village project was nearly completed so she had no fear of losing it, but she had always banked on Griggs being a good reference and she didn't want to end on anything but a winning note.

"Hi, Layla," she said when she reached her. "I just wanted to check in. The workmen have moved all the furniture back into the bedroom, right?"

"Yes, but the comforter hasn't arrived yet. I thought you said it would be here this week."

"It should have been. Let me investigate. Also, the rug is finally scheduled for delivery next week."

"My husband says they built the pyramids in less time than it has taken for that rug to make an appearance."

Kit forced a laugh. "It does seem like that, doesn't it? But it will definitely be there this week, and then we'll want to focus on adding a few very cool accessories. The icing on the cake."

Big sigh from Layla. "Good."

She tried Holt next. That situation particularly worried her because it was in its early stages. Holt already knew about the break-in and if he learned that a client had died in her stairwell, he might have second thoughts about going forward with her.

An assistant or office manager answered and when Kit gave her name, the woman murmured, seeming to recognize it.

"He's just finishing up with a patient," she added, "but let me check. He may be able to speak to you momentarily." She placed Kit on hold and then came back a moment later. "I'm sorry but he'll have to call you back."

"No problem," Kit said, but she felt a twinge of disquietude. Had she just been blown off? She reassured herself that it was probably her imagination. After all, Holt had probably spent his day dealing with patients, not reading the police blotter.

She phoned the remainder of her clients, finding an excuse to touch base with each of them. No one mentioned Avery's death. But there was a bump of another kind when she spoke to Barry Kaplan, her fifty-something bachelor. After she told him she was busy fleshing out the concept and would have ideas to him shortly, he responded with impatience, the first time she'd heard that from him.

"I thought there'd be something by now," he said.

"I'm so sorry," Kit told him. "I fell a little behind, but you're my top priority now."

Finished, she propped her elbows on the table and let her

chin rest in her hands. Clearly she needed to get her butt into freaking gear. And yet it seemed so pathetic to be shoring up things with clients, protecting her assets, while Avery's body lay in the New York City morgue.

She glanced at the time on her computer screen: 4:21. By now the person or people who had killed Avery must have heard the press reports and recognized their mistake They would be wondering where she was and how to find her, how to remedy their error. She felt her fear spike. But she knew she couldn't let herself be undone by it. The only way to stay safe was to keep her wits about her.

And part of keeping her wits had to be a willingness to face facts. She thought of the point Baby had kept pressing on her: that Kelman could be Avery's killer. She still hadn't heard from him, and that surely said something.

She'd assured Baby that Kelman knew what she looked like, and wouldn't have mistaken Avery for her. But the stairwell was dimly lit, and if Kelman had been hiding on the flight of steps to the roof and had pounced on Avery from behind, he might not have realized it was another woman.

There was something else, she realized. Kelman knew all about her stairwell. He'd hidden there last Sunday, waiting for her to return to her apartment.

And then, as she sat there brooding, her phone lit up. Kelman's number was on the screen.

chapter 17

"What's going on?" he asked, his voice almost hoarse with alarm. "I was scrambling today and just got your message."

"Something horrible. A client of mine died in the stairwell of my building last night."

She let the words just hang there, pressing the phone tight to her ear as she waited for his response.

"*How?* What happened?"

"I found her there this morning, at the base of the stairs. She had a large gash on her head."

She wanted to be vague at first, see how he'd respond.

"But what was she doing in your stairwell?"

"She'd stopped by to pick up a package last night and for some reason she took the stairs down."

"Could she have tripped?"

His tone was natural, authentic seeming. But she knew that was meaningless. He'd once convinced her that his name was Matt Healy.

"No." She waited a beat to drop the bomb, readying herself to gauge his response. "I heard one of the investigators say she must have been pushed. And there's something else. This woman looked a little like me, and she'd borrowed my trench coat before she left."

There was a sharp intake of breath on the other end.

"Please tell me you're not still in the building."

"No, I'm with a friend—at her place."

"Kit, I'm so sorry. This must be awful for you."

"That's the understatement of the century. Not only is my life in danger, but I'm also partly responsible for my client's death—we *both* are. You need to talk to the police as soon as possible and fill in the gaps for them."

"What have you told the police? Did you say anything about Ithaka—or about me?"

Of course that would be his big concern. Her frustration was starting to mount, pricking at her.

"I didn't breathe a word about you or about Ithaka, just about the burglary. But I can't keep withholding evidence from the cops. How will they find the killer if they don't have all the facts? They even asked what kind of relationship I had with my client, as if they were suspicious of *me*. You have to do something."

"You're right, Kit. And I will. It's definitely going to happen by the end of the week."

"That won't work anymore," she exclaimed. "You have to do it before then."

"There's a legitimate reason for the delay. It's one that will protect both of us."

"Are you sure it's not simply because you're the one who pushed Avery down the stairs, thinking it was me?"

There, she'd gotten it out on the table. Even through the phone, she could feel a surge of anger.

"Oh, you're back to me being a homicidal maniac now," he said testily. "I thought we'd established a bit of trust at this point."

"How can I trust you when you won't go to the police?"

"Okay, I can understand how upsetting this must be," he said, calmer now. "Why don't we meet again and I can explain in person. And I want to hear more about this woman's death. That will help me better assess if Ithaka's involved."

"Can't we just discuss this over the phone? I'm all ears right now."

"I think it would help if I actually showed you some of the evidence I've collected against Ithaka. Once you've taken a look at it, you might have an easier time seeing things from my perspective."

She digested his words. If she could *see* something, even just a few shreds of evidence, it would be worthwhile for her. And not just for the trust factor. Because if she ended up having to go to the police on her own, she'd have something to offer besides thin air.

"Where and when?" she asked.

"How about nine tonight. But I don't like the idea of you leaving the building you're staying in. Can I come to you?"

Not on his life. There was no way she was going to let him show up at Baby's.

"That's not going to work. Why don't we meet in a bar or restaurant again. And I could have the doorman hail me a cab so I'm not out on the street flagging one down."

There was a pause. What was he concocting now? she wondered.

"In light of what happened today, it's not smart for us to meet out in the open. I'm staying in a short-term rental in the West Eighties. Do you want to come here?"

An alarm went off in her head, ringing shrilly. But she had to chance it, take him at his word right now and see the so-called evidence. Tonight she needed what Kelman had as much as he needed what *she* had to offer—information about Avery's death.

"Okay," she said finally.

He gave her the exact address but suggested she have the driver let her off at the corner of 84th and Amsterdam, and he would meet her.

"Call me a minute before you reach there and I'll come down. Don't get out of the cab until you see me. And promise me you'll be careful."

There was concern in his tone as well as his words. Or was it just a master manipulator at work?

After ending the call, she set the phone down and leaned back in the chair, thinking. What if Kelman was totally legit? What if, just like her, he had accidentally become ensnared in a dangerous web? But there was also every chance he was a liar, a man calling the shots in an illegal and deadly scheme. She had only his word that he was a whistle-blower. The thought suddenly occurred to her that the flash drive might contain information that incriminated *him* and that's why he'd wanted it back so badly. Maybe he wasn't responsible for Avery's death, but how did she know he hadn't run down Matt Healy?

Earlier she'd decided not to return Sasha Glen's call, and to steer totally clear of anyone from Ithaka. But there might be something to be gained, she realized, from setting up another appointment, and doing it quickly. Though Sasha was a snoop, she seemed to relish dropping tidbits in exchange, and if Kit played it right, she could learn more about Kelman from talking to her—for instance, whether he'd left Ithaka under any kind of black cloud. She'd have a better idea then whether Kelman was dirty or not.

She scooted over to her laptop and typed an email message to Sasha.

"I'd be happy to reschedule our appointment," she wrote. "Do you have any availability this week?"

She'd barely turned away from the computer when a reply popped up.

"Tomorrow at 6:30 p.m. would work for me."

"Perfect," Kit typed back. "I'll plan to stop by then."

It would mean going out again, exposing herself. But Sasha's apartment wasn't all that far from Baby's and she would have the doorman find her a cab, just as she planned to do tonight. And as with her meeting with Kelman, it might just be worth the risk.

She rose from the table, wandered into the living room, and stood in a puddle of April sunlight by one of the windows, staring out at a purple-red brick apartment building across Park Avenue and the improbable strip of blue sky above it. She felt so safe up in Baby's apartment, with not only the doorman and concierge in the lobby but the two guards who stood just at the entrance to the courtyard with its circular drive. She might as well have been in an ivory tower. But she couldn't stay here forever, and she didn't want to. She longed to be back in her own home, her own bed, no longer fearful for her life. She had to figure out how to make that happen.

Lost in thought, she barely heard her phone ring from the dining room. Her heart skipped at the sound. It made her think of Avery's muffled ringtone echoing eerily from the stairwell that morning, beckoning her and Dara toward the gruesome discovery. She dashed back toward the dining room. Keith Holt's name was on the screen.

"Tell me you're okay," were the first words out of his mouth.

"Okay?" she said. Could he have heard about Avery already? Maybe, but she didn't dare let on until she knew for sure.

"My assistant said that a woman was killed in your building." So he *did* know.

"I'm fine, but it was actually a client of mine who died. As you can imagine, we're very upset about it."

"Was it some kind of freak accident?"

"The police are investigating, but we haven't been told any-thing yet."

She knew it was important to seem straightforward, but she had no intention of sharing the information she'd overheard.

"Well, I'm just glad to know you're safe."

"That's very nice of you, Keith. It's been a tough day, but we're coping. The reason I called earlier was to tell you that I had a chance to take a closer look at the clippings you pulled, and I'd love to share my ideas with you when you have a free moment."

"Terrific, and I'd like to hear your thoughts. But I'm going to have to call you in a few days. My schedule has gotten ex-tremely tight this week."

"Of course," she said. "Just shoot me an email when your time frees up."

After they'd exchanged goodbyes, she sighed in dismay. It sounded as if he was pulling back. She tried to tell herself she was overreacting, but up until now he'd seemed more than eager to meet with her at the drop of a hat. There just might be too much drama surrounding her for his taste.

She called Dara next, eager to know how she was holding up. Her boyfriend Scott had come home from work early to spend the day with her and she sounded less shell-shocked. There'd been at least ten more calls from press, she reported, even one from the British *Daily Mail*. Oh wonderful, Kit thought grimly, we're going international. She asked Dara to relay the informa-tion to the PR woman Baby had recruited.

At around six, Kit and Baby met to swap notes. So far, Kit told her, there'd been no confirmed casualties in terms of her clients, but she shared her suspicions about Holt.

"Does it sound to you like he's gotten cold feet?" she asked.

"Not necessarily," Baby replied. "I wouldn't read too much into it just yet."

The question Kit didn't raise with Baby, because there seemed no reason to worry her any more than necessary, was the one that incessantly repeated itself in her mind: What if something *else* happened? How much could their little boutique business endure before clients began to bail?

"How about you?" Kit asked. "Did you end up speaking to everyone you wanted to?" she asked.

"Yes, except the overly bronzed Steven Harper. I thought twice about calling him because, as you know, I don't want to seem too much in pursuit of the business, but I finally decided I'd just phone and inquire how he was feeling after his hypoglycemic attack. I probably should have done that anyway."

"But you never reached him?"

"No. He didn't answer his cell and when I tried his office, there was just a voicemail message from someone I assume is his assistant saying Mr. Harper was unavailable at the moment. I know the hotel is moving along—I drove by the site yesterday to check it out—but he may have been less interested in our firm than he let on."

"There's something else I need to share, Baby," Kit said. "I'm definitely meeting again with Garrett Kelman tonight—at nine. He wants to show me some of the evidence he's accumulated."

Baby sighed loudly. "I'm not going to say anything to try to stop you because I know I can't. But if you aren't back by 10:30, I'll be fit to be tied."

"I promise."

"I mean it, Kit. If you're not, I'm—I'm going to send out a tweet saying you tell all your clients to hang a disco ball above their beds."

Despite how wired she felt, Kit burst out laughing.

At 8:30, she rode the elevator down to the marble lobby and asked the doorman to hail her a cab. A few minutes later one pulled into the courtyard and she nearly leapt inside. As the car crossed Central Park on 85th Street, she glanced nervously behind her. Farther back, at least two car lengths, was a taxi slowly gaining on them, but when they reached Central Park West, the taxi swung left and hers continued straight. She was pretty certain she hadn't been followed.

She texted Kelman right before the cab pulled up to the corner, and as she swiped the card in the taxi's charge machine, she saw him emerge from a building a short way down the block. The second she stepped onto the curb, he took her arm and ushered her up the street. Even through her jacket she could feel the tension in his grip.

Reaching the small, non-doorman building, he hurried them both inside. The lobby was empty, except for the Mexican take-out menus strewn across the floor. He motioned her toward the elevator and jabbed at the call button. Gone tonight, she saw, was his black Ninja look. Instead he was in blue jeans and a navy V-neck pullover sweater, with a triangle of bare skin showing on his chest. It was hard to imagine that once she had touched that skin, run her hands over it urgently, and tasted it with her mouth.

The elevator arrived a minute later, announcing itself with a metallic creaking sound, and as she stepped into the tiny space ahead of Kelman, her heart beat nervously. He pressed the button for the third floor. They were standing so close she could see all the freckles on his face. She could smell something citrusy, too—a cologne perhaps, or maybe just the soap he'd showered with.

The apartment turned out to be a small one-bedroom. The décor was Japanese in flavor—sparely designed furniture, polished wood floors, and a sliding shoji door with translucent screen panels, behind which Kit assumed was a bedroom. How incongruous, she thought, to be standing in a Zen-like space when her life was in shambles.

She saw Kelman relax a little as soon as he had the door

locked behind them. But she didn't let herself relax. She needed to be on guard, keep an eye on him.

"Anything to drink?" he asked.

"No, nothing."

"Not even a cup of green tea?" he said with a faint smile. "I feel I should offer you that along with a bowl of edamame."

She shook her head. He was trying to establish a rapport between them, but all she wanted was to get to the business at hand.

"Let's sit down then," he said, gesturing toward the sofa.

It was long and Japanese style, built low to the ground on a simple wooden platform. She took a seat at one end, and Kelman settled at the other one. Scanning the room quickly, she saw that there were no possessions in sight, nothing at least that seemed to belong to Kelman. She realized he'd probably stashed his belongings away in the bedroom, mindful of what had happened in Islamorada.

"You said you had something to show me," she said.

"I do. I think it will help for you to see it. But tell me about your client first. I need to assess whether Ithaka was behind it."

He listened intently as she gave him the broad outlines. That was all he was getting for now. A couple of times as she spoke, Kelman looked off, his eyes narrowed, as if he were trying to fit pieces together.

"Is it at all possible that someone your client knew actually killed her?" he asked when she finished. "Like an ex-boyfriend? Or a disgruntled employee?"

Kit shook her head dismissively. "She probably wasn't a breeze to work for, but people seemed to respect her. And she told me she hadn't dated anyone significant in at least six months."

As she spoke, Kit felt something snag in her mind and then let go, like a sleeve caught momentarily on a piece of brush. What was it? she thought. But she couldn't retrieve the thought.

"I'm just trying to cover every base," he said.

"The base I need to cover right now is that there was no reason for anyone to show up at my building to kill Avery. But there does seem to be a motive for people to want *me* dead. In the dim light of the stairwell, Avery could have easily been mistaken for me."

Kelman crossed his arms, exhaling.

"It does sound like you may have been the intended target," he conceded. "And Ithaka could be responsible, just as they may be behind Healy's death. As I told you, these cases don't usually involve violence, but the conviction rates are high and they may want to guarantee it never comes to trial. Since they couldn't find the flash drive at your place, plan B was to kill you."

"And by now they must know that they killed the wrong person," she said. "Will they try again?"

"I've no clue, Kit. I assume it's possible. But it depends somewhat, I'd guess, on who the hell is doing this. If it's one of the two traders—Kennelly or Lister—going rogue and killing people in a panic, they may realize that the more havoc they create, the greater the chance of it pointing to them. So they may decide it's best to back off, at least for now. But if it's some kind of hired killer, I doubt he'll panic."

"Oh, brilliant." Without warning, she felt anger overtake her fear. She'd done nothing wrong, nothing at all, and yet people were coming after her. There was no way she was going to sit around like a total wimp waiting to see what their freaking plan *C* turned out to be.

"How do you know for sure that she was pushed?" Kelman asked. "The news items I read said it hadn't been determined."

"I've shared enough. I'd say it's your turn now."

"Fair enough."

He hoisted himself off the couch, crossed the room, and slid open the shoji screen. There was an aspect to the gesture that seemed to be out of a movie. A door sliding open. A revelation about to occur. But could she believe it? she wondered.

As she'd expected, on the other side of the door was a bed-room, one as sparsely furnished as the living area—a simple dresser and a duvet-draped mattress on a low, wooden platform. Kelman opened a closet and from deep inside pulled out a black knapsack. He walked back to the couch and this time sat within inches of her. He unzipped the main area of the knapsack.

"Here," he said, tugging out a sheaf of papers. "Let me take you through parts of this."

He started with the spread sheet on top, a list, he said, show-ing trades made by Lister and Kennelly. He dragged his finger down, explaining their significance. There were also several printouts of news stories. They reported on the disappointing results of tests on a highly anticipated drug meant to treat leuke-mia. As she listened to Kelman talk, she had a glimpse again of the confident, self-assured man she'd met in Florida.

"You've got clear links to Lister and Kennelly," Kit said. "What about Wainwright? Do you think he's involved?"

He shook his head. "That's what Healy was supposed to be digging into. My assumption is that Mitch *is* involved. As they say, a fish rots from the head down. At the very least, he must have been suspicious when he became aware of these trades and the killing the firm made. But that doesn't mean he's in legal danger himself. It's getting harder and harder to prosecute someone too many steps removed from the action. But still, he'd want to protect the firm's reputation, and make sure no one had a reason to incriminate him "

He took the pages from her and stuffed them back into the backpack. If it was all a sham, she thought, he'd gone to elabo-rate lengths to fool her. So maybe it *was* the truth.

"So is that one of the reasons you're delaying going to the SEC?" she asked. "Because you're still trying to find proof of Wainwright's involvement?"

"No, I have no way of doing that anymore. It'll be up to the authorities. It's what I told you the other night—I've switched strategies. The lawyer I'm working with has advised going to the U.S. Attorney's office rather than the SEC. Things will move much faster that way."

"There's a financial incentive to going to the SEC, isn't there? Does that hold true this way, too?

"No, but I don't care. That's not what this is about for me."

Interesting, she thought

"So you're going Friday?"

"Yup. At the latest Monday."

"*Monday?*"

"Only if the right person isn't available to meet with me on Friday."

She rose from the couch and dragged her hands through her hair.

"I can't believe this. It's an ever-moving target. Every time I speak to you, you're going on a different day."

"Kit, I know it's a very scary situation. But this is the smartest approach, for both of us. They'll move against Ithaka more quickly."

"It's not just Ithaka that worries me. It's the police. I'm withholding information from them."

"You're going to have to do your best to keep them at bay until Monday. And you're also going to have to be extremely careful. For now, don't leave the apartment you're staying at. After this, we can speak by phone."

His warning made her fear spike again. She glanced at her watch. It was almost ten.

"I should go," she said, "before it gets any later."

"Let me just put this stuff away, and I'll find a cab for you. Would you be open to me taking you home?"

"That's not necessary." The evidence he'd presented had

added to his credibility, but there was no way she was going to let him see where she was staying.

He started toward the bedroom and then pivoted, catching her gaze and holding it.

"I'm going to fix this, Kit. I promise."

She nodded, not in agreement, but just acknowledging the comment. He turned back and continued into the bedroom, slipping behind the screen.

Maybe he *would* fix it. She wanted desperately to believe that. Though there was one thing she knew for sure: he'd never be able to fix what had happened to Avery.

Avery. An image rushed Kit again. She could see the ugly gash on Avery's head, the mottled skin of her face and hands. And then Kit's mind was snagging on something again, but this time it didn't tear away so quickly.

"You know, there's a detail about Avery's death that completely confuses me," she called into the bedroom. "Why did she take the stairs?"

"What do you mean?" Kelman said from behind the partially open screen.

"The elevator was working that night." She stepped closer to the bedroom so he could hear. "Avery clearly came up on it and I rode it down later when I went out to see you. Someone could have forced her to the stairs, but I probably would have picked up the sound of any commotion in the corridor."

She peered behind the screen. Kelman was just closing the closet door and reading a text on his phone simultaneously. He looked up, surprised by her presence, and tucked the phone back into his jeans pocket.

"Sorry," he said. "I was just nudging my lawyer in light of everything we've talked about. . . . Doesn't your elevator have one of those emergency stop buttons?"

She bit her lip, thinking, "Yeah, it does."

"The killer might have taken the elevator to another floor, stepped out, and pulled the button, so it was temporarily out of commission. Avery would have been forced to use the stairs to go down. And then by the time you left, another tenant could have discovered the problem and undone it."

"So the killer must have thought I was leaving for the evening."

"Possibly. Or he might have been planning to lure you out somehow if you hadn't."

He started to close the screen, which resisted a little on the track. This wasn't his apartment, after all, and he wasn't familiar with the kinks. What had these past weeks been like for *him*? she wondered.

"Does anyone in your life know where you are?" she asked.

"Other than you and my lawyer? No. And it's been bizarre moving around the city, trying to be incognito. I feel like a character in a movie, someone people assume has been murdered but is really alive and has snuck back to try to figure out who wanted to kill him."

"What about friends? Aren't they worried about where you are?" She was curious to see how he'd respond, what it might reveal about him.

"When I left New York, I told friends I was going off the grid for a while, just trying to figure out my next move after Ithaka, so no one's expecting much contact. And as I told you in Florida, I'm not involved with anyone romantically."

"Family?"

"My sister's pretty much it, and she knows the bare outlines of what's going on. After Healy was killed, I paid for her to head out to California for a few weeks."

"It must be hard, living like this."

He smiled ruefully. "It's no picnic. I'm a person of interest in a homicide and the people who want you dead surely have the same agenda for me. But I'm not comparing my predicament to yours. I'm truly sorry for all I've put you through."

Ahh, an apology. On the surface at least it sounded heartfelt. She started to move toward the front door, buttoning her coat.

"Well, once you go to the authorities, things will begin to turn around, won't they?" she said, her back to him now. "You can go back to your old life."

He came up behind her and turned her around toward him. She felt an electric jolt at his touch.

"One way or the other, my life is never going to be the same again," he said. "I knew that when I decided to expose the illegal trades. But my situation is different than yours. You *will* be able to go back to your old life, Kit. It may just take time."

She said nothing, but he must have detected a look in her eyes.

"What?" he said. "Do you not believe that, or is something else on your mind?"

"It's just, I don't know—I love my work, and I want that to thrive. But as for my personal life, I don't actually want to go back to the way it was."

"Because?"

"Remember when I came around the corner and saw you talking on the phone at the hotel? You said something I couldn't get out of my mind: 'I'd rather have a few regrets than none at all.' I want to live my life that way for a change."

"Right, I was talking to Matt then. Is that why you were willing to go to bed with me? Because you didn't care if there'd be a few regrets?"

"Not exactly," she said. "That night I was hoping there *would* be no regrets, that it was something I'd always be glad I'd done."

Catching her by surprise, he reached up and cupped her

cheek. She didn't flinch, just stood there, finally allowing her face to settle into his hand. He leaned forward and kissed her, softly at first but then more urgently, his mouth seeming to devour her. She let her body relax into his and kissed him back, giving in to the sheer pleasure of it, and hoping she wouldn't regret it.

chapter 18

Baby was waiting up for her, dressed in a padded, blue silk robe and slippers and sporting, to Kit's surprise, a head full of pink sponge rollers.

"It's 10:37," Baby said, hurrying into the foyer. "I was *this* close to sending out that disco ball tweet. And then I was going to do another saying you recommend that every kitchen have a row of rooster figurines."

Kit smiled. "Sorry to be late, but I had a chance to see some of the evidence he has against his old company."

"And?"

"It reassured me a little—though not completely."

She recounted the meeting with Kelman, leaving out the part about the kiss. She didn't want to think about that at the moment—the feel of his mouth on hers, the way she had kissed him back before finally pulling away.

"Do you really buy his reason for waiting?" Baby asked when she was done.

"I'm not sure. I mean, maybe. As of right now, the things he's told me add up. Of course, looking at all those trading records was about the same as me trying to read Sanskrit. I had to take his word for most of it."

"You'll go to the police after he's approached the U.S. Attorney's office?"

"Yes, and I've been considering what you said about me hiring a lawyer. I *do* need one. I have a lot of 'splaining to do, as they say."

"You have to find someone really good, a criminal lawyer."

"I know, but the only lawyer I've ever used is the woman who helped me when I started my business. Offering guidance during a homicide investigation isn't quite the same as helping someone set up an LLC."

"Let me ask around, okay? My attorney doesn't handle criminal—and he's about as ancient as Matlock—but he's in a big firm and there may be someone there you can use."

Kit cringed, thinking of the expense, of the need to reach deep into her savings. But she didn't have a choice. Her life was on the line.

They turned in after that. Kit was too exhausted to even change into nightclothes so she just stripped down to her underwear and the T-shirt she'd worn under her sweater, and crawled into bed.

She lay in the dark for a while, listening to the spring wind rattle the windows. She thought of the kiss again. Part of her regretted letting down her guard, and yet she couldn't deny how strong the urge had been to reciprocate. And on the way home in the cab she'd realized that the desire had not just been physical. Despite the fact that she couldn't fully trust Kelman, she felt drawn to him. Not Death Star drawn to him the way Baby had suggested, but *something*. He absorbed what she said, seemed to read her mind at times, seemed to *get* her.

She thought for a while about what she'd confessed to him. It was utterly true, not just words spoken in the drama of the moment: she didn't want to return to her old life. As much as she was still reeling from Avery's death, and from Healy's, as well, those events had woken her up, forced her to be more aware, made her take charge. That didn't place her in the same league as the kind of badass, ruby-lipped characters Angelina Jolie played in movies, but she didn't feel like Miss Goody Two Shoes anymore.

She'd come to realize, too, that she was stronger under adversity than she would have anticipated, and the potential to be so may have been there all along. She didn't have a single regret about the career path she'd chosen, but she could see now that if she'd really wanted to attend college, she could have pulled it off somehow. The reason she hadn't was that she'd lost her nerve, curled up in a ball. There was no way she'd let that happen again.

From sheer exhaustion, she fell asleep more quickly than she had in many nights.

She was up by six, roused by a dream she couldn't recall. After showering and dressing, she made her way to the kitchen and dropped a piece of bread in the toaster. A few minutes later Baby strolled in. If she was feeling overwhelmed by everything, she was doing her best not to show it. And thanks to the rollers, her head was now a crown of champagne blond curls.

"I spoke to Dara and she's coming at ten," Baby said. "Since you're cooped up here, why don't you use her to do as much shopping as possible?"

"There's only so much I can delegate to her. I need a few small items to finish off the Greenwich Village apartment, but they have to be absolutely perfect."

"What about Barry the Bachelor's pad? I thought you were behind on that. Could Dara shop for that?"

"Yes, but I don't even have a concept for him yet. How *is* Dara, anyway?"

"As we know, Dara's a trooper, but I could sense from her voice that she's still quite upset, and not just about Avery. I explained to her that we were concentrating on only existing clients at the moment, and I'm sure she's worried her job is in jeopardy."

"I can't let it be."

But that wasn't all that concerned Kit in relation to Dara. She regretted withholding so much from her. She'd been trying to protect Dara, but all the mystery had only added to her assistant's anxiety. And even worse, every day Dara worked with Kit she was in some ways vulnerable, just like Baby.

Kit set herself back up in the dining room and checked online for any updates regarding Avery's death. The story seemed to be everywhere now. Avery's PR business had serviced just enough boldface name clients for her death to warrant coverage with the kind of hysterical tone usually afforded to cheating politicians or celebrity butt-crack sightings. Most of the press items now pointed out that Avery had died leaving the office of Finn-Meadow. And the most recent ones contained a chilling detail: the police considered the death a possible homicide.

Kit had suspected that even before she'd overheard the investigator, but seeing it confirmed made her heart skip.

Glumly, she checked email next, something she'd neglected to do last night. There was a frantic email from her friend Amy saying she'd heard the news and had tried to reach her several times to no avail. There was a message from Chuck, as well: "WTF. Are you OK? Call me right away." She quickly emailed her friends back, reassuring them she was fine and would be in touch when she had the opportunity.

For a moment Kit wondered if she should give her parents a heads up. Though they could hardly be categorized as Internet surfers, they did go online at times, and there was a chance they would stumble on the story. But she decided to chance it and not breathe a word. In the years since her father's bankruptcy, their protectiveness of her had mushroomed, and if she shared the story with them, they'd be totally wigged out. They'd probably plead with her to flee the city with a U-Haul.

Next she tried to focus on work, particularly on fleshing out a plan for Barry. She felt hopelessly stalled, unable to conjure up a viable concept for his place. Baby's suggestion came to mind. She decided that she would have Dara spend part of the day at the D&D building, gathering as many fabric samples as possible. Maybe seeing a ton of swatches would get her creative juices flowing.

Dara arrived shortly afterward and sat at the table with her, agreeably taking notes for the fabric-scouting mission and asking a few follow-up questions. But Kit could sense how fraught she was inside, still shaken from yesterday and surely wondering why Kit wouldn't be doing any of the legwork for Barry. It seemed like the right moment to come clean with her.

"Dara," Kit said, leaning forward, elbows on the table. "I need to be more honest with you than I have been. I know you've sensed lately that there's been more going on than meets the eye, and you're right. Since I got back from my first trip to Florida, it appears that someone has been under the impression—totally false—that I have information that could possibly send them to prison. I'm pretty sure that's why the office and my apartment were broken into. And it may be why Avery ended up dead. Someone apparently pushed her."

Dara looked stricken. "But—what *kind* of information? What could anyone possibly think you know?"

"I'll tell you at some point, but right now I just need you to be aware of what the stakes are. There's a decent chance these people will be apprehended soon, and yet there's no guarantee of that. There's even the possibility of more trouble."

"Okay," Dara said, bobbing her head a little, as if keeping time with her thoughts. "And thank you for telling me. You know how loyal I am to you and Baby, but I probably should give this some thought. Scott is worried about me, and so are my parents."

"Totally understood," Kit said, but she was even more disconcerted now. Was Dara thinking of quitting?

"In fact, do you mind if I leave a little early today?" Dara asked. "My parents want to meet with me after work."

As Kit nodded in consent, Dara's request triggered a memory: her six-thirty meeting with Sasha. She'd arranged it to see if she could gather as many crumbs as possible on Kelman, but seeing the evidence last night had ratcheted up her fear about leaving the apartment. It seemed too risky to venture out just for crumbs. She decided to call and cancel, promising to rearrange the appointment at a later time. That way it would still be an option for the future if necessary.

Sasha picked up her cell phone on the second ring.

"I've been planning to get in touch," Sasha said, "but it's been crazy here. . . . *really* crazy."

Crazy *how*? Kit wondered. She wanted to know, but if she were going to troll for information, she would have to proceed cautiously.

"I'm sorry to hear that. I bet you're always under a lot of pressure there."

"It's not the pressure that's bothering me," Sasha said, her voice hushed. "I'm used to that. It's the mood. The gloom here is so thick you could cut it with a knife."

"Is it because of Matt Healy?" Kit asked, trying to keep her tone casual. "I'm sure people are still upset about his death."

"Partly. You knew him, of course. I assume this hasn't been easy for you either."

How many times did she have to explain to the woman that she *hadn't* known Healy? Was Sasha just toying with her to elicit information herself?

"I'd actually met him only once, but still, it was disturbing to hear about his death. . . . You said 'partly.'"

"Excuse me."

"You said all the craziness was only partly due to Matt's death."

"What I meant was that it's not just that he died but *how* he died. Being murdered."

"Do the police have any leads yet?"

"Possibly."

"What do you mean?

"I can't really say any more at the moment. Are we still on for tonight?"

How could she *not* go now? Sasha clearly knew more than she'd just revealed and if Kit could worm it out of her, it might prove valuable to Kelman, and therefore to her in the long run.

"Of course, that's why I was calling. I just wanted to verify the time."

"I need to make it 7:30 instead of 6:30."

"Not a problem."

"And I need to do it downtown, near Wall Street. I've got a late appointment down there. Why don't we meet at a place called Harry's Bar on Hanover Square?" Not good. Wall Street would place her way out of any safety zone.

"But—I have to see your apartment," Kit insisted. "I only got a peek at the living room the other night."

"There's really nothing more to see. The two bedrooms are as bare as everything else. What we need to do now is talk about a game plan. We can do it over a drink. Now, I really do need to go."

Kit was sure that if she tried to change the location, she'd blow the opportunity.

"Fine. I'll see you then, Sasha. I'm looking forward to it."

She set the phone down and let out a shaky breath. Sneaking over to an apartment building on the Upper East Side was one thing, but an expedition all the way downtown was another entirely. She wasn't second-guessing her decision—there was stuff

Sasha knew and Kit had to lay her hands on it—but the idea of traveling so far away scared her.

Baby was still out at an appointment when Kit departed—and Dara had long since gone home—so she left a note saying she had an important matter to take care of and would see Baby around nine. Dismissing any need to impress Sasha this time, she dressed as nondescriptly as possible: a black velvet blazer, jeans, and boots.

Once again the doorman set out to flag down a taxi for her, but it took longer this time, probably because she was leaving toward the end of rush hour. As she paced the lobby waiting, she chided herself for not factoring that in. She was going to be at least ten minutes late, and Sasha was the type who might decide not to wait.

Finally the doorman came trotting toward her, announcing that the cab was just outside. She thanked him and nearly flung herself into the back seat. As they headed east and then south, Kit turned to look out the rear window. No sign of any kind of tail.

Surprisingly the FDR wasn't backed up, and the city flew by, a rush of lights and towering buildings against an inky blue-black sky. They exited at South Street, and the driver maneuvered his way farther west and then into the dark, foreboding canyons of the Wall Street area.

"Here we go," the driver said at last. After swiping her credit card, Kit peered out the window. The building was Renaissance style, probably constructed over a hundred years before, and she could see that the bar and restaurant were one flight down, in the basement.

She stepped outside, taking a split second to get her bearings. Though the address was Hanover Square, the building was actually on the corner of Stone Street, and she realized suddenly that she had been here once before several years ago. Not this restaurant but one down on Stone Street. In the summer, the taverns on the block set out rows of wooden tables that were always packed at night with people in their twenties and thirties, and she had sat there one night with friends, drinking beer and eating hamburgers, and simply people watching. Right now it was hard to imagine ever having another night like that.

She quickly descended the steps in front of her and swung the door open, anxious to be inside. Though the adjoining restaurant looked spacious, the bar itself was small, with low ceilings and brick walls painted a metallic color, gold-like and glistening. Votive candles twinkled on the tables and on the dark wooden bar. She spotted Sasha immediately, perched on a stool and looking almost preternaturally still, cradling a martini glass the size of a hot tub. As Kit approached, Sasha caught the movement and raised her chin ever so slightly in greeting.

She also gave Kit's outfit a quick once-over. But Kit couldn't care less. She had come only for dirt and was determined to leave with it.

"My week so far demanded a martini, extra dry," Sasha said as Kit slid onto a stool next to her. "How about yours?"

That was funny, Kit thought. If she were relying on that calculation, there wouldn't be enough gin in the bar to make all the martinis she was due.

"I think I'll just have a sparkling water," she said and gave her order to the bartender.

"Suit yourself. Thank you, by the way, for coming downtown. I have to meet up with some people in Brooklyn Heights after this so I knew I wouldn't have time to go back to the Upper East Side beforehand."

"I imagine you're in this area a fair amount during the week, because of your work."

Sasha took a long, slow sip of her martini before answering. She was in black pants again, today with another gorgeous silk blouse, this one fir green. Her large emerald earrings matched it perfectly. Kit realized for the first time how deliberate and restrained the woman's movements always were. There was nothing wasted, no nervous gestures or self-pacifiers—like brushing her hair back or touching a hand to her throat.

As Sasha set her martini down, her eyes briefly resting on the bar top, Kit glanced quickly behind her and scanned the room. She wanted to make certain no one new had come in since she'd arrived.

"One would think that, yes," Sasha said, looking at her again, "but most of the big financial firms have moved uptown, and I'm actually down here very little. Tonight was unavoidable, though. Some of my colleagues and I had a big powwow with a fund of funds we're hoping to do business with."

"I hope it was worth the trip."

"We'll have to see. A few people stuck around for some post-meeting chitchat and I'll have to catch up with them tomorrow and hear their take."

On the drive downtown Kit had warned herself again not to pounce on Sasha, that the woman relished cat-and-mouse play in conversation and if she came on too strong, Sasha would shut down. But here was a small opening and she decided to grab it.

"I'm sorry things have been tough at work."

"Tough?"

"You mentioned it on the phone earlier. That the mood there had been bad. Gloomy, you said."

"Oh yes, *that*."

Sasha let the word hang there. Okay, here we go with the kitty-cat tactics, Kit thought with irritation.

"It sounded from what you were saying on the phone that there might be a suspect in Matt Healy's death."

"I'm not sure. But there's *something* going on. Lots of closed doors. I assume it involves the police investigation."

"Do—"

"Oh, here's your bubbly water," Sasha interrupted as the bartender delivered Kit's drink. "I shouldn't have been indulging before you had it. That was rude of me."

Sasha had deliberately dropped the topic and Kit was reluctant to press any more right then. She told herself to switch gears and circle back later. There was something Sasha knew, Kit was dead certain, and she had to find a way to extract it.

"That's not a problem," Kit said. "So tell me about your apartment. It's a nice big space. Was there a decorating fantasy in the back of your mind when you bought it?"

"Nothing specific. I mean, that's why I'm talking to you, isn't it?"

"Of course. But it's important to start with what works for *you*—colors you like, the type of furniture, the vibe. And you don't have to have a grand scheme in mind, just a starting point. Maybe there's a home in a movie you found captivating. Or a hotel you can't get out of your mind. One client of mine started with just a piece of fabric she'd brought back from India."

"Well, as you saw, the apartment's modern. I definitely want to work with that, not fight it."

"Good. It can be interesting sometimes to go against the grain, but it's much simpler not to. Tell me about your last place. What did you like and not like? It can be helpful to consider what *doesn't* work for you."

"It was a duplex in a brownstone, my reward to myself after my career took off. But by the time I'd lived there five years, I'd been on one too many buying binges. There was just too much stuff, and it felt awfully, I don't know, *girlie* all of a sudden."

"Ah," Kit said. "And you'd like to get away from that."

"To be perfectly honest, it's partly because of a guy." Sasha had plucked the plastic toothpick from her drink, the one plunged through the chubby green olive, and she swished it slowly several times through the gin. The type of unnecessary movement she didn't usually make. "I've been seeing someone for a while—someone quite special—and I sensed he felt too cramped in the brownstone with all my girlie junk. I wanted a place we both would be comfortable in."

It surprised Kit to think that Sasha would acquiesce that way for a man. But maybe she didn't view her decision as acquiescence, just the outcome of a negotiation, like the kind she probably engaged in regularly at work.

"He's a fan of modern?" Kit asked.

"Yes, very much. In fact, he creates modern sculptures in his spare time. These gorgeous copper pieces."

A sense of dread overpowered Kit before the memory had fully unfurled. But then there it was: Kelman at the table in Islamorada describing the copper sculptures he loved to make.

"Well, it's nice you found a partner who's so creative," she said, trying to keep her breathing even. "How—how did you two meet?"

"This is *entre nous*, right? We actually met at work—another portfolio manager."

Was Kelman Sasha's *lover*? Maybe it was some bizarre coincidence.

"So you two have to be very discreet at the office, I would guess," Kit said.

Sasha lifted her fir-green shoulder, barely a shrug.

"Actually, he left the firm a month ago. He wants to shift careers, and he's been taking time off to figure it out."

There was hardly room for doubt now. Her fears about Kelman, the ones she'd longed to let go of, had been confirmed. He'd claimed he wasn't involved with anyone, but he was a brazen liar about that and probably more. She felt both fury and despair.

"What's his name?" Kit asked. She needed to be sure.

"Oh, it's probably best for me to stay mum." She smiled coyly. "Though as far as I know, you might have met him through Matt. They were buddies."

Why did the woman insist on playing this sick game, constantly suggesting she'd known Healy? Perhaps Sasha was even in collusion with Kelman.

"I told you," Kit snapped. "I didn't know Matt Healy." She grabbed her purse and nearly tore it open. "I'm really sorry, but I have to go."

As she fished for her wallet with one hand, she signaled for the bartender with the other.

"Right *now*?" Sasha asked. "What about the apartment. Don't you want to discuss it anymore?"

"Modern's not really my thing. You really should find someone else."

"What? But on your website . . ." Her gaze suddenly shifted to a spot past Kit's shoulder. "Oh, my. We have an Ithaka contingent arriving. They must have just finished up."

Kit swiveled around. To her shock, Mitch Wainwright was sauntering toward the bar. There was a jolt of recognition in his eyes when he registered her presence.

"I see you had the same idea we did," Wainwright said, nodding toward Sasha's martini when he reached them. There was another man with him—tall, dark haired, probably mid-thirties, dressed in a suit but no tie. Not someone she recalled seeing from her visit to the main floor of Ithaka.

"Progress?" Sasha asked Wainwright as he reached the bar.

"Yes, I think so. We thought we'd grab a bite of dinner in the restaurant here."

"I believe you know Ms. Finn," she said, glancing at Kit. "We've been discussing a potential decorating project."

He turned to Kit and burrowed into her with his copper penny eyes.

"Is that right?" he said. Beneath the slick charm of his tone was a hint of menace.

Kit didn't say anything, just nodded.

"And have you two met yet?" Sasha asked, indicating the stranger. She didn't wait for an answer. "This is another of our portfolio managers, Gavin Kennelly."

Kit's heart seemed to freeze in her chest as she processed the name. Kennelly was one of the two men Kelman had told her about. One of the two men who probably wanted her dead.

chapter 19

Kennelly narrowed his eyes, taking her in. Then he nodded in greeting. The longer he stared at her, the more his gaze hardened. And though she wasn't looking at Wainwright now, she could feel him studying her.

Kit slid off her bar stool. She needed to get out of there *now*.

"Don't rush off on our account," Wainwright said. "Let me buy you ladies a second round."

"I have to go now," Kit said. "If you'll excuse me."

As she started across the room, she remembered the warning she'd once heard about dealing with a threatening dog. Don't *run*. If you run, you will only provoke the dog even more, tipping it off that you're terrified, and then it will give chase, drag you to the ground, and tear you limb from limb.

So she walked as calmly as possible, yanked open the door, and mounted the stairs to the street without ever looking back.

But as soon as she stepped onto the sidewalk, the fear that she'd momentarily kept at bay broke free, nearly knocking her over.

She wondered if the whole evening had been nothing more than a set-up, with Sasha commissioned to entice her into the bowels of Manhattan, within striking distance of Wainwright and Kennelly.

And yet that idea didn't really fit. Wainwright had seemed stunned to see her. But coincidence or not, he knew where she was now and so did Kennelly.

She darted away from the entranceway of the bar, so that she couldn't be seen from inside, and looked anxiously up and down the street. There were no cabs in sight, not even many pedestrians. That meant the subway. She was going to have to hightail her way through the crazy labyrinth of streets down here and find the Wall Street station.

She barely knew the area, but she thought she could reach Wall Street by heading north. But the subway stop was farther west, where Wall met Broadway. Turning left on Stone Street seemed like the fastest option. Plus there were two people up that way, puffing on cigarettes in front of one of the taverns.

She took off in that direction. The two smokers stepped inside and she was alone on the street. She moved faster. Before long Stone came to an abrupt end with no apparent sign for the street running perpendicular. Smack in front of her was a large office building with a sunken plaza.

She swung right and she saw that this street quickly ended too, at a hulking parking garage. She'd turn left at the next intersection, she decided. She was pretty sure that was west and that she'd soon end up on Broadway, close to the subway stop.

And then behind her, she heard a footfall. She twisted around. No one. She picked up her speed. A few seconds later she was certain she heard the scrape of a shoe on pavement and she turned again, this time not even stopping. The street looked deserted. Were her nerves playing tricks on her?

Now, almost running, she reached the intersection. There wasn't a soul in sight, not even an attendant at the garage. Crap, she thought. And then she heard footsteps once more.

When she spun around this time she spotted him. A tall, slim figure far enough behind her that she couldn't see the face, but from the outline of his body in the dark, he appeared to be dressed in a suit. Was it *Kennelly*? she wondered, her heart pounding even harder. As she stared down the street, he stepped down into the dark maw of that the sunken plaza.

She started to really run, plunging left at the intersection, her shoulder bag slapping against her body. She'd been crazy to ever come down here.

Finally up ahead she saw a small cluster of people discharging from an office building, people working late and rushing to get home. With her lungs searing, she closed the gap and sidled up to an older black woman, dressed in a denim blazer with a soft leather briefcase.

"Excuse me," Kit said, nearly breathless. "Am I headed the right way for the Wall Street subway stop?"

"Yes, it's just two or three blocks away," the woman told her, pointing loosely.

"Thank you so much," she said, ready to cry in relief.

Another glance behind her. There was no sign now of the man in the suit. She rushed along the street and made the next right, trying to hug tight to the people who'd just left the building. Soon, though, the group splintered—two men crossing the street, another man moving quickly west, and the woman with the briefcase jumping into a car that was waiting for her.

Kit started to run again. And then, checking back once more, she noticed the car, a small black limo nosing up the street behind her. Something about the movement triggered an alarm. The car was moving slowly, but deliberately, like a predator inching through high grass. Suddenly it edged to the side of the road and stopped, just yards from her.

It was *them*, she realized. Before she could turn away, the rear door by the sidewalk swung open and a man slid out.

The streetlight was behind him and she couldn't make out the face at first, but there was no mistaking the barrel chest. It belonged to Mitch Wainwright. Kit took two steps backward, nearly stumbling. Her body felt electrified with panic.

"Can I offer you a lift, Ms. Finn?" Wainwright asked, his voice as inviting as the tip of a knife. She began to make out his features in the darkness and saw his lip curl. "It's not really safe to be running around down here at this hour."

"No."

There was no one else within sight now, and she knew if Wainwright chose the right moment, he could force her into the car without anyone noticing.

"That's a shame. Because it seems like it's time for us to have another little talk."

"There's nothing to talk about," she called toward him.

"Is that so?"

"Yes. For some reason you think I have something you want but I *don't*. I'm irrelevant to you."

"And yet you won't leave my employees alone. Here you are tonight, gabbing with another one of them."

She could see then how it must have appeared to him: that she was trying to pump Sasha, which was exactly what she *had* been doing.

"She—she wanted to hire me as a *decorator*."

"I'm not sure what game you're playing, Ms. Finn," he said, "but I can assure you it's a dangerous one. *No one* targets me, or my company, or my employees. Do you understand what I'm saying?"

"You have to believe me, I—"

And then, improbably, a cab appeared, crawling up the street behind the limo, its roof light on. Kit shot up her arm. Seconds later the cab pulled ahead of the limo and stopped. Kit nearly tore open the door and heaved herself inside. Out of the corner of her eye, she saw Wainwright jerk in surprise.

"I just need to get out of here," she blurted out to the driver. "That man—he was harassing me."

The driver, his head wrapped in a turban, studied her in the rearview mirror.

"You want me to call 911?"

"No, no. Just head north, okay. The east side. Once we get away, I'll give you the address."

She crouched down in the seat and peered out the rear window. Wainwright was darting back into the limo.

"Take the FDR, okay?" she told the driver. "It'll be faster."

When Kit checked a few seconds later, the limo was behind them but by the time the cab driver had made a couple of turns, it had vanished. Of course, she told herself. Wainwright wasn't going to engage in a car chase and risk being stopped by the cops.

Kit's heartbeat finally slowed, the sound of it no longer pounding in her head. She smiled for just a second, imagining what the expression on Wainwright's face must have been when she bolted into the cab.

But then the realities of the night came crashing back. Wainwright had obviously skipped his dinner and started searching for her right away in the car, perhaps even sending Kennelly on foot to increase the chance of locating her. She replayed Wainwright's words to her: "*No one targets me. . . .*" Standing there on the curb with his legs slightly straddled, he'd looked like a beady-eyed Terminator.

For the first time since she'd fled the bar, Kit fixed on Sasha's ugly revelation. As she'd raced through the streets, she'd been too panic-stricken to dwell on it, but now there it was in all its ugliness. Kelman was involved with Sasha.

Last night, Kit had finally let down her guard with him, allowing the infatuation she'd sandbagged behind some barrier to seep through again, and it turned out she'd been a crazy fool to do that. Clearly, Kelman had strung her along, pretending to have a romantic interest in order to serve his own ends. What if, as she'd suspected in the past, he'd been involved in the insider trading scheme himself and had later double-crossed his partners, enraging them. He may have used her as a distraction for the people at Ithaka, a distraction that had put her life in danger and led to Avery's death. He'd conned and manipulated her but fed her enough truth for her to believe his story.

What he'd never anticipated, however, was that her path would cross with Sasha's.

Four blocks from Baby's apartment building, Kit shifted in the seat and checked again out the back window, straining to see in the darkness if any of the car lights behind them belonged to a limo. There were only taxis and a few regular cars. When she entered the apartment a few minutes later, Baby was hunkered down in the living room, a book in her lap and a near-empty cocktail glass beside her on an end table. Kit had texted her en route to let her know she was okay, but Baby looked up anxiously at the sight of her.

"I thought you were going to stay under wraps until this whole awful business was resolved."

"I should never have gone out," Kit admitted, collapsing into an armchair. "I ended up being accosted by Wainwright, the head of Ithaka."

She told Baby about the two encounters with him.

"Do you think this Wainwright fellow is the mastermind behind the criminal activity at the firm?" Baby asked.

"He didn't come right out and say so, of course, but his tone was really threatening, like a man who knew how much was at risk, and was going to make sure I didn't do anything to bring him down."

"Would he have tried to hurt you—or, for God's sake, abduct you—if the cab hadn't come along?"

"Uh, I don't think so. At the time I was petrified that he was coming after me, but in hindsight I doubt he would have dared. Besides, I sense that tonight was all about scaring me, giving me the warning from hell."

"Is there any way to signal to him that you heard the message loud and clear so that he'll leave you alone?"

Kit shook her head slowly.

"I have no clue. . . . But wait, there's something I don't get. Why would he bother giving me a warning?"

"Because as you say, there's so much at stake. He's desperate."

"But it seems like an odd tactic at this stage in the game. Two people are dead, and suddenly he's generously offering a warning."

She thought of what Kelman had suggested, that Kennelly and Lister could have gone rogue.

"Maybe Wainwright isn't in the loop about the murders," Kit said. "He's simply telling me to back away from his business because I keep popping up on the scene. The men that Kelman talked about—Kennelly and Lister—could be the ones behind the two deaths, with Wainwright none the wiser.

"But even if Wainwright isn't a murderer, wouldn't he have heard about the deaths and wondered what was gong on?" Baby asked.

"Well, he definitely knows about the hit and run with Healy, but he may have no idea who drove the car. And there's a chance he hasn't heard about Avery's death. Even if he spotted a headline on it, he might not have read the whole story and learned how it was tied to our firm."

"Are you going to share all this with Kelman?"

"No," Kit said bluntly.

Baby's blue eyes widened in surprise.

"What's going on, Kit?"

"You know how I told you I was starting to trust him. Well, I take it all back." She shared what Sasha had revealed.

"*Bastard*," Baby said, reeling back in disgust.

"I'm sure it's him—how could it not be?—but I'm going to give him a chance to respond. He may not come right out and admit the truth, but I have to see how he handles the question."

"And if you find out he *is* involved with her?"

"Then I'm on my own."

"Do you think there's a chance he killed Avery after all?"

"The factors that make that unlikely haven't changed. He knew I wasn't going out then, he needed information from me. But he may have been in league with Kennelly and Lister initially so indirectly he'd be responsible."

She rose from the couch, ready to make the call but dreading the thought of it at the same time.

"Kit, promise me," Baby said, "that you won't let him talk you into meeting again tonight."

Kit smiled wanly.

"Don't worry, you're stuck with me. I have no intention of going anywhere."

After starting for the door of the room, Kit hesitated and turned around.

"I haven't even asked you about your day. How was everything?"

"Pretty good. And I have the name of a lawyer for you. He's not a partner so his fee is more reasonable, but he comes highly recommended for this type of situation."

"Great. And what about on the work front? Any new wrinkles?"

"We have plenty of time to catch up on that tomorrow."

There was a hint in her voice of something not being right.

"Wait, what's going on?"

"I hate to lay this on you now, but Dara called and asked if she could take a leave of absence for a few weeks, until things are resolved. She understands that this might result in us hiring someone else and letting her go."

"Oh no," Kit said, disheartened by the news. "I know she was meeting with her parents and I'm sure they urged her to do that."

"Yes. Dara has plenty of gumption, but I think she tends to follow their lead. These Millennials are so entwined with their parents. It's a bit hard for me to relate to since I was raised pretty much by four Mexican maids."

"Well, those women did a fantastic job," Kit said. "Should we hire a temp, do you think?"

"I've got a few ideas, but as I said, we can talk in the morning. Do what you have to do now."

It was all unraveling, Kit thought as she trudged into the bedroom. She was too afraid to work out of her office, Dara was probably leaving, Holt, her hottest new client prospect, appeared to be backing off. And her brain seemed incapable of generating a single worthwhile idea for the bachelor apartment. She felt as if she was staring at a river rushing over its banks.

In the guest bedroom she dumped her phone out of her purse. How could she worm the information out of Kelman? she wondered. If he'd lied to her about his relationship status, it seemed only likely that he'd deny any connection to Sasha other than a work one. Her only hope, she decided, was to catch him enough off guard that he wouldn't be able to disguise how flustered he was by her question.

As she picked up the phone off the bed, she saw from the screen that she had a missed call from Kelman and a text, neither of which she'd noticed when she'd texted Baby from the taxi. If he'd been playing a sick game with her as a pawn, he was still all in. She tapped his number and he picked up after the second ring.

"I was expecting to hear from you earlier," he said. "Is everything okay?"

"More or less."

"Meaning?"

"I'm just still trying to adjust to everything that's happened."

"This will be resolved soon, Kit. I promise you. Things are moving along quickly at this point."

"I have a question for you. Just a loose end I'd like to tie up."

"Of course. Shoot."

"Tell me about Sasha Glen."

A long pause followed. He'd confirmed the truth without uttering a word.

"How do you know about Sasha Glen?" he said finally.

"I asked *you* the question."

"What exactly do you want to know?"

"Are you two lovers? That's what I want to know."

Another long pause. Even more portentous than the first. And then just one word.

"Yes."

chapter 20

She'd prepared herself for such an answer and yet his words were as good as a kick in the gut.

"I need to explain, Kit," he said in a rush. "It's not what it seems."

Right, she thought, why don't you spin yet another tale for me and try to trick me into swallowing it whole.

"I'm not interested in your explanation."

"Kit, give me five minutes. That's all I ask."

"No. I'm going to hang up and I want you to stay away from me, do you hear? Nothing good has ever come from any contact I've had with you."

She disconnected, and after fighting off an urge to fling the phone across the room, dropped it on the bed instead. For a few moments, she just sat there, letting the truth echo in her head. He and Sasha were together.

Underneath her fury, there was also an undeniable pang of disappointment. She had *wanted* to believe Kelman, *wanted* to trust him, and yes, as tough as it was to admit now, *wanted* to rekindle that crazy connection with him she'd felt in Islamorada.

The phone rang again—it was him calling back—and she jabbed at the decline button. A moment later the voicemail icon indicated a message had been left. She ignored it and put the phone on mute.

Was he just a cad and a player? she wondered. A guy who while laying low in Florida had seen the opportunity for some easy sex with her and decided that his chances would be better if he claimed to be completely single? Maybe. And then later, once their lives became entangled in a nightmare and he knew he needed her, he might have decided not to make things even messier by fessing up to having a girlfriend after all.

And yet the other possibility loomed large, that he was a liar in *every* regard. Not a whistle-blower as he claimed but a criminal who'd simply kept her close—and hinted at an attraction to her—so she would provide a constant flow of information.

There was something that needed to be considered: Sasha's possible role in all that had transpired. Kelman's admission reframed the cat-and-mouse play the woman seemed so fond of. Maybe Sasha was part of the insider trading scheme and Kelman had asked her to keep tabs on Kit from a separate vantage point, trying to determine if she had a secret agenda. Sasha could have even tipped Kelman off that Kit was coming by her apartment. That was the day he'd followed her.

Of course, Sasha could have decided to keep tabs on Kit all by her lonesome. Perhaps Kelman had admitted to forging a bit of a relationship with Kit for the sake of scoring information—skipping any mention of naked bodies and all-night sex—and Sasha may have worried that there was more going on. There'd been all those weird suggestions from Sasha that she knew Healy better than she did, even the question in the ladies' room at Ithaka about whether she'd *dated* Healy. That could have been her way of reassuring herself that a certain decorator had no designs on *her* man.

But all the wondering in the world, she knew, wasn't ever going to provide any answers. What she needed to do instead was take action, and that meant finally going to the cops. She had promised Kelman she would wait for him to make the first move but in light of her discovery—and all it implied about him—the time for that kind of cooperation had passed. She needed to protect herself, maybe even from *him*. For all she knew, Kelman might never have even intended to divulge anything to the authorities.

She rolled over on her back and stared at the ceiling for a few moments. It was pale blue in color, probably Benjamin Moore's Robin Egg, and a slightly different shade than the rest of the room. Baby subscribed to the idea that people slept best in spaces painted in muted hues of blue or green. Kit loved the bedroom but she loved her own more. The sooner she spoke to the cops, the better her chances of finding her way home again.

As she was swinging her legs off the bed, Baby passed the open door to the guest room and poked her head in.

"Did you talk to him?" she asked.

"Yeah, and it's true. The creep actually admitted it."

"I'm sorry, Kit. What will you do now?"

"I'll call the lawyer first thing in the morning. Then schedule an appointment with Detective Burke. He looks like the kind of guy who uses waterboarding for anything beyond a routine interview, but I assume he's the one I'll have to deal with."

First thing in the morning she made contact with the lawyer, Nat Naylor. He sounded young to her, like someone who might still play beer pong on the weekends, but if Baby's lawyer had recommended him, she assumed he was qualified. After she'd explained to him that she had serious concerns about her safety, he agreed to meet with her at Baby's that day.

She tried to work after she hung up from the call, but her concentration was shot. To make matters worse, there was a worrisome email from her client Barry Kaplan: "I've been thinking since our phone call, and though I understand that you're busy, I really need to get moving on this project. If you're too jammed up to handle the job, it might make sense for me to find another designer."

Oh *lovely*, she thought in despair. At the rate things were moving, she'd have no clients at all by the end of the month. She replied, saying that she could understand his frustration but she would definitely have ideas to present to him in person early next week and requested that he send her available time slots. She opened her iPad and poured through photos of previous jobs she had done, hoping one of them might spark a concept. At this point she wasn't opposed to brazenly ripping off an idea she'd executed for someone else. But nothing seemed right for Barry.

Nat Naylor arrived at three, dressed in a pinstripe suit and carrying a black briefcase. He was thirty-two or thirty-three, she guessed, and though his bright blond hair hinted at endless summers, his six-foot-four frame and serious demeanor undercut the sun-bleached locks and made him read smart and lawyerlike.

He gave only a cursory glance around the apartment, obviously impervious to the full impact of Baby's jaw-dropping style, and positioned himself on one of the leather sofas. He asked if he could use her first name and urged her to do the same with him.

"Why don't we jump right in," he suggested, unsnapping his briefcase with two sharp clicks and removing a fresh new yellow legal pad.

She related the full saga, trying to be succinct but not omit any pertinent details. She admitted going to Kelman's room in Islamorada for a drink but left it at that. If Naylor's head was spinning from all the bizarre permutations and the roller coaster aspect of her tale, he gave no hint, just took notes with firm, fast strokes of his pen. Here and there he shot questions at her for clarification.

When she'd finished, feeling unsettled from rehashing it all, Nat leafed for a few minutes through his pages of notes, his look pensive. She wondered if he was simply trying to grasp all the details and commit them to memory, or pondering what truths might be tucked away beneath the story, truths that Kit had hesitated to disclose. Or maybe he was really sitting there thinking, "This woman needs to get herself a normal life."

Finally he let out a breath and looked up.

"Kit, tell me why you want to go to the police," he said.

The question stunned her. *Why?* She couldn't imagine the reason for asking that. "Well, because a homicide occurred in my stairwell and I have information that might prove valuable to the detectives in charge of the investigation, information I should have provided them with sooner. Why *wouldn't* I go to the police?"

"I see why it's your first instinct. But you never want to entangle yourself with law enforcement unless you absolutely have to. Once that happens, you have no control. There are just some very good reasons not to do it."

"But if I don't report this, aren't I guilty of obstructing justice? I'd be withholding critical information."

He hesitated for a moment, as if he was picking his words.

"Actually, I don't believe you would be. Obstructing justice is when you actively make it difficult for the police to do their job, such as destroying evidence or deleting relevant emails. But failing to divulge that you know a man who is connected to a company whose employees may have played a role in the victim's death doesn't fall into that category."

So what was he suggesting? she wondered. That she do nothing and let sleeping dogs lie? But the people who were after her weren't sleeping dogs. They were hounds from hell that wanted to eat her alive.

"But if I don't go to the police, they won't have everything they need to figure out who killed Avery. I'm partly responsible for her death, and I can't bear the thought of her murderer never being caught. And I have to also consider the fact that I'm a sitting duck right now."

"All right, I just wanted to put it out there. There's one more question I need to ask. Did you have sex with Garrett Kelman?"

She should have known it was coming.

"Yes," she said, looking him in the eye. "But I don't understand how that matters."

"If you're going to speak to the authorities, it's critical not to shade the truth or to leave out anything that could be relevant."

"But how is sex relevant?"

"As far as the cops are concerned, sex can be a motive. They might decide you feel jilted and that you're exacting revenge by going to them with your story."

"I'm not," she said, annoyed that it might come down to having to defend herself against that kind of a suspicion. "I just want the police to know who the possible suspects are. But if it's necessary to admit I spent the night with Kelman, I have no qualms about doing so."

"Good. Why don't we try to set something up for early Monday? I can accompany you."

"Nat, is there any chance we could go down there later this afternoon?"

A part of her had been wildly hoping that he'd suggest dashing to the precinct right now so that it would all be over and done with.

"I think we need to do some prep work," he said. "I want you to run through your story again to make sure there are no inconsistencies. And I need your phone."

"My phone? I don't understand."

"I want to make a record of all your calls to Kelman so we

don't miss one. And then we're going to create a spreadsheet, listing them, plus every encounter you've had with him. We'll review it all so when you talk to the cops, you leave nothing out."

"Why don't we sit in the dining room then?" she suggested. "It will be easier to go through everything there."

For the next hour they worked side by side at the table.

"I see," Nat said at one point, "that Kelman left you two voicemail messages that you haven't opened. "And he's tried twice today to reach you without leaving a message. What's that about?"

There was no way she could tell him about the Sasha development. That would only complicate matters, perhaps even cause the cops, as Nat had mentioned, to cast her as a spurned and vengeful lover.

"I gave Garrett Kelman plenty of time to go to the authorities ahead of me, but he hasn't, and I can't wait any longer," she said. "I'm not interested in getting into another discussion with him."

"Okay," Naylor said, though Kit wondered if he sensed that she'd just done what he'd warned her against—shading the truth. "But you should listen to his messages before you speak to the authorities. So we know everything that's going on."

Next they ran through her story again. It was draining to repeat it, but at the same time she felt a fresh surge of determination. She was *doing* something finally, taking concrete steps to protect herself. The idea of Naylor's fee made her cringe, but she could see how foolhardy it would be to act without an attorney.

When they'd finished their work, Nat took a minute to organize his notes. As he tucked them in his briefcase, Kit saw him look off, as if he was weighing something.

"I have a thought," he said, looking back. "After reviewing everything with you, I'm wondering if it would be better to skip the police and go straight to the FBI instead."

"I don't understand," she said, totally caught off guard again.

"If you're worried about me being entangled with the New York police, couldn't the FBI be even worse?"

"I actually think they'll be easier to work with. And besides, you'd have to deal with them eventually. Insider trading is a Federal offense and since the murder may indeed be related to that, the FBI will need to be involved. They'll work alongside the cops but they'll be the ones calling the shots."

Kit exhaled slowly, considering his words. She hadn't a clue what the best strategy was—how could she?—so it seemed like the smartest course of action was to follow her lawyer's lead. At least this way she'd be able to avoid Detective Burke's squirm-inducing stares.

"If you think that's the right move, fine," she said.

"I'll call you this weekend and let you know for sure. I just want to give it a bit more thought before we pull the trigger."

Love the analogy, she thought grimly as they both rose from the table.

Once she was alone again, she plunked down on the sofa, allowing herself to decompress and relish the relief she felt. Naylor, despite the blond surfer locks, seemed very together, a good hire. And though the idea of speaking to the authorities on Monday—whether it was Burke or the FBI or whoever—wasn't pleasant, she would get through the experience. And there'd be no more endless fretting about whether to do it or when.

She knew, of course, that instant results were way too much to hope for—she might be stuck hibernating at Baby's for days more, and it would be a long time before she stopped looking over her shoulder—but she was now at least setting events in motion that would begin to free her from the cordoned-off di-saster area her life had turned into. And if she were lucky, any damage her business sustained could be managed.

Unbidden, Kelman muscled his way into her head. Though most of her two-hour conversation with the lawyer had focused on Kelman and the events that had unfolded because of him, she'd stayed fairly detached, as if she were discussing a character she'd only read about in a book. But now she couldn't help but think about him. Her decision to go to the authorities was going to impact him big time. They would want to know where he was staying and she'd have no choice but to tell them.

What if he *wasn't* involved in the insider trading activity or any other crime? What if the only thing he was guilty of was being a player and using her as a fount of information? Well, there was nothing she could do about it at this point. His lies about his romantic entanglements had made it impossible to trust him and she needed to look out for herself.

And if he *were* innocent, she would have complicated matters for him, but he should have enough evidence to defend himself with.

Later, over coffee in the kitchen, she filled Baby in on the meeting with Naylor. She seemed even more relieved than Kit.

"I got a peek at him, by the way. Now *that's* what I call a Nordic god."

Kit snorted. "Are you thinking that should be more my type than lying, scheming, redheaded men?"

"Just planting the seed."

"Enough about me. How was *your* day?"

"Overall, things seem to be holding steady on the business front. Though I got a weird vibe from the Beekman Place woman I was shopping with this morning. She had a sourpuss look on her face all morning"

"You think she heard the news?"

"Possibly, though she could just have been having a bad hair day, knowing *her*. As for our hotel man, still not a peep from him. Who knows? He may be trapped in a tanning bed and unable to lift the lid off. Maybe it's our duty to contact every Sun Tan City boutique and ask them to check."

Kit tried to smile. She then took the moment to relate the contents of the email from Barry.

"Ouch," Baby said. "Can you use all day tomorrow to just knock out a step-by-step plan for him?"

"Yes, but I'm stuck. I still don't have a concept yet."

"Maybe you're overthinking it, trying to shoot for something totally original or cutting edge when it's not really necessary. Go back to who he is and what he's looking for. From what you said, he sounds like a man of fairly simple needs."

"Right, good point. He's a tax lawyer, and one of his buzz words for his fantasy place is masculine. Quote: 'No teensy towels in the bathroom or candles in a bed of rocks on the coffee table.' He wants it to be sophisticated enough to impress these new women he's dating, but he also wants to feel relaxed there."

She thought suddenly of Nat Naylor's suit. "Maybe I should just go with a kind of lawyerlike vibe. Give his place a menswear feeling. I could do the sofa in a soft flannel pinstripe. Of course, it might be hard to tell where Barry ends and the sofa begins."

Baby chuckled. "But I bet he'd love it. And the flannel keeps it easy and relaxed. Ralph Lauren makes a nice fabric for that, by the way. Navy Walker Pinstripe."

"Or I could put plain gray flannel on the sofa and do the pillows in tie fabrics—like houndstooth or herringbone. That kind of thing has been done before, but as you say, he doesn't need me to reinvent the wheel."

"Exactly."

"Okay," Kit said grinning, "tell me if this is too over the top, but Farrow and Ball has a red paint they call Blazer, based on a Cambridge University jacket. I could do the entranceway in that color."

"Love it!"

Kit started to rise, anxious to start fleshing out the concept, but Baby reached out and touched her arm, indicating she should stay.

"There's one other thing I need to mention. While your lawyer was here, I heard from Bianca, our PR guru, and she had some disconcerting news to share."

"Is somebody doing a big story?"

"Possibly. Interest has spiked since the police announced that they're considering Avery's death a homicide, and Bianca thinks reporters will start digging. It could end up being covered in a place like *New York* magazine, and then we'll be front and center."

Kit shook her head in dismay.

"But the really troubling news is a tidbit she learned from the police. Bianca managed to cozy up to one of them—trust me, the woman's got major-league tits and she knows how to use them—and the guy dropped hints that Avery wasn't just pushed. The person who shoved her down the stairs finished the job, as they say."

"*How?*" Kit asked.

"He implied that her neck had been snapped."

Kit fought the sickening image, but it took hold in her mind anyway, two hands twisting hard around Avery's neck. Her client had died because of her, and the person who'd done it was still out there. Please, she thought, desperately, let Monday make a difference.

She went to bed early that night and woke just before six. It was pouring out, the rain thrashing against the windows from the wind. Despite how inclement the weather was, she hated the idea of being cooped up inside all weekend.

Midday Saturday Naylor called.

"I talked to a couple of colleagues and everyone agrees that the best course is to go straight to the FBI," he reported. "I'll call my contact there first thing Monday."

By Sunday she had two more calls from Kelman, one with a voice message and one without. She dreaded the thought of listening to them, but Naylor had told her to do it and she was running out of time.

She started with the very first one Kelman had left on Thursday night, after admitting to his involvement with Sasha. It was a second plea for her to give him five minutes, a promise that his explanation would put everything in perspective. Yeah, right, she thought.

The next message, she could see, was far longer. She tapped the play arrow.

"Kit, even if you refuse to call me back, I need you to understand what really happened," he said. He claimed that he'd had a very brief fling with Sasha not long after his break-up with the Australian. They'd spent no more than three nights together, but she had become fixated on him and had begun implying to people that they were seriously dating. He thought there might be something wrong with her.

"Remember," he added, "when I told you that I had become disenchanted at Ithaka, that it no longer seemed like the right fit for me. She was a major factor in that."

Oh, that's clever, Kit thought. He's using the Alex ("I-won't-be-ignored, Dan") Forrest defense, from that movie, *Fatal Attraction*.

His voice sounded much different in the voicemail message he'd left today: flat and emotionless, almost cold.

"This is my last call, Kit. You won't hear from me again. But I've done what I promised I would. I thought you should know."

Did that mean he'd gone to the authorities finally? It sounded like that. But how could she be sure?

· · · ·

Nat Naylor texted her at nine the next morning, saying he would be speaking to his contact shortly and would circle back after that. While the phone was still in her hands, it rang again, a number she didn't recognize.

"Ms. Finn," the male caller said when she identified herself. "This is Special Agent Frank Taft from the FBI. How are you doing today?"

"Um, I'm fine," she said, confused. There was no way Nat could have made the call already.

"We've been informed that you have information you want to share with us. I'd like to arrange for you to come in today and talk to us about it."

"You spoke to my attorney?"

A pause.

"No, I did not. You can bring an attorney if you like, but it's not necessary."

"But who told you about me? We were planning to call today ourselves."

"I'm not at liberty to say at this moment."

But she knew without a doubt. It had been Kelman.

chapter 21

So he'd done what he'd promised. He'd gone to the U.S. Attorney's office—and they had clearly instructed him to speak to the FBI as well. She explained to the agent that things were already in motion for her to make a statement, hopefully that day, and she would have her attorney call him momentarily. She phoned Naylor back and shared the latest development. In the end, the meeting was set for three o'clock.

When it was time to go, Kit resorted to the diving-into-a-cab method she had relied on twice before, instructing the driver to leave her at 26 Federal Plaza in Lower Manhattan. As the city whizzed by, she tried not to fixate on the interview ahead, knowing that, per Nat, it was best not to sound rehearsed. But she couldn't keep her mind off Kelman. On the phone, Nat had warned her that they couldn't rely on the fact that Kelman had told the FBI the same exact story he'd shared with her; there might be landmines she couldn't anticipate. But due to the fact that he'd gone on Friday, as promised, she sensed that he hadn't hung her out to dry in any way.

Crowds of people crisscrossed the plaza, and she looked behind her several times as she dashed across it. It was gusty out again today and the wind whipped strands of hair around her face.

Due to security measures, it took her at least ten minutes to make it from the lobby to the designated meeting room on the fifteenth floor. Naylor was already there in the company of two agents. The room was sparsely furnished—nothing more than a table with chairs beneath a portrait of the FBI director. Naylor introduced her to the two agents, who both rose from their seats. One was Taft, the man she'd spoken to on the phone, and the other was Michael Woo, Nat's contact. Each looked to be in his mid- to late forties.

"As you're aware, we'd already placed a call to the Bureau when Agent Taft reached out to my client," Nat said after Kit had taken a seat. "Garrett Kelman had asked her to give him a chance to get everything on the table before she contributed what she knew, but she didn't want to wait any longer. Now it appears you have had contact with Mr. Kelman."

"Nat, as you know, we're not at liberty to talk about other witnesses," Woo said.

"Michael, my client's life may be in danger. You don't have to tell us what Mr. Kelman said in his statement—Ms. Finn is here simply to relate her side of events—but we'd like to know, for her safety, that Mr. Kelman actually made good on his promise to speak to you."

Woo took a second and then nodded.

"I don't see any harm in that. Yes, he was here. Now Ms. Finn, we'd love to hear what you have to share."

She started at the beginning, with Islamorada, and worked her way from there to Avery's death and the meetings she'd had with Kelman. Taft took notes, and while the two agents weren't what she'd call friendly, they were polite enough.

It wasn't until she finished that they asked most of their questions. They wanted her to go over every aspect of Avery's visit and what she knew, if anything, about Avery's personal life. It made sense—they were trying to determine if the murder might be unrelated to the insider trading.

"You don't have a picture of Ms. Howe, do you?" Taft asked.

"Well, I can find one," Kit said, taking out her phone and pulling one up quickly online. "Her hair in this shot is much fuller than mine, but it was straighter the night she came by. She was also around my height and build. And as I said, she was wearing my coat."

Neither man registered any reaction to the photo, but Kit knew they must be recognizing how in the dim light of a stairwell, Avery would have born a resemblance to her.

Next they went back over each of her encounters with Kelman. She figured they were trying to compare what she said with what he'd disclosed, note what matched and didn't. Any discrepancies would be telling. She'd told them on the first go-round that she'd been to bed with Kelman, and during the question period they asked if that had been the extent of her sexual relationship with him.

"Yes," she said. She was taking the kiss in front of the shoji screen to her grave.

What threw her was how much interest they appeared to have in the mix-up with the pen. Taft asked her to describe more fully how she'd knocked everything to the ground and why she hadn't realized her mistake. She read skepticism in his eyes. Part of him, she knew, was wondering if, just maybe, she *had* been looking for the flash drive after all.

"I shouldn't have picked up the pen," she said, keeping her voice even. "But I guess I'm more sentimental than I realized and I was struck by the fact that his was the same as mine. And then when I heard the key in the door, I was too flustered to pay enough attention."

When they finished, both agents thanked her for her cooperation and stressed that they would be in contact with the homicide detectives. They also made clear that her discretion was of utmost importance. She was to discuss the case with no one, not even Mr. Kelman.

"Understood," she said. She couldn't imagine Kelman ever reaching out to her again anyway.

"We also need to discuss your personal safety," Woo said. "That's a priority."

"I was just about to raise that," Nat told him.

"We advise you to be extremely cautious," Woo said. "Consider staying with a friend for the time being, avoid going places alone. And we'd like to schedule a weekly call with you, just to make sure you're feeling secure."

For some reason his comment almost made her laugh. His tips were about as comforting as knowing that when your plane crashed in the middle of the Atlantic, the seat cushion could be used as a flotation device.

"That's it?" she said.

"I'm afraid there's not a lot more we can advise."

"But will it at least be safer for me now? I assume Ithaka will learn that the evidence has been turned over to you, and that I am not a threat to them."

Taft shook his head. "Unfortunately it's not going to work like that. The Bureau will need to conduct an investigation and that takes time, often months. If there's been criminal activity, people at Ithaka know they are in danger of being exposed, and we want to give them as little chance as possible to batten down the hatches. It's important no one learn that you've come forward. If there's a trial, you may be called to testify."

"So I'm still in danger?" she said, feeling her heart begin to drum.

"Possibly," Taft said. "Like Agent Woo said, you need to be cautious. If there appears to be a serious threat to you as the case moves along, we can also discuss relocation."

"*Relocation?*" she exclaimed. "You mean one of those witness protection programs?"

"It wouldn't have to be forever."

"But I couldn't leave my work, my life here." She could feel herself growing agitated, angry even, and she willed herself to calm down. The two men sitting across from her weren't to blame for anything.

"Why don't we table any discussion of relocation for now," Nat interjected. "I'll review everything with Ms. Finn later."

The first chance they had to speak privately was when they reached the plaza outside the building and set off on foot across it.

"You handled yourself really well in there," Nat said.

"Even when I looked ready to bitch slap someone at the very end?"

"The idea of leaving everything behind can't be fun to consider."

"Are you saying I *should* consider it?"

"Two people are dead. You can't lose sight of that. You'll want to stay as careful as possible until this is all resolved."

"I wasn't naïve enough to think that the second I left here the FBI would go charging over to Ithaka and arrest people. But I never thought it was going to take *months* for anything to happen."

"Let's hope that for your sake they move more quickly than that."

They'd reached the street and Nat shot up his hand for a cab.

"Why don't I drop you back at the apartment and then I can head to the office from there?"

"Oh, that's not necessary," Kit said. She glanced around, surveying the people hurrying across the plaza. She would have liked to say yes, but not at five hundred dollars an hour.

Nat smiled. "No charge for escort service," he said, guessing the reason for her response. "I'll use the ride to review notes for another case."

"Well, then that's an offer I can't say no to," she said, smiling.

As soon as they were in the cab and headed north, Nat opened his briefcase and Kit fell silent. Her mind kept replaying that one awful word over and over: *relocation*. It would mean going to a whole new place, away from her friends, her business, her partnership with Baby. She wouldn't be able to stay in touch with anyone, maybe not even her parents. And how would she support herself? By trying to start another business from scratch?

In a split second, she realized for sure that she'd never do it. Once before, at seventeen, she'd been run out of the life she'd known—her lovely bedroom, her home, the college she'd dreamed of going to. There was no way she'd allow that to happen again. Yes, there was danger, but she would have to chance it.

"You doing okay?"

She was so lost in thought, it took a moment to register that Nat was speaking to her.

"Yes, thanks," she said. "And thanks for all your help today. It was such a relief to have you there."

"One point I just want to reiterate. It's critical that you not discuss the case with Kelman."

"Yeah, well, that's not likely anyway."

"At least it seems he didn't throw you under the bus. And that what he told you was probably true."

He was right. For days she had clung to the idea that Kelman could be caught up in a dangerous and illegal scheme and that he might have killed Matt Healy when parts of the scheme soured. And yet it now seemed that he was what he'd claimed to be for so long: simply a whistle-blower.

And what about Sasha? she wondered. Had he been telling the truth about her in his voicemail message? It was unlikely she would ever know. She wasn't really sure how that made her feel, but she sensed something begin to gnaw away at her. It bore a resemblance to disappointment.

Once they reached Baby's building, Nat walked her into the lobby and suggested they touch base by phone the next day. As he strode back to the cab, she watched the flaps of his navy suit lift. His might be taking a bite out of her savings, but at least he'd sparked an idea for Barry Kaplan's apartment.

"Tell me everything," Baby urged as soon as Kit had walked in the door.

"Well, I could tell you, but then I'd have to kill you."

She explained that going forward, she wouldn't be able to divulge information about the case. But she relayed basic details of the meeting and also the fact that the notion of relocation had been raised.

"What are they talking about for God's sake?" Baby said. "Sending you off to some place like Fort Wayne or Fargo with a wig and a new name?"

"It doesn't matter because I'm not leaving New York. Ithaka may have upended my life, but I'm not going to let them out-and-out destroy it. I'll just have to do my best to stay out of harm's way."

"I don't want you in Fargo, Kit, but are you sure this is the wisest course?"

"I don't know if it's the wisest, but it's the only choice I can live with. And now that I've gone to the authorities, I'm going to put all my attention into shoring up my end of the business."

"I'll help you as much as I can."

"But I do have to find a place to live for a while. I can't just bunk down here indefinitely."

"Why not? To be perfectly honest, I've liked having the company. And once May comes, I'll be in the country most weekends and probably working Fridays from there like I did last summer."

Kit felt her eyes well in gratitude.

"Are you absolutely sure, Baby?"

"Yes. Besides, it will save me from doing something stupid, like getting a cockapoo."

"Is that a *bird*?"

"No, a cocker spaniel–poodle hybrid. I was considering it because it doesn't shed."

"Ha. Okay. Why don't we say that for the time being at least I'll stay and then we'll play it by ear. There's one more hitch, though. I'm going to have to recruit a freelancer to do a fair amount of legwork for me since I'm staying undercover."

"I have feelers out for someone to fill in for Dara. In the meantime, why don't I do the final shopping for your Greenwich Village clients. I've seen the photos of what you've done so far, and I'll pick out the last few accessories they need. I could even bring the items down there myself and see how they work."

"Oh, I'm sure they'd love that. I suspect they've told most of their friends that you're actually the one doing the decorating anyway."

"Any other fires to put out?"

"Well, there's Barry, the not-so-happy bachelor, but I have the concept now at least, and I'm going to finish making the presentation boards today. I'm waiting to hear if he can meet with me midweek. It'll mean going out, but I'll be careful. So far no one seems wise to the fact that I'm staying with you."

"Here's a thought. Why don't you have him come here? I'll do one of my famous salmon balls rolled in slivered almonds and I'll serve him a martini that will knock him on his ass."

"Oh, that would definitely work. And then that just leaves the doctor. I'm going to call today and see if I can reel him back in."

Kit sprang from her chair, ready to move into action, but she could see that Baby still had something on her mind.

"I see your wheels turning."

"I've been wondering about X. The infamous Garrett Kelman. He who rules by the spear."

"You mean, has my view of him changed?"

"Yes, now that you've learned what he's done. Will you follow up with him?"

"I don't think he wants anything to do with me at this point. And maybe that's for the best. I'm pretty sure he's not a murderer or thief, but he may still be a scoundrel."

But when she returned to the guest bedroom, she realized that despite what she'd said to Baby about Kelman, the pang of disappointment she'd been feeling had intensified, like a burn exposed to sunlight. From the moment she had met Kelman in Florida, something had stirred in her, and it hadn't just been lust. There'd been an emotional undercurrent as well, which for weeks had been burrowed beneath her anger and fear. When they had kissed the other night, it seemed to suggest that there might be a chance for them to restore that connection in spite of the chaos all around them. But by failing to believe him, she'd eliminated that chance.

She changed into jeans and set up shop again at the dining room table. Over the past two days, she'd felt an inertia gaining hold on her, but it was gone now, as if swept away by a blustery gust of April wind. She left a message for Keith Holt. She emailed the Greenwich Village clients with updates on the missing rug and duvet and to say that Baby had offered to add her input during the final stage and that she would be picking up a few small pieces and accessories to show them for consideration.

Then she set to work on the plan for Barry. Baby used one of her large walk-in closets as a workroom and Kit found enough pinstripe and herringbone fabric swatches in one of the plastic tubs in there to give Barry an idea of her theme. She also went through old shelter magazines and tore out pages that showed the kind of furniture shapes and accessories she had in mind. In a near frenzy, she mounted everything onto boards. Close to finished, she emailed Barry again, this time inviting him to come to Baby's apartment for cocktails and a presentation on Wednesday at six if his schedule permitted.

At around seven, when she was stapling the last pieces onto the boards, her phone rang and she saw that it was Holt's number. Okay, good, she told herself.

"Nice to get your message," he said. "How've you been?" Pleasant enough, but definitely not as engaged sounding as before. If she were going to regain her footing with him, she'd have to play it carefully.

"Good. I just thought I'd check in and see how you were doing. I'd love the chance to talk more about your clippings when you have the chance."

"I'd like that, too," he said, warmer now.

"Shall we set a time?"

"It's probably best if we hold off for a couple of weeks. I've decided to go ahead with that idea I mentioned to you. I'm seriously considering buying a new place that's more open and modern. In fact, I've even seen a couple of lofts this week."

"How exciting," she said, disguising her dismay. He'd mentioned the idea as a possibility, but it had seemed fairly remote. If he did go through with purchasing a new apartment, he wouldn't need her services until after the closing and that could be months away.

"Yes, and I'm going to see if I can sell my place with most of the furnishings. That way, I start totally fresh. I should probably redo the clipping file once I settle on a place."

"That makes sense." She could feel the project slipping out of her grasp, like water through her fingers. "But the clips you pulled could actually be of value as you look at lofts. They can help direct you to a place that has the right vibe for you."

"Good point," he said.

"Here's an idea," Kit said, scrambling a bit now. "When you

narrow the hunt down to a few choices, why don't you have me take a look with you and offer my input. I'd be happy to do it free of charge."

"I'd hate to have you go to all that trouble."

"It wouldn't be any trouble. And I might have some insight that proves valuable."

She could almost hear him deliberating.

"All right then. I may actually be taking a second look at a spot this week. Thursday night. Are you free?"

"Yes, actually I am. I'd love to join you."

"Okay, I'll call you with the details later in the week."

Ten minutes later she wandered into Baby's study, where she was just wrapping up a call herself.

"Well, to borrow one of your favorite phrases, I think I've managed to pull my ass out of the fire. I just heard back from Barry and he's coming over Wednesday—so get the cocktail shaker ready. And the good doctor may be back on board."

"Excellent. How about dinner then?"

"Let me fix it. I ordered groceries online and they should be here shortly."

There was still, however, one call she wanted to make before the meal. Even as she'd torn through her work that afternoon, she'd found it hard to put Garrett Kelman out of her thoughts. She might not have total trust in him, but she believed him far more than she had a day ago, and things just felt unresolved between them. She decided to call him, to at least thank him for doing what he'd promised. Grabbing a breath, she tapped his number on her phone.

He didn't answer. She reached only the automated voice asking that she leave a reply.

"Garrett, please call me," she said. "I know you did what you said you would. I realize we're not supposed to discuss the case, but I'd like to just touch base."

The evening passed with no return call. Five hours later, as she switched off the light on the bedside table, she was pretty sure there wouldn't be one—tonight or ever.

And though Kelman would be out of her life, the crisis he'd instigated would continue to cast its pall over everything. She'd be looking over her shoulder for as long as she could imagine.

chapter 22

She tried to stay busy over the next two days, fixating on work, but it grew harder again. There was only so much she could accomplish holed up at Baby's, and many of her files and supplies were back at the office. She decided that on Thursday, after her presentation to Barry was out of the way, she would sneak downtown to her apartment. She'd pick up fresh clothes, as well as the stuff she needed for work, and the ton of mail that must have accumulated.

The idea of going home, even for a short while, frightened her. As far as she knew, people from Ithaka were keeping an eye on her place, banking on the fact that at some point she'd have to return. She called Andre, her super, and asked if he could meet her there at ten on Thursday and hang around while she let herself into the apartment. That would at least provide an ounce of security.

Wednesday was a good day for business. Holt called to confirm meeting her in Tribeca Thursday night to view the loft he was interested in. She smiled in relief, anxious to hold on to the assignment. Because the building had no doorman, he suggested she wait at a nearby coffee shop and that he'd call when he was close. That suited her just fine. It meant she wouldn't be left alone in the foyer of a strange building.

The bronzed hotel man finally returned Baby's call and asked for a Friday appointment. He wasn't expecting a presentation at this point, he said, just more discussion. Baby suggested that on Thursday afternoon she and Kit spend at least an hour brainstorming so that they had a few ideas to dazzle him with.

The meeting with Barry that night went off perfectly. He arrived exactly at six, went wide-eyed when Baby's housekeeper entered the room hoisting a silver tray of sparkling cocktail glasses, the famed almond-crusted salmon ball ringed with water crackers, and a silver bowl of multicolored olives. He looked even more stunned as Baby swept in a moment later in a cream-colored caftan, parts of it billowing like sails on a schooner.

Kit and Baby exchanged amused glances when they realized that Barry was wearing a tie in a fabric practically identical to one Kit was suggesting for a throw pillow. She took that as a good omen, and it turned out to be one.

"Well, this was certainly worth the wait," he told her after he'd reviewed the presentation. "It's fantastic. When can we get started? This is my busiest season, but I don't want to delay."

"We'll begin immediately," Kit said. A lot of shopping would have to be farmed out, but he didn't have to know that.

After he departed, she sighed and turned to Baby.

"Well, there's one down at least."

As soon as she woke on Thursday morning, she could feel her apprehension start to build, like the distant roar of a train that would soon come tearing through a tunnel. She'd be heading downtown, and not only would she be exposed, but she'd also have to face the place where Avery had died.

At least Andre was good to his word and was waiting in front of the building when her cab pulled up. As Kit stepped out, she quickly scanned the area. The only people around were the types she was used to seeing in the neighborhood day in and day out—black-clad, unhurried-looking Nolita residents and a cluster of tourists with a huge city map.

Andre greeted her, opened the door to the lobby, and immediately pointed out the security camera he and his son had installed.

"It's such a terrible thing, the murder of that girl," he said as she dug out the letters and catalogs jammed in her mailbox. "The police—do they have any suspects?"

"Not that I'm aware of, Andre. Have they been around?"

"Yes, here and there. Asking questions of tenants and me and my son. I'm just thankful my son was in Brooklyn that night and people saw him. You know how innocent people can get snared in these things."

"Don't I," she said ruefully.

Andre had summoned the elevator. As they stepped inside, Kit's gaze flew first thing to the red stop button on the brass panel. She wondered if the police were working with the same theory that Kelman had suggested, that someone had stopped the elevator that night, forcing Avery to use the stairs.

As they exited on the fifth floor, she couldn't help but glance at the stairwell door. Her guilt over Avery's murder was still raw. Part of her longed to be rid of it, but that seemed callous.

Once they reached her apartment, she saw that the customized door had been installed, and Andre handed over the new keys. She unlocked the door and after they entered, they both looked cautiously around. Nothing had been disturbed since she was last there.

"You haven't seen anyone suspicious around, have you?" she asked Andre. "Any men who don't look like they should be in the building?"

"No, and I've made a point of being here a lot. My son, too. And I check the tape from the camera each day. Nothing suspicious."

She sighed. What he'd shared wasn't good for much, but it smoothed the edges on her nerves just a little.

"It will probably take at least thirty minutes to pack up my stuff. Do you mind waiting around? I could use your help taking everything downstairs."

"Of course. I have work to do on the third floor. Just call me on my mobile when you're ready."

A moment later she had her apartment to herself. Her response, as she wandered through the space, surprised her. She had thought her fear would color everything, ruin it for her. But it felt so sweet to be back inside, to see and touch her possessions. The air was still faintly redolent with the scent from the fig candles she burned most nights when she was home alone. Unexpectedly she felt a surge of anger. They wanted to take all this from her, she thought. But she wasn't going to let them.

She packed quickly, jamming as much as possible into her backup suitcase, including clothes she'd need as the weather warmed up over the next couple of weeks. When it was time to retrieve items from the office, she felt herself go on higher alert. But after letting herself in, she discovered that everything appeared as she'd left it. Still moving quickly, she loaded two tote bags with files and supplies, including sketching paper, fabric samples, and extra fan decks of paint chips.

Mission completed, she called Andre. As good as it felt for her to be home, she didn't want to linger. He returned immediately, carrying several packages, one of which was a long packing roll addressed to Baby that she realized was from Colin, the main draftsman they used. Dara had been sending messengers down to collect any packages that had arrived, but the drawings must have slipped through the cracks.

"Oh, thanks, Andre," she said. "I'd appreciate it if you could keep holding on to packages as they arrive, and we'll arrange to have them picked up."

"Are you ever coming back, though?" he asked. With a super it was impossible to tell if questions sprang from genuine concern or a need for information that might impact him in the long run.

"Of course, I'll be back," she answered hurriedly, though she hadn't a clue what the future held. "I'm just staying with a friend for now and working from her apartment."

"That reminds me, a client came by the other day—on Tuesday, I think. A woman."

It must have been one of Baby's, Kit realized, because she couldn't imagine which of hers it could be.

"Did she leave her name?"

"No, not a name. She was tall, with long black hair. A very attractive lady. The type with money. She said she wanted to see you."

Sasha, she realized with a start.

"What did you tell her, Andre?"

"That you were away and she should try you by phone."

She'd never thought to caution Andre to keep quiet.

"That's all?"

"She wanted to know where you were," he told her. "I told her you'd left with one of your co-workers. But that I didn't have any idea where you were staying."

Kit let out a ragged sigh, feeling her fear spike. The word co-worker might prompt Sasha to put two and two together.

"Nothing else? That was all she said?"

"There was just one other thing," he said, his brow furrowing. "She asked a funny question."

"Did she want Mrs. Meadow's home address?"

"No. She asked if a man with red hair had been staying with you. If you now lived together."

Kit stared at him, stunned by the craziness of his revelation. Sasha had come down here trying to figure out if Kelman was camped out with her. If Sasha was really involved with him, how could she be wondering where he was living? It suggested that Kelman had told her the truth. Sasha was obsessed with him.

But what *else* did it mean? Was Sasha also doing Wainwright's bidding, attempting to suss out her whereabouts?

"What did you tell her?"

"I told her I didn't discuss my tenants' personal affairs. But *will* there be someone living with you? I need to know for the lease, of course."

Kit shook her head.

"No, no one is going to be living with me, Andre. And certainly not a red-haired man."

"All right then." He shrugged. "You know what my son says—though I don't think it's true. Most people are descended from monkeys, but redheads are descended from cats."

She laughed in spite of herself. Maybe that explained a few things, she thought.

She and the super lugged her belongings downstairs. Before she closed the door of the taxi, she pressed twenty-five dollars into Andre's hand for his efforts, and urged him to say nothing about her to anyone. As the taxi made its way north, Andre's revelation ate at her. If Sasha had deduced from his comment that Kit was at Baby's, she might be watching the apartment building on Park Avenue, and that meant Baby was exposed, too.

"What's she up to, do you think?" Baby asked after Kit shared the new development.

"I don't know. It could be that she's in the thick of things and has been told to play detective and figure out where I am. As a potential client of mine, she's got a cover. I'm just worried she may have deduced I'm staying with you."

"This place is like a fortress, but we should take extra precautions. Write down a description of her and let me go speak to the concierge. I'll tell him to be on the lookout for anyone like that. I'll say it's a client who's gone off her rocker."

After Baby headed downstairs, Kit wandered into the guest room. There was an urgent call she needed to make, one she'd considered the entire cab ride north. She dug out her phone and tapped Garrett Kelman's number. It didn't surprise her when she reached his voicemail.

"Garrett," she said. "I know you're not keen on speaking to me, but I need your advice. Sasha Glen has been snooping around my apartment building. It's important that I understand more about the problems you had with her. Can you get in touch with me, please?"

He called back two minutes later.

"What do you mean snooping around?" he asked. His voice was cool, distant sounding, but she could detect a note of alarm.

She related what her super had told her.

"Did you ever listen to the voicemail message I left you—the one about Sasha?" he said.

"Yes. But I admit, I was reluctant to believe it. Until now."

"You need to watch out for her, Kit. Stay as far away from her as possible."

"Do you think she's involved in the insider trading?"

"I was wrong about Matt Healy so who am I to say for sure, but my guess is that she's too much of a loose cannon for anyone to have included her in that kind of scheme. There's something truly off with her."

"What could she want with me?"

"She may have figured out, from things she's overheard, that we've been in contact. And she sees you as a threat."

"But why would she jump to the conclusion that we're in-volved?"

"It wouldn't take much for her to decide that. Like I told you in my message, I went to bed with her just a couple of times and she became fixated. She imagined this whole relationship with me that didn't exist."

"And now she's imagining you and I are together."

"Sounds like it. What were you doing down at your apartment? I thought you were going to be careful. I know this is frustrating, Kit, but you just have to be patient and watch your back at all times."

"I *am* going to watch my back. But I refuse to shut my entire life down. Who knows how long this is going to take."

"I think things will start to move," he said, reiterating what Nat Naylor had said. "Ithaka is wise to this, and the FBI will want to get in there, look at records."

"If Ithaka has already destroyed records, will your evidence be the only thing the government has to go on?"

"Ideally, they'll find corroborating evidence. My guess is that they'll try to get a doctor to flip, someone who provided info to Kennelly and Lister."

"That old guy you spoke to on the phone?"

"Yes, or maybe someone else on the advisory committee who might have been in on it."

She sensed he was ready to end the call. No, she decided. She couldn't let him go.

"Garrett, would you be willing to meet? Just to talk. Not about the case, but I feel there are things we need to say to each other."

"Do you think you can finally trust me?"

"I think so. It's been hard because everything went to hell, but I want to clear the air."

There was a long pause, and she found herself holding her breath.

"Where? And when? We have to be careful."

"I'm going to sneak out tonight to meet a client. In Tribeca. If you're still at the same apartment, I could come by after that."

"I don't like the idea of you leaving wherever you are."

"I won't be going out a lot, but there are appointments I *have* to keep. Otherwise, there'll be nothing waiting for me when the case is resolved."

"What if I meet you downtown when you're done. We can find a place to talk and then I can bring you home."

"Okay, I should be finished at about eight or so."

"All right, I'll wait at a bar or restaurant in that area. Call me when you're wrapping up."

When she disconnected, she was surprised at how much relief she felt. So she would have another shot at seeing him after all. And maybe there was a tiny chance she could make him want to renew their connection. Because that was what she wanted. Weeks ago when she'd asked Baby how she could have done such a bad job judging X in Florida, Baby had told her to think back about the warning signs she'd missed, but in hindsight Kit had never seen any. She'd been drawn to him. She had wanted something from him. And she still did.

She spent the rest of the afternoon brainstorming with Baby about their meeting with Steven Harper and reviewing a shopping strategy for the bachelor apartment with the freelancer she would be using. At six, she changed for her meeting with Holt.

"Any tips you'd recommend on how I should play this?" she asked Baby.

"Yes, stay home," Baby said. "Let *me* go."

"You've already been doing far more than you should. And I don't want to throw him any more curveballs."

Baby sighed. "Okay, then I'd say you want to regain the power position. Be happy to help but not needy to please. And seem busy with work. Toward the end you might even glance at your watch and say, 'I'm so sorry but I need to meet another client now.'"

"Do you use this same kind of technique with men, as well?"

"I would if I could meet one who didn't write his Match profile in all caps or tell me that his main goal in life is to seize the day."

They hugged goodbye and Kit took off. Though she'd managed to squash her anxiety as she'd worked and brainstormed that afternoon, the minute she was in the lobby, it began to bully its way back. She still meant what she'd said at FBI headquarters, that she wasn't going to let her life be destroyed, and yet she felt far less nervy each time she actually went out into the world. This time when she surveyed the courtyard, she was on the alert not just for strange men but also for a tall, dark-haired woman with a less-than-sane look in her eyes.

She arrived ahead of schedule at the small café and took a seat at the counter, where she ordered a cup of tea. Lost in thought, she finally glanced at her watch and saw that it was ten minutes past when Holt was supposed to call. She drank more tea and recollected how good it had been to be back in her apartment, even if only for a short while. She thought about Kelman, too, and what she would say to him later. She didn't want him out of her life.

Once again, she glanced at her watch: 7:22. She wondered if Holt might have been forced to contend with a patient emergency or if the two of them had gotten their signals crossed somehow. She was just about to call his office when her phone rang.

"So sorry for the delay," he told her.

"Not a problem."

"I was dealing with the real estate agent. She was originally going to accompany us, but then she couldn't get away this early. She's entrusted me with the keys so we can get in ourselves. I'm in the lobby right now, over on North Moore Street. Shall I swing by and pick you up?"

"That's so kind of you, but it won't be necessary. I'll just run over there now."

He gave her the exact address, and after paying her bill, she headed there, checking twice behind her, just making sure. North Moore was a charming street, just several blocks long, she realized, running between West Broadway and West Street.

The building itself was fairly nondescript but attractive enough, the limestone painted a creamy off-white. Kit guessed that before a major renovation, it once had contained small, floor-through factories or industrial offices.

As promised, Holt was waiting inside the foyer and he smiled in greeting. His gray-tinged hair had grown a little longer since she'd last seen him and he'd brushed it back against the sides of his head. He was wearing an overcoat today and thin, brown leather gloves. Dapper looking. Doctor in charge.

As Holt fiddled with the keys, she peered through the glass door into the lobby. A large roll of brown builder's paper was leaning against one of the walls and sheets of it had been spread on the floor. Her guess: none of the apartments were even occupied yet.

Holt finally selected a key, inserted it into the lock, and when that one didn't work, tried the other. He cursed under his breath. After a few moments of jiggling, the lock finally gave. Holt turned the handle, gave the door a push, and then turned to her.

"Sorry to seem so aggravated," he said. "I just assumed the real estate woman would be helping us. She at least promised to stop by later."

"Don't worry about it. I've been a bit crazed myself lately."

He paused and looked at her.

"I have to ask. Are you still interested in the project? I've been concerned you've had too much else going on in your life."

God, she'd been right. He *had* been pulling back in the last week, drawing certain conclusions about her ability to manage the job.

"Oh, no, I'm totally game," she said, flashing a big grin that she hoped he wouldn't read as forced. "I'm really looking forward to collaborating."

"Good, so am I. And I could really use your input on this place."

"If you're seeing the apartment for a second time, it must have spoken to you."

"It did," he said, as they tramped over the sheets of builder's paper toward the elevator. "Lots of light. Lots of walls for art. And the loft I'm looking at is on the sixth floor—the top one—so there's access to a roof deck."

"What about the commute from here, though?" Kit said as they boarded the elevator. "Even if you use a cab or a car service, it's probably going to take close to forty-five minutes to reach the hospital."

"True, it's not as convenient as my current place, but I can always read in the cab each morning. My main goal is to find a space I love."

When they reached the floor, she discovered there were just two apartments. Holt motioned to the one directly across from the elevator. He had a key for that door, too, but it turned out they didn't need it.

"The agent mentioned it might be unlocked," he told her, swinging open the door. "There were workmen here today apparently. It's all been remodeled."

The place appeared to be about two thousand square feet in size, with large windows capturing a vista of downtown roofs and old, shingled water towers. Because of the remodeling there wasn't a lick of furniture, and that meant no floor lamps either. Holt reached for a light switch and flicked on a series of pin lights in the ceiling, which did a semi-decent job of illuminating the room.

She didn't love what she saw. There was a shotgun feeling to the main room, less of a loft, really, and more just an apartment that seemed to go back forever. One of the walls was exposed brick, which was a throwback to another era, when people wanted their living spaces to have the cozy feel of a brick-walled tavern. But based on Holt's comments in the lobby, she decided to proceed carefully. She didn't want to dampen his enthusiasm or risk losing the job.

"Wow, you're right," she remarked. "The light in the daytime must be fabulous."

"And the walls? Terrific for art, aren't they?"

"Um, sure." If he ever really bought the place, she'd recommend painting the brick white at least.

He narrowed his eyes, curious. "There's something you're not saying."

"I'm just taking it all in."

"Let me show you the rest then."

She followed him to the rear of the apartment. Midway back on the right was a poorly conceived, windowless middle room, which she couldn't imagine being good for anything other than a nursery; to the left were storage areas, a small laundry room visible through an open door, and a service entrance to the apartment.

At the far back, side-by-side, were the two bedrooms. The master, which he showed her first, was spacious, and yet there was something off about the dimensions. Too big a room for simply a bed and a couple of dressers and yet not quite big enough to also accommodate a reading chair and ottoman. The master bath at least was nice—floor to ceiling gray and white Italian marble.

"So what do you think?" Holt inquired, his tone not disguising how pumped he felt about it.

"It would certainly be a big change from where you're living now. But that seems to be exactly what you're aiming for."

He raised an eyebrow.

"That's it? I thought you'd have more to say."

She felt momentarily flustered. She might want the business, but there was no way she could out-and-out lie and let him choose a place that ultimately wouldn't suit his needs. She quickly searched for the words that would strike the right balance.

"Well, I'd be happy to give you my feedback. But I have the sense that you're already leaning toward this place and you may not want me to throw a wrench in the works."

"I do love the apartment, but I'm not an expert. I could really use your input."

"Okay, to be honest, I think you could find something much more special than this." She swung her arm around the room. "It feels a bit constrained, as if the walls are pressing in. I love the idea of you in a loft, but one with a truly spacious feel."

He chortled. "Well, at least you're not one to mince words. As long as we're here, why don't you check out the second bedroom? Then I'll take you out for a bite to eat and we can discuss the pros and cons over a nice meal and a bottle of wine."

"Um, I'm sorry," she said. She had told Garrett she'd be free by eight. "That's very nice of you, Keith, but I have to meet with a friend in a bit. What if we did lunch tomorrow instead?"

He looked at her, and to her surprise she saw the muscles around his eyes tighten, as if a screw had been turned on each side. "Oh, just like last time then," he said, his voice strangely cold, almost hostile. "You had to dash off for a rendezvous."

That's right, she thought, wincing internally from his tone. She'd turned him down for dinner before, on the day they'd met for espressos at the café. Did he actually have a romantic interest in her? She'd wondered that briefly before, even entertained what it would be like, but had dismissed the whole idea.

"But like I said, we could grab lunch," Kit told him. "If you really love this place, we can talk about how to make—"

Before she could finish, a noise startled her. Holt heard it, too, and they turned in unison toward the front of the apartment. It had sounded like the elevator being called back to another floor.

"What was that?" Kit asked, her heart skipping.

"Let me check."

"Wait," she said. What if, even after all her precautions to-night, she'd been followed to North Moore Street. "Maybe we should go together. I've had some problems lately. . . ."

"I'm sure it's just the real estate agent." He touched her arm reassuringly. "Take a look at the second bedroom and I'll bring her back."

"All right," she said reluctantly. As he turned, something stirred in her, like water being swirled in a jar.

She watched for a moment while he hurried down the long hallway to the front. What if it *wasn't* the real estate agent? she thought, feeling her body tense. But no, she was overreacting, she told herself. The woman had promised to come, so it must be her.

Grabbing a breath, she left the master bedroom and poked her head into the room next door. It was incredibly small, a space suited for either a child or a houseguest grateful just for a bed.

She backed out of the bedroom and looked back toward the front of the building. No sign of Holt. She wondered if he'd gone down in the elevator looking for the agent.

Something continued to stir in her as she stood there, wait-ing, wondering what to do. She realized how much she disliked the curt, icy tone Holt had used when she'd told him she'd have to pass on dinner. His remark had been weirdly proprietary.

Had she been reading him wrong these past couple of weeks, failing to suss out an attraction on his part that might be propel-ling him to work with her? When he'd asked her for dinner the first time—the day they met at the café—she'd been a little concerned his intentions weren't purely business, but no alarm bells had gone off. She'd been meeting Garrett that night, and when she'd explained to Holt that she had to run out at seven o'clock for a meeting, he'd seemed to take it in stride. No harm done.

And then, like a rogue wave, fear quickly engulfed her. Ever since Avery's murder, an end that had been earmarked for *her*, Kit had been mystified as to why the killer chose to wait in the stairwell just before seven. Who could have assumed she was going out at that time?

But there was one person who surely would have assumed it. Keith Holt—because she'd told him that was her plan.

chapter 23

No, she thought, shaking her head, it couldn't be true. It was too absurd, too improbable. But memories tumbled forward in rapid succession: Holt popping up as a new client without a specific referral; Holt seeing her in the trench coat the day of Avery's murder; Holt not taking her call the morning afterward, even though he was in the office. Was that because he'd assumed he'd killed her and was too stunned by the fact that she was on the line?

She recalled a comment that Garrett had made earlier, that there could have been more than one doctor involved in the insider trading situation. But Holt was an orthopedic surgeon, not a cancer doctor.

And if he'd lured her down here to kill her, why go chasing noises. Another thought rammed her. Maybe he'd arranged for a confederate to meet him here, someone from Ithaka.

Again, she told herself that it was all too farfetched. And yet the panic coursing through her overrode every argument her brain was making. She couldn't take any chances. She had to get out of there.

She rushed the few steps back to the entrance of the master bedroom and glanced down the larger hall toward the front of the apartment. Holt was still not in sight, and the loft was utterly quiet. She didn't dare sneak out the front door—he would be coming back in. But there was the service exit.

She inched as quietly as she could down the hallway, past the laundry room and the storage units, until she reached the service door. Please be unlocked, she begged. She tugged and the door flew open. It was dark in the corridor and she had no clue where the light switch was. She patted the wall frantically with her hand without any luck. After a moment, outlines emerged. She could see a door that was clearly to the stairs. She rushed toward it, yanked it open, and began to descend, holding tight to the handrail.

On the landing she jerked to a stop—to listen, to get her bearings. If she just kept going, she would reach a door that opened onto the lobby and from there she'd be free. She thought of the phone in her purse. She needed to call Garrett, to get him to come, but she didn't dare lose the seconds it would take.

She started to move again, quickly reaching the next floor. Just five more floors, she told herself. She listened again, straining to hear over her thumping heartbeat. A faint noise made a tear in the silence. It was the sound of a door being quietly opened and then sucked closed. Someone had stepped into the stairwell. But she couldn't tell if it had come from above her or below.

Hide, she commanded herself. She eased open the door to her right and tiptoed into the corridor. Once again she was engulfed in darkness, but after a moment she could make out the doors to two apartments. She prayed they'd be unlocked like the one upstairs. She reached the closest and twisted the handle with trembling fingers. It opened.

No lights were on, but the windows were curtain-less and there was just enough illumination from outside for her to pick out shapes. The place was nearly empty, no furniture. And floors here were laid with builder's paper, too. She closed the door behind her and started toward the back of the apartment. An aluminum ladder had been propped against the wall just outside the bedroom and as she rushed by, her elbow caught the edge of it.

She knew from the apartment upstairs that there was a walk-in closet in the bedroom and she hurried toward it. She opened the door and stepped into total blackness. Her body brushed against something hard and metal—another ladder she realized. She could feel paint cans with her feet, a cluster of them on the floor.

After tugging the door shut, she tore open her purse and searched for her phone. Where the hell is it? she wondered desperately. Finally she had it clutched in her fist.

But first she listened. Making sure the apartment was empty.

Kelman answered on the first ring.

"All set?" he asked.

"I'm in trouble," she whispered, the words barely forming.

"*Where?*"

"North Moore Street." In her terror she struggled to recall the number. "I think 22—" She realized she wasn't alone in the apartment. She could hear footsteps advancing toward the bedroom, making a swishing sound on the paper that lined the floor.

"Kit?" Kelman called.

"Shhh—" she told him, dropping the phone into her coat pocket.

A bar of light popped beneath the door. Two more footsteps.

And then, horrified, she watched as the door swung open. Keith Holt was standing there.

"My goodness," he said. "Are we playing hide and seek now?"

There was menace in his tone. She knew what she'd guessed upstairs was probably true, but she couldn't let him see that in her eyes.

"I'm sorry," she said, her voice choked. "I was frightened."

"Frightened?"

"I told you upstairs. Some things have happened to me. Then we heard that noise."

He pursed his lips.

"I thought someone had gotten off the elevator," he said, "but when I came back inside, I realized we'd simply heard the wind rattling the windows up front."

"Well," she said, forcing a smile that she knew looked fake, "another reason this might not be the perfect place to live."

"Ah, yes."

"What about the agent?" she asked, shifting a little to the left. She was still in the closet and she needed to get out. But he was standing squarely in front of her, like some kind of colossus. "Maybe we should see if she's in the lobby."

He pursed his lips again. "Actually, no agent was ever coming. To be perfectly honest, I needed a little time alone with you tonight. I'm still trying to figure out what kind of game you're playing."

Her knees went soft, ready to buckle. Yes, she'd been right. He was one of the doctors, in the middle of everything.

"You need to let me leave, Dr. Holt," she said, raising her voice slightly in the hope that Kelman could hear her and realize who she was with.

"No, I can't do that. Because I see you've figured it out now. I'm not sure how you did it, but I can read it in your face."

"I don't know what you mean."

"Oh, yes, you do." Holt's whole body tightened. "If you're smart, you won't play any more games with me."

Maybe, she thought desperately, there was a way to bargain with him.

"Please, I'm not playing any games. But tell me what you want."

"For starters, I want the fucking flash drive," he snarled.

There it was again. The freaking flash drive.

"Who told you I have that?"

"Matt Healy. And don't dare tell me you have no clue what I'm talking about."

She shook her head.

"No, I'll be straight with you, I promise. But—but I want to understand." She realized she needed to keep him talking, give Kelman a chance to try to reach her, to call the police. "You worked with Healy? You told him about the drug results?"

He scoffed, shook his head in disgust.

"To my utter regret, yes. Oh, he was all wine and dine and big bucks when we first met. Wanted to pay me nicely for my efforts. And then months later he ends up in a fucking panic. One of his co-workers had stumbled onto evidence of the illegal trades, wanted to take it to the SEC. Healy was trying to manage him, trick him, but then the guy suddenly admitted that he'd put all the evidence on a flash drive and some girl he'd screwed had stolen it. He swore there could be nothing about me on the drive, but I couldn't take any chances."

"And he told you my name. That's why you called me that Friday, to set up an appointment."

"Someone had to take charge. Healy was out of control. Losing it. I had no idea why you took the drive, but I had to get it."

"But first you followed him to Florida."

"He vowed he was going to try to shore up the situation. But I couldn't trust him to do it. I parked by the place he was staying, asked him to come out and chat in my car. I could tell from what he was saying that he'd be more than willing to throw me under the bus to save his own hide."

"And so you ran him down," she said. The words emerged in little more than a whisper.

"Do you think I was going to let him *ruin* me?" She saw his hands clench, still in the brown leather gloves. "Make it so I could never practice medicine again?"

He paused, curling his lip malevolently. "And I wasn't going to let *you* ruin me either, whatever your game is. You left me no choice than to hack my way into your apartment."

"But I never planned to ruin anyone, I swear. I took the flash drive by mistake. I didn't know anything about the trades."

"Oh, is that right?" he said snidely. "The day after the break-in you were practically gloating that the thief hadn't gotten what was most important. It was like you were sitting there mocking me as I fixed you a fucking espresso."

She remembered the moment suddenly. She'd begun to sense at that point that the thieves had wanted more than her iPod speakers and she'd made a vague comment to that effect.

"I didn't—"

"It was all I could do to resist reaching out and smashing your face in."

She felt a fresh surge of panic. Had Kelman called the police by now? Couldn't they trace her location through her phone?

"You killed Avery, thinking it was me."

"Let's just say you gave me quite a shock when you called my office the next morning. But I've said enough. I want to know what your little game is. Were you planning to blackmail Healy, or anyone else you could find?"

"No, like I said, I—I just stumbled into the whole thing. The flash drive was in a pen and I took it by mistake."

She was scrambling now, trying to figure out how to buy more time. How to save herself.

"Oh, please. What do you take me for?"

"If you want the flash drive, I can give it to you," she said hurriedly. "I have the pen with me."

He narrowed his dark eyes, studying her intensely.

"All right," he said, eerily calm now. But that wouldn't be enough, she knew. He would try to twist her neck the way he'd done to Avery. That was why he'd worn the gloves.

"Let me get it," she said. "Let me get it right now." She jabbed her hand in her purse and started rooting desperately. Holt yanked one side of the purse toward him and peered in.

"Don't tell me you've got something like a gun in there."

"No, I just want to find the pen for you." He let the bag snap back toward her. Finally, she felt the smooth, cool barrel of her father's Mont Blanc.

"Here it is," she said, yanking her hand from the bag. She held it out, showing him. He started to reach for it. And when he did, she stepped back and flung the pen in his face.

He jerked back defensively, but the pen still caught him in the left eye, then bounced off. His hand flew to his face.

In a split second Kit reached down and grabbed one of the paint cans by the handle. It was half full, still heavy. She hoisted it up and swung it hard at Holt's head.

It hit with such force that it made a huge thwacking sound and ricocheted, almost hitting her, too. Holt moaned in pain. As he reeled back, Kit dropped the can with a thud, stepped around Holt and began to run, toward the door to the stairwell.

Within seconds he was behind her, grabbing her by the shoulder. As he yanked her backward, she swung around, striking him with her open arm. She started to run again, but he hurled himself at her, sending her sprawling to the ground. Pain shot from one end of her body to the other.

Before she knew it, he had her by both feet, dragging her backward, her arms outstretched. "Help!" she screamed.

"Shut up," he said, "or I'll make you regret it."

She let her body go limp, trying to think. He'd nearly reached the bedroom, gripping her hard by the ankles. She could feel his rage surging through his hands. He was going to kill her, she knew, snap her neck in two.

She saw the ladder then, propped against the wall. She reached for it with her hand, bringing it toppling down on both of them. It rammed into her head and her arm, sending a bolt of pain through her. Behind her Holt yelped and let go of her feet. She sensed him falling backward. She scrambled up, then bolted toward the stairwell door. This time she reached it. After flinging the door wide, she clattered down the stairs. Her lungs felt as if they were about to explode.

In no time he was behind her again—she could hear his feet pounding on the stairs. She made it down to one landing, and then another flight of steps, but as she reached the next floor, he caught up to her, yanked her hard again by the back of her jacket.

Her body lurched backward, the jacket choking her. She wrestled away from him and spun around. Blood was running into his eyes from a gash on his head.

Kit clenched her fist and tried to strike out, but the blow only grazed him. He grabbed her arm and shoved her against the handrail. With all the strength she could muster, she brought up her foot and kicked him hard in the knee. It thrust him backward. He reached out, trying to grab onto her for support, but he couldn't reach her, couldn't even see with the blood in his eyes. He staggered backward and went tumbling down the stairs.

He landed in a heap on the next landing, groaning. She couldn't take the chance of trying to maneuver by him. Grabbing a breath, she tore up the stairs, one flight, then another and another. She was on six finally. She burst into the apartment and raced to the main door and into the hallway.

She jabbed frantically at the elevator button and saw to her dismay it was on one. But there was no sign of Holt behind her. Finally the elevator reached the floor. She threw herself inside and pressed one. When she reached the ground floor, she held her breath and peered out. Still no sign of Holt. She charged through the lobby and out the main door.

It was dark, but there were people in the street. She ran toward Broadway, her lungs on fire. And then up ahead, rushing toward her with his phone in his hand was Garrett Kelman. Tears of relief welled in her eyes.

"Are you okay?" he yelled.

"Yes." She touched her head. There was already a lump from where the ladder had rammed into her.

"The building number you gave me was wrong. I was rushing up and down the street trying to find you."

"He tried to kill me. My doctor client. He was involved with Healy."

"Where is he?"

"Still in the building, I think. He's injured. He fell down the stairs."

"I called the cops. They say they're coming."

"He killed Healy. And Avery, too."

He pulled her into his arms, pressing her against his chest. The leather of his jacket was cool from the night air.

"I felt so helpless," he said. "I could hear you, but I had no idea where you were. Just tell me you're really okay."

She pulled back for a moment and looked at him.

"Yes," she said, a smile forming on her face. "I kind of managed to beat the shit out of him."

He smiled. "Way to go."

And then, not far from them, they heard sirens.

"It must be the cops," Kelman said. "I told them to come midway down the block. We better go meet them."

chapter 24

Two and a half weeks later Kit moved back to her apartment.

Baby came down with her that day, along with her housekeeper, who Baby had enlisted to help not only haul bags but Swiffer away the layer of dust that had settled over everything. Kit thought how nice it would have been to have Dara in the mix, too, but she was still on leave and they weren't sure if she'd ever return.

After they'd organized the office and the housekeeper had departed, Baby opened a bag of sandwiches she'd packed and a bottle of rosé. She and Kit settled on the sofa.

"Your apartment looks great, but just say the word and you can be back at my place in a heartbeat," Baby told her. She was dressed for spring today, in cream-colored pants and a pale pink blouse. Her nails matched the blouse perfectly.

"Thanks," Kit said, "but I'm ready to be home. You know what's really going to kill me, though? Sliding into my sheets tonight and remembering what yours feel like in comparison. But it's given me something to aspire to."

"At least now I know what to get you for your next birthday."

"Don't you dare think of getting me *anything*. I owe you so much, Baby."

"You would have done the same for me, Kit—though, God

forbid I ever get to meet some dashing male stranger with a dark secret. But in all seriousness, do you really feel safe?"

Holt had survived the fall down the stairs with only a broken arm, cracked ribs, and a mild concussion, but he'd been arrested immediately and was being held without bail.

"Yes, I think I feel safe," Kit told Baby.

"That sounds tentative."

"Let's put it this way, with Holt out of the picture, I don't feel in imminent danger. As for Ithaka, there's enough evidence against them on the insider trading front that I'm low on their list of concerns. I'll probably look over my shoulder sometimes just out of habit, but I'm ready to get back to my life."

Well, not exactly, she thought. As she'd already realized, she didn't want to return to the old way. She wanted something new. Gutsier choices.

Baby took a swig of her rosé, appeared to briefly relish the taste, and then turned pensive.

"I'm still troubled by the fact that I was such a bad judge of men. I practically had you engaged to Keith Holt."

"I never saw anything sinister about him either," Kit admitted. "He seemed intense at times, but I always expect surgeons to be that way."

"And I take it he never had any intentions of redecorating?"

"No, no, that was all a big fat lie. On the same day that Healy reported to him about me taking the flash drive, he called and asked for an appointment so he could assess me and try to figure out what I was up to. The only thing he ever intended to redecorate was my neck."

"And was the apartment hunting story all a ruse, too?"

"Yes. I'm sure when he first mentioned the idea to me he was just planting a seed in case he ever needed to lure me alone someplace."

"I accept that you can't tell me why he wanted you dead or

how it connects to the case, but I have to say, it's torturing me
not knowing. I can't stand the thought of how close he came to
hurting you."

"One day in the not too distant future I *will* be able to talk
about it, and I'll share everything."

Baby sighed, drumming her fingers softly on the arm of the
sofa.

"Well, we might have been wrong about Holt, but there's
one man you guessed right about from the start. He who carries
a big spear."

Kit laughed.

"Yeah, I made plenty of mistakes along the way, but my
initial sense of Garrett Kelman was right. That he was a man
worth knowing."

Kelman had gone with her to the police precinct the night
she'd been attacked, waited with her for Nat Naylor, and then
dropped her off at Baby's later. By that point her body felt like
one huge, throbbing bruise—from her being knocked to the
floor and dragged, from being conked by the aluminum ladder.
She'd slept that night as if she was drugged.

She'd seen Kelman again the next morning. He'd come to
Baby's briefly just to check on her. A day or so later he'd taken
off for Florida with his attorney to straighten matters out with
Molinari and her partner, and to spend time with his sister,
whom he'd given the all-clear to come home.

Since he'd left town, Kit had heard from him just twice—
brief phone calls to see how she was doing. She had no idea
what the future held for them. She trusted him now, and felt as
drawn to him as she had that night in Islamorada, and yet she
had begun to wonder if he was distancing himself, not because
he didn't experience the same connection but because it was
all too complicated, and there was too much cold, black water
under the bridge.

And then he'd called today to say he was back and was hoping to see her, as soon as tonight. She had suggested he come by her place and that she'd fix them both something simple for dinner.

"I should probably let you settle in," Baby said. "I'll see you tomorrow for work."

"Now that you've gotten a taste of working from home every day, would you prefer to do more of it."

"God no. I feel energized coming down here. Oh, by the way, if you have the time tomorrow, I can take you to the hotel. The building's not more than a shell right now, but it will be good for you to see the exterior and the neighborhood. That needs to be considered as we start to brainstorm."

Last week, much to their satisfaction, they'd learned that they'd landed the hotel job. Harper would be a challenge, but Baby said she would do much of the heavy lifting when it came to dealing with him personally.

"Oh, I have a piece of good news myself," Kit announced. "Last night I heard from a friend of Barry Kaplan's, another single guy. Barry showed him the boards and he wants me to do something similar at his place."

Baby laughed. "Well that's an insider trading tip we could pass along if we wanted to. There's about to be a huge run on pinstriped flannel."

After Baby took off, Kit wandered back into her office. Despite the awful associations the space had with Avery's death, it was good to be back there, too, and to realize that her business wasn't going to go down the tubes. The next weeks were likely to be insane, but she was also determined to work smarter than she had in the past, to leave time for both play and travel.

For the rest of the afternoon, she tackled a backlog of emails, spoke on the phone to her parents—whom it had taken four days to calm down once they learned about the incident with

Holt—and had her friend Chuck over for coffee. Like Baby, he was frustrated by not being able to hear many details about her situation, other than what he'd read in the *Daily News* and *New York Post*, but he was relieved she was safe.

"They were all abuzz about you at work," Chuck said. "You know how Mavis is. She thinks the only coverage that matters is in *World of Interiors* or *Architectural Digest*. But she seemed totally intrigued. You may have turned her into a *New York Post* reader."

Kit laughed. "Well, at least I gave her a glimpse of another side of life."

At seven Kelman arrived.

He was wearing jeans and a dress shirt, with his navy pull-over sweater loosely thrown around his shoulders, not like some preppy gesture but more of an afterthought. His face was clean-shaven, and she noticed that there was little trace remaining of that awful weariness. At the sight of him she felt a crazy mix of relief and desire.

"How are you, Kit?" he said, embracing her in a hug.

When he pulled back, she saw him glance around the apartment, taking it in. She knew he must be thinking the same thing as her: that it was strange for him to be standing there under such different circumstances than the last time.

"Good."

"You sure?"

"Uh huh. Like I told Baby, it's going to take a while to get my sea legs again, but I'll be fine. Tell me about Miami. It didn't seem like you wanted to say much on the phone."

"Sorry to be so guarded when I spoke to you. I doubt the FBI has your cell phone bugged, but I can't help but feel a little paranoid these days. And I didn't want to say anything about the case since they warned us not to discuss it with each other."

"Do you feel comfortable talking about it now?"

"Actually I do. As you'd expect, I promised not to divulge any specific information I've shared with the FBI about trades and phone calls—and I won't—but I don't see any harm in the two of us doing a postmortem. The only way I can make sure you're out of danger—and I am too—is to keep communicating with you about what's going on."

"That works for me," she said. "So then tell me, do you feel you righted things with Molinari and her partner?"

"Yeah, I'm pretty sure I'm out of the woods with her. She'd been in touch with the FBI and the cops in New York. And I assume she talked to you?"

"Yes. I gave her a statement and she seemed satisfied with it, though she was far from pleased that I'd been in contact with you and had never updated her."

Kelman dropped his sweater on an armchair and they'd settled on stools in front of the island.

"Would you like a glass of wine?" she asked. "I actually have a decent Bordeaux I've been saving."

"I'd love that." She brought out the bottle and two glasses, and as Kelman uncorked the wine, she set up a plate of olives and Parmesan cheese, items that had been in her fridge since before she moved in with Baby.

"I think this cheese is okay," she said, smiling. "It said 'aged thirty-seven months' or something like that on the label, and I've added only an extra month to that."

"I'm famished so I'll take my chances," he said, grinning back. She realized how little she'd seen him smile since Florida.

"This may be getting too close to the area that's off-limits, but did Holt's name ever surface when you first learned about the insider trading?" Kit asked.

"Never. But it had been a fluke for me to intercept the call from that one doctor, and the chances of me stumbling on another player were slim. There was nothing about Holt in the records I logged into. And any payments to Holt would have been made in cash."

"Do you think Healy was in cahoots with Kennelly and Lister or was he working all by his lonesome?"

"The three of them must have been working together, because it's hard to imagine two sets of them concocting basically the same scheme. And I still think Wainwright knew about it all. I'll bet they came up with the plan with Wainwright's approval or even at his instigation."

"But if they'd already seduced one doctor, why go to the trouble of paying a second for the same info?"

"They probably divided up the work and each went after various members of the advisory board, hoping to corrupt just one of them. And then, lo and behold, they landed two fish."

"There's one thing I still don't understand. Holt's an orthopedic surgeon. How did he end up on an advisory board for a cancer drug?"

"I know next to nothing about medicine, but I did a little investigating online and the drug that was tested is meant to treat blood cell disorders beyond leukemia. It's apparently also being tested on lupus and rheumatoid arthritis. I saw that one of his areas of expertise were problems caused by arthritis so he would have been a legitimate candidate for the advisory board."

"It seems so insane for him to have put his career in jeopardy."

"His need for money clearly overrode any fear of the risk he was taking. I'm sure Healy paid him well for his information."

"But how could Holt presume that killing Healy and stealing the flash drive from me would solve his problems? Wouldn't he have realized that there were other ways for him to be implicated?"

"Maybe not. I suspect he believed Healy was working solo and had no idea there were other players in the mix. So Holt told himself that once he eliminated Healy and made sure the flash drive didn't come to light, he'd be safe. I was still in the picture, of course, but without the flash drive, I obviously didn't seem like a threat to him."

"Is there any chance the person who broke into your place in Miami could have been Holt?"

"No way. I didn't manage a good look at the guy, but I could tell he was on the young side—and definitely not an amateur."

"Then you still think it was Ithaka?"

"Yes. They probably sent someone as soon as Matt tipped them off to where I was staying. He must have told them I had the flash drive, but they surely wondered what else I had that could prove damaging to them. Remember how you thought someone had been in your apartment a week before the big break-in? I bet Ithaka was behind that, as well. It was done by a pro who made only one tiny mistake with your pillows."

"That makes sense. Holt talked about hacking his way into my place, which suggests he was there just once."

Kelman took a final swig of his wine and set the glass back down.

"So are you still up for some dinner?" she asked. Part of her was worried he might find an excuse to split now that they'd completed their postmortem. "I haven't had a chance to stock up on groceries yet, but I thought I'd throw together something super simple."

"Sure, I'd love that," he said.

"Good."

She reached into the cabinet and took out a large pot, filled it with water, and set it on the stove. When she turned around, Kelman was taking her in with those riveting blue eyes of his.

"There's one thing I can't figure out," he said. "Holt planned to kill you that night, so how was he going to guarantee that he wouldn't be connected to your death? He's smart enough to know you would have probably told Baby who you were meeting and where."

"He took a couple of precautions. First, he arranged for me to go to a coffee shop rather than the apartment. He could have said later that we were supposed to meet at some other building, and we got our signals crossed and I never showed. Also, he managed to gain access to the building without ever giving his real name to the broker."

"How do you determine that?"

"Once I realized no one was going to cough up any details to me, I did some snooping. I dropped by the realtor for the building and the only person in the office was this young woman who couldn't have been more than twenty-seven. I told her who I was and said I was trying to figure out what had happened. She apparently had no clue she shouldn't be talking to me and said that Holt had emailed them posing as a foreigner who wanted to view the apartment but didn't have much time. They left the keys for him to pick up. I suspect because it wasn't a furnished apartment, they weren't super worried."

"It sickens me to ask this, but what would he have done with your body? He couldn't leave it in the apartment. The police would wonder how you'd gained access and that might lead back to him."

"Maybe he planned to come back late at night and drag it down to the street. It could have appeared as if I'd been followed on my way to meet him and killed by the same person who'd snapped Avery's neck. There was a real arrogance to the man. I'm sure he felt nearly invincible."

Kelman shook his head in disgust. "He won't ever have another chance to hurt you, Kit."

"What about Sasha?" she asked. "What kind of threat does *she* pose?"

"I've been tempted to contact her and tell her to back off. But after I had my fling with her, I learned that the smartest strategy was to not engage her on any level. I think she'll back off. Plus, she'll be busy trying to do everything possible not to be tainted by the scandal that's about to swamp the firm."

Kit slid off her stool and began to root through the fridge for garlic. Among the rotting lemons and carrots, she found a head of it with only a few tiny green shoots sprouting out of the top.

"What are we having anyway?" Kelman asked.

"It's called *aglio e olio*. It's really just spaghetti with garlic and olive oil and then you toss in lots of Parmesan." She offered a playful grimace. "Like I warned you, my larder is a bit depleted at the moment."

"Well, those are four of my favorite foods in the world."

She grinned. "Glad to hear it. In the cookbook it says that this is the dish that Rome's chic insomniacs depend upon to see them through the wee hours of the morning—when they're out and about."

He held her eyes tightly with his own.

"So, tell me," he said. "Does that mean I get to stay until the wee hours?"

"Yes," she said. "I'd like that."

acknowledgments

I always love researching my books, but this one seemed particularly exciting and fun to work on in terms of collecting information. I spoke to everyone from decorators to hedge fund managers, and I also had a fabulous three-day trip to Islamorada.

My heartfelt thanks to: Denny Daikeler, design consultant and author; John Eric Sebesta, interior designer; Tate Kelly, real estate advisor; Dick Furlaud, Principal, Artorius Management; Nathanial White, attorney; Susan Brune, Esq.; A. John Murphy, partner Murphy & Weiner, Palo Alto and San Francisco; Barbara Butcher, consultant for forensic and medicolegal investigation; Dr. Chester Lerner, Associate Chief of Infectious Diseases, New York-Presbyterian/Lower Manhattan Hospital; Ed Petersen, retired FBI agent; Caleb White, police officer; Andrezj Wojtowicz, contractor; and Elias, who is on such deep background I can only use his first name

A huge thank you also to my wonderful editor, Carolyn Marino, who I have thoroughly enjoyed working with, and to Laura Brown, who helped so much through the entire process. Thanks as well to Mary Sasso and Rachel Elinksy for all their support and efforts on the PR and marketing front. And then there's my amazing agent, Sandra Dijkstra, to whom I've owed so much over the twenty years I've been writing books! I want to also offer my gratitude to her terrific team: Elise Capron, Thao Le, and Andrea Cavallaro.

About the Author

Kate White, the former editor in chief of *Cosmopolitan* magazine, is the *New York Times* bestselling author of the stand-alone suspense novels *Hush*, *The Sixes*, and *Eyes on You*, as well as the Bailey Weggins mystery series. She is editor of the *Mystery Writers of America Cookbook*. She is also the author of popular career books for women, including *I Shouldn't Be Telling You This: How to Ask for the Money, Snag the Promotion, and Create the Career You Deserve*. You can contact her or learn more about her at katewhite.com.